THE
HOUSE
OF
FOOTSTEPS

THE
HOUSE
OF
FOOTSTEPS

MATHEW WEST

Harper
North

HarperNorth
Windmill Green,
Mount Street,
Manchester, M2 3NX

A division of
HarperCollins*Publishers*
1 London Bridge Street
London SE1 9GF

www.harpercollins.co.uk

HarperCollins*Publishers*
1st Floor, Watermarque Building, Ringsend Road
Dublin 4, Ireland

First published by HarperNorth in 2022
This edition published by HarperNorth in 2022

1 3 5 7 9 10 8 6 4 2

A catalogue record for this book
is available from the British Library

HB ISBN: 978-0-00-847293-1
TPB ISBN: 978-0-00-851919-3
PB ISBN: 978-0-00-847296-2

Printed and bound in the UK using 100%
renewable electricity at CPI Group (UK) Ltd

MIX
Paper | Supporting
responsible forestry
FSC™ C007454

This book is produced from independently certified FSC™ paper
to ensure responsible forest management.

For more information visit: www.harpercollins.co.uk/green

For Monica

1.

It all seemed to happen very quickly after I decided that I should try to find a job. First of all, the job found me, and then hot upon its heels came my first assignment, and then – well, everything else. I remember it distinctly: the thick, crisp office paper with the company letterhead, and the brief summons below calling me to Thistlecrook House. That name. Something about it struck me as unusual, right from the off. Perhaps it was its somewhat Scottish character when my appointed task would, in fact, send me travelling south of the border. I must have read the stiff paper at least three times over to assure myself that I had parsed it right: Thistlecrook House. Perhaps I only wondered for so long over the property's name as a distraction from the daunting significance and opportunity that this assignment represented for me. I even remember the date at the top of the summons, 13 May, and I remember that it was a Friday.

It was 1923 and less than a year had passed since the formal conclusion of my postgraduate studies at the University of Edinburgh in the field of art history. With the rigours of academic life behind me, I had permitted myself an idle winter to enjoy the unusually fine and clear weather that shone upon the capital that brisk season. My time had been engaged with coffees and long lunches; bracing walks up and down the royal park under the shadow of Arthur's Seat in the fresh afternoon air; and whiling away evenings lounging in the cosy warmth of friends' living rooms, smoking, drinking and engaging in earnest discussion with my peers: not so much setting the world to rights as astutely and mercilessly tearing the major questions of the day to ribbons through what we were quite convinced was incisive discourse. The perilous state of the economy and national debt, rising unemployment, military manoeuvres in the Ruhr valley, the virtues and deficiencies of Joyce's *Ulysses* – which we had by that time all read, almost – we took them all to task.

I suppose that the world at that time seemed pretty hopeless and without direction. The bruises of the Great War that had dominated our formative years were still all around us to see, even if no one really spoke much about it then. And my fellows and I must have made for a pretty hopeless, directionless bunch as well – wrapped up with a sort of normless ennui, though we were far too full of the self-confidence and brash invincibility of young manhood to recognize it within ourselves. The newspapers may have been printed front to back with death, inflation and revolution, but we were ready to live. Yes, we were without fear as we turned over the folly and ineptitude of our parents' generation and let their shredded remains drop, floating down onto carpeted New Town floors, to lie discarded among the cigarette burns and fallen sandwich crusts.

As you might imagine, for me that winter was a high point of youthful extravagance and irresponsibility, and I was having a devil of a time. But as someone once said, nothing can last for ever. My parents had found considerably less to enjoy in my seasonal pursuits, and by, I think, March their cheer and goodwill for all men – and their son in particular – was all used up. My mother had written to me frequently, at times it seemed almost weekly and in an increasingly perpendicular script, to impress upon me the importance of securing good and reliable employment, not to mention a mortgage, a pension, and a wife and children to boot. She seemed to be determinedly under the impression that I might still change career path to become a lawyer, that being a profession I had once expressed a mild curiosity about when still at boarding school. The considerable time and effort I had put into studying and achieving my actual qualification did not appear to have diminished her hopes at all.

My father, as a general principle, preferred not to involve himself directly in parental matters concerning his sole child and heir, and instead opted to funnel all communication to me via his wife – my mother. So when the male parent took it upon himself to telegram me direct in early April, advising that we would meet for lunch the following afternoon, and at said lunch – over a course of smoked salmon and devilled eggs – gruffly inform me through his moustache, 'Simon, I think it's time you found yourself a job', I knew that he meant it.

I had been born and raised in the estimable Edinburgh suburb of Morningside where I spent the entirety of my childhood, save a period between 1916 and 1917 when my mother and I moved to stay with her sister just outside the city after the Kaiser's zeppelins dared to drop bombs on the capital; and again for six months in 1918 when the influenza was stalking every urban street in Europe like some ghastly revenant. The span of my childhood years might have accounted for some of the most remarkable and turbulent periods in recent history, but of course I was hardly to know that at the time. I was a jolly schoolboy for most of it and, between youth and – yes – some measure of privilege, matters like the war in France did not affect me much at all. Not that we Christies were aristocracy or anything like that, I hasten to add. Father's income was really pretty modest compared to many of my friends' families. Of course, Father had gone abroad to fight for a time, until he came back with a limp and a lifelong enmity towards the Germanic peoples. But to me, the war, the Spanish epidemic, the rising tide of Bolshevism, they were all little more than headlines on a newsstand.

Having received my father's edict, I quickly came to realize that I had been in academia for so long, and had so few employed friends, that I wasn't sure precisely how one went about getting a job. Fortunately – and as previously intimated – it was not long before a job found its way to me. In short: at a friend's party I was introduced to a casual acquaintance whose uncle had been tasked with opening a Scottish branch of a well-established London auction house, and so happened to be on the active hunt for a man educated in art history to provide some manner of expert advice and so forth. I quickly arranged a meeting with said uncle, we each found the other's manner to be agreeable, and, as easy as that, the vacancy was mine.

Which brings me back to Thistlecrook House. The ancestral home of the Mordrake family, seated in the very north of England, so close to the border that one might hit it with a flung pebble. The master of the estate had expressed an interest in selling off a chunk of a sizeable collection of artworks that had been accumulated by his family over the centuries, including a number of old masters and even, reputedly, an original sketch by the hand of Leonardo da Vinci. The family had approached my auction house and, as the geographically nearest employee with a knowledge of the subject area, I was directed to visit the house and carry out an assessment and initial valuation of the collection.

It was a terrific opportunity, a chance to lay my hands and eyes upon a much-rumoured but long-unglimpsed artistic treasure trove. The Mordrakes were legendary collectors and appreciators, but, supposedly, a family of habitual recluses, and first-hand accounts of the full contents of their hoard were vanishingly, tantalizingly, rare. It was said that no one outside the family had seen the collection in its entirety for at least a century, if such a thing could even be possible. Of course, in such circumstances their gallery had developed a mysterious, close-to-mythical status, and was the subject of no small speculation, and in some quarters scepticism, throughout the art world. And here, I had been invited to witness the collection, in full, for myself. To provide a critical analysis, no less! Who knew what long-hidden masterwork I might uncover? It was a tall order but one I felt confident I was up to the task of. The received wisdom was that the Mordrakes of old had held a particular fervour for ecclesiastical art, and most of all for the lives and deaths of the assorted saints. Theirs was supposed to be one of the finest assemblies of classic martyr-dom imagery to be held in private hands outside of Italy. My own postgraduate thesis had been on the subject of icono-clasm and the secular eye in theological artworks of the High Renaissance. Who better, then, for the job? I was confident that, north of The Wash, I could match or outclass any comers on the subject area. I knew, too, that this would be a test of my mettle at the auction house, and that a posi-tive outcome – and a hefty sales commission – would surely make or break my budding career.

It had all been arranged: the Mordrake family would put me up for the duration of my stay, and meet any and all expenses – which should be as minimal as discretion could allow, my employer had advised me in no uncertain terms. And so it was with mingling feelings of giddy enthusiasm and trepidation that I departed from Waverley Station, armed with a set of cases stuffed with changes of clothes and bulky reference books, bound to cross the border into England and from there on to Thistlecrook House.

I remember well the head-spinning nervousness and excitement that gripped me as the train heaved out of the station with a wheezing shudder of steam. 'No turning back now,' its scraping gears seemed to wail. I had done my fair share of holidaying around Europe, naturally, but always for pleasure, never for work, and now a sudden and urgent reluctance to leave the familiar comforts of my home city, even for the temporary duration of my assignment, rushed through my being. I stared gloomily through the train window up towards the castle, perched high above me on its throne of black rock against a sky burnished steel-grey with cloud, with a strange and unwarranted superstition that I should never lay eyes upon it again.

I admit I have always been a sort of a one for a spot of introspection. A deep thinker, to reference another's words describing my demeanour. But, for some reason, this general mood of pessimism, that began as the train left the station, went on to hit me particularly hard on the first leg of my journey south. If you had seen me in my gloom, you would never have guessed that I was embarked on a journey of such academic and vocational opportunity for a fresh and untested young postgraduate.

The roundabout routes of the rail system obliged me to take the train first as far south as Newcastle, and from there north again to a small town called Cobsfoot, from where I should be able to secure passage to the Mordrake house. At the ticket desk of Newcastle station, the young clerk had to ask me to repeat the name of my destination, and then called over his manager, apparently stumped.

'Oh yes, Cobsfoot,' the manager told me brightly. 'The eleven thirteen to Dumfries will take you there. Only, you should ask the conductor when you board. Most trains won't make the stop unless requested.'

'Cobsfoot station is so rarely used?' I asked, slightly dismayed as an image of a minute, quaint town with old ladies peering nosily from their windows began to take form in my mind.

'Very rarely indeed. Not much call for travel to Cobsfoot. The town itself is nice enough, though. My wife and I once spent a pleasant week there,' the manager informed me with an encouraging smile, before smartly returning to his work.

My ticket purchased, I found that I had an hour and a half to kick about in Newcastle on an overcast and drizzly day. I wandered around the town a little, mulling over the undertaking I had set off on. For the first time, it hit me that I could be holed up in this obscure corner of northern England for some long while, if the family's art collection was really as extensive as believed. The master of Thistlecrook House, Mr Mordrake, might at least provide some agreeable company, I reflected, although in my mind's eye a portrait had already been formed of a fusty old gent with a gut, dressed in tweeds and with a shotgun permanently broken in the crook of his arm: an image not entirely unresembling my father, I realized. The fact that he could even consider selling off his family's long-held art collection surely indicated that he had no interest in the contents himself. I doubted that I would be able to find much in common with the man.

Who else resided at Thistlecrook House – whether there was a wider family – I did not know. Nor did I know precisely how far from Cobsfoot town the house was, nor what else there was to be found in the locale. I consoled myself that what countryside I had observed from the train so far was pleasant enough and, when not working, I could surely enjoy some long, rambling walks. Perhaps I could take advantage of the solitude to begin to write my book, as I had intended to do over the winter that had just passed. And of course, I told myself, I could not downplay the attraction of the collected artworks themselves. Although my visit was in a professional capacity, art was my passion, and to sort through the collection's treasures would surely be such a pleasure it could hardly resemble work. That prospect brightened my mood considerably.

The time finally came for my departure towards Dumfries. As advised, when I boarded I put a word in the conductor's ear that my final destination was to be Cobsfoot. He nodded conspiratorially at the information. The rails on this part of the journey must have been unusually bumpy and uneven, probably aged and in disrepair, and I was bounced around for an hour or so while keeping a tight hold on my jostling luggage before the conductor found me and leaned close to murmur, 'Cobsfoot is the next stop, sir.' He licked his lips, a touch too close to my ear for comfort, and added, 'The platform is short, so you should detrain via the further door, if you please.'

The conductor helped me to unload my cases, the train pulled away, and I found myself standing on the platform of Cobsfoot station, quite alone in an unfamiliar setting and feeling alarmingly dislocated. No one else had disembarked, and the platform was deserted. Before me was a small station building. On all other sides the station was enclosed by dense, green, leafy woodland that the train tracks seemed to cut a swathe through. I gathered my luggage clumsily in my arms and struggled through the station building, finding it just as deserted as the platform. Passing in one door and out the other, I emerged to a view down over the town of Cobsfoot itself from the top of the hill upon which the station sat. The town was, to its credit, a little larger than I was expecting, having a number of crisscrossing streets, at least two larger buildings that I took to be inns, and a distant church spire stretching towards the clouds and set some way back from the cluster of rooftops that seemed to make up the town proper. I stood for a while, basking in the bright sun that had now emerged and listening to the humming chirrup of insects that hung in the air around me. I had been given to understand that Thistlecrook House stood some distance outside the town, and my journey was not yet complete. From my vantage point I could see as far as the surrounding countryside, though there were no visible manor houses that might have been my objective.

Outside the station, I realized with prickling embarrassment that I had forgotten to telegram ahead from Newcastle and announce the time of my arrival, which might have allowed Mr Mordrake to send a vehicle to collect me. I had, at least, messaged my anticipated arrival date before I departed Edinburgh, to which I had received the single-word and somewhat peculiar reply: 'CAPITAL'. There was nothing for it now but to find someone in town who could provide directions and onward transport, or else could send a message to Thistlecrook House to let them know that I had arrived. Adjacent to the station was an inn, as might be expected, but the lights were out and the door shut and barred. Strange, but it was still early afternoon and midweek – and in the country, folk often kept more conservative hours, I had heard. I loitered outside the wide windows at the front of the hotel until I was sure there was no one inside, and then my luggage and I began our struggle down-hill, following the steep road that led away from the station.

My first impression of Cobsfoot, from the squat and silent houses that lined the road into town, was that I seemed to have inadvertently stepped back in time by some hundred years or so. Old Edinburgh was hardly the model of a modern, swinging twenties city, but it seemed as hot as New Orleans in comparison to this quaint little berg. Low grey stone houses with thatched roofs, an unpaved street lined with cart tracks, a bucolic backdrop of rolling fields and lowing cattle. I felt like I was walking into a novel by … well, I don't know who, but someone pretty cheap and sentimental. At first, I was relieved that none of the net curtains twitched as I passed, wary locals peering suspiciously from behind them at the newly arrived stranger. But this relief soon turned to an odd sensation that the entire place seemed to be completely and utterly deserted. There was not a sign of life about. The day was clammy and warm and, by the time I reached the bottom of the hill and the town proper, I had worked up a decent sweat through a combination of physical exertion and mounting panic, as I wondered just where on earth I had allowed myself to end up. Had I alighted at the correct station, or had I inadvertently stranded myself at some abandoned village in the middle of nowhere? What sort of town was so devoid of life in the middle of the working week?

Perhaps it was this fretting that distracted me, but I heard nothing of the commotion that lay around the next corner. I blundered around it with my cases, following a faded, hand-painted sign that pointed towards the town square, only to find myself face-to-face with a pair of towering black horses, capped in long-feathered headdresses equally dark in colour, pulling behind them a sombre carriage. The carriage, too, was black as obsidian. Seated at its head, a grim-faced man in a top hat raised his eyebrows in mild surprise at my sudden appearance, stomping directly into the intended path of his vehicle, but he provided no other reaction, nor did he pull his horses to rein. To either side of the carriage trudged an escort of similarly black-attired men, their heads bowed low, except one or two who were peering at me through confused and indignant eyes. It was a full funeral procession, and I was standing slam in front of it, a human roadblock with a suitcase under each arm and one in either hand besides, huffing and sweating and utterly red in the face.

There was nothing for it but to drag my person as quickly as possible to the side of the road and bow my head while the assembly passed, trying to summon any quiet dignity

and respect that I could find left within me. The horses and
carriage tapped past, followed by a long trail of men, women
and children, shuffling slowly, some sobbing quietly. I
pretended not to notice the few furtive glances that were
shot my way by some of the more curious members of the
congregation – though I confess I allowed myself to do some
glancing of my own to take in the colour of the local populace. They seemed a ruddy, hearty lot, in shabby but clean
Sunday best, with the honest, open faces characteristic – or
should that be caricatured – among rural folk. I dared to
glance at the funeral carriage, too, and with a chill saw that
the neat little coffin it bore was not more than four feet
long. A child's death, then, and no doubt a grievous blow
for the entire community. No wonder the streets were
emptied and the local businesses stood closed to custom.
Any initial prejudices I may have formed concerning the
people of Cobstoot evaporated at the sight of that small, sad
wooden box, and the empty space left behind filled with
nothing but empathy for their loss.

The procession trailed off up the road in the direction of
the distant church. As the sound of the final dragging feet
faded away, I was left with little to do but continue towards
the town square, where I found a spot to sit and wait for the
townsfolk to return so that I might make some enquiries
about onward transport. I sat there for perhaps an hour or
so brooding upon the temporality of man and so on and so
forth, and then my mind turned once again to Thistlecrook
House and what and who might await me upon my arrival.
The Mordrakes, I understood, owned much of the farmland
around here and most of the townsfolk directly or indirectly
owed their employment to the family. Perhaps I had just
witnessed the master, or his kin, passing by among the
funeral procession.

At length I was relieved to see men and women wandering down the hill from the church, and life began to filter

back into the town. The people returned slowly, reluctantly. Some still wore pale, aggrieved faces and wept forlornly, but most had already loosened their ties and unbuttoned their collars against the unsympathetic heat, and now dawdled in pairs or small groups, talking quietly and sharing gossip and jokes, evidently uneager to return to the usual business of their daily routines after such a strange and sad diversion. As they drew closer and passed me by without a glance, I was curiously surprised to hear in their voices the soft lilt of the borders accent. It somehow seemed wrong to hear them talk in such familiar tones when it was a St George's Cross, and not the Saltire, that fluttered from the flagpole outside the town hall. Such was the nature of these border towns, I supposed: neither one place nor the other.

From where I waited, I faced directly towards a largish tavern with a sign that named it the Whistle and Duck. It had sat quiet and dormant for the duration of the funeral, but now I watched as the proprietor unlocked its door and entered, followed closely by a good number of the town's men who appeared to have decided that, at this point of the afternoon, work and routine could wait until tomorrow. I took up my suitcases once more, struggled over, followed the crowd inside and pitched up at the bar, where I waited until the locals had all been served and then ordered myself a cool ale and commenced to question the man behind the bar.

'I wonder if you can help me – I'm looking to procure some transport to take me and my luggage outside of town,' I began, having taken a refreshing sip of my beer.

The barkeep clucked his tongue thoughtfully. 'That could be difficult done today, sir. Normal circumstances I could certainly recommend a few names, but the whole town has been turned out for wee Maggie Hall's funeral.'

'So I gathered,' I replied, then paused, unsure whether it would be insensitive of me to pursue that topic. It seemed the fellow was keen to talk about it whether I asked or not, however.

'Aye, it's a terrible tragedy,' he continued, polishing a glass with the close attention that is the special reserve of barmen and butlers. 'You weren't here for the funeral?' he asked. I told him I had only arrived that afternoon. 'I didn't think the Halls knew many out-of-towners,' he agreed, looking me up and down. 'Aye, a terrible tragedy – the poor child was barely six years old.'

'Terrible,' I agreed. 'Did you know the young girl?'

He shook his head. 'Only to see her playing about town with the other bairns, but she seemed a bright wee thing.'

'It's an awful tragedy for the family.' I took another sip of beer.

'Aye, they lost another wee one around ten years ago as well. A bitter shame for them. I suppose that's the way of life, though. You know, sir' – he leaned forwards – 'they sent a coroner all the way from Carlisle. He had a drink in here before he made the return trip – sat right where you are now, as miserable as they come with his face all creased up in a frown – and he said he hadn't a clue what he was going to write in his report. Not a thing wrong with the wee girl, he said, nothing that should have caused her to drop dead like she did. Especially at her age. I suppose it's just one of life's mysteries at that.'

'I don't suppose you happen to know if the Mordrakes were in town for the funeral?' I ventured.

'Mordrakes?' – the man's eyebrows raised in surprise, 'You mean Master Mordrake, from down at the old house?'

'I suppose I do: Thistlecrook House, yes? That's where I need to get to, you see,' I said, hoping to draw the conversation back to the question of my transport.

'Aye, Thistlecrook, that's the old house. But the master didn't come for the funeral. He doesnae come in for much at all, truth be told. He keeps to himself for the most part – not really involved in the community, you know. I can't recall the last time I saw old Master Mordrake around. Eh, you've some business with him, then?'

'That's right,' I replied, slightly more haughtily than I intended.

'It's none of my business, of course, sir. It's only that it's a rare thing that we get a visitor looking to go out to the house. Let me think …' He tossed his cloth over his shoulder and stroked his beard thoughtfully. While I waited, I could not resist questioning the man further; the one or two crumbs of information about my host that he had already dropped were quite intriguing, and I saw no harm in scrounging for a few more.

'Does Mr Mordrake live alone? He has no family?'

'Aye – just himself and his staff. And not many staff for such a large house, either. You know' – he glanced about warily, licked his lips – 'more than once I've had lads sitting at the bar here, drowning their sorrows before they head on home, having quit their service up at Thistlecrook House. It's a strange place, and the master takes dark, wild moods, to hear tell.'

I think I actually laughed at that, a little. 'Oh yes, a bit of a tyrant, is he?'

'I suppose so. Of course, I only know what I've heard. I couldn't say for myself. But you … you've never heard tell of Thistlecrook House, then?'

'I only know of the Mordrakes by reputation. A little eccentric, a little reclusive, perhaps? But you make it sound like I'm on my way to Castle Dracula,' I said, sure the fellow must be pulling my leg with all of this.

The barkeeper gave me a slightly long look, then smiled. 'Well, yes, it's just local legends, I suppose. Lord knows we've enough of those. People have always talked about the old house, and the family there, all sorts of things you wouldn't believe –'

Now a girl who had been busying herself nearby laying tables turned and interrupted. 'Away and leave poor Mr Mordrake alone.' She tutted. 'It's a sad story what happened, and besides, how he runs his house is his own affair, and no one else's.' Yet despite her scolding she seemed eager to add her own account into the mix. 'Mr Mordrake is a widower, you see,' she said, turning to me. 'He had a wife, once, a pretty wee thing she was, and kind, too. She used to come to town – they both did, in those days. I was just a wee girl then, but I remember seeing them out walking happily together, dressed all smartly, not at all like the people round here. They looked like they'd arrived from another world entirely. But then, there's a small lake – more of a pond, really, or somewhere in between what would you call that?'

'I'm not sure,' I confessed.

'Well, there's a wee lake close to the old house, one that freezes over every winter, and the wife was skating on it, but the ice broke under her and she fell through, and she died.' The girl shuddered at the imagined chill of such a fate. 'That was during the war, while the husband was over in France. He didn't return until the war was finished, and they say that he was a different man when he came back. The poor soul. No one has seen much of him since.' She glanced around, then leaned towards us over the bar and added in a hushed voice, 'They say the ice froze again over her head, so no one could find where she had disappeared to. They all thought she had run away – until the lake thawed in the spring and her body floated to the surface, looking just as she did the day she died, for the ice had kept her beauty.'

'Now who's telling tales, Mary?' the barkeeper chuckled.

'Well, fair enough. But people are just superstitious about the old house, and I don't think it's right to speak badly of the lonesome man who lives there now, on account of old stories,' Mary concluded.

'There's more to be superstitious about than one drowned wife,' the man said, but before he could elaborate, his attention was caught by the swing of the tavern door. A young lad who could have been no older than fifteen had entered. 'Oh, here now, Laurie,' the barkeep called to him, 'this fellow is looking to get up to the old house. Will you take him in your cart?'

The boy hesitated and glanced longingly towards the cluster of men drinking at the far side of the room. He was still dressed – as they all were – in his black trousers and white shirt from the funeral.

'Here, Mary, you ask him and he'll be sure to say yes.' The barkeeper laughed, nudging the girl with his elbow. She smiled too, and the poor boy, Laurie, turned a bright crimson.

'Aye, I'll take ye,' Laurie muttered and hurried back outside, his eyes fixed upon the ground.

'And there you have it.' The barkeeper smiled, holding his palms out triumphantly.

I thanked him, quickly finished my drink and gathered my things to follow Laurie outside. I would have gladly stayed and heard more about the mysterious Mr Mordrake – not to mention enjoying another ale – but time was pressing on and I didn't want the first impression I made to be one of tardiness. The initial character sketch that I had formed of my temporary employer and host, that of the blustering country gentleman, now gave way to one of a sombre, moody widower given to sullen silences and long evenings sat alone staring into the glowing embers of the fireplace, brooding intensely while his harassed staff waited in mute discomfort. I had no doubt that the new image was as wildly inaccurate as the first – but I found I was eager to discover the truth for myself.

Outside the tavern, it was still a bright and sunny after-noon, although the sun was a goodish way dipped towards the horizon. I set down my cases and waited, and presently the young lad Laurie returned, sitting atop a rickety cart pulled by a single plodding grey horse. If a horse can appear shiftless then I would say that this one did. I had not expected the lad to arrive in a shining automobile, but still, this was less enthusing than I had hoped. But there was not much for it, and so Laurie and I loaded my luggage into the wagon and I took my place bunched onto the single narrow seat beside him, and we were away.

The horse clopped slowly out of the square and up one of the roads leading out of town. Archaic houses gave way to rugged, rocky moorland populated by thin herds of cattle and sheep dispersed across craggy fields.

'Is Thistlecrook House very far outside town?' I asked. I could not catch my companion's first mumbled reply and had to ask him to repeat himself.

'A wee ways,' he said.

The trail led down a slope, and the farmland vanished as we entered into a wood of densely twisted, gnarled old trees. I could see no road signs nor markers of any kind. 'Do you make this journey often?' I asked, to break the long, uncomfortable silence as much as anything.

'Aye, sometimes,' my sullen driver responded. After a pause he offered an elaboration. 'Makin' deliveries an' carryin' messages an' such.'

'Oh yes? Do you know Mr Mordrake at all?'

He shook his head. 'I'd say no one does, 'cept maybe his butler. Mostly I deal wi' him.'

'With the butler?'

'Aye.'

I observed a faint curl of distaste flicker upon young Laurie's lip. 'And Mordrake's wife – did you know her?'

I do not know why I asked the question. Something

about the story, the image of the beautiful young wife vanishing through a crack in the ice into the frozen lake below, was playing on my mind.

But Laurie only shook his head grimly. He was surely too young to remember anything about it, I supposed. The conversation petered out, and I found myself in no hurry to resurrect it. I tried to content myself with peering into the dark woods that surrounded us, and attempting to identify the bird calls I heard, though I was not much of a one for ornithology. The trees might have been willows and ash. Sprinkled among their knotted roots, bright, pleasing flowers were blooming in their hundreds, creating colourful patterns that spread across the forest floor like so many Persian carpets. Even under the shade of the trees, the air was hot and humid and swirling with the dusky perfume of the wildflowers. The last days of spring were in full blossom, and the hazy months of summer hot on their trail, I thought with a trace of wistfulness.

'I seen him before,' Laurie piped up suddenly. 'Mr Mordrake. He used to come into town on Sundays, for church. Me an' the other boys would run up and look in the windows of the motor car after he'd gone into the church. That was when I was a bairn,' he added quickly, defensively, as though dismissive of such childish notions now, and I suppressed a smile. The lad was still so fresh-faced that he could have been speaking of a month past. 'He sat at the front o' the church, in them covered boxes for gentry, ken? Well, my friend Iain Jameson used to sneak down to take a look at him – at Mr Mordrake – an' told me he always had his eyes closed like he was asleep, all throughout the entire service. An' so we wondered why would he come all the way to town jus' to sleep through the service? Only … I snuck down once mysel' to have a look, an' when I peeped roun' the corner I seen him, an' his eyes wisnae closed at all … they was wide open, big an' round and not blinkin', an' he was grinning like a madman watchin' the vicar, and his whole body was sort of heavin', like he was laughin' to hissel', laughin' at what the vicar was saying. An' then he turned his head, and looked down at me peeping at him round the corner, and his eyes were red, like with tears from all the laughter. He looked right at me and his grin went even wider and he nodded his head – like, like he was sharin' a great joke wi' me, or something. Only I couldnae ken what he was laughin' at, at all.'

Young Laurie had delivered this story very quickly, speaking so fast I struggled to follow the words as they rattled from his mouth. I turned to look at him as he spoke, but his eyes remained fixed upon the trail ahead. His face had grown quite white. He shook his head. 'I ran back an' never snuck down to spy on Mr Mordrake after that. Only, he disnae come to church at all any more, anyway.'

I didn't know quite what to say to all of that, and Laurie seemed to have spoken as many words as he intended to make use of that day, so we trundled the remainder of the journey in silence. Again, I found myself wondering if these curious stories were some sort of joke, if the local populace were having a laugh at my expense in some fashion, though I couldn't see much humour in it. And neither Laurie, nor Mary, nor the barkeeper at the Whistle and Duck had struck me as insincere with their words. Whatever the case, I reflected, Master Mordrake seemed to be a character that inspired an unusual amount of wonder and speculation among the people of the town.

It was not too much longer before a first glimpse of my final destination became visible through the tightly knotted branches, though I did not initially appreciate the nature of the building I saw. Some way distant, a large, dark structure emerged slowly into view, standing alone at the centre of an expansive clearing: it was a grand, aged thing with a high, sharply gabled roof and severe gothic arches along its sides, appearing more like some sort of church or cathedral than a place of residence. Indeed, on first glance that is what I took it for: an abandoned church that had been left standing in the forest in favour of a more conveniently located place of worship. But, as the cart drew closer to the monolithic construction, I observed the long, raked gravel driveway that wound through an open set of gates towards the building, the neatly arranged flower beds outside, and the opened windows with curtains gently wafting in the breeze that were all telltale signs of habitation. This, then, must be Thistlecrook House. A shining motor car was parked off to one side of the house – somehow, it seemed starkly and entirely out of place there, a modern anachronism that had intruded on this quaint bubble of antiquated Britain that I seemed to have been delivered into.

Laurie dropped me off just inside the estate gates and helped me unload my cases, then quickly hopped back to his seat and was gone without further word. A stroke of luck, as I had been unsure whether or not I would be expected to provide some sort of payment for his assistance. I left my luggage where it stood and walked through the gardens towards a large arched doorway that I assumed was the main entrance. For some reason, that walk felt one of the longest of my life. Perhaps it was nervous anticipation of my first paid assignment, or perhaps it was the consequence of a long and somewhat trying day of travel. Or perhaps the unsettling stories I had heard in Cobsfoot, serious or not, were playing upon my mind. Whatever the cause, I could not seem to will my lethargic legs to carry me with any haste up the long gravel driveway.

And then finally, suddenly, I was there, and the tall dark door was standing imposingly above my head. I rang the bell.

2.

I waited under the monumental door for what felt like a long time. If the bell had made a sound then it had not reached my ears. Perhaps the bell pull was out of service and I should knock? I doubted my fists could elicit more than a faint thud against the door's sturdy oak panels. I raised my hand to pull the bell a second time and, as if in response to my motion, the door suddenly clunked and swung slowly inwards. I was met by a tall elderly man, with skin the precise colour of the pages of an old library book and thin wisps of white hair radiating about his scalp. He was dressed in a dark suit, evidently almost as old as its wearer and somewhat frayed at the seams – yet he held himself with a rigidly upright bearing in a dignified attempt at defiance of the natural and unavoidable stoop of his age. 'Yes?' the servant asked, taking in my own doubtless dishevelled and ruddy appearance in a sweeping gaze.

'My name is Simon Christie. I am here to see the art collection,' I introduced myself. 'I was sent by Southgate's auction house, I mean.'

'Yes, we received the telegram,' he said, looking me up and down once more for good measure, and making no move to invite me inside.

'Is Mr Mordrake home? This is Thistlecrook House, is it not?'

'Indeed the master is at home, and this is your destination.' The old man forced his features into something resembling a courteous smile. It looked like a painful process. 'We received your telegram but you did not say what time you were to arrive. We did not know when to expect you. I suppose you have luggage.'

'Yes, I'm sorry, I had intended to send a message from Newcastle but I had to rush for the train,' I lied. 'I left my luggage back at the gate; the boy Laurie dropped me there.'

The butler peered past me in the direction of said gate. 'You came in Laurie's cart. I see,' he said, as though the information came as some great personal disappointment. 'Well … come in. I will send a boy for your cases.'

At last, he stepped aside to permit me entrance, with no abundance of welcome or good cheer. I found myself in a grand entry hall of dark wood and deep-green furnishings, with a large staircase opposite that curved upwards to the left and right, leading to the upper floor. Tall, narrow windows set above the staircase parting allowed some of the evening's sunshine in from outside, but overall it was so dark inside the house that upon stepping across the threshold I found I could see nothing at all for the few seconds before my eyes adjusted to the gloom. I was still reeling when I was ushered into a room to my right, a sort of sitting room with plush settees in some type of severe floral upholstery, roses I think. A large window faced out over the driveway and the gardens through which I had just passed, and beyond that the gate leading off the property.

'I shall inform the master that you have arrived. We did not know what time to expect you,' the butler repeated, rather hammering the point home, I thought. 'We are in the middle of preparing dinner – will you be joining Mr Mordrake?'

I had not realized how late in the day it had become, but as soon as the man mentioned food, I remembered that I had not eaten since morning, and my stomach began to raise a growling demand. 'If it's all right with Mr Mordrake for me to join him, then yes, I would be obliged,' I said.

'Unless you packed some dinner in those cases of yours, I expect you'd better eat with the master,' the butler replied, quite sharply. He delivered the words so quickly and matter-of-factly that I was not sure whether to be offended or not, and he had turned and excused himself from the room before I could find any reply. I wondered what I could have done to affront the man so, aside from the evident slight of failing to telegram ahead my anticipated hour of arrival.

I seethed a little for just a minute, and then remembered that I was here on business and could not afford to foul my first impression, and so I tried to cast the rude butler from my mind and distract myself by looking about the room. Like the entrance hallway, the furnishings were tasteful but austere, and all dark, muted reds and greens: sombre colours that would aid the widowed master's introspective brood-ing, I imagined. I made a quick circuit around the room, looking for and inspecting things of interest to me. Naturally, my first ports of call were the paintings hanging on the walls, though they were few in number, and I was disap-pointed to find they were limited to inoffensive rural landscapes, along with two unremarkable still lifes of vases of flowers. Among the landscapes there appeared to be no local scenes. They were all sweeping mountains, lakes and rivers, represented in all the seasons and dotted with pictur-esque cottages and cabins with curls of white smoke puffing from their chimneys and tiny colourful figures representing the farmers, shepherds and itinerants that dwelt in such far-flung places, all dwarfed by the vast majesty of nature. The pieces were tasteful and accomplished enough, but I saw little of any significance or value. My hopes for the famed Mordrake collection did waver a touch based upon my impression of this single room – though I curiously noted that the wallpaper between these humdrum paintings bore the telltale faded markings where frames had been hung once, and then removed.

The one exception to the landscapes and still lifes, and the only work in the room to capture my attention for more than a glancing inspection, was a quite singular, sizeable portrait that hung over the fireplace, showing an intense-looking man staring straight down at the viewer from crystal-blue irises beneath bushy black eyebrows and a mop of dark unruly hair that – the artist had picked out with precise detail – was just greying at the temples. I spent some time admiring this piece while I waited for my host. The face in particular had been passed off with a remarkable vivacity and lifelike quality, and the piercing eyes glared demandingly out from the canvas with a quite unsettling effect. There was no indication who the sitter might have been. His dark hair, the swarthy cast to his face, his drooping eyelids, and slightly elongated features gave him an almost exotic appearance – whoever he was, he was certainly striking and probably handsome, I decided.

Still alone, I moved to an inspection of the numerous bookshelves that took up the majority of two of the walls. To my surprise, the titles on the spines were all in different languages: a small number in English, some in French and Latin that I could clumsily decipher, varied other European languages I might have hazarded a guess at, and even some in letters and alphabets entirely unfamiliar to me. The works were all jumbled together in no discernible order, and seemingly with no regard for the authors nor subject matter, nor even the language of the text within. The titles that I could translate seemed to be a bemusing mix of prose and history, reference books on a wide array of scholarly and scientific subjects, and even a copy of the land register for the region dated to 1764. Either my host was a scholar of rare talents, or else the Mordrakes had habitually collected rare and esoteric books as avidly as they had paintings.

Hearing the door behind me open, I turned, and for a moment was taken aback to be confronted by the spitting image of the man in the portrait above the fireplace. The same dark hair and thick brow, the same pronounced nose, and slender stately jaw that I had just been admiring in oils now stood before me recreated in the flesh. The only differences were a tidier, slicked-back haircut and a thin pencil moustache darkening the upper lip – and, perhaps, a marginally more youthful complexion.

'Ah, Bannatyne told me he had shoved you in here,' the man said, moving towards me swiftly and extending his long arm. 'I am Victor Mordrake. It's a pleasure to meet you. You are my man from Southgate's, yes?' His voice was cool and level, and without a trace of an accent.

'Simon Christie,' I said, receiving his firm handshake. 'That's right, Southgate's assigned me to carry out your valuation. I am sorry for my late arrival.'

'Are you late? It's of no matter to me. Bannatyne tells me you will join me for dinner.'

'If that's all right. I had intended to telegram from Newcastle, but did not have the time. I'm afraid I've caused a bit of an inconvenience,' I said, laying it on a bit thick, being anxious to make a good impression and all.

'Not at all. Did Bannatyne say so? Don't mind the old man, he loves to complain about anything and everything. It's just his way – he would call the grass an inconvenience for growing. You'll get used to it, don't worry. In any case, I insist you join me for dinner, so it's settled.'

As he spoke, I could not help but wonder at how different the man's cheery words and easy demeanour were to any of the notions I had formed on my journey here. This was neither the crusty landed gentry, nor the tortured, bereaved husband I had been expecting. I marvelled, too, at how closely his features resembled those of the face in the portrait. The eyes most of all: like the painting, his were a very pale blue – almost white, like diamonds – and seemed to shimmer with energy and vitality even as he spoke about dinner plans. Unconsciously, my gaze darted from his face to that in the painting, and back again – he must have noticed, and laughed.

'It's a remarkable likeness, isn't it?' he said.

'Uncanny. Is it your grandfather, perhaps?' I asked.

Victor Mordrake raised an eyebrow. 'Indeed. Most take it for my own portrait, though I am not so vain as to hang my image in the parlour and require my guests to regard me in duplicate. What tipped you off?'

'Well, the technique, and the condition of course, and the frame, which is not much in style any more – although an old frame may hold a new painting, naturally. But most of all the clothes give it away – your ancestor's style is almost a century out of date.'

My host laughed with delight. 'I can see Southgate's has sent the right man for the job. You pass your entrance exam, and may proceed to the old family collection that is held in such reverence and wonder – or so I am told.' He winked. 'But look, the sun is already setting. Your work can wait until tomorrow, can't it? Bannatyne has sent your luggage to your room – here, I will call someone to show you up.'

'It's very good of you to put me up for the duration.'

'Not at all.' Mordrake waved my words away, and pulled on a cord to summon help. 'You could hardly stay else-where – we are quite isolated in the woods here, as you may have noticed. And in all truth, I look forward to having another soul about the place, even for a short while. Yes, I have a good feeling that we shall enjoy each other's company. We will eat in half an hour,' he told me as a servant boy arrived. The three of us exited back into the main entrance hall, from where I was escorted up the winding staircase, while Victor Mordrake wandered idly away down one of the ground-floor corridors, without another word nor a glance after my direction.

The young servant showed me to my room – or rather, rooms, for I discovered that I had been accorded an impressively capacious suite of chambers more fit for some sort of visiting dignitary. My parents' Morningside home had been spacious enough for the three of us, as far as Edinburgh townhouses go, but I had spent the last several years crammed into student flats with one or two fellows, living practically on top of one another. The suite Mr Mordrake had provided me with was almost as large as any of these flats, and I was to have it all to myself. The bedroom smelled fresh and newly cleaned, and its windows were still flung wide open when I entered, though by this time a twilight coolness had definitely begun to settle. I went to the windows to close them, admiring as I did a view over the rear of the estate. The grounds were bounded on all sides by the same twisted trees that had overlooked my journey here, though the forest was kept at bay by a considerable expanse of neat green lawns that stretched a good distance in every direction. Close to the house, almost underneath my window and to the right, I could see a walled rose garden that appeared to be in full spring– summer bloom. As I pulled the shutters closed, the air swept in with a heady intake of the garden's fragrance. When time allowed, I would certainly have to make a walking tour of the grounds.

Just as I was about to turn away from the view, I caught a glimpse of a reflective glint in the distance; looking again I could see a shining streak of silvery-blue flashing just above the treetops, directly opposite my window. Out there must be the lake I had heard tell of, I realized – where Mordrake's young wife had met her frozen end below the ice. I turned my back to the window with a shudder.

Victor had told me dinner would be half an hour, but after I had washed my face, changed my clothes, and lain on the bed to ease the headache that was beginning to press upon my temples, the clock showed that thirty-five minutes had passed and no one had come to collect me. My stomach was becoming quite ferocious in its grumbling by now, so I decided to venture out and investigate. From my room I could find my way back to the central hallway easily enough, and back down the staircase, but from there I had no clue where the dining room was. The shady hall was silent; I could hear no telltale clinking of cutlery nor glass-ware that might guide me. I briefly considered returning to the front parlour and pulling the bell for assistance, but thought this might be presumptuous – and besides, I didn't want to put myself even more in the butler Bannatyne's bad books than I apparently already was. So I set off down the corridor that I had seen Mordrake wander down some half hour earlier. For such a large house, the corridor was strangely narrow, so that two people approaching from either direction would have had to squeeze past each other, and walking two abreast would have been an impossibility. The staff must make use of a network of hidden passages while going about their work, I assumed.

Every door I passed was closed, with no sounds audible from within. By the time I had made it halfway down the lengthy corridor, I was convinced that the dining room could hardly be found so far in this direction; nonetheless, the sight of an open door ahead of me, and the faint sound of movement within, spurred me onwards to investigate. As I drew closer, I could see a kitchen through the crack in the door, though there was no sign of anyone inside. At its far side was a heavy door embedded in rough, ancient-looking brickwork – the footsteps I could hear came ringing from within. Realizing how far off my intended course I had wandered, I decided to withdraw, but before I could, the aged door swung open suddenly and the butler, Bannatyne, emerged, clutching a bottle of wine in his long fingers. He stopped sharply when he saw my gawping face peering at him through the gap in the door.

'Can I help you, sir?' he asked, with the tone of one who considers that their help is most undoubtedly required.

'I was looking for the dining room,' I explained, feeling for all the world like a schoolboy who has been caught snooping after curfew.

I thought a slight smirk crossed his features. 'The dining room is back the way you came, just off the main hall.' Bannatyne pointed behind me. I nodded, turned, and we made our way back, he walking slightly behind me and hovering just over my shoulder, owing to the narrow construction of the corridor. From the corner of my eye, I could see his head jut back and forth as he walked, like some tall, strange bird.

'No one told me where the dining room was, you see,' I mentioned, feeling that, after all, the fault was hardly mine. Bannatyne said nothing, just continued to bob his head silently, until a moment later he signalled with a small gesture that we had arrived at the door I was after.

In the dining room finally, I found my host already seated and eating. He looked up and saluted me with his knife. 'Please, sit down, Simon,' he said between mouthfuls of quiche. 'Help yourself'.

Not even my gnawing hunger – nor a lingering, resentful embarrassment at my inadvertent detour and Bannatyne's begrudging rescue – could keep me from noticing and admiring another large painting that hung on the wall over the dining table, a domineering focal point for the room. Its sheer size was its first notable feature, stretching almost from floor to ceiling. The content, too, struck me immediately as unusual – at first glance, it was nothing more than an abstract configuration of dark colours, lathered onto the canvas in thick strokes, very modern and surreal and quite out of place among the house's more classical decor. Looking closer I realized that this in fact appeared to be another landscape, of a kind. Row after row of jutting green hillsides rose and fell in rippling lines, like columns of waves colliding and overlapping one another, in a landscape that corresponded to no real-life scenes that I knew of. More than that, something about the sharp verticality of the hillsides and their swarming, almost oppressive closeness struck an unreal chord, creating, on the whole, a quite primitive and unsettling effect.

It was a curious choice to hang over the dinner table, and I tried not to let my surprise show too apparently. In any case I was so hungry that the spread of eggs, pastries, and bowls of steaming vegetables laid before me provided ample distraction, and I hovered over the table searching for something to satisfy my ravenous appetite.

'I take it your rooms are to your liking?' Mordrake asked casually.

'Oh yes, more than I need. Again, I am very grateful,' I replied vaguely, my eyes still moving from dish to dish but somehow not settling on anything to put on my plate.

After a few seconds I realized that my host was watching my hesitation with a twinkle in his eye.

'I suppose I should have warned you,' he said, 'though I forget it's something that bothers other people. We serve no meat in this house. You shall have to exist on vegetables and dairy while you stay here, though you shall not go hungry, I assure you.'

I looked to Mordrake, then back at the table, and realized that this indeed was the source of my indecision. 'No meat at all?' was all I could think to say.

'None. I abhor dead things. I shall have none under my roof. You may think it an eccentricity, perhaps, but the Pythagorean diet is not so unusual. And it has been proven time and again that it can provide all the necessary vitality a man requires, with certain benefits to the constitution besides. Try the eggs: a new recipe that has worked rather well, I think.'

Of course, I had known several fellows in Edinburgh who had gone vegetarian at some time or another with varying degrees of enthusiasm and success. Even so, it was somehow not a philosophy I had expected to encounter out here, from the master of a country estate. I must confess I was somewhat disappointed, but I was hardly in any position to protest and so I piled a little of everything onto my plate to make the best of the situation.

'The housekeeper, Mrs Pugh, does insist on bringing flowers inside to decorate the house, especially at this time of year,' Mordrake continued while I tucked in. 'I will allow that they make a pleasing sight for the first day or so, but I cannot stand to see them wither and die. I make the girls collect them up and burn them before that can be allowed to happen,' he said, his voice flat and grave.

It occurred to me that this quite extreme aversion to any reminder of mortality must surely be related to the loss of his wife, and perhaps also to the sights he had witnessed in France during the war – terrors that my generation could only infer from the heavy silence of the men who had been there. I decided that it might be prudent to change the subject.

'The house is a fascinating building,' I said. 'Has your family always lived here?'

'Oh, no. The building was here long before we arrived, in one form or another. I doubt that anyone could hazard a guess at how old it is, truth be told. It has been built and rebuilt time and time again, and what we sit in now is no doubt unrecognizable from its original construction. We Mordrakes have been here for many, many years, mind you. I must give you a tour of the house and grounds at some point. Feel free to wander the estate as you please.'

'I should like to,' I agreed, then added diligently, 'if my work allows the time, of course. And the name, Thistlecrook House: it is quite curious as well. I shouldn't have thought to find such a name so far south.'

'You see, where we are, the border between England and Scotland has moved frequently over the centuries,' my host explained. 'For long periods of history there was scarcely a border at all, and the entire region was mostly an uncontrolled frontier. A place caught on the borderline between whims of nationhood. The house has been English, Scottish, and back again, until such designations become meaningless. I've no idea who came up with the building's name, but I assume that it was a sort of patriotic attempt to imprint the place with a distinct character at some point in its history. Ironic, now – but I think it has a certain ring to it, doesn't it?' He smiled, his pale eyes glinting.

'Yes, it's certainly distinctive.'

'Do you know much about the history of this part of the country, Simon? It is tied closely to the history of the Mordrake name, you know. Hundreds of years ago the borders were entirely lawless and feral. The reivers – you have heard of them, I assume?'

I allowed that I had, albeit vaguely.

'Yes, well, the border reiver clans made their living raiding or robbing anyone who passed through these parts, or tried to settle here – each other included. It really was a wild place back then. Murder, kidnapping, torture, arson, it all went on; women and children too, everything and everyone was fair game. For the best part of three centuries the border reivers ruled these lands, in their fashion. Of course, the only time any sort of army passed through was when they were on their way from England to wage war on the Scots, or vice versa, and they would kick up such a trail of destruction on their way that they left the place worse off than they'd found it. No wonder the people here took matters into their own hands – and who can blame them.' Victor chuckled dryly. 'The Crown held no jurisdiction. In such circumstances people must rely on themselves, and exist on their own terms. Religion, society, civilisation – they all fall away, and older, more primitive wisdoms take hold. These are truths we can all recognize. People began to practise strange rituals in the hills all around here: beliefs that had been long forgotten and then remembered, which would later be called witchcraft. I'm afraid these parts were lousy with covens.' Victor paused here for what seemed like a long time, his brow furrowed, staring away into space, as though he were repeating an old school recital and could not call to mind what came next.

My budding headache was beginning to pinch ever more viciously into my temples. 'How fascinating,' I murmured, rubbing my eyes. 'You seem to have a keen interest in the area.'

Victor looked at me, and a spark of animation returned to his eye. 'It's just family history, as I say. This is where the Mordrakes come in. After the Crowns were unified, the new King James determined to put an end to the reivers, once and for all. He called on aspirant young families to go north and make their name bringing the King's order and justice to the lawless. Any land they could carve out by blood would be theirs to keep. The Mordrakes were one of the families that answered that call, rounding up the brigands and pagans and bringing the border region to heel. That was hundreds of years ago, of course, and we have remained here ever since.'

Victor's voice faded out, his initial enthusiasm quite abruptly drained. As for me, the long journey of my day had caught up with me and, having listened to my host's story, I felt bowed by exhaustion. My head was pounding, and a rising nausea was rendering my much-anticipated meal tasteless in my mouth. I wanted nothing more than to return to my room, lie down and close my eyes.

Conversation faltered. Mordrake seemed content now to brood in silence, and, for me, thinking of anything to say was a chore. I was seated opposite the enormous painting of the undulating hillsides and, during the lengthy pause that followed, I found my attention drawn to it again. Its dark, uncanny peaks and vales I have already described. Above those, forming a stripe along the top of the painting, a deep violet sky was swirled in heavy brushstrokes with tiny white dots picked out for stars. When I had first sat down, one of the oddities of the image that had struck me was the blank featurelessness of the alien landscape – I had thought that no trees or rocks or people clung to the steep slopes. Now, though, I observed there were, in fact, minute red figures interspersed across the scene, dwarfed beneath the rising hillsides they apparently stood upon until they were almost lost within the image entirely. More than that, though, their tiny details seemed to actually be deliberately hidden among the thick splodges and folds of paint the artist had used for the landscape, in a most curious effect. I concluded that the striking, disquieting imagery certainly had some merit to it; the careless execution was not to my taste, but others had more of an appetite for that sort of thing.

The food was cleared away but, as much as I wanted to make my excuses and retire, I felt that good manners dictated I should stay a while longer at least. I lit a cigarette. 'I must admit, I am exceedingly eager to get started on my work tomorrow and discover just what is hidden in your family's collection,' I said. 'I have already admired a small selection about the house. That piece' – I indicated the painting opposite – 'is really quite singular.'

Mordrake looked at me and sighed unenthusiastically. 'That piece,' he said, 'is not for sale.' By now he was slumped in his chair. Perhaps he was feeling as washed out as I was, I thought.

'I was admiring it, trying to make out what it might depict.'

He gave the painting the briefest of sideways glances. 'It was the work of a friend of mine, a scene he once saw – or rather, imagined. I keep it out for sentimentality as much as anything, I suppose. Most of the collection proper I had moved upstairs, some time ago. It doesn't hold very much interest to me any more. In the past we Mordrakes collected obsessively … as I suppose you already know. My ancestors almost made a vice of it. But I haven't looked at those old paintings in years. I forgot I had even asked for the examination, truth be told. I mentioned it to Southgate's out of curiosity and they practically bit my hand off.'

I shifted uncomfortably in my chair. 'Well, of course there is no expectation that you will sell anything. I am only here to make a valuation.' I smiled, my hope of securing a hefty commission seeming to vanish before me. 'Not even a full valuation, in truth: that wouldn't be possible here. I will just catalogue the collection, and identify any pieces of interest – exceptional interest, that is. I am a little surprised it has not been carried out before, actually – for financial reasons, insurance and so on,' I suggested vaguely.

'They have tried, from time to time. Southgate's won the jackpot, I suppose.'

'And of course, it will be an honour for me just to see the artworks,' I added.

Mordrake yawned.

My headache was practically unbearable now, and I judged that there would be no offence in excusing myself – in fact, by this time, Mordrake seemed to be positively willing it. He waved a disinterested hand at me, and I left him at the dining table in his moody fog and returned to my rooms. Pain throbbed like so many needles behind my eyes, and I desired with my entire being to just lie perfectly still, in absolute darkness. I closed the curtains, undressed, fell onto the bed, shut my eyes and willed sleep to wash over me like a cleansing tide.

As exhausted as I was, sleep would not come. It never does when we crave it the most. My mind was turning over and over, churning like a grindstone, replaying and repeating snatches of conversation and glimpses of faces I had encountered throughout the long day, in a meaningless and disorienting performance. And, of course, the more I tried to clear my mind, to concentrate away my dizzying thoughts, the more intensely they pressed upon me.

Of all the faces and voices that recurred in my imagination, none was more dominant than that of my host, Victor Mordrake. In person he had been nothing like my expectations. He was cultured and witty, and, judging by his bookshelves, a rare intellectual – rather old-fashioned, certainly, but with a classical sort of appeal. Undoubtedly an eccentric and I could understand why the townsfolk would feel compelled to whisper stories about him. The innkeeper at the Whistle and Duck had mentioned his moods, too, and I supposed I had seen a glimpse of that in his dip into moroseness at the end of the night. I would have to keep on my guard not to frustrate him with some innocent, inadvertent action. I could not, after all, forget that I was here in a professional capacity, in spite of my host's charming lack of formality.

I must have drifted off eventually, for I jerked back to consciousness sometime later with a start. The pale evening twilight that had filled the room had turned to absolute black. The night had grown hot and fetid, and my sheets were soaked with sweat and bound around me most suffocatingly. I untangled myself, threw them off and lay there in the stifling warmth of my room, throat dry and heart racing. My head still throbbed with a dull ache. Somewhere in the house I could hear footsteps ringing, though the hour must have been well past midnight. Surely the staff were not still up and working? Perhaps someone else was finding the night as sleepless as myself and roamed the halls in search of a quiet mind. The footsteps grew louder, seeming to draw closer to my door, and then softer again as the night walker moved off to more distant reaches of the property. I shut my eyes and listened to their volume rise and fall, rise and fall, until eventually, finally, they faded completely – or else I merely drifted to sleep against their steady, rhythmic beat.

3.

Between intrusive footsteps and my own whirling thoughts, I enjoyed little rest that first night. And yet, as long and arduous as the sleepless hours had been, I could barely believe it could be morning already when the first rays of sun came peeking through the curtains. I groaned and pulled the sheets over my still-throbbing head, then, a few moments later, squinted out at the clock, which told me it was time to rise. Not wanting to delay my first day's work – in truth, the first honest day of paid work of my life – I dragged my reluctant body from the bed and made myself ready.

I soon felt better for having stirred myself into action and, while I dressed, a nervous enthusiasm began to take hold at the prospect of today, finally, laying my hands upon the Mordrakes' artworks. Who could say what I was about to uncover? Me, the first outsider to witness the family's near-legendary trove for who knew how many decades – centuries, even! The work I would begin that morning would establish the first foundation for a proper catalogue of the collection that might expose its secrets to the wider world. My imagination began to run away with possibility.

I was soon skipping down the main staircase two at a time when I encountered the butler, Bannatyne.

'Oh, it is you,' he said, summing up the situation succinctly. 'The master has not yet risen.' His eyes sloped to the hands of the grandfather clock and then back to me. 'I suppose you will want breakfast.'

It was not a question but a resigned statement of the inevitable; he pointed me to the breakfast room and then lurched off in the direction of the kitchens. 'Just some toast and tea would be marvellous, thank you,' I called after him. He turned back, looked for a moment as though he was on the cusp of saying something further, and then resumed his course.

I settled at the breakfast table, wondering what I could possibly have done to offend the man so. He returned shortly with my order, and I ate in silence, alone. When Bannatyne returned to clear my dishes, I asked, with as much joviality as I could muster, 'Mr Mordrake is not an early riser, I take it?'

'Not today, sir,' the aged butler replied. I gave up.

'If you could just show me to where the art collection is stored, then, I will begin my work.'

'Yes, sir.'

Bannatyne escorted me back up the stairs, along the corridor that passed my own bedroom, and up another set of stairs to a previously unseen upper floor, where the ceilings sloped tightly with the angle of the roof. This part of the house seemed musty and undecorated, and appeared to be little used. The air was close, the climate several degrees more heated than in the lower parts of the building, which was already pretty balmy.

We had walked to the far western end of the building to ascend the second staircase, and we walked back now until we must have been somewhere roughly above the central hallway, when Bannatyne jerked open a door and held it ajar, indicating that I should enter. A blast of hot and stale air greeted me from the sealed and unventilated room; inside, I saw a space so large that it must have taken up at least a quarter of this uppermost floor, with a sharply inclined ceiling that almost sliced the room's vertical aspect in two, so that to move about much of the area one would have to stoop. To my astonishment, the entire vast floor-space of this attic room was crammed absolutely full with boxes, crates, rolled up canvases, loose statues and ornaments, and frames – frames everywhere, far too many to count, stacked against each other in long domino rows or piled up one atop the other in haphazard columns, all mismatched corners that jutted out sharply. A single small window set into the slanted ceiling allowed a spotlight of sunshine to illuminate the mess, with little effect except to cast jagged, angular shadows among the maze of heaped artworks.

I could not help but exclaim in horror. 'This is the Mordrake collection?'

'It is,' remarked Bannatyne.

'But … this is how they are kept? Has no care been taken at all?' I asked, my wide eyes bouncing frantically over the crazed clutter and imagining all kinds of ruinous damp and rot setting in, vibrant colours fading in the direct sunlight that beamed through the small window, and rodents and vermin destroying by nibbled inches whatever masterworks may be hidden among the heap. 'You might have consulted someone about proper storage – the proper care and attention with which these works must be treated!' I chided, unable to contain myself. Bannatyne stood just behind me, out of my view, but I could sense his shoulders rising in indignation.

'The master took a dislike to the majority of the collection and had them moved up here several years ago,' he replied. 'We do as the master asks. You may wish to take up the matter with him. Now, I expect you have much to get on with – I shall leave you to it.'

I did not even notice him depart. I took a few anguished steps into the mess – as far as I could into the scant clear floor space available – and wondered despairingly how I should even begin to sort through the chaos. Given how inaccessible most of the artworks were, my choice was rather made for me, and I started by picking hopelessly at the frames heaped closest to the door. To my surprise, at first inspection, the paintings within appeared to be in good condition, with only a faint tracing of dust and no immediate signs of damage. The atmosphere in the attic space was thin and airless, which may have aided their preservation – though for me the heat was stifling, and already my shirt was clinging with sweat. In any case, regardless of their actual state, my heart thudded with indignation at the cavalier lack of care or respect shown for these historically and artistically valuable pieces.

Quickly, though, once I began looking over the paintings themselves, my initial desperation gave way to fascination. This was, after all, the Mordrake collection – at long last! And though I could see now that I had my work cut out for me, I could not lose sight of the professional and academic opportunity this random jumble represented. I began looking through the paintings one by one – not appraising nor inspecting, but only admiring with a freshman student's enthusiasm. Almost at once I discovered that the collection was vast not only in quantity but also in content: a head-spinning mix of styles and eras, all muddled together with no apparent logic or sequence whatsoever. Renaissance biblical studies sat beside medieval woodcuts, next to classical scenes in the Romantic style; while others were much more modern, stark and abstract. A rustic and rudimentary pictorial sequence of rural witchcraft was followed by a sweeping tableau of Samson raining bloody massacre upon

the Philistines with a jawbone; next came almost modernist
depictions of men and women contorted in existential
anguish. In fact, the only common factor that very quickly
became apparent appeared to be a taste for the morbid,
sensationalist, even. Here, a goat-faced preacher clad in
violet recited unholy verses to a slavering congregation;
there, one soldier killed another, impaling him on his spear
in some dusty city street. An apocalyptic vision showed
bizarre demons assembled from incompatible animal parts
gleefully dragging their sinful prey to a fiery and very literal
hell-mouth. A stern-faced scientist performed an experiment on a small animal; next to that, a portrait of a man or
woman in extreme closeup, seemingly grasped and distorted
by a terror so absolute that their features were rendered
barely recognizable as human. I turned over a series of small
medieval allegories, painted directly onto dry wooden
boards, that depicted rotting, worm-ridden corpses and
sickly grinning skeletons arrayed in simple lines, dancing
and joining hands with the living in mad exhortations
towards the grave. The quality varied massively. In some I
saw styles that brought tantalizingly to mind the hands of
Blake, or Goya, El Greco or Caravaggio; others were
amateurish scrawls or wild, almost uncontrolled splodges of
paint that struck me as the works of madmen.

As I looked upon each canvas in turn, the more depictions of slaughter, degradation and savagery that passed
before my eyes, the more I found I had to keep looking. I
began sprawling over the stacked frames, reaching into
corners and pushing my way through the piles in a
compulsive trance. Images of murder, execution, dissec-
tion, experimentation, ritual sacrifice and suicide flashed
before me in a sickly blur of reds and whites, midnight
blues and blacks. Every outrage of biblical or classical
legend was accounted for, from the familiar to the obscure:
from Cain slaying Abel, right through to Judas Iscariot's

lonesome suicide. Brave Judith beheaded Holofernes, Jezebel was torn at by red-muzzled dogs in the street, Caesar died in shock under treacherous Roman knives, while Prometheus was disembowelled nightly upon the slab. A triumphant Odysseus massacred his rivals in love, and poor heartbroken Ophelia lay drowned among the reeds and lilies. The martyred saints were represented in their masses, flesh sickly green and red in their death or dying. Sebastian hung limp and bleeding and stuck through with innumerable arrows; Catherine was tortured and broken on the wheel time and time again, sometimes pierced by turning spikes, sometimes crushed under its roll or stretched over it like a rack; Lawrence sizzled and seared upon a red-hot iron grille; Jeanne d'Arc's innocence was ravaged by diabolical flame; Bartholomew stood crimson and dripping, clutching his flayed skin around him like an elegant lady's shawl. John the Baptist's severed, staring head was served up on platter after platter as though at some nightmarish pagan banquet, while Salome and Herodias looked on with disgust, or indifference, or malicious satisfaction.

For every scene that I could recognize there were at least two more where the subject was too vague, or obliquely depicted, for me to identify. Armies massacred each other by sword, pike and musket in the thousands. Grotesque, absurd devils squatted on beds and whispered heinous knowledge into willing ears. Shrieking victims burned alive in smouldering infernos. Prisoners were sliced and flayed by expressionless torturers. Suicides hanged anonymously in stark, bare rooms. My head spun with every human cruelty. Delving deeper into the hoard, I found exotic, inexplicable images from the distant east, graphics from beyond the limits of my education, depicting many-faced demons with blank, inhuman stares; dream-beings and hovering spectres with wild eyes and gaping maws that demanded sacrifice.

Unflinching harem scenes revealed vices of such sadistic depravity that I could barely comprehend.

It was too much. I realized that I was slick with sweat, and my head felt somehow heavy and light at the same time, as though it would either float away or fall to the floor like a weight. The room was so airless and stifling, and as hot as a furnace in the early summer heat. I gazed about myself as though I were drugged, and discovered that I had clambered almost the entire length of the attic in my frenzied searching through the nightmarish gallery. I needed air. There was barely space to manoeuvre as I edged my way back towards the distant door, picking a path through the hoard; halfway across the room I passed under the hot glare from the window in the ceiling, and I had a thought to open it and permit some fresh breeze in – but upon reaching upwards to paw ineffectively at its frame, I found there was no handle nor hinge by which it could open. Stretching for it only made my light-headedness worse, and I almost reeled and fell completely into the sea of jagged frames. My tongue felt fuzzy and too large for my mouth. In lurching, barely controlled movements I swayed desperately for the door, knocking and tripping over artefacts and canvases as I went.

Finally, barely conscious, I reached the door and burst out into the comparative cool of the corridor. Fortunately, there was no one about to see as I squatted down and cradled my head in my hands, letting the blood course back through my brain and trying in vain to clear my mind of the vicious litany it had just witnessed. I stayed there for some time, hunched foetal-like and sticky with sweat, conscious of the absurd figure I must have appeared but unable to make myself move. What kind of person – what kind of family – could assemble such a collection of horrors? To single-mindedly seek out depictions of such brutality, such inhumanity, seemingly without any regard for or concept of the beauty or the aesthetic quality of the art? I could see now why Victor had shut the collection away – I shuddered at the thought of a respectable house decorated with such nightmares. After a time, I don't know how long, my blood cooled and my pulse slowed, and I felt my lucidity return. Even when recovered I could not bear to go back and face the hateful room again, and so I decided I should walk outside and refresh my head with some open air. I slowly made the descent, keeping a firm hold on the banisters as I went. It was only when I arrived outside and saw how high the sun sat in the sky that I realized how much time had passed – I had spent the entire morning in the heated confines of the attic, obsessively turning and devouring its bloodthirsty contents.

Standing in the cool shadow of the house and smoking a cigarette, I felt more like myself again. In fact, after the shock of the moment, I began to wonder with confusion and embarrassment at what had come over me. Images of the morbid and macabre were hardly unusual in my field of study. Any one of the paintings I had encountered in the Mordrake collection would have been entirely unremarkable, taken on its own. Indeed, most would hardly have looked out of place hanging on the walls of some museum of the fine arts, where the great and the good would no doubt have nodded in appreciation at the stark, unflinching subject matter. But something about the sheer volume of images amassed together, the unrelenting viciousness and detail of their content – not to mention the fetid, oppressive atmosphere of the attic space – had overwhelmed me, and I now found myself deeply reluctant to make my way back upstairs to return to that ghastly room and resume my work. Furthermore, the longer I stood there smoking and thinking the matter over, the more the sheer, startling obsessiveness of the collection struck me. For all of the religious imagery amassed in that dank space, I could not recall witnessing a single portrayal of Christ himself, nor a hint of the eternal salvation or redemption that such art typically promised in exchange for temporary, earthly suffering. No, the focus never wavered from the cruelty of the deed depicted. The Mordrake ancestors must have been truly discerning in their pursuit of the sadistic.

As I brooded and sucked the last puffs from the stub of my cigarette, the master himself appeared from around the corner of the building and greeted me with a cheerful 'Hello, Simon.' At his heel followed a set of dogs in a range of shapes and sizes, trotting obediently – at the back of the pack came the diligent servant Bannatyne.

'Hello, Mr Mordrake. I was just taking a short break from my work – getting a little air,' I explained, though if he was surprised to discover me loitering then he did not show it.

'Call me Victor, I insist,' he said with a wave of his hand. I was relieved to see that his mood had improved again since last night. He walked right up to me and stopped, seemingly waiting for me to say something – I wondered nervously if any pale cast to my face, or darkened patches of sweat around my collar remained as revealing signs of my recent discomfiture. The dogs massed around Mordrake's ankles, the older ones snuffling his dangling hand, the younger pups watching me curiously.

'Your family's collection is truly … something to behold. The, er, scale alone is far greater than I had expected. Even its grand reputation could not prepare me for such an extensive set.'

'Hmm, it does take up quite a lot of space,' Victor replied mildly. 'I don't believe it has been displayed in full, ever. I used to have a few pieces around the house, but I took them down some time ago.'

'I suppose I can see why, if you don't mind me saying. There is a distinct theme that runs through the works. Your ancestors seemed to have had rather a taste for the morbid.'

He chuckled softly. 'Yes, there are one or two pieces that would raise an eyebrow, aren't there? You understand why I removed them from public view – though, I seldom have visitors, living with no near neighbours, here. And I did used to enjoy looking through them when I was a younger man – it seemed like an illicit thrill, you know? Like I was looking at things forbidden. I have rather lost the taste for it all, now.'

'I can imagine.' Once again, I was struck by the thought that Victor's change of heart and attitude to the paintings may have coincided with his return from France, and the war – his return to an empty home. I wanted to ask more, about the contents of the collection and how it had come together, but thought that perhaps now was not the opportune moment.

'I know that the full collection has never been catalogued,' I said instead, 'but is there any record at all of some of the pieces included? Records of sale, and so on? Household finances, even family trees, they could be of immense help to me in identifying pieces of value – verifying their authenticity, and all that. Not that – Well, there are a number of pieces that caught my attention, you see, but there is a limit to what my eye alone can ascertain.'

'I don't believe so,' Mordrake hummed. 'There used to be books of old household accounts and such, there may be some sort of record there – what happened to those, Bannatyne?'

'They were moved to the upper library, sir,' the elder answered swiftly. 'It is on the same floor as your rooms, Mr Christie, in the eastern wing of the building. You will find the upstairs library through the final door on your right.'

'There you go – you can look there. Help yourself,' Mordrake told me, bringing his hands together in a decisive clap that made the jostling dogs prick their ears and stand alert.

'I shall, thank you. Anything I can find could help speed my work considerably. And of course, a clear record of provenance can enhance the value of a piece immeasurably.'

Thinking on my feet, I added, 'I wonder, the attic space which the collection is kept in is quite … cramped. It will be quite a challenge to inspect the works properly up there, and with little natural light. Is there perhaps another room I could work in, bringing the paintings down in sets?' I surprised myself with the perfect plausibility of my excuse, when in reality my sole motive was not to have to return to that sweltering room surrounded by the hateful collection in its totality.

Mordrake's brow furrowed slightly. 'Well, we have plenty of unused rooms in the house. Any suggestions?' He again deferred to his butler.

'The western bedchambers are currently unused, sir. Perhaps they might be adequate? They receive a good amount of sunlight from around ten o'clock onwards. I suppose that you shall need help moving the works. I shall make space in the boys' schedule,' said Bannatyne, wrinkling his nose at me – just a fraction – over his master's shoulder.

'I should be much obliged, thanks.'

The pair departed, followed by the mob of canines. I finished my cigarette then decided to take a look into the upstairs library and its household records, before I plucked up the nerve to return to the paintings in the attic.

Following Bannatyne's directions, I took the stairs up and to the right, then walked along the eastern corridor until I came to the final door. All was silent as I turned the handle and entered into a bright, spacious room with a few armchairs and settees scattered about. Daylight streamed in through two tall windows, though this room was protected from the sun's full afternoon glare by the building's shadow and retained a pleasant coolness. Between the windows a wide desk was set up, and covering most of the walls were extensive bookshelves that had been crammed to overspilling with countless volumes piled tantalizingly on top of one another.

I unhurriedly walked across the room, pausing at the desk to run my hand over its shiningly polished surface, then gazing out of the window absently for a time, thinking I could perhaps spend the afternoon here perusing the books and avoid a return to the suffocating attic, when a slow realization, a sort of creeping sixth sense, told me that I was not alone. I turned, slowly, filled with a sudden and strange apprehension. Huddled on the far side of the room, and hidden from my view by the open door when I had entered, my peripheral vision picked up a blur of blue and the recognizable pattern of a face and two dark eyes staring towards me from the corner. With a start and an involuntary gasp, I turned sharply from the window to face this unknown other. Sat curled in an armchair was a young lady, around my age or perhaps a year or two younger, in a simple blue dress, with long dark hair curling loosely down her shoulders. Her legs were drawn up beneath her in a disarmingly girlish repose. In her lap, her hands lay rested upon the open pages of a book, and her head was dipped towards the words therein, but her round eyes were peering up at me with an expression of surprise, curiosity and, perhaps, faint amusement.

However discreetly startled she looked, I expect the same expression was plastered across my own face amplified tenfold, at the very least. 'Oh! Excuse me! Well! I am sorry.' I have no doubt I looked and sounded a complete fool. After a moment, her eyes lowered back to her text and she recommenced her reading without saying a word.

'I am sorry to intrude upon you, only, you see, I didn't know …' I tried, letting the sentence trail off as she failed in any way to react. For several long, awkward seconds I stood there while she read. I expect I had turned bright red.

At last, she spoke, without looking up. 'You didn't know what?' she asked, turning a page slowly.

'I … I don't know,' were the words I managed to utter.

'You don't know what you didn't know?' the girl said, finally lifting her dark eyes to regard me once more, while the amused curl of her lips spread into a full, sardonic smile. 'Well, I'm afraid I cannot help you with that. It is a burden we all must bear, I fancy.'

I laughed. 'I didn't know anyone was in here, was what I meant to say. I'm sorry, I didn't mean to interrupt.' To my relief, my faculty for speech appeared to have returned. Her eyes were really quite remarkably large, and extremely dark brown, I thought to myself.

'You haven't interrupted. Don't mind me – no one else does,' she said quickly, pursing her lips and returning to her book. Her voice was light, soft, and spoken with what I thought might have been a Home Counties pronunciation – she was certainly not local.

I hesitated for several moments, but the conversation seemed to have ended. I wandered from the window to the library shelves, and stood inspecting the books contained there blankly, my eyes roaming across the titles written upon the rows of spines without communicating a mote of information that my brain could make use of; all of my thoughts were on the girl sitting behind me. I had understood that there was no one else in the house. Hadn't Victor Mordrake said just as much, that he lived here all alone? So who could she be? I realized then that I had not introduced myself – I almost turned and did so that moment, but something made me hesitate, and then it seemed I had stood there for too long and an introduction after such a pause would surely appear absurd. Or would it? Somehow, I wasn't sure. I wondered if she was watching me from behind, equally curious as to who I was, and what this stranger was doing in the house, staring for minutes on end at the bookshelves?

Eventually, out of sheer confused embarrassment, I reached up and plucked a book at random from the shelf with a nod, as though this was indeed the one and only volume I had set out to find. When I turned once again to face the room, I was disappointed to see that the girl was still engrossed in the pages of her own book. She did not appear to be wondering about me at all.

I gave a little cough as I crossed back towards the door, and nodded and smiled a polite goodbye to her when she looked up.

'Oh, wait,' she said as my hand fell upon the door handle. I stopped and looked into her heart-shaped face framed by tresses of shining dark hair.

'You will be staying here for a while, will you?'

'That's right.'

'Would you do me a favour and not mention that you met me? It would be … easier, for both of us. Say nothing to the master, and nothing to that butler, either. Telling one is the same as telling the other, you can be sure.'

'I … well, of course, if you say, but –'

'Just, please don't mention me,' she said simply, her previously disinterested eyes growing wide and imploring.

'Look here, I hardly understand –' I began, but I could see that this was, for whatever reason, an important matter to her. Perhaps this room was in some ways off limits, or perhaps she was one of the household staff, taking an illicit break? Though, this woman did not strike me as any kind of servant, in appearance or manner. Whatever her reasons for making such a request of me, it seemed like a trivial thing to agree to, and I found myself all too happy to tell her what she wanted to hear. 'As you would have it. It is our secret,' I said with a small bow. Her expression relaxed and she gave a faint laugh. I left the room, beaming like a fool and clutching my useless book, though my mind was reeling with unasked questions.

With no more reasons to prevaricate, I made my way back upstairs to the attic room and its gruesome collection; mercifully, the air had cooled off somewhat since the morning, though the place still held an indistinct dread to me. I looked at the book I had taken: it was some aristocrat's account of a walking tour of castles in and around Wales, from the previous century. With a sigh, I dropped the useless tome on top of a nearby stack of paintings, and finally, as the clock hands were beginning to tick into early evening, began my work for the day. I started with the piece nearest to me, turning my back upon the wider room and trying to divert my mind from the accretion of terrors that I shared the attic with. The painting in question was a largely unremarkable, somewhat sensational depiction of the rape of Lucretia. I flipped open my notebook, touched my pencil to paper and wracked my brain for a single meaningful word to write.

4.

After the disorienting series of events that had dominated the morning and early afternoon, I felt that I had only just begun my work in earnest when one of the boys – I believe his name was Arthur – came to inform me that dinner was soon to be served. I half expected to see the young lady I had met in the library seated at the dinner table when I entered, but she was not there, and Mordrake and I again dined alone. My curiosity had been piqued but, even if the mysterious lady had not sworn me to silence, I could see immediately that my host was in no conversational mood. Once again, the evening hours seemed to have rendered him sullen and uncommunicative. I tried to foster some incidental chatter, mentioning again that his family's collection was much larger and more varied than I had anticipated, and that in a first survey I had spied more than a few pieces that I thought could really be of some significant interest. Mordrake grunted few words of reply. Then I made the error of suggesting that I could help the staff ensure the paintings were stored properly, wrapped and protected from wear and tear, nibbling vermin, and the humidity of the oven-like attic.

'I'll store them however I damn well please,' he snapped. 'They are perfectly fine where they are: did you see any signs of damage?' I had to admit that I had not. 'Well, then,' he said, and we passed the rest of the meal in silence.

Mordrake disappeared almost as soon as the food was finished and I was left to my own devices for the evening. In the end I flicked idly through the book on Welsh castles that I had taken from the library. It proved to be a fairly interesting read, though the words on the page could only command half my attention. The other half was twisting and turning over the events of the day. I still grimaced with embarrassment at my extreme reaction to the gruesome paintings, and wondered whether my nerve was up to the task of making a meaningful account of them all. And my encounter with the lady in the library had thrown me off guard too – I had to admit, it wasn't the first time I'd found myself tongue-tied when confronted with a pretty face, but, even so, I found it difficult to account for just how awkwardly I had blown the encounter. Why on earth had I not introduced myself and asked who she was? Neither would have been in any way remarkable or unreasonable. And why was I so surprised and intrigued by her presence, anyway? True, my limited enquiries in Cobsfoot had led me to believe there was no one besides Victor in the house, but it was hardly beyond imagination that he might be joined by a relative, or a second wife, or a young ward even. But then – why on earth should she implore me to keep our meeting secret? I retired to my rooms that night with an unpleasant, foreboding churn in my stomach.

As a strange bookend to the day, I changed out of my clothes and noticed for the first time a painting hanging opposite the foot of my bed. It was not especially large or distinctive, but even so it seemed unusual that it should have escaped my attention the previous night. For a moment, I even wondered if Bannatyne or another had added it to the room during that very day, or else if it had been obscured by a sheet or some such, but that seemed unlikely. The painting itself was nothing very remarkable, yet another landscape, but this one depicted the recognizable shape of Thistlecrook House itself. The perspective was from what I took to be a rear view, and seen through trees, so that the object of the painting was largely concealed by twisting branches in the foreground, and only the roof and a portion of the upper floors of the house could be made out. The angle of the composition was quite curious – why anyone would choose to paint such an awkward, obscured image was a mystery, though the finished effect was of equal parts frustrating and haunting. The brushwork, too, was of some interest: small, tight, swirling strokes of an almost impressionist style, though in my opinion the painter lacked flair.

I climbed into bed and lay staring at the painting opposite, with little hope for a restful sleep. My prospects were not helped by the commencement, as the night before, of noisy footsteps pacing back and forth through the building, sometimes ringing so loud they could have been in the hall directly outside my door, sometimes fading until they were barely audible. I would listen intently to the silence, wondering if they could have ceased entirely at long last, only for their echoing thud to return from some new and distant corner of the house. That went on for several hours, until perhaps two or three o'clock in the morning. A brief period of peace was then broken by a faint hum that seemed to come from outside: a low, vibrating pitch that gently lifted and fell in timbre, and which I could not account for. After a time, curiosity drove me to rise from my bed and pull aside my curtain so that I could peer out over my view of the estate. The moonlit grass glinted and swayed in the quiet night. A lone figure, tall and slender, whom I believed I could recognize, even over such a distance, as Victor Mordrake, moved at a hurried stride across the lawns, away from me and away from the house, gliding in a direct line towards a gap in the seething, dark trees that bounded us on all sides. Above the treetops, I could just make out the lake's distant surface as it glimmered and shone in the starlight.

I let the curtain drop and climbed back into bed. A short time later the footsteps resumed.

I was hardly surprised when Mordrake again failed to join me for breakfast the following morning, considering his forays across the estate under the darkness of night. The man must suffer terrible insomnia, an affliction I myself had struggled with at times of stress – the last two nights included, no doubt brought on by the anxieties of my current errand. I therefore had some sympathy for his plight. Only, I had found that a little warm brandy before bed, followed by quiet, meditative contemplation where I accepted – rather than fought – my inability to drift to sleep, had been the answer. I did not think that stalking the grounds by moonlight could be an advisable practice. Perhaps I would mention this to him when I next found him in an agreeable temper.

These were the thoughts that drifted through my mind as I buttered and ate my toast and drank my three cups of coffee in silence. Also, I wondered how soon I might return to the upstairs library in the hope of encountering the young lady there again. I had still to locate any records that could help me trace the contents of the art collection, after all, and I therefore had a perfectly reasonable excuse to visit a second time. The scene played out over and over in my imagination. 'I don't believe I introduced myself yesterday, my name is …' Or, 'I fear I blundered quite rudely when last we met and passed over introductions completely. I am …' Or, sometimes, with a simple bluntness I could only achieve in my mind's eye, 'My name is Simon Christie; who are you?'

Any immediate return to the upstairs library was thwarted by Bannatyne, who, after breakfast, summoned the lads Arthur and Joseph to begin assisting me in moving some of the paintings from the attic to the spare room that would serve as a sort of makeshift study. The staff had already been busy while I ate breakfast, removing the furniture from the room or pushing it to the side, and spreading old sheets over the floor so that I had a wide, open space to work on. The elderly Bannatyne watched and supervised, a constant looming presence tutting 'mind the corners, Arthur,' and so forth, as we three younger men between us carried a selection of works down. This task took up much of the morning, and I was obliged to spend the afternoon at work on the pieces we had moved. The selection had been plucked at random from those most accessible from the doorway: a varied assortment of romantic witchcraft studies and gilded martyrs meeting their gory ends. I found nothing of particular interest, though there was a quite crude piece that I thought must represent Socrates being executed by hemlock poisoning, which may have held some curiosity value.

Regardless of the quality of the art, the work was diverting and the day passed quickly, though it took some effort of will to keep my mind focused on the task at hand. Whenever I permitted my thoughts to wander, they seemed to find their way to those same dark round eyes staring out of a heart-shaped face – curious, laughing, imploring. I shook my head and chuckled at my own schoolboy fascination for this momentarily glimpsed creature. Remember, reader, that I was still a young man then, and – leaving aside two or three student flings that burned out as quickly as they flared up – I was quite inexperienced in matters of the heart. Who isn't, in their early twenties? Try not to judge my impulsive infatuation too harshly.

Sometime late in the afternoon Bannatyne knocked quietly and loomed into the room. 'Has this space proved more accommodating to your work, sir?' he asked.

His tone was marginally more civil than usual, so I possibly overdid it with the enthusiasm of my response. 'Oh yes, first rate! The light really is much better, it suits my purposes perfectly. And much more space to move about, and breathe – that attic is quite claustrophobic, don't you find? It is much cooler and fresher here. And – just as you said – I have had all of the benefit of the afternoon sunlight. I must thank you again for suggesting this room, and helping me move the pieces down, it really is much appreciated.'

'How gratifying,' Bannatyne offered, after a small pause. 'I only interrupted to inform you that Master Mordrake shall regretfully not join you for this evening's meal – he has business to attend to. As you shall eat alone, we can serve dinner whenever would suit you.'

'Oh, I see. Well, perhaps in an hour? I'm just about finished here … I thought I might take another look in the upstairs library for those household accounts.'

I do not even know why I told him that much. The butler offered no reaction, however, and simply nodded and withdrew. Impatiently I finished what I was doing, packed away my things for the day, and made my way down the first-floor hall, which was almost the entire length of the house, from my workroom at one end to the upstairs library at the other. Somehow, my feet couldn't seem to carry me fast enough – fool that I was, I was almost running. As I neared the library door, though, the thought came to me suddenly that she may not even be in the same room today – after all, why should she? I swallowed, opened the door and entered as gracefully as I was able, and shot a swift glance to the corner of the room, where I was relieved to see the girl, dressed in yellow today, sat curled in the same armchair with a book in her lap. She raised her eyes to me, and smiled – my juvenile heart did a backflip for joy.

'Ah, hello again. I wondered if I might find you here today,' I began, confident and assured.

'And so you did. I'm here most of the time,' she replied, tapping her fingers on the open pages of her book.

'I, er, believe I neglected to introduce myself yesterday. My name is Simon Christie. I am here with the auction house, Southgate's, to value the Mordrake collection,' I recited, stepping towards her and extending my hand in formal greeting. She was slumped so far back in her chair that she had to shut her book and put one arm behind her back to awkwardly prop herself forward with her elbow and place her other hand into mine. I regretted putting her to the trouble immediately – but the touch of her fingers, warm, small and delicate, was electricity.

A brief, painful silence followed before she realized that I was waiting for her to introduce herself in turn. 'Oh, my name is Amy,' she told me neatly.

That appeared to be all I was getting for the time being, so I stepped back and gestured towards the bookshelves. 'Bannatyne told me I might find some household accounts among these volumes. I hoped I might be able to locate some records of what is contained in the collection, or accounts of purchases. Anything to help me establish the provenance of some of the pieces, really,' I explained while she looked up at me with polite attention.

There was another muted pause, and I turned to the bookshelves to resume my search in quiet despair. But a moment later the girl – Amy – spoke again. 'Oh! You're talking about those terrible paintings!' she exclaimed, her eyes widening in comprehension. 'I can hardly even stand to look at them – ghastly, vile things. They can't be of any value, surely?'

I laughed. 'It's a singular collection, I give you that. I was quite taken aback myself when I first saw the content. Not to everyone's taste, and, yes, well, some of it may struggle to sell. But there are undoubtedly pieces of value in there – I think even a piece or two of real academic significance as well.'

'But who would want to buy them?' Amy continued, wrinkling her nose. 'They used to hang downstairs, you know, in the dining room, the parlour and so on … Not the very worst paintings, but still, nothing you would want people to see. Goodness knows what visitors must have thought.' She knew the house well, and was no temporary visitor like myself, I noted.

'Many of the scenes depicted are quite common subjects, particularly for the times that they were painted,' I told her. Somehow, I seemed to have found myself defending the very artworks that had inspired such revulsion in me the preceding day. 'Art is often a way to make sense of the horrors of the world around us. And, to trot out the old homily, beauty lies in the eye of the beholder. Although,' I added quickly, 'I would have to agree, there was not much in the collection I could fairly describe as beautiful.'

Amy said nothing but continued to stare at me, the ink-dark pools of her eyes dancing with something I fancied was close to amusement. I shifted uncomfortably under her gaze, and with a smile and bow I returned to the book-shelves. As before, I was deeply conscious of her sat behind me, and the possibility that she watched me while my back was turned – only, today I was almost certain that this was the case.

Eventually her voice broke the silence once more. 'Did you say you are an art dealer?'

'Not exactly. I work for an auction house. We sell art on behalf of others,' I said, turning back to her and standing in a way I thought might appear distinguished.

'And that is different to a dealer?'

'Well – yes. Although, I suppose, in some ways there are certain similarities between the two,' I conceded.

'Because you both buy and sell art,' she said quickly. Then, 'I don't know very much about it, myself. You must have a keen interest though, to be in your line of work?'

'Yes indeed, since I was quite young. My mother used to take me to the national galleries when I was a boy. I think I inherited much of my taste from her. Art has always been my greatest passion.'

'The national galleries?'

'In Edinburgh.'

'Of course. That is where you grew up?'

'Indeed. And you – you were not born here in Cobsfoot, I daresay?'

'No, no, I moved here from far to the South, quite some time ago, now. So, let me see, you visited the galleries with your mother and developed a passion for fine art. And now it's your employment. How lucky for you.'

I hadn't thought of it on these terms before. 'I suppose it is lucky. Although … it's a different thing, appreciating art at the gallery, and studying its history and significance, and the biography of the artist and so on. Sometimes I worry my individual tastes have been eroded by years of academic study. And attaching a price to it is another matter entirely – it feels disrespectful, somehow, as though it cheapens the whole thing.'

'Oh, so you don't enjoy it after all?' She seemed genuinely disappointed at the news.

'I do … it just doesn't feel like a hobby any more, is all I mean to say. I imagine it's the same with any employment.' I shuffled my feet slightly. 'And you,' I cast about my mind for some witty or incisive question to put to her, which might keep the dialogue going at a lively pace, but all I came up with was, 'do you have any interest in art at all?'

Amy considered the question carefully. 'I enjoy it … I appreciate it … if I see something I like, it pleases me. But I couldn't claim to have a precise interest, or any real knowledge. You would think me very ignorant, I suppose, if we tried to discuss it.'

'I cannot believe I would.'

She smiled coyly. 'What if I told you I liked landscapes the best? That's terribly dull, isn't it?'

'Ah, an appreciation you share with Victor, judging by the decoration around the house.' I very nearly said 'your brother', for that was the relationship between the pair that I had decided to be the most likely, but I caught the words moments before they left my mouth. Amy's brow creased momentarily, reflexively, at the mention of Victor's name, her mouth twitched slightly, and then her expression was serene once more.

'Mm, perhaps,' she said, and then with distaste, 'although he always had a soft spot for those ghoulish paintings upstairs. He would bring them down to show to me, and ask me what I thought, what I saw in them.' She shook her head as though to dismiss the memory, making the curls of her black hair wave, and wafting a cloud of perfumed scent into the air.

'Victor … Victor,' she repeated thoughtfully, and then laughed. 'You know that's not his real name?'

I laughed with her. 'It isn't? Then what is it?'

'He called himself Domhnall when I first knew him, if you can believe it – as if he could trace his heritage to anything remotely Celtic. I doubt that's any more true than Victor, though,' she said, confusingly. Perhaps not his sister, after all.

'Goodness. I wonder what caused him to change it?'

'Oh, he was full of his own self-importance back then.' Amy was still chuckling quietly to herself, and if she heard my question, she did not answer it. She pulled a handkerchief from somewhere and wiped her eyes, then said, slowly, deliberately, 'Simon Christie. Do you have a middle name?'

'I do: James,' I said, laughing now at the strange abruptness of the change to her line of questioning. Amy nodded thoughtfully.

'And your mother, who took you to the national galleries when you were young: what was her maiden name?'

'Well, she was a McGregor. Do you have an interest in family histories?'

'I have an interest in names,' Amy replied, her eyebrow arching minutely. 'I think you can tell a lot about a person by their names.'

I opened my mouth to reply when my eye fell upon the clock on the wall. An hour had passed already, and Bannatyne would be searching for me for dinner if I did not present myself. I did not want him to find me here, with Amy. 'My goodness, is that the time? I had better report for dinner, before Bannatyne sends a search party,' I said.

'How disappointing,' Amy replied, to my endless gratification.

'You will not be joining me for dinner?' I asked, hopefully.

'Oh, no ... I shall dine privately,' she told me, and then laughed as if she had made a joke, and I laughed too, even though I did not understand at all. 'You should come back and visit me again, tomorrow evening after supper. I think the books you are looking for are there.' She lifted an arm languorously and pointed to the far side of the bookshelves. With a step closer, I saw that she appeared to be correct. 'You could make a study of your household records, and I shall read my book.'

'I would like that.' I smiled and bowed, and hesitated for a moment.

'I will be here tomorrow,' Amy told me, the corner of her mouth twitching so that I thought she might laugh again – whether with me or at me I could not be sure, but I did not think that I minded. 'Only … it remains our secret, yes?'

I bowed a final time and left.

5.

I found Bannatyne waiting in the dining room, looking at his pocket watch conspicuously. The evening's meal was served, a cursory affair of cheese, bread and eggs – I supposed the staff had their feet up tonight, and I couldn't really blame them.

'No chance of a steak and ale pie while the master's away, I suppose?' I asked, by way of some small joke.

'I am afraid not, sir,' the stiff informed me humourlessly.

I didn't mind. I was in light spirits. I even caught myself humming a little tune while I ate, and wouldn't let Bannatyne's sideways glower put me off. I had a name, now, to associate with the round eyes and dark hair that possessed my thoughts so: Amy. And we had held a conversation, a good conversation, I thought, easy and natural. She had seemed interested in me, she had asked questions, she wanted to know more … had I presented her with enough questions in return? I had asked some, though I could not now recall what answers she had provided. I still had little clue as to what position she held in the house, the nature of her relationship with Victor, or even her second name. Had she worn a ring upon her slender finger? That might have offered some hint, but, fool that I was, I had not thought to look. In any case, she had laughed a lot, which I found a pleasing and comforting thought.

For all my high spirits, I confess that I was feeling quite perplexed about the whole situation as well, and it took some effort not to throw some questions in Bannatyne's direction while he stalked quietly about the room. I would not have betrayed Amy's confidence by mentioning her to the butler, of course, but I supposed that a few innocent questions about the master and the household couldn't do any harm – even if I was unlikely to get any helpful advice out of the man, and might ruffle his feathers a little. I've never been very good with uncomfortable silence, anyway, and by the time my plate was nearly clean I couldn't stand it any longer.

'Have you been in the service of the Mordrakes for long, Bannatyne?' I asked in as disinterested a voice as I could manage.

'I have been with the master for thirty-three years,' he told me, with a hint of pride.

'That's so? Goodness, that's a span. You must have known him man and boy, then.'

'Yes … I was a young man myself when I first arrived at Thistlecrook House. The master was much different in those days. When first I came … when first I came, I arrived here in much the same way you did,' Bannatyne told me.

I looked at him. 'As an art historian?'

'In a pony cart,' he said, and then, rather pointedly, 'sir.'

I let it slide. 'Did you serve his parents as well?'

'No, sir. They died when the master was quite young.'

'Oh dear.' I couldn't resist pursuing the topic – where was the harm? 'And does Mr Mordrake have any siblings – brothers or sisters?'

'No, sir. Though he did have a sister, but I understand that she also died.'

'Goodness, how terrible for him.'

'Indeed.'

'How … did some illness sweep through the family, or some such?' I asked.

'The parents died of illness, yes. The sister some years later – I understand it was an unfortunate accident. There is a lake just behind the house that freezes over every winter. She fell through the ice while skating, and drowned.'

I almost choked on my mouthful. 'His sister did?'

'Indeed, sir.'

'But – I had heard he lost his wife the same way,' I said, cautiously. 'Surely they can't both have fallen through the ice?'

The butler's craggy features tightened with surprise and suspicion. 'His wife? Mr Mordrake has never married. Where did you hear that? Did you speak to someone in town?' he asked, jutting his chin towards me.

'I – yes, that's right, I heard it in town. But I must have confused myself, I think. Perhaps they said sister. Not to worry.' I waved the matter away, suddenly fearful that I had said the wrong thing. But the girl, Mary, at the tavern in town had told me that it was Mordrake's wife who had drowned, I was certain of it. Bannatyne watched me carefully and cleared the table with his lips pursed tight – evidently there was a mutual feeling that too much had been shared.

After dinner I needed time, and space, to think things over. The sky was still a bright, blue-grey twilight and the climate was warm, so I decided to use the evening to take a walk of the estate and, I hoped, clear my head. Exiting by the front door, I took a little time to admire the well-tended gardens with their rows of colourful flowers that I could not name. As I wandered, the crunch of gravel alerted me to the footsteps of another – looking up I saw that it was only Mrs Pugh, the housekeeper. The cheerful lady waved hello as she made her way to the gates of the estate, where her husband's cart was waiting. I returned her salutation with a wan smile. From the front gardens I walked in a wide circle around the house, admiring its architecture in more detail than I had previously been able. Mordrake had mentioned that the site had been inhabited since time immemorial, and that the ancient core of the building had been renovated and expanded many times; gazing upwards, I thought I could see the signs of its changing style even in its current facade. Architecture was not my forte, but even I could observe how the windows of the upper floors were distinguishably more modern than those of the ground floor. Around the back of the building, I could see what looked like ancient, weathered battlements where the tops of the walls joined with a slanted roof that looked to have been added later. Those with a more expert eye would have found much to fascinate in the mishmash of techniques and styles that were fused into the structure of Thistlecrook House, I mused.

I deferred for now from entering the walled rose garden that I had observed from my bedroom window, and instead followed a trail towards the woods that surrounded the estate's expansive lawns. What I desired most of all was to tramp over some rough, uneven ground and enjoy the untamed benefits of my remote location. A lungful of fresh country air, an earful of evening birdsong, and some splashes of mud on my trousers would surely help to cleanse my mind and bring some order to my confused thoughts – or such was my hope. The trees were old and gnarled, and, though showing some signs of greenery, were still curiously sparse for the time of year. I followed a winding route beneath, between and around their twisted branches and trunks, unsure whether my feet were being led by an estab-lished but barely visible trail, or if I was beating my own untested path across the terrain. In either case it felt good to walk.

Even as my physical self moved further from the looming arches of Thistlecrook House, my mind never left its quiet, crumbling walls. 'It remains our secret, yes?' The words echoed, repeating over and over again in my memory. And the smiling, mischievous, teasing expression on her face, yet her dark eyes betraying her sincerity, an edge of desperation behind her coy words. But why should Amy be so anxious that I not mention our fleeting acquaintance to Victor, when, after all, we all shared a single roof? It surely could not be unexpected that we should meet – and wasn't it Victor himself who had directed me to the upstairs library, which Amy seemed to favour? Strange ideas and insinuations were beginning to overrun my imagination, none of them good, and none with much grounding in reality.

Under looming boughs and between tall, upright trunks as white as bone, my wandering route brought me to a small structure hidden within the woodland. I first glimpsed it through the branches from some distance away, and diverted my path so as to take a closer look; drawing near I could see that it was some sort of circular, colonnaded building placed atop a slight elevation. Its design and location were intriguing enough to distract me from my thoughts of Amy and Victor, momentarily at least, and I clambered up the small hill to inspect the strange ruin.

The building itself was a squat, oval shape, ringed by columns that were now overgrown by creeping vines and foliage. Some sort of memorial, I mused, or perhaps one of those anomalous so-called temples sometimes constructed within the grounds of such noble houses. The entire structure had been completely consumed by nature and neglect, and had evidently stood abandoned for many years. Through small gaps between the overwhelming mosses and ivies I could see that it had once been ornately decorated, with a frieze of apparently classical scenes of merriment and debauchery engraved around the circumference of its

domed roof. Beneath the vegetation, the columns were
patterned in spiralling, winding motifs; leering grotesques
and pagan green men had been sculpted into every nook
and cranny, their mocking faces wreathed in bounteous
abundances of stone foliage, fruit, and berries. I walked a
circuit around the small building and found a doorway, shut
and barred by heavy chains and an intimidatingly large and
well-rusted padlock. The door was weathered and battered
by the elements, though despite its evident age remained as
sturdy and solid as they come. Through a thin, splintered
crack between the door and its frame I could just about peer
inside, but I could make out nothing but shadow within.

The strange abandoned place gave me a sense of foreboding, and after I had lingered there for only a short while,
long enough to conduct my cursory inspection, my senses
began to prickle with the sensation that I was somehow
being watched. Filled with superstitious aversion, I left the
curious construction behind and resumed my trek.

No sooner was the old temple out of my sight than it had
left my mind, my thoughts returning to the house and its
inhabitants, the confused and conflicting accounts I had
heard, and those troubling, bloodstained artworks in the
attic.

As much as I desired to place some distance between
myself and these concerns, and seek some respite from the
mounting volume of questions in my head, I nonetheless
kept Thistlecrook House's looming shape – visible through
the twisting branches – upon my right-hand side while I
walked, so that I should not lose my way and find myself
far from the house when darkness fell. In so doing, I inevitably beat a wide circumference around the building, and,
on such a course, it was not long before my path took me to
the rear of the estate and I spied through the trees ahead the
flashing, silver surface of the lake. I had not set out with the
intention of arriving at that place, but having caught its

reflective glint through the silhouetted trees, I was drawn to take a closer look. I pushed through the foliage on a direct course towards the water, heedless as the branches scraped and scratched at my face and clothes, until the overgrowth fell away and I stood on the dried mud of the bank. The body of the lake was not very large – it could hardly be called a lake at all, in truth – and it might only have taken half an hour to walk the full irregular circle of its shoreline, even at a leisurely pace. The water rippled coolly in the shimmering evening heat, and a hazy vapour seemed to beat off the surface, though the early summer sun had by this time descended almost behind the treeline and out of sight completely. Drooping yellow-green willow trees leaned over the water all around, their bowing fronds almost dipping to the surface, like tentative worshippers reaching but not daring to touch the object of their adoration. All around me, the air buzzed with insects moving in eccentric, dancing circles, filling the atmosphere with a trance-like droning sound, above which I could just faintly hear a gentle gurgling, lapping of water, though I could see no stream or river that fed this reservoir. I stood on that spot for a long time and, while I stood and watched, the sky by infinitesimal degrees changed from dusky blue to pink, then crimson, then deep indigo with the sunset; its dazzling hues were reflected and magnified back towards the heavens with even greater vibrancy upon the vast looking-glass of the lake's surface. The colours and the sounds seemed to wash over my senses completely, and saturate me, and at that moment I thought the view over the lake on that hot evening was more beautiful an image than I could ever hope to see captured by oils upon canvas.

My reverie was broken only when a slight breeze rustled through the branches, whipping across the mirrored waters to break the calm with a pattern of ripples, and then whispering down the nape of my neck, causing me to shudder and recall once again the words of the barmaid in the Whistle and Duck, and – almost – repeated by Bannatyne that afternoon. This lake, so idyllic in the light and warmth of this moment, froze over every winter. A young wife, or a sister, fallen through the ice, to a chilling grave deep beneath the water's surface, her frigid resting place perhaps not to be discovered until many weeks after her disappearance. It seemed difficult to fathom, looking over the placid, inviting waters on this hazy evening, that this spot could hold such grisly association. On the far side of the water from where I stood, I could see a small cabin or boathouse, but even from this distance its appearance was dilapidated and abandoned; not far from me, a small green rowing boat was sucked into the mud on the lake's edge. Despite its natural splendour, it appeared that no one came here any more.

The sky had by now turned to a deep azure of almost total darkness, and the dizzying heat seemed to have all at once turned to a nipping chill. How long had I stood there on the lake's edge? I could not be sure. Whether anyone would notice my absence I did not know, but I had no keys and did not want to risk being locked out. My legs felt tired and heavy, and my eyelids were beginning to droop as I commenced my trudge back towards the house, following the bank of the lake a short way eastwards before turning south when there was no more shore to follow.

As I turned my back on the shining lake to face the house, I chanced to look up. Something about the view of the distant house, partly obscured behind the line of trees, made me stop with a sense of that alarming trick of the senses known as déjà vu. Only – it took a moment to come to me – this was no precognition, no mental illusion; I had indeed witnessed the house from this very angle once before. Hanging on the wall of my room, opposite my bed. The painting in my bedchamber depicted this view, almost exactly. But not quite – the angle was different, the perspective slightly elongated: whoever's hand had created the work must have been positioned some small distance north of where I now stood. The scene depicted in the painting hanging upon the wall of my room was of the rear of Thistlecrook House, as viewed from the centre of the surface of the lake.

6.

When I reported to the breakfast room the following morning, rubbing my raw and hollowed eye sockets after another unsatisfactory night's rest tossing in the heat and listening to the thudding, ceaseless footsteps of the unknown insomniac wanderer as they made their way to and fro about the house, I was surprised to find Victor Mordrake already seated at the table. A hearty plate of eggs and toast was piled in front of him, and a coffee cup was held poised halfway between the table and his lips. 'Good morning, Simon!' he called, in a voice so enthusiastic I might almost have called it insensitive at such an early hour.

I returned the greeting, albeit with less gusto. 'I was not sure whether to expect you back today,' I said.

'Oh yes – just some trifling local business that detained me. No matter. Provincial concerns that come with my position, you understand,' he declared casually, while I helped myself to toast, butter and jam. 'I must apologise for leaving you to your own devices yesterday. I trust you were able to find some diversion in this old place?'

'Yes, of course – it was no inconvenience at all. I was able to locate the household records, which I hope may benefit my work considerably.'

'You know, I have to remind myself that you are here on business,' said Victor – looking at him now, I found I could not think of him as a Domhnall, whatever the truth of the matter. 'I have already come to think of you as an old friend come to visit, Simon. Perhaps it is because I so seldom entertain these days. It seems strange to think, but once, the rooms of this house buzzed with conversation, visitors, energy. All sorts of interesting people used to come and go. Ah, I wish you could have been here then! But that was a long time ago. Now I fear I have become reclusive in my old age.' I must have raised my eyebrows at that. Victor's physiognomy was hard to pin an age to, but I felt sure he could be no older than fifty, or perhaps mid-fifties – and he certainly had the vigour of a younger man.

'I am quite enjoying the solitude, I must say,' I replied. 'I think I can enjoy my own company more easily than most people – I always have.' Even as I said the words, an image of long black hair, brown eyes, formed guiltily in my mind.

'Have you explored much of the house, yet?' Victor asked suddenly, then continued without waiting for a reply, 'I can't remember if I said, but you must make yourself at home – feel free to poke around. It would do the place some good, I think. Shake the cobwebs off, you know. Have you looked around much, already?' His crystalline eyes flashed at me piercingly – was there a suspicion behind his words, I wondered? Did he already somehow know that Amy and I had met? But why, then, the subterfuge?

'Well, a little – not very much, to be honest,' was my answer.

'Only, if you could avoid the western wing on the ground floor, the kitchens and so on, that might be best.' He leaned closer and added in a low voice, 'Bannatyne likes to maintain that part of the house as his own little kingdom. Not much to see there, anyway, ha.'

I thought I would take advantage of his cheerfulness that morning to satisfy at least one aspect of my burning curiosity and asked, 'I thought I heard someone walking around the house, quite late into the night. In fact, I have heard footsteps every night since I arrived, I think. I supposed that it might have been the servants working late?'

'Is that so? Well, like most old buildings, the house can make a terrible racket of creaks and groans. I expect it was just that – don't pay it any mind, you'll soon get used to it. Although, now that I think about it, old Bannatyne does work quite late sometimes – and I am a bit of a night owl myself, I suppose. We'll try to keep it down for you. Oh! Did you enjoy your walk across the grounds yesterday evening?'

'Why, yes, I did, thank you,' I replied, surprised and a little confused by his jarring turn in questioning. 'It was a pleasant evening, so I thought I would venture around the estate a little and enjoy the country air.'

'Quite right! I saw you from my bedroom window,' he explained. 'I must have returned home sometime after you set off. You were crossing the grass, back towards the house. You had been out at the lake.'

'Yes … that's right. I found I had walked there without meaning to,' I said. It sounded almost like an apology. The reports I had heard – inconsistent though they might have been – would indicate that the spot must hold some sort of tragic association for Mordrake; but, if it was so, then he showed no indication of the fact now.

'The sunsets are exceptionally beautiful there, particularly at this time of year,' he said, leaning back in his chair casually. 'Though the insects can bite something rotten,' he added, flicking a toast crumb from his knee so that it arced through the air and landed on the carpet a good three yards distant.

'Yes, it was very beautiful,' I agreed, cautiously. Casting my mind for some other, safer territory towards which I could steer the conversation, I recalled the wild and derelict ruin I had found, not far from the lake. 'I meant to ask, actually,' I piped up, 'on my walk I came across a strange old building in the woods – round, and surrounded by columns. It looked to be completely abandoned. I was curious to know what it might be?'

'Ah yes, the old folly,' Mordrake told me, his eyelids drooping. 'Built … who knows when? A couple of centuries ago, I think. No one goes there now. We had to lock it up tight, to stop children sneaking in to play – some time ago, a couple of youngsters came to some harm out there, I understand.'

'I see,' I answered, wondering just how many tales of woe and misadventure a single house could accommodate.

Mordrake soon excused himself from the breakfast table, muttering about yet more indistinct 'business' to attend to, and I was left to set about my work. That day, and the several that followed it, settled into a routine that felt at once comfortable, familiar, and deeply satisfying to me. I breakfasted either alone or with Victor, following which he would inevitably vanish to whatever oblique concerns kept him occupied through the day. For my part, I spent my daylight hours engrossed in the paintings of the Mordrake collection – examining, assessing, and carefully scribbling down notes regarding their quality, style, possible provenance, and any other points of interest. In truth, this being my first assignment for the auction house and my having received no real training on how I should proceed, I had very little idea what I was doing. But I followed my best instincts and tried to establish a basic foundation that could form a catalogue of the collection, while also sifting out any pieces of possibly significant interest from the wider batch – although, to my disappointment, nothing I examined in that first week struck me as having any particular artistic merit whatsoever: lurid, gruesome or blasphemous scenes with more shock value than quality. Of the lost and forgotten masters the Mordrakes were popularly supposed to have squirrelled away – the reputed da Vinci that no one had seen for one hundred years – I found no evidence at all.

Even so, the work was interesting and the hours passed quickly – which was well, for it was the evenings that were the true source of my pleasure at that time. They began by dining again with my host, which was a more or less enjoyable experience depending on his fluctuating mood. Some days he was cold and uncommunicative, but more often than not he was in good spirits, and would ask me for news from Edinburgh and beyond, enquiring about recent events and current affairs, and listening with amused interest to my attempts to explain or put across a particular point of view. Once or twice, I thought of suggesting he direct Bannatyne to arrange for some newspapers to be delivered, rather than relying on my spurious reports – but of course I said nothing so presumptuous.

On other nights he would talk to me about his own interests: history, astronomy, mathematics, and physics, and other technical and scientific subjects – unusual hobbies for a man of his class and position, certainly, although his interest seemed to be of a purely theoretical nature with no practical application. When I asked him how he came to know so much about such obtuse matters, he only laughed and waved the question away. 'Just a hodgepodge of formal and informal training, old boy. I've picked up bits and pieces, here and there. But really, I know very little at all, in the greater scheme of things.' Despite his humble protestations, he made for a passionate and erudite lecturer – although more often than not I found that, try as I might, I was unable to follow his lines of reasoning. Nonetheless, the depth of his knowledge and infectious enthusiasm made him quite enthralling to listen to.

Or, it would have, if there had not been one other, over-arching concern that indomitably took foremost position in my mind. As soon as the plates had been cleared and I could politely and discreetly excuse myself, I would sneak to the upstairs library to pass the twilight hours in Amy's company. I would knock and enter, and look to the corner where she sat curled in her enveloping armchair, and she would raise her eyes and smile or say a word of greeting. Then I took my place at the desk and we would pass the evening together, her reading quietly while I pored over the household records in search of any accounts relevant to the art collection. She was always there in the library; I never saw her anywhere else.

From our very first such evening, we spent much of our time in comfortable silence, neither of us feeling, it seemed, the need to fill the quiet with idle chatter. To read silently in a room with another might have been awkward – with Amy it was not. Between these wordless periods, though, we chatted, we discussed, we compared our interests and attitudes and perspectives on the world – and for the most part found that these converged most edifyingly. Usually, Amy would begin the dialogue by asking me something – about my childhood, my family, my education – and I would find myself talking at length on these and a myriad other subjects as she, with rapt attention and wide-eyed interest, encouraged additional disclosure from me with a seemingly endless pool of further questions. I had never imagined my comparatively restrained and uneventful life could have sounded so fascinating as it did when I described it for Amy's pleasure. I told her of my – limited – travels around Europe, both with my family before the war and as a roaming young student in the months between university semesters, and of my impressions of the various cultures and peoples I had encountered and the small yet significant differences in their ways of life from our own. Amy, it seemed, had not travelled, and I fancy that the evenings she enjoyed the most were the ones when I spoke of these places. I described at length, with misty reverence, my time in Rome, with its startling juxtaposition of modern urbanity alongside ancient rubble on every street corner; Paris, and the cynical pleasures of Montmartre nestled beside the striking, strident Gothicism of Notre-Dame; and Florence, highest in my estimation of all the destinations I had visited. I told of how my pulse had raced as I trod the halls of the Uffizi, flanked on every side by masterworks, so many assembled together that I might have lived under its roof for a week and still wanted for more time to discover all of its treasures; crossing the Ponte Vecchio, with its curious merchants who seemed to have stepped from another era completely; sitting on a Tuscan hillside, sipping wine and watching the sun set over the city; and, best of all, the sublimity that overcame me as I entered the city's Duomo and gazed up at the painted interior of its dome, the scale and aged majesty so vast that my senses could barely comprehend. Amy's eyes seemed to grow rounder and wider still with every new wonder I recounted; her dark locks bobbed as she nodded her head in mute encourage-ment for me to go on, go on. Recounting these experiences to Amy, I felt that I experienced them afresh myself.

For all of her assertions to the contrary, Amy's artistic knowledge proved good, and she was more than able to hold a conversation on such topics. She had clear and considered opinions and preferences that, when they agreed with my own, were pleasingly insightful; when we differed, her views intrigued and stimulated. But, for Amy, it was literature that stood chief among her pleasures. She devoured books in weeks or even days, reading and reread-ing in an almost trance-like state of total immersion, so that even in that first week I saw at least four different volumes pass through her fingers. Her preference was for novels –

leaps of imagination that flung the ordinary and familiar into the reaches of the extraordinary; but she also had a taste for histories and biographies, often all the more thrilling for the truth of the far-fetched tales that lay within their pages. The theatre she enjoyed, though she lamented its inaccessibility from her remote location; opera and ballet were fine enough when the opportunity presented itself but hardly worth seeking out. She seemed only vaguely familiar with the popular music hall and variety songs of the day, which I confessed to having a certain guilty partiality for. She did not even recognize any of them when I blushingly regaled her with a few verses – quietly, of course, so as not to alert the whole house. Given this evident isolation in which she lived, I did not expect that she would have seen any moving pictures yet, and, indeed, she listened to my descriptions of them with an almost childlike wonderment that bordered on incredulity.

She spoke of an eagerness for outdoor activities when she was younger that now went unindulged. 'Surely the estate grounds provide plenty of space for riding and so on?' I asked, and she responded with a vague shrug and acknowledgement that provided no real answer. 'Come now, you surely can't spend all of your days cooped up in this room?' I asked, trying to sound offhand and inoffensive – yet clearly hitting upon the point rather too boorishly.

Amy turned her eyes upon me sharply and said, 'I enjoy spending my time in here, reading – if it is any concern of yours at all'.

Sagely, I dropped the subject on that occasion. Yet as the hours and days passed, I found that as much as I talked and revealed the full extent of my passions and my hopes, fears, and dreams, my experienced past and my anticipated future, any attempts to draw similar information from Amy were deferred time and time again by polite and witty answers of no substance. Put simply, I had told her all about myself, and she had told me virtually nothing of herself. I knew that she had spent her childhood in the south of England and had come to Thistlecrook House in the blossoming of her adult life; but how or why, what her place was here, and why she remained always alone in this room remained a mystery. By her cryptic entreaty for secrecy when we first met, and her obvious evasiveness and unwillingness to speak when directly questioned, it was abundantly clear that the subject was a sensitive one. I feared charging in with blunt interrogation would only upset or anger her, which my own discretion – not to mention my fear of losing the pleasure of her company – could not entertain. This might sound foolish to you, reader, but as I have said, I was young and largely innocent when it came to matters of love, then. I suppose that I probably still am. In my case, that innocence took the form of a quite overpowering excess of cautiousness, in fear of saying or doing the wrong thing and risking alienating the object of my adoration.

Nonetheless, and with predictable inevitability, my burning curiosity eventually overstepped my delicacy. I forget how many evenings we had passed together peacefully by this point. It began when I asked her, innocently enough, what she was reading that night. It was Austen's *Northanger Abbey*, a firm favourite of hers. 'I must have read it a dozen times over, and I shall read it a dozen more,' Amy told me happily.

'I'm not sure I have ever reread a book that I'd finished. Not since I was a child, anyway,' I said. 'I suppose I should not be surprised that you do, though – I daresay you have read every book in this library at least ten times by now.'

'What do you mean?'

'Only that you are always to be found in here, ensconced in your chair. I have yet to encounter you outside this room.' I smiled, speaking lightly to show I meant no offence, but perhaps my motive was too clear for all that. Amy's face fell into a cold frown.

'Well, I like it here,' she said flatly, and returned her attention to the pages before her.

'I have offended you; I am sorry,' I said, sincerely. 'It is only –'

She cut me off. 'I know what you mean to insinuate,' she said, not unkindly. 'I … cannot doubt that you are curious, and have questions. I do not blame you. You are no fool, and I hope that you do not think one of me –'

'I never could!' I cried.

'We both know that there are … that aspects of my –' The corner of her mouth twitched as she struggled in vain to find the words. 'Let us put it that things have been left unspoken. But you will have to be patient. I will tell you that it is by my own choice that I spend my time here, in this room; I remain secluded out of free will. And now I would ask you, as a gentleman, to change the subject.'

So put, what option did I have but to comply? I attempted to introduce a new topic – I forget what specifically – but the conversation faltered, and we fell to silence for a time.

If I give the impression that those evenings Amy and I spent together were uncomfortable, or strained by frustrated dialogue, it was not so. For the most part, I was perfectly contented to sit and work while Amy read, to answer her questions when they came, and to satisfy her curiosity about any and all aspects of my person and life. I felt – unusually, considering the brevity of our acquaintance – perfectly at ease in her company, and it was enough to simply sit in the same room until the sky had turned claret red with the sunset and, with a yawn, Amy would discreetly signal that it was time for me to excuse myself.

It was only when parted from her that the questions would begin to form, and burn upon my mind, at times consuming my thoughts so absolutely I fell into a sort of mute reverie, a paralysis of anxious mystification. Who was this young lady who read alone night after night, never seeming to leave her quiet library? Where and when did she eat, or sleep, and who among the meagre household staff waited upon her needs? And what was the nature of her relationship to the master of the house? I shall spare you the half-formed essence of my own speculations on the subject, in favour of a recitation of the events and facts as I encountered them. I cannot doubt that you, too, in reading my attempt to recount these circumstances, have formed theories and suppositions: all I will say is that whatever suspicions you may have developed are likely not far off my own, at this point of my story. And if you wonder at my course of action during this account, why I said or did the things I did – well, all I can say is that you were not in my situation, and I proceeded as I thought I must. I would allow that, perhaps, I am a more cautious man than most. Yet it seems to me that most people, in most situations where the best means to proceed is unclear, will favour a careful, restrained approach over wild impulsive action based on an assumption that all of one's darkest suspicions are the unvarnished truth. How often does a person shrug off the most bizarre events as mere coincidence, or happenstance, or good or ill fortune, without giving any serious consideration to a deeper meaning, or a deliberate design, or sinister intent? So it was for me. And now there is nothing for me to do but look back; to relive and re-examine all that happened, and marvel at how, but for some small action here or an inaction there, things might have turned out so very, very differently for me.

7.

Sunday brought a conclusion to my first full week at Thistlecrook House. I did not know what the day's routine would be for the household, if indeed it had one, but I rose early in case I would be expected to attend church – though on the whole that struck me as unlikely. My head was groggy and thumping from yet another sleepless, sweat-soaked night, and I was grateful for breakfast and coffee, though Bannatyne seemed greatly perturbed to see me up so early. I thought he might insist I wait for Victor to appear before food would be provided – but thankfully not, for come twelve o'clock there was still no sign of the master of the house.

I idled around at leisure, admiring some of the curious and exotic ornaments scattered about the ground-floor rooms, and making a more detailed inspection of the artworks displayed on the walls there than I had previously had opportunity to. As I had observed on the day of my arrival, with the exception of the elder Mordrake's portrait in the parlour, the paintings were limited exclusively to landscapes both real and imaginary, as well as plain object studies, in the most part depicting pots and vases of colour-ful, blooming flowers – a substitute in the absence of the

real thing, I supposed, given Mordrake's aversion to wither-
ing petals in his home. It was only then that I realized there
were no other portraits anywhere upon the walls, as one
might expect to see in such a historic home: no family, no
relations, no one. The pieces that did hang were pleasant
enough to look at, and a superficial comparison of their
widely varying styles and methods provided me with some
small distraction, but they could not hold my interest for
very long. I thought of returning to my workroom and
continuing my efforts there, but I felt that I was entitled to
my day of rest. Instead, I quietly made my way to the
upstairs library.

It was empty. The windows were closed, the curtains
drawn, and Amy's habitual armchair sat unclaimed. Absent
of the bright sunlight, and its usual bibliophile occupant, the
room seemed hollow, still and lifeless – an empty shell. It
was dusty, too, I noticed; thick, furry trails of the stuff lay in
heaps on the shelves, and on the backs of the faded settees.
A faint taste of revulsion curled in my throat, and I
wondered that Mrs Pugh's housemaids could be so slovenly
in their duties. My arms pricked with goosebumps and with
a shiver I turned and left the room. It held nothing for me
without Amy's presence. But where could she be? I
wondered if she, alone, might have made the trip into town
to attend church, and felt a pang of sorrow at the notion
that she might do so without inviting me to join her –
though, somehow, I doubted that was indeed where she
was to be found.

I stood now in the dark hallway outside the library. The
house around me was entirely hushed, and apparently
deserted. My gaze passed up and down the corridor, over
the numerous doorways that lined it on either side, and I
found myself wondering what they might conceal. Logically,
given I had never seen her in any other part of the house, I
had to assume that Amy's chambers must lie in close prox-

imity. Behind one of these very doors, in fact. And hadn't Victor told me that I had the run of the house, that I should make the place my own? There would be no harm in looking. With a dry throat and slick palms, I raised my hand and knocked lightly on the door immediately in front of me, directly opposite the library. There was no response. My fingers dropped to the handle and turned it gently – it gave way and the door fell ajar, just a crack.

I hesitated. What business had I in snooping, when I was a guest here, staying under the terms of my employment? And if these were indeed Amy's rooms, what good did I possibly expect to come from my intruding?

After a moment's pause, I pushed the door open more widely, and peered inside. Within lay another suite of rooms much like my own, though bare and unmade, devoid of the warmth of human habitation. Motes of dust swirled through the air, illuminated in the beams of daylight that seeped through the gaps in the closed curtains. Not Amy's chambers, after all. I was at once relieved that my curiosity had not led me into any dishonourable action, and yet my relief was mingled with the bittersweet tang of disappointment, and red-cheeked foolishness.

I wandered into the empty room, taking in its solemn, minimalist furnishings. The parts of Thistlecrook House that I had seen so far had hardly been decorated in modern styles, but this room seemed antique even by the rest of the house's standards. The faded wallpaper, peeling in places, might have been hung a century ago; the dented and chipped furniture looked to belong to the century even before that. The walls and shelves were bare, the bed stripped – I thought I was perhaps the first person to set foot in here for a great length of time. The only sign of decoration in the room was a single small painting in a frame, which stood balanced on a medium-sized dresser. In the gloom, I could not make out its subject; stepping closer, I discerned it was a small portrait depicting a young girl. I picked it up and looked down at her youthful face – I thought she might perhaps have been eight or nine. Her deep, serious brow, and a slight pronunciation of the nose reminded me somewhat of Victor's features – but then her dark hair, drawn tightly with faint curls that fell across the porcelain skin of her forehead, put me in mind of Amy. She could have been a relative of either, or both, or none. There was nothing to be learned from the image.

And yet someone had placed it here, sitting prominently in the otherwise bare, undecorated room, in this house where portraiture of the former inhabitants was almost non-existent. I held the small frame up, turned it around and about before my eyes, looking for – what? Secret notes scrawled on the back of the canvas? What did I expect to see? I returned the painting to where it had stood, then quickly, compulsively, slid open each of the drawers in the dresser one after the other. They glided out easily, unburdened by any contents: each and every one was bare.

A sound echoed from downstairs and startled me into a swift withdrawal from the empty room. Back in the corridor, I sighed at the futility and childishness of my search. What justification could I have for poking around Victor's, or Amy's, affairs, after all? I had to remember my position.

So self-rebuked, I made my way back downstairs and passed the rest of Sunday in solitude. I might have taken another walk around the grounds, but a persistent drizzle was keeping the region thoroughly soaked. There was little for it but to spend my time browsing the downstairs bookshelves and making an attempt to read a selection of their contents. I shunned the more cryptically scientific tomes on offer in favour of the small selection of histories – but even these proved so dry and obscure in their arcane subject matters that I soon slid each one back into its empty space on the shelf with an exhalation of defeat. Eventually, I retired to my chambers.

When night finally came, I had scarcely placed head to pillow before the inevitable footsteps began to echo through the house – more mystifying than ever given how still and deserted the building had been all through the day. On this night they seemed to be worse than I had heard them before: the sleepless walker, whoever he or she might be – my finger of blame ranged inconclusively between three key suspects – seemed to be roaming the entire length of the house and back again at a manic pace. I tossed and turned in bed, my covers flung aside and the mattress damp with perspiration, listening to the ringing steps with a rising sense of indignation. Who could be so inconsiderate to make such a noise at this hour, heedless of the needs of the rest of the household for a good night's sleep? I listened, and fumed, but I did not rise from where I lay.

The night was otherwise so still and silent that I fancied, by sense of sound alone, I could somewhat trace the foot-steps' progress back and forth about the property: from somewhere below me on the ground floor, up the central staircase, fading from earshot as they roamed to the eastern wing of the building, then growing louder again as they drew closer to my own rooms. I rolled over in my bed so that I faced towards my chamber door – I could practically feel the floor reverberate as the steps drew closer, and louder. Between the door and frame, thin cracks of faint moonlight shone through, and as I lay, and watched, the narrow strip of light below the door was broken by the shadow cast by two pacing feet that passed by my room and continued down the hall. I listened to them trail off, and then thud once more in the cramped attic rooms where they seemed to sound directly above my head. Then all fell quiet for a time. Just as I began to drift from consciousness,

I was roused again by the return journey. The footsteps stirred above me, then descended the staircase, then increased in pitch until they passed by my room a second time, where, I fancied, the two dark shadows visible below my door paused, just for a moment – or was that only my imagination?

Monday saw a welcome return to routine after Sunday's restless agitation. Victor greeted me cheerfully at breakfast, brushing off his absence the previous day with the usual vague word about having affairs to deal with. Half by way of conversation, half with genuine curiosity, I asked what sort of business he'd had to take care of on a Sunday.

'Oh, you know. I have various responsibilities as the primary landowner in these parts – and all sorts of titles that are mostly ceremonial, but occasionally require me to sign some papers or make some decisions,' he explained lightly. 'I hope you weren't too aimless on your own again. Did you go for another walk?'

'No, the rain and the humidity rather put me off.'

'Yes, of course, it was a rotter. So, you looked around the house some more?' he asked, fixing me with a friendly but intent stare.

'That's right. There are plenty of books and artworks to divert me,' I told him.

'Mm, indeed – well, that's good. You must make yourself at home, you know. Look around, only remember – it is a very ancient house, and it has its own peculiarities. Some people have found –' he cut himself off suddenly. 'Oh, damn it! I had meant to tell Bannatyne to offer to drive you into town yesterday, in case you wanted to go to church. It completely slipped my mind to mention it. You're not religious, are you?'

'Not really, no. It's not a problem. I don't usually go to church.'

Victor grinned at me and nodded. 'I thought not,' he said.

'Although, if it's all right, I probably should make a trip into town at some time or other, to send a message to my employers and let them know how I'm getting on. But there's no rush.'

'Of course. Use the car when you like – Bannatyne can drive you. Or, can you drive yourself?'

'I'm sure I can – I used to borrow my father's car fairly regularly,' I told him, just a touch defensively. The prospect of a drive, and a change of scenery – and perhaps the opportunity to ask some further questions in town – was really quite attractive to me at that moment. But I still had work to do, and some instinct told me that Victor might not be appreciative if I seemed overly eager to get away. So I made a mental note of the offer of the car, and went about my business for the day as normal.

After breakfast, my daytime hours were passed in contemplation of a series of saintly decapitations depicted in gory, painstaking detail. Disembodied heads with their golden halos still intact rolled about on canvas after canvas, some with their eyes dramatically turned upwards into their sockets and their skin the sickly green of death, others quite serene and philosophical about their sudden change of circumstance. The body of Saint Denis reached out to retrieve his detached cranium as though the execution had been nothing more than a mild inconvenience. The paintings were all fourteenth or fifteenth century, and though I could not have said that any were rediscovered masterworks, my mind boggled to think they should have been shut away in this remote English estate, unobserved and forgotten for such a length of time.

With the evening, I made my way to the upstairs library to look for Amy. I found her nestled in the usual spot, and she greeted me with a quiet hello and small smile, saying no more until I spoke.

'I came to see you yesterday but couldn't find you. Were you occupied?' I asked, speaking offhandedly but watching her reaction closely from the corner of my eye.

Amy closed the book she was reading and ran her fingertips over its cover. 'Hm? Oh, yes … yes, I was elsewhere,' she answered vaguely, then, seeing something more was required, added, 'I'm sorry if you were looking for me.'

'Are you religious at all?' I asked. Amy frowned at me, then raised her eyebrows with a laugh.

'What a strange question! No, I'm not, are you?'

'Not particularly. I asked because it was Sunday – I thought perhaps you were at prayer or some such.'

'Oh. Oh, I see. No, that wasn't it … I just wanted some solitude, that's all.'

'More solitude than you can find here?' I asked, smiling, and Amy pursed her lips in a way that expressed she was not offended by but did not appreciate my humour.

We settled to our reading, she her novel and me my unstimulating lists of numbers, orders, and receipts that were largely meaningless. Bored, and desiring Amy's attention, I picked up the thread of our initial conversation. 'My mother used to drag me to church every Sunday. I hated it; the sermons were so indescribably dull. I can still hear the Reverend Gilhoolie's voice droning on now – God, what a dusty old bore he was.'

Amy chuckled. 'I'm sure he tried his best. I expect you weren't much of an audience to preach to, after all. Were you a choirboy?'

'Ha! No, not me.'

'That's a shame. I can just picture you in a cassock. Is that what choirboys wear?'

'I'm not sure. And in any case, I never wore anything like that, I'm sorry to disappoint you. I did like the art in church, though – of course. I remember a big painting that used to hang in our church, of Jacob and a line of angels climbing the ladder up to heaven. I used to be fascinated by it. I couldn't really understand what was going on, but it seemed magical, so strange and mystical. Perhaps it was that painting that ultimately led me to the job I do now … funny to think. It was probably just some local artist of no significance.'

'When did you last go to church?' Amy asked, drumming her fingers.

'Oh, probably at the beginning of the year sometime. I still accompany my mother every so often.' I think I blushed a little at the admission – Amy seemed to enjoy it, however, and smiled at me fondly, tilting her head slightly. 'What about you? When were you last in a church?' I asked.

'Oh, a very long time ago – well, I suppose it must have been the wedding –'

She fell abruptly silent, and stared down at her book. Her fingers ceased their rhythmic tapping.

'What wedding was that?' I asked.

'I … It was nothing. Oh, please, forget I said anything,' Amy said quietly, not looking at me.

'Your wedding?'

'Please, Simon.'

Without realizing it, I had risen from my chair, and now stood over her where she sat, staring down at the veil of raven hair that fell over her face. 'Who was married? It – it was you, wasn't it? You meant to say your wedding?' I demanded. Her dark locks quivered slightly as she shook her head, but I knew that it was so. Certainty burned in my pounding breast like a hot coal. And then, another certainty, one that I did not want to put into words. I heard my own voice tremble as I spoke. 'It was Victor, wasn't it? You were married to Victor. But you don't wear a ring now,' I added, quietly, lamely, claiming victory in some insignificant battle while the world around me roared with flame.

The hair shook again, and Amy lifted her head. Her jaw was set against me and, with a defiant dignity that scorned my pride, she said, 'You know better than to ask me these things, Simon. I cannot answer your questions – you know this. I wish I could, but … not yet. You must believe me when I say it is better for both of us this way. I … I like you well enough, Simon Christie, but if we are to remain on good terms, I must have your promise that you will not ask such questions.'

For a moment, her quiet, level tone, her moral superiority to my own ungallant prying, flared an indignant anger within me, and I thought that I could be just as stubborn as she. But there was a pleading glint in her tear-rimmed eyes that checked me, and caught the hotly formed words in my throat.

'You must understand –' I began, my voice thin and reedy, like a whining child. My protestations fell silent as Amy lifted her hand quickly, and placed a cool palm against my cheek.

'I do understand,' she told me emphatically. 'I do not blame you for your curiosity – but I cannot answer you, either. Please, Simon, just promise me. Be patient, and promise you will not ask me about how I came to be here, or about my past. Will you do that? Will you?'

I bowed my head. 'You are right – I am sorry. I should not have pushed. Please, let us be friends again.'

'But will you promise me you won't ask again?' she insisted.

I only hesitated for a beat. 'I promise,' I told her. I took her hand from where it rested against my face, held her fingers tightly in my own for a moment, then let it fall. I returned to my desk.

No words passed between us for some time after that. I worked on in silence, trying not to let my frantic thoughts distract me from my labour – trying, but failing. Equal parts of fascination and frustration filled my mind. What sort of promise had I just made – and could I hope to keep it? It

seemed absurd to refrain from asking any questions whatsoever about another person's past. Why would Amy even
demand such a thing? What was it about her background,
and her current situation here in Thistlecrook House, that
made her so secretive?

Secretive, yes, but also fearful, I believed – for surely
there had been an awed terror behind her tremulous voice,
her tearful eyes, as she implored me to silence. There was a
fear and a desperation that – when I thought of them –
made me believe I should not and would not betray her
wish. It was better for both of us, she had said – but how so?
Did she fret for her safety, and mine also? I could not yet
fathom the strange and obtuse truth of the web that Amy
was caught up in. But in that moment, I made another vow,
private but no less significant to me than my verbal promise: I vowed that I would discover the truth of Amy's
situation, and that, if it were within my meagre powers, I
would help her.

Even as I made such a noble pledge, my emotions reeled
at the knowledge, all but confirmed to my mind, that Amy
and Victor had been – were – married. True, Amy had not
said as much – and hadn't Bannatyne asserted that
Mordrake had never married at all? I could have come up
with one hundred alternative explanations to fit the facts I
had collected, but this had to be the most likely, and it was
the one I felt in the knot of my gut to be the truth. My mind
whirled with doubts, apprehensions, and questions: questions which, upon my honour, were bound to go unasked
for the present time.

Almost more pressingly than any of this, though, I
wondered how deeply I might have offended Amy this time
with my blunt inquisitiveness. I had pushed so tryingly that
she had been forced to extract a pledge of silence out of me;
whether she had accepted my word on its own value, or yet
harboured some lingering doubt and resentment towards

my conduct, I could not be sure. The thought that it might be so drove me to distraction.

I could see her in my peripheral vision, seated in her armchair at an angle perpendicular to where I sat. After a short time had passed, I became aware that her head kept bobbing up and down in some curious motion, so that from the corner of my eye I could see her face raised to look at me, then dipping below the falling curls of her hair, then lifting again to watch me furtively once more – all while her hands made a series of small, mysterious movements in her lap. This went on for several minutes – twice I glanced slightly towards her only for her to freeze, and wait motionless until I had returned to my work, only to resume her activity a few moments later. The third time I turned my head, I caught her mid-glance, and she stared at me through wide, playful eyes, a smile dancing upon her lips.

At first, my relief that she was cheerful once more, and seemed to bear no grudge against me, was so overwhelming I forgot my initial curiosity. But another movement of her hand brought my focus back – I noticed that her lap contained not one of her small novels, but a taller and wider book, which was held firmly in one hand angled up and away from me, while the other clutched a pencil.

'What are you doing? Are you writing something?' I asked.

'No, it's nothing – go back to your work.'

'Go on, what do you have there?' I persisted. Amy giggled musically, making me laugh also, though I could not comprehend the joke. I turned in my chair and half rose, but she drew back and clutched her book to her chest in a secretive motion. I sat back down and shifted once again to my work, waving my hand at her. 'Well, go on then. I can see it's a secret. No matter, I shall just assume that it is a joke at my expense, in some form or other.'

'It is no joke!' Amy protested. 'It is … Well, I'm embarrassed to say.'

I turned, resting my arm upon the back of my chair. 'Why should you be embarrassed?' I asked. 'You are writing something, or else drawing a picture?'

'Yes, it's a picture, only … Well, it's the subject that embarrasses me. Oh, I might as well say, for you'll drag it out of me sooner or later – it's a little sketch of you, is all.'

'Of me? I did not know you drew. May I see it?'

'No!' Amy hugged her sketchbook tight and drew backwards into her chair defensively, though I had not moved from my seat and we had the space of half the room between us. 'It's just a hobby. You would be embarrassed for me, if you saw my scribbled attempts.'

'I can't believe that.'

'I haven't drawn in a long time, I'm so out of practice But, well, I thought you looked – picturesque, seated at the desk by the window there. And you were so serious, so deep in thought at your work … I thought I might just take a sketch of you.' She shrugged. Her pale face had turned quite pink.

'Well, I am flattered. I look forward to seeing it when it is done.'

'Oh, I'd be too ashamed to show it to you. I really don't have any talent – and you know so much about art …'

'It's quite bad form to draw a picture of someone and not let them see it, you know,' I teased her. She frowned at me in sincere concern for a moment, then smirked.

'Now you're the one making a joke of it.' Amy tutted. 'You shall never see your picture if you laugh at me. I'll tear it up once I'm done. Now, you just get back to your important work, and let me finish in peace, if you please.'

I laughed, and did as she bid, trying to return my attentions to my books – and for the next half an hour I stared blankly at their columns and numbers and scrawled words

without a single detail contained therein managing to penetrate the chaotic squall of thoughts, questions, and hopes
that spun about my mind.

Night fell, and unfolded in the fashion to which I had
already become accustomed – though not yet acclimatized
– in my time at Thistlecrook House. I tossed and turned
under a muggy blanket of heat that quickly turned to
uncomfortable chill whenever I threw my sheets to the foot
of the bed, and then the pacing footsteps commenced their
march up and down the building, seemingly returning time
and time again to the hall directly outside my room. In my
sleep-starved confusion, I imagined more than once that I
rose and crossed the room to fling open my door and
confront the mystery ambulator, only to discover the hallway deserted and silent – and then I found myself back in
bed, without having stirred at all.

My insomnia brought unsettling new significances to the
hushed sounds of the house at night. The whisper of a light
breeze around the building, over its roof tiles and round its
corners, became the indecipherable language of distant
chants and incantations recited outside my window, deep in
the secret woods. Taps and groans in the house's frame,
among the pipes and in the woodwork, to my ears became
scuttling, unseen things that lurked and skittered in the
darkness – beings that scurried between the gaps. I dreamed
that the house and its grounds had frozen over in thick
layers of unnatural ice, and that I was frozen too, fixed in
place within my bed, while outside great leviathans swam
through the icy vapours hanging thick in the air: vast enti-
ties that moved with an infinite slowness in steady, arcing
circles, their forms cresting and falling in glacial motion
while long tendrils flowed and fluttered behind. Around
and around they went, in an endless, rotating patrol of the
house under the twinkling night sky.

I woke seized with a sudden and deep-rooted panic. It was still the darkest depths of the night. The house was silent now, save for the heaving thump of my heart that felt fit to leap out from my chest. My dreams had been intense, and real, and I thought I had been writhing and crying out in my sleep, though what had startled me enough to wake me from such a deep slumber I had no recollection. I thought I might have heard the footsteps resuming – if their march had ever ceased – though lying there now, staring at the ceiling, I could hear nothing. I rolled over in my bed and tossed and turned, trying to find a comfortable position, until I settled upon my side facing my chamber door, and the familiar pale halo of moonlight that shone around it. It took me a moment to comprehend that something in what I saw there was not right. As I looked now, the strip of light glowing beneath the door was not one, but three. The line was interrupted by a pair of shadows, perfectly still and unmoving: two shadows below my bedroom door – shadows that could only be cast by a pair of feet standing directly outside.

The creeping realization of what I was looking at gripped me with an uncontrollable, almost unaccountable, dread, overwhelming and absolute. Who stood there, outside? How long had they been standing, waiting while I slept? And why – why did they wait outside my door? I was wide awake now, still lying on my side, transfixed with terror, my eyes wide and bulging, unable to blink. I might have called out, asked who was there; I might have risen from my bed and flung open the door in confrontation. As I recount this now, these actions seem simple, obvious even. But as I lay in the dead of night, sheets pulled up to my chin and blood curdled cold, staring at those two dark shapes below my bedroom door, the only thought I could conceive was that whatever stood on the other side was something that I did not – ever – wish to lay my eyes upon.

I watched, and watched. The shapes shifted slightly, motions almost imperceptible except to my electrified senses; they teased their weight from one foot to the other, but did not move from where they were planted. After a duration that might have been mere seconds, or might have stretched on for hours, they withdrew suddenly, slipping into the night and restoring the glow below my door to a single, uninterrupted line. I remained fixed in the same position, continuing to watch it for a long time after. Finally, the worst of my panic subsided and I found I could breathe again, and tear my eyes away. The house felt at peace once more. I rolled away from the telltale light and onto my back, from where I could just make out the painting of Thistlecrook House that hung at the foot of my bed – the painting of the view from the lake. Through the darkness, it seemed not to show the estate in the bright blue and green of a summer's day, as it did in my memory of the image; the colours in the painting now were muted, the sky was overcast and grey, and the branches of the trees were bare of leaf. Blanketing the ground was a thick covering of white snow, as in the deepest chill of winter.

8.

When morning streamed into my room, I sat up at once and, after rubbing my burning eyes, looked to the painting that hung opposite. It showed green grass, budding trees and blue skies overhead troubled by just three – I counted them – wispy clouds. I told myself that the snow-covered scene I had glimpsed last night had been a mere trick of the light, the painting's usual vibrancy washed out in the dim half-light so that all I saw were white fields and black, crooked trees. And the feet at the door … a chance shadow cast in the hallway, or nothing more than a dream brought on by the maddening nightly footsteps. Rational explanations in the clarity of the morning's light, which I offered up as consolation against the things that I knew I had seen.

I mentioned nothing to Mordrake at breakfast, of course, and for his part he was oddly uncommunicative – not moody and sullen as he sometimes became, but, seemingly, distracted by his own inscrutable thoughts. I felt little compulsion to talk with my host, anyway. As my attachment to Amy grew closer, I felt that I equally drifted further from Victor's acquaintance – like a man overboard floating between two life rafts, unable to swim for one without leaving the other behind. Well, I had made my choice. The silence suited me just fine, and the meal passed swiftly.

That afternoon I was in my makeshift studio, hard at work in the study of a new selection of paintings that the lads Arthur and Joseph had helped me carry down from the sweltering confines of the attic room: some fresh slices of repulsiveness from the butcher's shop above. Immersed as I was in my examination, I was surprised to hear the door open and, upon glancing over my shoulder, see Mordrake himself enter. 'Please, please, continue. Don't let me bother you,' he declared as I straightened and turned to face him.

I resumed my study of the painting I had at hand, and tried to relocate the thread of my interrupted thoughts, but quickly discovered it was a fruitless endeavour in the other man's presence. He moved about behind my back, tiptoeing in a conspicuously exaggerated imitation of stealth, all the while humming a faint, tuneless extract to himself and looking over the room's contents.

'Do you know, I haven't been in this room for, I should say, over five years,' he announced, after several minutes.

'You have so much space in the house. I shouldn't wonder some remains unused,' was my reply.

'Yes, far too much empty air for just one man to bounce around in,' he said. I glanced at him curiously, but his manner betrayed nothing.

He moved to my side and looked at the work I had propped up – an unsophisticated woodcut, angled carefully to receive the best portion of the morning's light through the windows. An unidentified man was being sawed in two from the groin downwards, having been strung upside down by his feet by hooded captors. Victor stared at the image for a time without comment. Then he turned to the neat stack I had yet to work on, and chuckled with delight.

'I remember this one! Goodness me, I haven't seen this for the longest time,' he told me with a boyish enthusiasm, lifting the top-most frame from the pile and holding it out to appraise at arm's length. Over his shoulder, I could see that it was a small work, a strange piece showing a well-dressed man playing a fiddle while three squat, corpulent, dun-coloured demons danced around him. It had been accomplished in thick, careless strokes, giving the impression that the piece had been completed in a hurried frenzy. 'Isn't it marvellous?' Victor asked, turning to me, his eyes flashing.

Personally, I found it tacky, and a little repulsive. 'It's a curious piece, certainly,' I said, making up some generic critique on the spot. 'I think it's most likely the work of an amateur – talented, of course. Probably not much value in the auction house, I'm afraid. But, of course, if you enjoy it then therein lies its true value.' Victor didn't seem to be listening, in any case. He was still looking at the small painting, chuckling to himself. I stepped closer and joined him in contemplating the piece, wondering what he could see in such crude, unrefined brushwork and sickly colours.

The longer I gazed upon the piece, the more its intended meaning seemed to speak to me. 'I think it is intended as a study of melancholy, after a fashion,' I said, almost to myself. 'Look at the anguish on the player's face: he seems to take no joy in his music, or the company he keeps. And yet, we might assume that it is his playing that keeps the demons dancing by his side. He tortures himself – perhaps out of ignorance, perhaps by masochistic tendency. Perhaps he is simply … compelled to continue playing.'

Victor looked at me strangely, his pale eyes flashing white in the bright afternoon sun that flooded my workroom. 'D'you think? How interesting. I never gave it such close attention, I suppose. I just thought it looked jolly.' He laughed. 'You must think me an uncultured boor.'

'Not at all,' I swiftly flattered. 'If you enjoy it, then, well, isn't that the single truest aim of the artist? I can think of no greater credit than that.'

'I find your insight fascinating, Simon. I should like very much to hear your thoughts on some of the other pieces, sometime. What intrigues me', Victor mused, 'is what drives an obviously ill man or woman to devote their time, and energy, and meagre resources, to creating such an absurd and pointless image. Why bother? Is it ... some need to describe our world around as we see it, in the forlorn hope that others might bear witness to one's own unique perspective? That they might be acknowledged, and remembered, even after they are gone: a form of immortality? Or is it perhaps a compulsion to multiply and share misery – so that others might see, and acknowledge, and perhaps take on their own fraction of the suffering. Like a starving man handing out his last crumbs.' He laughed dryly. 'What a remarkable condition. No wonder so many of the greatest artists were raving lunatics.'

Mordrake's point eluded me – but I did not particularly appreciate his demeaning my entire field of study in this way, so I thought I would steer the conversation elsewhere. 'A good number of these pieces seem to be by amateurs,' I said. 'And yes, likely some of them were madmen too. I can't imagine they came through regular dealers. And the styles are from all over Europe – all over the world, in fact. It must have taken your family an age to collect them all. To locate such unique images, with such ... attentive dedication to the subject matter.'

'Hm? Why, yes. For generations, hunting the globe for quaint and obscure artworks was chief among the Mordrake hobbies,' Victor said. 'Until I grew bored of it – and so ended that tradition, ha! I think this one is marvellous fun, though,' he beamed at the crude image.

'Well, anyway,' he continued abruptly, 'I only interrupted

you to invite you for a spot of shooting tomorrow. The weather has been so fine and I am restless to tramp around in the sunshine a bit. I rarely have the pleasure of company, besides old Bannatyne of course, and his conversation is limited. So what do you say?'

I stared at him in surprise. The invitation was unexpected, and I found myself lost for words for a moment. I must have dithered in uncertainty for too long, for Victor frowned at me. 'You don't want to? Or – do you not shoot?' he asked, in a somewhat offended tone.

I was not an experienced nor passionate shooter by any measure. My father had dragged me out onto the grouse moors with his business associates a handful of times, but the so-called sport was not to my taste. And I had been a probationer for the university shooting club for a few months, though that had only really been to gain access to their private bar. To Victor I explained, 'Yes, I shoot, a little. It's just – well, I'm a little surprised that an avowed vegetarian would enjoy such a pastime.' In truth, my hesitation owed as much to my uncertainty over whether I should accept his invitation or not, being assigned to the house in a professional capacity, after all. But surely to refuse his offer would be a worse offence than to lose a day's work to leisure?

'Ah, that,' Victor actually seemed a little surprised at my logic. 'Well, I don't eat the stuff, but I have no objections to a little sport. I have the utmost respect for nature, and what is more natural than the predator hunting the prey? Besides, the game makes a good gift for the servants.' He winked.

'Oh, I see. Only … Well, surely the predator only hunts so that it may eat?'

Victor shrugged. 'Well, in any case – you will join me tomorrow, yes? I insist. Good, then it's decided, and I'll have Bannatyne make preparations.'

So agreed, he spent the next hour or so looking through the stack of paintings, and my work had to be put to one side while I listened to his commentary on each. Some he shrugged at and set aside, but most he seemed greatly entertained and fascinated to see, and would declare that he had forgotten all about this one, and thrust it before me with an enthusiastic entreaty to agree it was a fun or amusing piece – adjectives that, given the content of the images, were not altogether appropriate, to my mind.

It was some relief when the pile of available artworks was finally exhausted and he left me in peace. Mordrake's presence had come to feel less and less agreeable to me the longer I stayed within his household. The man himself was charming, and an undeniably entertaining companion to pass the time with – when he was in a favourable mood – and, at times, I allowed my guard to slip and found myself basking in the easy enjoyment of his company. Until, that is, I recalled to mind the varied and grievous suspicions I was harbouring. If, as seemed clear to me, Victor and Amy stood on opposing sides of some wide – yet at this moment unidentifiable – rift, and if, just as surely, my sympathies and my loyalty lay devotedly with Amy, then that must unavoidably place Victor and myself in opposition. I had no evidence, no tangible proof whatsoever, and yet I was confident that Amy's plight, whatever its true nature, must in some way be accountable to Mordrake. The sense of foreboding that the house and its tragedy-touched history invoked seemed to be echoed through the lean form of its master. And then, the question of Amy and Victor's relationship, the wedlock that I now bleakly and jealously suspected to bind them – what was I to make of that? It was true that many married couples lived quite separate lives, often with considerable success. My own parents had quite efficiently reduced their interactions to a handful of clipped communiques per year. But Amy and Victor … their nuptial ties were something else entirely.

Even so, for all these misgivings, I somehow could not bring myself to fully dislike Victor, and the thought of spending a day in the countryside in his company was not altogether objectionable. I did not mention the invitation to Amy later that day. I wanted to – a part of me did – but instinct made me hold my tongue. Surely she would not have welcomed the news. In fact, that evening we scarcely spoke at all. Amy hummed contentedly while she continued at her drawing, and I worked at my desk.

'Is something the matter?' she asked, peering at me closely over her sketch pad after a period of melancholy silence. I assured her that nothing was – she nodded, and did not ask again, but I could feel her gaze upon me still, watching, reading my features and my movements. After a time, she set aside her pad with a gentle sigh. 'You look too withdrawn to draw tonight, Simon,' she told me.

That night I collapsed onto my bed, and – with my back turned resolutely upon the bedroom door and its ominous sliver of light, and the ceaseless beat of pacing footfalls that sounded outwith – fell into an exhausted, nervous sleep. My dreams were of a fiery day of judgement, a sombre scene of ash and smoke, where the unworthy burned in heaped crimson pyres or were shovelled into gaping hell-maws by grotesque-faced demons with heavy, well-muscled bodies that dripped with sweat and grime. I watched the scene from above, with that omnipotent perspective only afforded in our dreams. After a time, I found that I was not alone, for I stood waiting in a line with an amassed representation of the holy saints. They stood apart from me, watching me mistrustfully, saying nothing but pointing to their gory and exposed wounds with a solemn meaningfulness. Some bore scars from axes and swords; some had been burned in a fire. Here, one had been cut through by machine-gun bullets, while another smiled at me sadly from behind her influenza mask. They stared expectantly, as though challenging me to prove my worth among their number, to demonstrate how I had suffered, what I had sacrificed to earn my place in their ranks. All I could do was hold my empty palms open to them helplessly.

9.

My mood of melancholy and apprehension was in no way dispelled come the following morning. My first action upon waking was to rise and throw open the curtains, in the hope that the fickle weather might have turned once more to rain, and my shooting excursion with Mordrake should have to be called off. But the morning was glorious, and my attitude remained sour.

Victor chattered away to me at the breakfast table, not seeming to notice the taciturnity of my responses, or perhaps merely being too well-mannered to draw attention to it. I only half listened as he told me of the day's arrangements and debated with himself as to where we might take the car. He seemed excited, and eventually, after a good dose of coffee, his excitement became infectious, and I found myself nodding along as he weighed the pros and cons of different routes and destinations until he had settled upon a plan. The opportunity to see some of the local countryside was certainly welcome, and I told myself that there could be no harm in perhaps getting to know my host a little more closely – it might even allay some of the tenuously founded prejudices I had been formulating against him. My reluctance was primarily that

I had never much taken to shooting, hunting, nor fishing as pastimes, in spite of – or perhaps precisely because of – my father's gruff efforts to see my masculinity fitted to the mould of his bygone ideals. The world of the twentieth century was changing, and I was a new man to fit a new age – or so I liked to think. Besides which, I could not help but feel an uneasy tangle in my innards that I was, in some way, betraying Amy by offering Victor my temporary companionship, even on such a trivial and harmless outing.

As a final half-hearted attempt to waylay the inevitable, I asked whether we were not out of season for any good game. Mordrake waved the question away impatiently. 'Good game, yes, but there are always pigeons and rabbits to clobber, and if we can blast some blighted crows away, all the better,' cried the vegetarian.

In no time at all, the pair of us were whizzing along the empty country roads at speed in Victor's shining motor car. I wore my sturdiest trousers and a pair of borrowed walking boots – which fitted me surprisingly comfortably – for the occasion, though the weather was thankfully too humid to allow for a getup of full tweeds. Victor himself was at the wheel, I at his side, and a pair of his younger dogs sat restlessly panting and slavering in the back; Bannatyne had, to my relief and the old man's minutely registered chagrin, been left behind for the day. The landscape looked appealingly picturesque in the glorious sunshine, and Victor gave me a decent tour of the area: through the twisted forest where Thistlecrook House was hid; up the hills around Cobsfoot so that we could look down on the small town's neatly clustered buildings from above; then through the varied quiltwork of fields and hills that made up this part of the country; and past neat rows of swaying crops, and cattle that lifted their heads and gawped in mute shock as we hurtled past. While I would never have admitted it to my companion, there was a certain thrill to be had in clapping through the sleepy countryside at such a pace.

We stopped on a hillside seemingly picked at random and began our trek, up and down the gently flowing terrain. Victor made for an impulsive, some might say reckless, gun: as we walked, he would suddenly and without warning swing his shotgun from the crook of his arm and blast into the distance at some quarry I had not yet even spied. Sometimes the dogs would charge off and retrieve a limp rabbit or bird from the grass, other times they simply raised their heads momentarily, then continued scampering about our feet, seemingly already aware of whether his shot had found its mark or not. The man's squeamishness for dead things did not apparently extend to the open countryside, and he soon had a decent haul of rabbits swinging from his belt.

My own takings remained at precisely zero, which suited me, generally preferring to admire the scenery without peppering it with missiles as I did. But after a while, my host seemed to grow concerned that I was not enjoying myself, and began pointing out targets to me with a cry and a jab of his finger as they disappeared fleeing into the undergrowth. I aimed and fired off a few shots, and, to my relief, hit nothing. 'Too bad, Simon,' Mordrake consoled me, with a slap on my shoulder. 'Close one. Quick little rascals, aren't they?' And we marched on.

Soon after I had begun to wonder how long we would continue to trudge through the high afternoon heat, we came to a small hollowed-out ruin of a building, nestled on a hillside in the middle of nowhere. There was nothing left but a rectangle of grey, weathered stone walls, flooded by tall grass and overgrown with purple and green moss, and at one end so collapsed that the stonework stood only waist high and the gable wall had vanished completely. We stopped here for a while and wandered among the ruins, eating the provisions we had brought. Mordrake told me that this had been a church once, built by local families in the sixteenth century; but a rival clan had barred the door from outside during a ceremony and set the building ablaze while there were sixty-seven people trapped within, mostly women, children, and the elderly, massacring them all in retaliation for some long-forgotten slight. Sitting there among the hollowed-out stone skeleton that remained, on a glorious afternoon dappled by the sun that shone down from behind lazily drifting clouds, it seemed almost impossible to credit so cold-hearted an atrocity being committed in such a sleepy and pleasant land.

From our elevated vantage point, I watched as a low breeze travelled over the landscape below, bending the long grass in a wide arc, sweeping around towards us and then up the hill and whispering hollowly through the spaces between where we stood and the patient stones – a cooling moment of relief from the afternoon humidity.

'I had no idea the history of this part of the country was quite so infamous,' I said, breaking the serene silence.

Victor spoke to me over his shoulder from a short distance away, where he stood surveying the land. 'It is not so remarkable. Go anywhere in the world and you will find the same sorts of stories. There is a single scarlet thread of brutality that runs through the history of every culture, every nation – through all of human experience,' he proclaimed.

'I suppose that may be true,' I agreed uncertainly. 'You do seem to be interested in this area in particular, though. In its history, I mean – there are many books on your shelves downstairs.'

'There is always more to learn. I have not read them all, yet,' he replied, quietly so that his voice was almost lost in the gentle rustle of the grass and the thrum of buzzing insects. I wondered in that moment whether an interest in the darker annals of our island's history was connected to the nightmarish art collection the Mordrakes had amassed over generations: a fascination in man's capacity for cruelty to his fellow man, that ranged from history, to art, to who knew what else?

'Your family has always held an interest in the brutal nature of man.' The words had left my lips before I knew what I was saying.

Victor half turned his head, so that he stood before me in profile; against the brightness of the sun I could not make out his features, but his voice told me he was smiling his wolf's grin. 'Just so. It is not something that everyone can understand. Most would turn their heads from the cruellest human deeds, without seeing the inherent honesty revealed therein. It is not the brutality that fascinates, but the truth that it reveals. If you wish to truly get the measure of a person, any person ... then you need only behold them in the indulgence of their most depraved desire. Witness them at their worst, and you witness their soul. Most do not appreciate this – but, Simon, I think that you do.'

I thought that I did not. But even as the content of Mordrake's words, spoken over his shoulder in a slow, steady intonation – a voice that was somehow predatory – shook and revulsed me, the tone of those words, the way in which they were spoken, held me fascinated. I recognized then and there that Mordrake was revealing something to me, something that had until this moment been kept concealed. The corner of the veil was being lifted, and it was for me to reach out and pull the rest away. I thought of the art collection, all ruddy and crimson, and black as the abyss; I thought of roving footsteps at night; the solemn, lonely lake; and I thought of Amy, her curling raven hair, and the pools of her dark round eyes set deep in a heart-shaped face gazing into my own, imploring me. If I asked now, I believed, then Victor would tell me all.

I looked up at the half-silhouette of his aquiline face, opened my mouth, called to him, 'Victor –'.

He turned to face me, his eyes widened with surprise, and he held up his hands. 'Good lord! Have a care, aim it downwards, man!' he cried, his tone a mixture of laughter and command. I followed his gaze and saw, to my astonishment, that the gun I had been carrying broken over the crook of my arm was now held raised, with both barrels pointed directly at my host.

I hesitated. Some wily impulse at the back of my mind raised its voice. How easy it would be, it said, in that moment, to pull the trigger. An instant's decisive action – out here in the middle of nowhere, just the two of us and the two unheeding dogs – and Mordrake would be blown away like the crows he had pelted out of the sky that morning. And, perhaps, Amy would be released from whatever hold the man had on her – she would be free, to be with me.

My target was scowling at me now. He didn't seem overly concerned, more frustrated at my lack of caution. A flicker of pain moved across my skull – a shadow that seemed to jolt through my nerve endings like ice. I winced, feeling the cold sensation of the trigger pressed against my finger. Beads of sweat needled my brow. With an effort, I exhaled the breath that I had been holding suspended in my lungs, and lowered the gun so that it aimed into the swaying grass below.

'I'm sorry ... I don't know what I was thinking,' I stammered feebly, and quickly broke the weapon once more.

Victor shook his head. 'Do have a care, old boy,' he muttered, and squinted at me suspiciously in the bright sunlight.

* * *

Dusk had just commenced to shade the sky as we returned to Victor's motor car and began our journey back towards the house, taking a southerly route through the winding, gnarled forest while the dogs panted and yawned contentedly in the back seats. In the boot was a mass of corpses: limp rabbits and two fat pheasants that were Victor's takings to be gifted to the household staff, and nothing from me. Neither of us spoke very much on the return journey.

I gazed out of the window sleepily, watching the old and wild trees glide past in a jittering slideshow of flashing dark and light. I thought that I caught a fleeting glimpse of the shadowy form of the old Mordrake folly, that colonnaded and overgrown shell of a building buried deep within the woods, almost invisible among the wilderness it had been surrendered to. Not far beyond that, a spark of silver caught my eye, and then, from behind a flickering curtain of trees, the expanse of the lake appeared to our right, a sweeping, mercurial looking-glass under the blushing pink of the evening sky. I leaned forwards in my seat to watch it as we sped past. Victor must have noticed me staring out of my passenger window, for he remarked, 'It's a beautiful sight at this time of day, isn't it?'.

'It is. Hard to believe what happened there,' I heard myself saying dreamily. It took a moment for the words I had just spoken to register; when they did, I was seized by a sudden panic. I looked at Victor, who stared straight ahead, his face creased into a frown. 'That is –' I began, feeling the need to make amends for my incautious words, yet unsure what precisely I was apologising for. 'Well, only that I heard, in town, that someone had drowned in the lake, that they fell through the ice, and ... I ... don't know why I brought it up.'

Victor nodded once, slowly, then answered in a brisk voice, 'Yes, I've heard that too. It's an old story around here – just a myth, I think, to stop the children playing on the ice in winter.' His eyes remained fixed on the blurring road ahead, and if his expression betrayed any emotion, then I could not read it.

Frantic curiosity emboldened me to push the subject, now that it had been broached. 'I think I had been under the impression it was something that had happened more recently, for some reason.'

Victor said nothing, and the reflective basin of the lake moved past us and vanished into the trees. The car slowed to a trundle as we approached the house.

'They used to drown witches, there, you know,' Victor told me.

'Pardon?'

'At the lake. Another strand of humanity's scarlet thread in this part of the world.' He smiled humourlessly. 'At the time when the witch-hunts were all the rage. I told you before that there were covens all around these parts – or, allegations, anyway. Neighbours accusing neighbours, you know, a way of settling old feuds. They held the trials at the lake. And perhaps there were some real witches too. Innocent or guilty: by their dozens, they all drowned in the lake.'

The wheels of the car crunched over the gravel as we drew up to the entrance of Thistlecrook House. In the twilight, I could see the figure of Bannatyne already waiting for us beside the open front door.

That evening Victor remained at the dinner table for a long time talking, pontificating on a wide range of subjects even once our – delicious – risotto had been devoured and the plates tidied away. He sat back in his chair, smoking, and telling me stories of the great many places in the world to which he had been. It seemed that in his younger days he had been something of an adventurer, and had borne witness to most of the great cities of Europe – far more than my meagre travels had taken me to – but also to disparate dusty locales all around the Mediterranean, and the Middle Eastern cradle of humanity, as well as to lands even further to the East, distant and exotic; he talked of cities and land-scapes, and of castles and palaces whose names I had never heard before and sounded directly out of the pages of some works of fantastic fiction.

'I suppose I should not be surprised to hear you are well travelled,' I said. 'I have seen the great range of languages on your bookshelf.'

He shook his head modestly. 'Most are ornamental; I could not read them any more. I am lucky enough to have a good ear for languages, and when immersed in them so that there is no choice to revert to my native tongue, I pick them up quickly – the basics, anyway, enough to get by. But I forget them just as quickly, I am afraid.'

He sighed with satisfaction, loosening his shirt collar. 'It does me good to reminisce about these things, to recall the exploits of my youth. I have become stuffy, a shut-in. I am glad you came here, Simon,' he said, dropping his piercing gaze upon me. 'I feel a younger man, just by having you around. But, what of yourself, you must have seen a decent portion of the world by your age?'

Embarrassed, I admitted the small number of not-so-distant cities I had ventured to, with my family or as a student. Victor knew them all intimately, of course, and his eyes glowed with enthusiasm as he pressed me for details of the precise locales I had visited, and the sights, and sounds, and tastes that I had enjoyed there. 'You still have your youth, and plenty of time. You must make the effort to see, and experience, all that you can while you are able, Simon. The world is truly so much smaller than most people think – but the opportunities that it presents are very nearly limitless,' he told me. 'You are too young, I think, to remember much of what the world was like before the last great war. So much can change, and so quickly, for the better and for the worse. You must experience all that you can before it is gone forever.'

I only hesitated for a moment before asking, 'I was told that you fought, in France?'

'Naturally. For King and Country, eh? Bannatyne came with me, too. I had to pull some strings for that, now that he's getting on in years. But there was nothing very remarkable in my small part. I was there, I suppose, and I saw for myself; that was enough.'

Victor's eyes took on a faraway glaze, and I thought better of pressing him for details that were not offered willingly. You have to understand that at that time, men who were old enough to have been there simply did not care to speak much about the war. And we younger men, we did not much care to hear about it. At that age, living just for yourself seems a complicated enough thing, without being reminded of those lost souls whom you have already outlived. Meanwhile, even as such thoughts sped through my mind, I confess that my eyes shifted towards the clock on the wall. The hour hand was approaching eight, and I was long overdue for my standing appointment with Amy.

While I watched the clock, Victor watched me with a mischievous twinkle in his eye. I caught his gaze, and for a moment imagined that he had read my thoughts and was smiling mockingly at my anxiousness to quit his company in favour of my covert rendezvous. But then he said, 'Come through to the parlour with me, there is something I want to show you'.

I fumbled to find some excuse, but my thoughts were sluggish after the day's excursion followed by a hearty meal with wine; besides, my host was in effusive spirits, and I had to admit I was enjoying myself. I allowed him to lead me from the dining room to the parlour, where we sat upon the ornate settees under the unimpressed glower of the Mordrake ancestor's portrait.

'I had Bannatyne pull these out from somewhere or other, 'Victor said, picking up a small box from the side-board. 'I expect that it would come as some relief to you to learn that this particular piece is not kept with the rest of the collection. Even I have some inkling of its value.' He laid the box on the table and bid me to lean closer. 'I want to watch your expression when you see it.' He smiled. 'You are about to witness the famed da Vinci of the Mordrake collection.'

'Then it's true – you really have one?' I think I gawped at him.

'See for yourself,' he said, and lifted the lid with a quick movement: a magician's flourish. Nestled inside was a small scrap of very old paper, a modest half-page torn from a notebook, but almost the entire sheet was covered in scrib-bles. A series of three drawings dominated most of the space, surrounded by faint handwriting in a compact, precise script. The drawings were, perhaps predictably, anatomical in nature: a human face, then that same face stripped of skin, veined eyes bulging and teeth bared in a shocked grimace, and finally the skull, devoid of all muscle and sinew, its now empty eye sockets wide, dark and star-ing. I gazed down at it for a long time, taking in the details, the composition, the care with which the facial features had been recreated and deconstructed with each successive image. Beside the three proper sketches was a smaller one, a tiny doodled caricature of some sort of ugly crone, facing back across the page at the other images as though in distaste. The room seemed to fall silent as I contemplated the page, only the soft tick of the clock and Victor's breath-ing to accompany my thoughts. I studied each line, each ink-stroke, searching for the marks of genius. For some reason, I felt more drawn to the doodle of the old woman than the other sketches; there was something in its hasty, irreverent nature that appealed. My heart thudded in my chest as I took in the academic significance of the work, but, at the same time, I admit that a shadow of doubt loomed in my mind, that I could never have picked this page out from a folio of one hundred sketches by lesser mortals.

'You know, you are the first person outside the family or the staff to see this, for a very long time,' Victor said quietly.

'I am honoured, truly,' I told him.

'It is not a very remarkable work, perhaps – just a sketch, really, an idle scribble.'

'An idle sketch by the hand of a genius is a rare and remarkable treasure,' I gushed, and Victor seemed mightily pleased.

'Here, something else you might be interested in,' he said, picking up another item from the table – a small book, with a cross on the cover: a bible. 'It is not as remarkable as a da Vinci, but it is a curiosity nonetheless. And I think … yes, I am sure, it will appeal to your sensibilities.

'I told you that the Mordrakes arrived in this part of the country many centuries ago, at the behest of the unified Crown, to put down the border reivers and bring peace to the region. Naturally, force was met with force, and savagery encountered no mercy – the only way to outroot lawless viciousness is to overmatch it tenfold. So it has ever been. The Mordrakes, my ancestors, rode down hard on the reiver clans and brought them to heel, all across these lands. It is even said that it was a Mordrake who led the raid on the wretched Sawney Bean and his clan of cannibals – though I think that is mere legend. In any case, it is true that a Mordrake led the charge against one of the most brutal raiders in the area, a man known as Garvey Little, and cut him down in combat.' He held out the small bible to me, and I took it. 'To commemorate that victory, of order over lawlessness, of good Christendom over wild barbarism – and, I think, to send a message to the other reiver clans – my ancestor had the body brought back to the capital and flayed; and with the bandit Garvey Little's skin he ordered his bible be bound in human leather.'

It took me a moment to realize what I held in my hand. When I did, I almost dropped it with an instinctive revulsion. Instead, I think I said, 'Oh!' and stared at it dumbly. In truth it looked like any other leather-bound book, but somehow it suddenly felt warm and wet against my fingers, seemed to pulse with its own sickly heartbeat, and I had to fight my impulse to place it down or hand it back to Mordrake – anything to put it out of my own grasp.

'Yes, that is the book,' Victor affirmed with relish. 'Quite morbid, I suppose, but I think it's an interesting piece. And I thought you might appreciate it, too, given your interest in the local history.'

'Morbid, indeed,' I said. 'It is … a unique family heirloom. And, I think, a remarkable legacy of a less civilized time.' I passed the book back to him, finally, wanting it in my hands no longer. He opened it at a random page and stared down at the words, a faint smile on his lips.

'I must say … Well, it seems a little strange you would keep such an object in the house, but you will not tolerate dead flowers,' I observed.

Victor gave me a sideways glance and raised his eyebrow. He did not reply for so long that I thought he was not going to, and when he did it was merely to softly growl, 'Do you know, I hardly think it is the same thing.'

By the time Mordrake had shown me these prized possessions, it was too late into the evening for me to reasonably make my way to the upstairs library, and so I offered no objection when he instructed Bannatyne to open another bottle of wine. Briefly, I entertained the idea of contriving to send Amy some sort of message, or apology, but it was impossible of course – and besides, I consoled myself as I took a sip of my fifth, or perhaps sixth, glass of the evening, I had never sworn that I would spend every evening with her, after all. If she missed me, she could always come downstairs and find me.

'Do you have somewhere you need to be, Simon?' Victor asked quietly. I must have been staring at the door, lost in thought.

'Why, no, of course not,' I lied clumsily. 'Only ... I am not used to drinking so much ... on a week night ...'

'What does the day of the week signify?' he replied. 'I am enjoying drinking with you. If you enjoy it, continue – if it does not please you, then by all means cease.' His tone was not malicious, nor defensive – he was simply stating an obvious truth.

'No! No, I enjoy it plenty,' I declared, draining the last of my glass in a hasty gulp.

Victor refilled it at once.

'Then let me oblige your pleasure.' He grinned as the glass in my hand clinked unsteadily against the long neck of the bottle. 'I believe that a man must above all things please himself – and the same goes for a woman, too, for nothing is more equitable than pleasure. What else might be given so freely, and so freely received? What – tell me, what do you believe in, Simon?'

'Well, I believe ... yes, one should do what one pleases, what makes one happy, that is ... if it is not malicious to others. Because, surely there must be some form of moderation? For the sake of ... for the sake of society, functioning society.'

Victor laughed. 'As you may have observed by now, I do not put much stock in society. But you mustn't mistake me. Base carnality will breed misery in time, I am only too aware – first for others, and then for oneself. But simple pleasures ... Pleasure can be harmless, and pursued freely. It is a wonder to me that so many seem to devote their lives to anything and everything other than that which brings them joy.'

'I suppose ...' I looked about the room, with its austere furnishings and empty, silent spaces, filled only by our two meagre voices. Once again Victor seemed to watch, and read, the narrative of my gaze with precision.

'You are thinking this retreat is a strange place for a self-proclaimed hedonist to seclude himself,' he said, his voice falling to a low hush. 'And you are right. I have had my reasons for keeping my own company for some time. But I have been thinking, for a little while now, that it might be time again for me to open these doors, and to reacquaint myself with the world outside.'

Victor and I stood swaying by the fireplace – my glass was full, again, somehow. Our conversation took us long into the evening hours, covering a wide range of subjects that I cannot now recall – subjects of no consequence, I fancy, although they seemed fascinating and significant at the time. After we had discussed, and debated, and laughed together for I do not know how long, Victor fell abruptly silent and seemed to watch me with a curious regard. When he finally spoke, his voice was low and serious; I knew then that he had come to his intended purpose of the evening.

'You have been my guest in this house for some time now, Simon,' he began, speaking so soberly that it made me suddenly conscious of my own drunkenness. 'You appear to have taken to the place better than most. Many struggle to stay here long. I do not know if it is the seclusion, or some aberration in the atmosphere here, or even the magnetic influence of the rock beneath our feet – I have read of the remarkable effects such things can have on the human brain. Whatever the cause, it disorients and upsets. Bannatyne has a devil of a time finding staff that will stay.'

Blearily, I began to wonder if Victor was leading to an attempt to deceive me into revealing my hand, if he was telling me these things in the hope I would confess all that I had to tell of Amy. But he continued, 'Perhaps you heard stories in Cobsfoot, no? Perhaps they warned you against this place, told you tales of tragic misfortune. I shouldn't wonder. But this house and all its oddities don't seem to have deterred you. No, you are fascinated by them.' He was not inviting me to agree with his assertion; it was not a question. 'An ancient site like this, it is filled to overflowing with history. With memories. Memories walk these hallways; they echo through this house like so many footsteps.'

'Footsteps?' I repeated, the hairs upon my neck rising.

Victor's eyebrow raised by a fraction. 'Indeed. Tell me, Simon,' he said, turning the full prismatic intensity of his gaze upon me, 'what about this place intrigues you? I know that you have questions.'

'I … am not sure I follow you,' I slurred, startled at the rough and jarring sound of my own voice.

'Come now,' Victor picked up the wine bottle from the table and refilled my glass. 'I refuse to believe you have not seen anything unusual … that you have not wondered about me, and this place. You need only ask me, Simon.'

I swallowed, tried to think. 'The lake … What I heard … Did someone truly die at the lake?'

'I have already told you that. Many have died at the lake, too many to count.'

'But – your sister, or your wife? Who fell through the ice – was it them?' I seemed to be having difficulty organising my thoughts, or voicing them coherently. I knew I was being drawn into some sort of trap, I could feel it, but could not be sure of the design or the purpose. And I was not so sure that to fall would be the most terrible thing.

Victor only closed his eyes, moved his head in a motion that might have been a nod. He seemed to be standing very close to me, all of a sudden. As confused as I was, as hard as my heart raced, I knew what he wanted me to say; I knew the name he wanted to hear from my lips, but I would not give it. My solemn secret, my honour, was steadfast. A silence yawned between us.

'That's all right,' Victor said then, seemingly in response to nothing. 'This place confuses, it obscures. There is no shame in falling for its trickery. But it must be frustrating for you, Simon, to wonder, without resolution – to have so many questions, with no answers.'

'What about this place –' I blurted hoarsely.

Victor stepped away from the fireplace. At length he removed his dinner jacket, threw it casually onto an armchair, then lowered himself into the settee to recline there, one arm stretched across the back.

'Ah, it is of no matter. Let us continue to enjoy ourselves tonight. Come, sit with me, Simon,' he said.

'What … what is it about this place?' I asked, again. 'What is the lake?'

He smirked slightly, and I felt a hot rush of anger flush my face. He saw my frustration, my powerlessness, and he smiled wider; my burning intensified. 'Nothing but a reservoir, old boy,' he said. 'Yes, you are confused. There is no shame in it, Simon.' He rolled his head back, stretching his neck, arching his shoulders; the bulge of his Adam's apple showed over his starched white collar. 'Sit with me,' Victor said again.

I stood my ground, unsteadily. 'What is happening here – in this house?'

'Do you truly wish to know? No, I don't think that you do. Sit with me. What's the harm?'

My mouth was dry. I lifted my glass to my lips, but it was finally emptied. I knew that I should leave, turn away from the man sprawled across the wide settee opposite. But I did not. I opened my mouth to speak, and some sort of inarticulate groan emerged; but my words – my questions, and my excuses – were spent.

'Simon,' Victor called me from where he lounged, contemplating his fingernail with a theatrical attentiveness, 'we both knew it was going to happen.' The white span of his shoulders rose a margin of an inch, the most casual of shrugs. 'Why resist?'

I affected not to know of what he spoke – looked away, inhaled the muggy atmosphere of the room deeply into my lungs; but my attempt was to fool only myself, and was doomed from the outset. He was correct, I understood. And – after all – what was the harm? Slowly, my body allowing time for my murky cognitions to come up with some excuse – to find any compelling reason to resist – I placed the empty glass on the mantel, and took five careful steps across the room towards the settee. I sat beside Victor, under the fold of his outstretched arm. He chuckled softly.

'Yes. It is this place … it holds a powerful influence over us all,' Victor murmured, his voice very close to my ear. 'But there is no shame in succumbing.'

I felt his hand on my leg, his long fingers splayed across my thigh. My hand was on his chest, pressed against the stiff linen of his shirt, feeling the shifting strain of muscle underneath: pressing against, but not pushing away. He stretched over me, like a jungle cat pinning its prey; his face filled my vision, his bright-blue diamond eyes transfixed my own. His lips were upon mine, surprisingly soft – I met them willingly, hungrily. And then they were at my ear again. 'There is nothing she can give you that I cannot,' he whispered.

10.

I stood alone on the north side of Thistlecrook House, smoking a cigarette and gazing abstractedly over the grass in the general direction of the lake, hidden behind its obscuring screen of trees. I should have been working, but I found I had no stomach for the damned paintings that morning. They had begun to penetrate my dreams, the endless parade of saints and sinners, martyrs and monsters, demons and debauchers; my unconscious mind turned over troubling images like pages of a book, dark and suggestive messages that I could make no sense of, and which permitted me no rest. A hot shock of pain at my fingers told me my cigarette had burned to its end. I threw it aside.

Many had died at the lake, too many to count. Mordrake's words echoed in my ears, cryptic, significant, incomprehensible – another abstract clue for my meaningless pile. I had learned nothing of Amy, who she was and why she lingered in her library, nothing of the roving footsteps at night that waited patiently outside my door – I had tried to convince myself that I had not seen those shadows standing there, but I knew that I had. I had discovered nothing regarding a young body that slipped into the lake on a winter's day, a swirl of dark hair haloing below the fractured ice, white

skin turned to brittle porcelain and pink lips frozen blue.
Victor had offered to tell me. Twice over the course of the
previous day and its evening I believed that the opportunity
to ask him all had been presented to me, and I had not
taken it. Whether my resolution to keep my own counsel
had been judicious or not, I could not be sure.

Recalling what I could of the previous night's conversation, I flushed to think of the events that had followed. My
memory was a blur – I had drunk too much, and Mordrake's
words had confounded me, overwhelmed me. But all the
same …

I had not been with a man since school, not even thought
about it, much. Back then, of course, it had been a different
experience entirely. Grubby fumblings, hasty, almost
violent with embarrassment and inexperience. Scratching
an itch, a necessary, mutually beneficial exercising of bodily
functions. I had known chaps at university, too, who had
gone in for that sort of thing from time to time, and who
had even been quite frank about it all. Most of them had
wives or fiancées now. Once or twice, they had invited me
to join, in a roundabout sort of way. Back then I had never
had the inclination. With Victor it had all been different,
somehow.

I began to stride quickly around the side of the house,
trying to outpace my thoughts. It could not happen again;
of that I was certain. I could not again forget my suspicions,
and fears, regarding the man. And then there was Amy – I
could not help but feel I had betrayed her, in some way. It
was hardly the same as if it had been with another woman,
of course, but even so – and the fact that it had been Victor,
of all people. I might blame the wine, Victor's persuasive
words, whatever malign influences I imagined him capable
of – but in my heart I knew that these factors had only
weakened, but not broken, my resolve. I had followed his
lead willingly, done nothing that I did not myself desire.

In the morning, I had found myself in my own bed – that was something – and I skipped breakfast entirely, unable to face the prospect of encountering Victor at the table. But before long my stomach was grumbling unhappily, and I considered going to the kitchens to find some sort of snack, but the risk of running into Bannatyne dissuaded me – to see the manservant seemed one and the same as seeing the master. I lit another cigarette.

Come dinnertime, my hunger overpowered my aversion to company, and I reported dutifully to the dining room. To my utmost relief, Mordrake did not join me. The stony-faced Bannatyne dropped no clues as to where the master occupied himself, and I did not ask. I fancied that he sneered at me with even more unrestrained malice than usual, and placed my wine glass down heavily with a purposeful clunk – but perhaps by this time I had sunk too deeply into para-noiac fantasy, and these slights were all imaginary.

Mordrake's unexplained absence allowed me to proceed directly from the dinner table, up the staircase and along the east corridor towards the upstairs library. As I made the journey that evening, my emotions were a tangle of enthu-siasm and apprehension. Fewer than forty-eight hours had passed since I had seen Amy last, but it felt like an eternity, and I had to restrain myself from almost jogging the distance from the dining room to the library door with a lovesick excitement. And yet, my stomach fluttered with worry, too – I worried what I would say to her, to excuse my absence the previous evening. I worried that my words, or some-thing in my expression, would alert her to the guilt that clawed and gnawed in my chest. It seemed to me that she would surely read the embarrassment of last night's impul-sive foolishness written all over my face. For some reason, I worried, too, that I may not even find her in the library this evening – some unfounded premonition warned me that I might discover the room empty once more, Amy vanished, from all except my memory. I flung open the door and, unashamed and impudent, looked straight to her armchair. There she sat, in familiar repose with a book clasped neatly in her lap, wearing a yellow dress with her dark hair falling in one luscious wave over her left shoulder. My happy, foolish heart!

'Good evening,' I greeted her, with just a note of tremulous emotion in my voice.

She glanced up at me, after a pause.

'Oh, good evening,' was her murmured reply. I took my place at my desk and opened the household books to where I had last left off. I thought Amy might ask where I had been, why I had not visited the day previous, but she did not. After perhaps a minute or two of pregnant silence, I turned in my chair to face her and began to recite the excuse that I had been mentally rehearsing all throughout the day. 'I was sorry not to have seen you yesterday evening, but I was waylaid by Victor – the man quite demanded all of my attention. Completely unexpected. He kept me talking all evening, and then showed me a couple of his family heirlooms, which I expect you're familiar with. He showed me the da Vinci, which was quite something to behold, I will admit. I felt like an enthusiastic undergraduate again. And he had dug out his bible, too, the one bound in human skin. That, I was less keen on. You … Do you know the pieces I speak of, yes?'

'Hm? Why, yes, I know them.'

'By the time I was rid of him, well, it was late, and I didn't like to presume to call upon you. I didn't think I could send a message, either, after all … Well, I missed your company, even if it was for one evening,' I added, blushing.

'How nice of you to say,' Amy said blandly. Through my entire speech she had not removed her eyes from the page of her book.

Silence engulfed us once more. I had intended to refrain from mentioning the shooting trip, but to fill the uncomfortable quiet I found myself speaking on, confessing more than I had planned to – perhaps I felt compelled to admit to all of my minor misdemeanours, as if that might in some way unburden me of the nagging guilt of the major ones. 'We – Victor and I, that is – he quite dragged me out shooting yesterday, as well. Before he showed me the heirlooms, you see. I'm not a great fan of shooting, to be honest, I'd rather just enjoy the countryside without blasting it to bits … but, well, he insisted, and I could hardly refuse. It was … Well …' I floundered, and left the sentence unfinished, dangling awkwardly in the air between us. Amy offered no response at all.

I tried then to busy myself in my work, thinking that she perhaps simply wanted to read in peace, but found myself utterly vexed and unable to concentrate. Finally, I turned in my chair once again and said, 'Look here, is everything all right? You don't seem yourself, I hope you don't mind me saying.'

'I don't mind at all. I am quite all right, thank you.'

'Are you at an interesting chapter?' I asked.

'What?' Finally, the dark eyes lifted to regard me, for the most fleeting of glances.

'In your book. You appear to be engrossed. I thought if you were at an interesting spot, perhaps I am bothering you?'

'It is all interesting to me,' Amy replied archly. 'Every paragraph has me riveted. I am sorry if you are finding my company lacking this evening. Perhaps you would rather go and spend time with your friend Victor.'

'Well, now, I would hardly say friend. I told you, he practically demanded my presence – what excuse could I make to get away from him? And I missed your company, truly.'

'And I told you, I appreciate your saying so. You mustn't trouble yourself making excuses for my sake. It was … a little unexpected when you did not join me last night. But solitude is nothing new to me – if anything, I was returned to my natural state. I do perfectly fine on my own.'

Naive fool I might have been, but even I could recognize the icy tones of a wronged woman well enough when I heard them. 'Look here, I hardly sought out the man's company – in fact, to come to the point of it, I can hardly stand him.' Amy still did not look at me, but raised a meaningful eyebrow while her eyes remained fixed upon the page. I felt my cheeks burn redder and redder. 'I wish I could have spent the evening here, with you, as had become our routine.'

'Well, if we are wishing for companions, then I suppose I might do better, myself. You are pleasant enough company, as a matter of routine, as you put it. But I think the company of my own sex, over yours, would be much preferable to me. Yes, another lady, who could be my true friend, and a confidante and ally to me – who could really understand me – that is what I would wish for.' Amy had lifted her head and gazed out of the window while she spoke, a mercilessly sardonic smile upon her lips.

'Well now,' I said, 'I can see that you are hurt, so I shan't put any stock in what you are saying. Once again I say I am sorry that I neglected you –'

'Neglected me?' Her sudden glance in my direction, hurled like a hatchet, combined with her icy intonation told me I had once again said the wrong thing. How was it that every word I uttered, no matter how well intended, wound up flung back against me? 'Oh, you should like to think so, shouldn't you? You flatter yourself unduly, Mr Christie. I expect that you like to imagine me, sitting here, alone all day and pining for your company – don't you? Staring at the clock on the wall, and sighing that the hour hand has not yet passed six, which would bring my one salvation from my overwhelming loneliness – my fairy-tale isolation – which is your scintillating company? Well, you can kindly dispel any such notions from your mind. Ugh! Perhaps if you understood that, then you could also understand why I long for fairer companionship.'

There was no reasoning to be had with her, I could see that now. I could have turned and marched out there and then, but – ever stubborn, ever the fool – I soldiered on. 'I have already apologised, what more should I do?' I asked plainly, holding out my hands in supplication.

'Do as you please,' was her infuriating reply.

'But you haven't accepted my apology yet – I only want us to be as we were … I would be the friend you want, if you would let me.'

'I tell you, your sex cannot be a true friend to mine.'

I straightened my posture and summoned what dignity I had left. 'I disagree – but, call it what you will, know that I am on your side, and would help you, if you would accept it.'

This at least garnered some sort of reaction from Amy. She looked at me through wide eyes that shimmered darkly with surprise, or perhaps amusement. 'Help me? On my side? I wonder if you even … Do you truly mean it?' She seemed to ponder the matter for a moment. 'No. I would not come between you and your budding – friendship – with Victor,' she almost spat the name. 'He is welcome to you.' Her eyes bent back to her book.

'Damn it, he doesn't have me!' I cried, and flushed again to think of last night. My frustration overflowed at last. 'You say I do not understand – so, please, Amy, help me. I … I well remember my promise to you, and I shall not break it. I will not ask, but I would listen if only you would tell. And I would help you, too, if I could. I would be your friend and ally, and – and more … if I could only understand what was happening here, if you would just tell me the truth.' My voice was shaking, strained with desperate emotion. Amy regarded me once more, with the same unsettling blend of curiosity and mockery swimming in the inkwell darkness of her eyes. Her lips parted, the corner of her mouth twitched, and for a moment I thought she might relent – take pity on my naked pleading and permit me into her confidence.

Her long raven locks shook, and her gaze turned away. 'No. Perhaps another evening … but I think you should leave me now, Mr Christie,' she said.

I was just about ready to quit her company in any case, and accepted the dismissal gruffly. As I made to leave, though, sheer bloody-mindedness made me pause with my fingers on the door handle and turn upon the room once more for a final word. 'Oh, I have business to attend to tomorrow, in Cobsfoot,' I said. 'I expect I shall return late, so you shall be at liberty to enjoy your solitude, free from my disappointing company, for one more evening at least. Goodnight.'

I left without waiting for a reaction, and made directly for my chambers, where I paced and fretted for I do not know how long. Amy's biting words echoed in my ears, ringing so clearly she might have been hovered at my side, whispering them venomously at me once more. What had made her say such things? She was hurt that I had left her alone, and spent the day with Victor, that was clear – and the night, too, though she could not have known that. I sat upon the bed and wondered. Why should my actions have provoked such a reaction? I would have avoided Victor entirely, spurned his every invitation, turned a deaf ear to his conversation, if she had only asked me – but she told me nothing, and how then was I to blame if I misstepped? The more I thought it over, the more indignant I became, and the more convinced that Amy had behaved entirely unreasonably towards me.

And yet, even as my umbrage rose with each obsessive mental re-examining of the scene that had just unfolded, all

I could think of was seeing her again, and trying to make things right. Three times my pacing took me to my bedroom door, and my fingers reached for the handle that I might proceed directly to the library in the hope of making amends there and then, though by that time the hour had grown late and the moon was waxing high in the sky. Why had I told her I would be absent the following evening? It was true that I needed to go to Cobsfoot at some time in the near future, but I had not planned to make the trip tomorrow. I had even, in a happier mindset, entertained the notion that I might invite Amy to accompany me into town, and – even more ambitiously – supposed she might have accepted. But in my wounded pride I had wanted to have the last word, and, like a child, I had used it to cast a final stone in the hope that it would leave Amy stinging, so that she might know how deeply she had wounded me.

I must have slept that night, for I dreamed. I dreamed that I glided across a vast and white expanse; that I skated endless swooping arcs upon a great field of ice, sailing over the frosted surface like an angel, marking the perfect blank canvas with the indentations left by the bite of my blades; I followed the crisscrossing trails I myself had left behind in long, looping circles. Black trees bent heavy with snow marked the edges of my fantastical rink, my only audience. There was no one else upon the ice; I was completely alone, where no one would find me. In the house, all the people there, they would never find me. Silver crystals danced through the sky, flecked against my cheeks and upon my lips where they melted into dew and were absorbed. Only me, and my reflection, moving below. Moving beneath the surface of the ice, mirroring my movements in perfect synchronicity. A reflection, an endless reflection that followed wherever I would lead, shifting and writhing, formless and exquisite, stretching down, down through the frozen abyss to unknowable leagues. Upon the ice, I was alone and safe; they could never catch me – I was moving too fast – I was flying, I was a bird on the wing, I was a beam of starlight, and none of their plots and schemes could ever catch up with me.

The sound of a great echoing split, a crack like a thunderbolt, brought me rudely back to wakefulness. Immediately upon opening my eyes I was fully conscious and uncannily aware of my surroundings; the contents of my room seemed to shudder and vibrate around me, as though in a state of a sort of hyperreality. My heated nerves jangled with such pent-up energy I felt I was hovering an inch above the bed's surface; the entire room seemed to pulse and glow with sparkling lights, like Chinese firecrackers popping noiselessly. I sat up in the covers and stared about my room in the charged moonlight. Through the fizzing gloom I could make out the shadowy, lurking shapes and outlines of my room's familiar furnishings; yet in that moment they were unknown to me, the placement and ordering of things not correspondent to my recollection. Had those paintings always been on the wall, and in such an arrangement? Was it I who had left the wardrobe door standing wide like that, those drawers slid out as far as they would go? Why was the lid of my suitcase open, my books stacked about the floor in neat piles?

I blinked, and looked to the bedroom door and the broken crack of light below, where two shadows were cast – I wondered how long they had stood sentinel there, what they waited for. Did they guard my sleep, monitor my dreams? 'Who else can it be, after all?' I murmured softly to myself, or perhaps I merely imagined I did.

I averted my gaze and lay my head back upon the pillow. I stared up at the ceiling, then closed my eyes and tried to recapture the thread of the skating dream. I tried, but it would not come back to me.

11.

Victor was already seated at the breakfast table when I arrived downstairs the next morning. I hesitated at the door for a moment, embarrassed to see him for the first time since the night after our shooting trip. For his part, he did not react to my presence at all; only Bannatyne threw me the sneering glance that had, by now, become the customary greeting I expected from him. I took my seat with a sense of trepidation, offered a good morning and reached for the eggs. Mordrake returned my salutation absently, looked up at me and uttered with mild surprise, 'Good God, man, you look awful. Are you ill?'

I assured him I was only tired. He nodded, and pursued no further conversation. I was relieved, being in no mood to talk to anyone – least of all Victor. And yet a part of me was actually surprised, even wounded, at the sudden, cold detachment of his manner. I expected some sort of reaction from the man, considering what had happened between us. And I will admit, as I sat opposite him at the breakfast table that morning, I found that I actually wanted him to look up at me with his cool, hard, blue-white eyes, a faint smile twitching upon his lips.

Faced with Victor's disinterest, it was not long before I fell to my own brooding. My quarrel with Amy still weighed heavy on my mind, naturally; between that and my strange and vivid dreams I had enjoyed little rest. My temples throbbed and burned, my eyeballs felt strained and ill-fitted within my skull. At opposite ends of the same table, Mordrake and I sat and ate in moody silence, each ignoring the other entirely; for all the world we could have been seated on different continents.

After we had eaten all we would, Bannatyne brought in the day's correspondence for Victor. He carelessly tore open the letters and threw them aside with the briefest of glances. For a man with seemingly so little regard for the outside world, he seemed to receive a considerable number of communications, though none ever appeared to require any action or response from him. He sighed and tutted, his eyes absently roving the room. I wondered what could be driving him to such distraction. If his nights were as sleepless and troubled as mine then it did not show on his features. Could it be that he, too, felt as much disquiet and remorse as I did after what had happened between us? He had drunk as much as I, after all, and although he had been the initiator and the dominant partner, well ... perhaps he now regretted the impulsive deed.

Invigorated by hot food and several cups of coffee, by the end of breakfast I was twitching for some reason to break the sullen quiet that had hung over the room since I entered – some topic of conversation to dispel the atmosphere, and perhaps engage Victor's attention so that I might better interpret his attitude. I was loath to indulge in entirely inconsequential chatter, however, in case he might misinterpret my intent. Fortunately, I remembered that I had a legitimate question to ask, and with a small cough I disturbed the peace.

'I meant to ask, would you mind terribly if I borrowed the motor car today to drive into Cobsfoot ... we discussed it some days ago?' I said.

Mordrake raised his heavy eyelids to me. 'Hm? Well, hadn't you better get on with the paintings, don't you think? How much longer are you going to take, anyway?' he replied bluntly. I was taken aback. Nothing in our previous exchanges on the subject had suggested he foresaw a time limit on the extent of my stay; in fact, quite the opposite.

'Well, there are so many, in the collection, I mean – it is extensive, and so poorly catalogued, I still have a lot to do I'm afraid.'

'You've been here a long time already.'

'Yes, well … as I say, there is much to be done to make sense of the collection.' I felt a punch of panic in my gut as I was reminded just how precarious my position here was – how easily I might be sent away, dismissed from my appointed task, from the house, and from Amy.

'I … should hate to overextend my welcome, of course,' I stammered, 'but if you will allow a little more time, I think I can lay a good foundation for any future work, at least. That's why I need to go into Cobsfoot, to send a message to the auction house – to provide an update, and let them know when they might expect me back, you see.'

'Can't you send one of the boys?' he asked. I opened my mouth, hesitating while I tried to think of some excuse. The truth was that I could entrust a simple message to one of the staff, of course, but I had been keen to return to the town, and spend some time away from the walls of Thistlecrook House – and, I hoped, make some selective enquiries among the townsfolk. Before I could conjure a compelling argument, however, Victor waved his hand irritably. 'Oh, go on, take the car for today. I don't need the cursed thing anyway. Just speak to Bannatyne about the arrangements, won't you?'

So it was that around midday I drove Victor's car into Cobsfoot, rolling slowly and carefully through the winding forest that lay between the house and the town. When I had asked Bannatyne for directions, Victor, who had been within earshot, had declared tetchily, 'Just follow the road, it will take you there,' and his words did not steer me wrong. After perhaps twenty minutes or so of cautiously snaking along its twists and turns, I emerged from the woods and, driving up the hill out of the valley where Thistlecrook House sat, could see the spire of Cobsfoot church high above me.

As the road put distance between myself and the old house and its troubling occupants, and as the church spire rose like a beacon on the hill ahead, I felt some of the shadowy anxiousness that had weighed upon me for I know not how long – the restless, lurking sense of dread that jangled constantly against my tired nerves – lift from my burdened and fatigued soul. My heart raced a little slower, and the questions that spun endlessly within my brain reduced their pace by a fraction. A change of surroundings would be the tonic I so sorely needed, I told myself – and, perhaps, there would be answers to be found in town.

I puttered into the village and parked in the sunny square where I had passed the morning so many days ago. How long had it been since I was here last? The rigid structure of my own routine, followed daily almost without interruption, combined with the lackadaisical absence of any sort of coherence or pattern to the passage of time for the rest of Thistlecrook House, had made the days blur into one, and I had no clear notion of how long I had been away from home on this task of mine. Perhaps Victor was right – perhaps I had been under his roof for far too long a time.

The town square had struck me as quiet on my first visit and it was even more so now, the townsfolk being hard at work without the sorrowful occasion of a young girl's funeral to divert them. Except, apparently, for the post office clerk, for when I located that building I found it shut

tight with no sign to indicate why, or when it might reopen.
I loitered around the square, wondering if such a small
town would have a telephone by which I might get a
message to Edinburgh – and then, my stomach reminding
me of the hour, I decided to obtain some light lunch while
I waited for the post office to reopen. I made for the Whistle
and Duck. Before long, I was drinking tea and eating cake,
with what selection of the week's newspapers I could find
spread out on the table before me. After my indeterminate
period of seclusion, I had hoped to catch up on the events
of the last while in the wider world, but now I found myself
staring at the articles blankly, like a visitor in a foreign
country with only the faintest understanding of local
concerns and controversies. The newspapers reported polit-
ical manoeuvres in Westminster, speculated about events
unfolding overseas, and whispered idle gossip and scandal
among the aristocratic and artistic classes, but it all seemed
distant and irrelevant to me. At one point, having squinted
at the names in print until the penny finally dropped, I
lifted my head and cried to the fellow behind the bar, 'We
have a new Prime Minister!' It was half a question, half a
declaration of surprise. He only looked at me and shrugged
without interest. I forced myself to read on, but by the time
I reached the business sections I was just staring at words on
a page and gave up with a sigh. I stared out of the window
and my mind drifted back to Thistlecrook House.

Lunch consumed, I wandered back across the square to
find that, to my relief, the post office was open for business
once more. I commissioned my telegram to Southgate's: a
few brief phrases to indicate that the collection was more
vast than anyone had previously dared to believe, but also
in such a dire state of disarray that it might require me
several more weeks to complete my allotted assignment,
while also vaguely hinting that in the short time available I
had already uncovered several pieces of probable artistic

and perhaps historic importance, and that I was confident my time was being well invested in this exercise, which could prove a most fruitful and profitable venture for all concerned. That accomplished, I dashed off a word or two to my mother, to provide reassurance that her only son was well and fine and promising to send a longer message as soon as I was able.

With my communications sent, my goals in the village were achieved, and so I wandered back into the muggy open air and sat for a while thinking about Amy, and about Victor too. My mood was not a jolly one. I could only imagine just how ruinously my foolish actions had harmed my relations with them both. Did Victor really want me out of the house as soon as possible? And Amy – I recounted the ugly discourse of our last meeting with a fretful shudder, in spite of the hot climate. With the clarity of reflection afforded by distance and time, I was now more certain than ever that Amy had not taken such great offence at the mere fact of my absence for a single evening, but rather at the individual whose company I had instead kept. She was not hurt that I had missed our standing appointment – she was distressed that it had been Victor whom I had spent my time with. I might have dismissed such possessiveness as childish petulance. Yet I could not help but wonder at the language she had used: she had spoken of allegiances and sides, of Mordrake being 'welcome to me', as though I were some trophy, some pet, to be squabbled over by competitive siblings. What to make of this, I could not yet be sure.

When I conjured Amy's face to my mind's eye now, it was frowning, icy and merciless at my perceived disloyalty. I could barely stand to think of her so – yet somehow the image of her laughing smile eluded me. What could I do to make things right, to prove my worth and earn her forgiveness and trust? I thought perhaps of buying her some sort of gift from town, some small trinket to show that I thought of her – but what would she want? I still knew so little about her. I wondered vaguely if Cobsfoot had any kind of bookshop.

As I sat and pondered, from my vantage point at the centre of the town square I spied the serving girl, Mary, whom I had spoken to on my first day here, passing by with what I estimated to be the sunken shoulders and dragging walk of one who is headed for their place of employment with the prospect of a long shift ahead of them. Sure enough, she proceeded directly to enter the Whistle and Duck. In truth, I had been biding my time at that spot in the hope of spying just such a familiar face. I quickly abandoned my position and hurried across the square for the third time that day. When I re-entered the tavern, Mary was just taking her place behind the bar, so I made my way over to her and ordered an ale. As she poured, her eyes hopped uncertainly from the filling glass to my face – she recognized me, but could not place from where.

'Hello again,' I began.

'Hullo,' Mary said, and then, in an only slightly stilted attempt at familiarity, 'Well, this weather's not showing us any pity, is it? I can't remember the last summer so muggy.'

'No, indeed. You may remember me, I was in here quite recently, asking for directions,' I reminded her with a smile.

Mary pursed her lips and studied me with a soft hum of concentration. 'You were … aye, I knew I'd seen you before,' she said, and I wondered if she was only being polite, but then she added more brightly, 'Ah, you were the fellow asking about the old house, weren't you?'

'Yes, that was me. Simon Christie. I've been a visitor there since, at Thistlecrook House.'

'Is that so? You've been out there all this time? Are you a friend of Mr Mordrake's?' she asked, almost suspiciously.

'No. I was only sent there to appraise his art collection. I work for an auction house – Southgate's.'

'Oh aye, that's right, I remember now,' she said – though, I did not think I had told her the purpose of my visit when we first spoke. She smiled and handed me my drink; I lingered at the bar awkwardly, and after a moment Mary added, 'Mr Mordrake has quite a collection of old paintings, doesn't he? I remember hearing that.'

'Yes, it's quite famous, though no one has seen it for a long time. It has been the subject of no small amount of speculation among art historians. Having seen some of what it holds … Well, let's just say it's not quite what I expected. There are some fascinating pieces in there though, I think even some old masters that no one has seen or even known of for generations. His family must have been collecting and hoarding them for hundreds of years.'

'Is that so?' Mary said, her pleasant smile still fixed in place, though I saw her eyes roving the inn for another customer to serve, or a table to clear, that would provide a convenient excuse to terminate the conversation; fortunately for me the place was empty. I decided I should cut to the chase while I had her attention.

'I was glad to run into you again, actually, I –' My words faltered. Suddenly I found myself unsure of what to say, how to voice the fantastical fears and theories that had been forming in my mind for the past days and weeks without sounding like an utter lunatic. Where to even begin? Mary raised her eyebrows expectantly. I proceeded carefully, articulating each word with a slow deliberateness. 'I have been out at Thistlecrook House for some time now, and I have seen – that is, I have found it to be a quite remarkable place. Remarkable, and … surprising. I had been hoping to talk to someone who knows something about the history of the area – and the Mordrakes – to ask some questions.'

'Oh, there's plenty round here who know the area better than I do,' Mary replied quickly, but I pressed on.

'The last time I was here, you told me that people spoke strangely of Mr Mordrake – that there were stories about him. What kind of stories?'

'Well … not so much about Mr Mordrake who lives there now, but about the family. The Mordrakes have owned all this land around, more or less, for a long, long time, and they've always lived out at the old house.' Her voice dropped to a conspiratorial hush. 'People are leery about the old house. They say that hundreds of years ago – oh, I don't even like to talk about it – but there were stories they committed all sorts of crimes and terrible things out there. But that's all history – Mr Mordrake seems a quiet and gentle man.'

'What sort of crimes did his ancestors commit?' I persisted, imagining for a moment the stern portrait of Victor's grandfather glowering down from the parlour wall, hard and compassionless, and so uncannily resembling his descendant.

Mary hesitated for a moment. 'Oh … it's just stories to scare the wee ones. It's nothing to take serious. It's almost a bit of a joke, you know, as though every bad thing that happened in town could be blamed on the Mordrakes? Almost, but …' She relented, seeing I was not for dropping the issue. 'They say that the Mordrakes used to rule this place with an iron fist, back in olden times: murdering anyone who challenged them, burning down their houses and stringing up entire families.' She shuddered. 'And others who would just disappear entirely. And then … people say there used to be evil rituals at the old house, people coming and going from who knows where, dressed in robes and chanting into the night. And dreadful things in the woods down there, and the lake … But it's all just nonsense, really, from a long time ago. It's all long before anyone alive now was born. I suppose every town has its local legends, don't they? Stories for scaring the wee ones …'

'Things in the woods? What sorts of things?'

'I don't –' She sighed, and shook her head, but carried on. 'All sorts. Daft stories. Devils and beasties in the woods that will snatch you away after dark. It's all nonsense. They say witches used to meet in the woods, and at the wee lake there, and do dreadful things. Some folks'll tell you it was a Mordrake who was their master, and led them in their evil masses – or, in other versions it's the Mordrakes who rounded them up and drove them away. You could ask every person in this town and they'd probably tell the story different.'

Another question was already formed upon my lips, but Mary shook her head firmly. 'I don't like to talk about such things. I don't know much about it, and it's all nonsense anyway. If you're really interested, you should talk to Helen. She knows more about it, and she doesn't mind talking.'

'Helen? Who is that?'

'Helen Pugh – the housekeeper at Thistlecrook. You must have met her.'

'Oh yes, of course. I don't think I knew her first name,' I explained. Mary told me that by some good fortune this was Mrs Pugh's night off, and she would like as not appear at the inn later in the evening, if I could wait.

'I shall, thank you. I'm sorry, but just one more question, if I may? You told me that Mordrake lives alone at the house, yes? He has no family, or relatives that stay with him?' Mary agreed this was true. 'But he had a wife, once, who died – she drowned in the lake, yes? You're sure of it?'

'Aye, that's right.'

'Did you see her? Can you remember what she looked like?'

'Hmm, it was a long time ago, and I was just wee. I remember she wore lovely elegant dresses – I thought she must look like a princess. And, she wore her long hair down – beautiful black hair, she had.'

'That's all? You remember nothing else?'

'Not really. I only saw her a few times, when she would come into town to go to church sometimes. Her and Mr Mordrake both, they looked so happy together. It was a long time ago, now. Oh, and I think that she had an accent – she wasn't from around here, I suppose, though that's no wonder. Hmm … I think that's all I can remember about her. But, why are you so interested?'

'I found a portrait, at Thistlecrook House – I thought it might be of her, but I didn't know what she looked like,' I lied.

Some customers entered and Mary was finally able to excuse herself from my presence to serve them. I suspected I had exhausted her goodwill with my eccentric interrogation; I ordered a second ale as thanks for her time, and drank it quickly. As I moved to leave, though, she reached over the bar and caught me lightly by my arm.

'You'll find Helen Pugh here this evening, I'm sure of it, if you can wait. She might be able to tell you more. You'll be going back to the old house to finish your business, then?' I told her that I was, that I had more yet to do, and her eyes wrinkled with concern. 'They're just stories that people tell, from a long time ago, just to frighten the wee ones,' she repeated, and I wondered whether she spoke to provide reassurance for me, or for herself.

12.

The clock on the Cobsfoot town hall told me that the hour was not yet four, and I had some time to occupy myself before I could hope to locate Mrs Pugh and discover what information she might be willing to share that might help me to unpick the mess I had found myself in. I thought it wiser to try to speak to her beyond the confines of Thistlecrook House; here in Cobsfoot, and outwith her waged hours, she might be willing to discuss her employer more freely, I hoped.

My restless thoughts made for restless feet, and I decided to use my free time to take a walk about the town. I set off with the high steeple of the distant church as my arbitrary goal. After I had covered about half the ground from the town square to the house of worship, a peal of bells sounded from the direction of my destination: a pleasingly irregular, clanging din – the bellringers must be at practice. The sound seemed to stir something inside me, a distant memory of childhood, and I fancied that I had not heard the chiming of church bells for a longer time than I could remember.

I found the church itself a lumpen, aged building, well-weathered but apparently attentively cared for. I walked around the structure admiring its history and fortitude – I would have wagered it had outlasted any other building within the town. An elderly lady stood skulking outside the church doors, watching me. I smiled and waved, but she did not react. I entered the small churchyard and walked among the graves there, reading the names and dates from times long distant, and trying to imagine the faces they had once belonged to, their manners and their dress, their accents and attitudes from long ago – living, breathing wives, husbands, fathers and mothers, now nothing but carved names in stone. Some grave markers were so ancient and weather-beaten that the names had disappeared completely; some lay in collapsed heaps overgrown with thick, green moss. The sight made me unaccountably sad.

After walking solemnly among the stones for a while, I noticed that the old lady was still watching me, having followed me around the church building so that she could spy on me over the graveyard wall. I left the yard by a route that deliberately took me past her, offering a bright 'Hello,' as I drew near. She muttered some vague words that I could not interpret, but by their tone I thought I could recognize a grudgingly returned greeting.

Up close, the small elderly lady looked as ancient and decrepit as the church she seemed to be protecting. On a sudden impulse, I asked her, 'Have you lived in Cobsfoot all your life?'

My unexpected address seemed to startle her more than I could have anticipated. Her ancient, rheumy eyes opened in shock and her lips trembled for a moment, and then she nodded in affirmation.

'Did Mr Mordrake ever have a wife, and did she truly fall through the ice on the frozen lake?' I asked, leaning close to her small, crooked form. She opened and closed her mouth noiselessly for a moment before some quiet, trembling words emerged.

'Aye, the wife drowned … in the lake,' she murmured. She raised a gnarled finger of warning. 'I always tell them, stay away from the old house, and don't play on the ice, or you'll end up like Mordrake's wife.' The bells were still pealing overhead and I could barely hear her whispered words over the din. I leaned closer still.

'Who do you tell?'

'The bairns! Stay away from the old house. Just like my mother told me, stay away and don't play on the ice, or you'll go through like the wife …' She was shaking her head sadly.

'Your mother?' I asked, 'But … did your mother tell you not to play on the ice?'

'Aye!' she confirmed, seemingly a little affronted that I should question that it was so.

'She told you, years ago when you were only a child, that Mordrake's wife had fallen through the ice?'

The old woman nodded, but her thoughts seemed to have drifted back to the current generation of youngsters. 'You just tell those wee ones to keep away, or they'll be dragged off. The witchies will drag them up to old Mordrake's folly!' Her voice rose to a pitched cry, and then she giggled raspily, amused at some joke that was lost on me. I would have asked more, but I sensed that it would be useless; her conversation was not with me as much as with some vague half-memories. In any case, she was already turning away. I could scarcely hear her parting words, some sort of continued admonition to leave the old house be and not disturb the Mordrakes, but whether it was meant for me or some imagined gathering of children I could not be sure. I left the old woman shuffling towards the church and made my way back into town. By now my temples were beginning to throb with another headache, not helped by the bright sun that still hung in the sky – nor the two ales I had partaken of earlier, no doubt.

By the time I had wandered back to the Whistle and Duck, the hour hand on the town hall clock had passed five, and the inn was filling up with what looked like a decent portion of the working men and women of the village. I looked about the assorted patrons helplessly, but the only familiar face to be found among them belonged to young Lauric, who had driven me to Thistlecrook House in his cart some weeks previously; he returned my gaze momentarily, and without a flicker of recognition.

My good guide, Mary, appeared from somewhere and took my arm. 'Helen Pugh isn't here, yet, but she'll not be long – that's her husband, over there,' she said. 'She'll not be far behind him.'

I ordered another drink despite my aching head, and seated myself in the corner. I might have questioned the locals a little, while I waited, or interrogated poor Mary further, but the place had developed into quite a hubbub and I felt self-consciously an outsider among the friendly handshakes and embraces, the earnest debates and roaring laughter over local concerns that I could not appreciate. To my relief, as Mary had promised, it was not long before Mrs Pugh arrived arm in arm with another local woman. The cheerful housekeeper made for her husband and greeted him, and nestled among a group there; and for a moment I wondered how I might insert myself without causing offence. Once again, Mary came to my aid. Between serving customers and retrieving empty glasses, she tapped Mrs Pugh on the shoulder and pointed me out to her; I half raised my glass to the older lady from my inconspicuous corner. Finally, Mrs Pugh approached.

'Why, hello Mr Christie,' she greeted me, evidently somewhat confused at seeing me outside the house, and in a local drinking establishment, no less. Truth be told, I expect I probably made for something of a startling spectacle by this point, having wandered back and forth around the town in the swarming heat for most of the day in various states of nervous agitation. 'Is there – What brings you to town?'

'Hello, Mrs Pugh. I had some business in Cobsfoot today, and, well … I hoped I might meet you here this evening,' I said.

'You wanted to speak to me, Mr Christie? Whatever for? Is there something the matter at the house?' For the first time, I noticed that her accent was not local and came from somewhere south of the border – like me, she was not from these parts.

'No – that is, I do not yet know,' I answered, more ominously than I might have intended. If it was possible, the stout, motherly lady's eyes grew even wider and rounder as she gazed at me in confusion and concern. I opened my mouth to speak, but – just as I had with Mary – I found myself lost as to where to begin. The woman knew Thistlecrook House and its inhabitants far better than I did – heavens knew what she would think of me if I jumped at once too deeply into my wild and fantastic notions.

I offered to buy Mrs Pugh a drink, mostly by way of delay and to allow myself to gather my thoughts. At the bar, I leaned heavily on its smooth, well-worn surface, watching our glasses fill and trying to conjure adequate language to explain my mindset, while the busy babble of voices all around washed over me. Furnished with fresh beverages, I returned to the quiet corner and commenced my examination in a low voice that would not be overheard among the din.

'How long have you been in Mr Mordrake's service, Mrs Pugh?' I asked.

'Well, it must be coming up to five years, now. I joined his household not long after he returned from France,' she answered.

'Longer than most of his staff, I believe?'

'Yes, that's right, except Mr Bannatyne, of course. Staff do come and go so quickly at Thistlecrook.'

'Why is that?'

'Well, you know – Mr Bannatyne is such a precise man, he likes things just so, and he's strict with his rules. Some of the boys find him difficult, but he's always been fair with me. And the master ...' She paused, and I anticipated having to prise the information from her by degrees, but then she continued with a frankness I had not expected. 'You know, people around here are dreadfully superstitious about the house. They tell all sorts of stories – I'm sure you've heard. I had not long moved to the area, you see – that was after my George came back from France as well, thank the Lord – when I took the position there. People told me I was mad to work for the master. They said Mr Mordrake was a tyrant, a madman, and that strange things happened there, dreadful things. Pfah! They've no sympathy for the poor soul. He just wants to be left alone. But the young folks, they believe the stories, they get fanciful notions, and never stay for long. I swear I spend half my time nursing the youngsters about some foolish worry or another – and teaching them just how Mr Bannatyne likes things done.'

For a moment, I heard Mordrake's voice at my ear again, felt his hot breath on my neck. 'You seem to have taken to this place better than most, Simon,' he was saying. I shook the memory from my thoughts.

'The stories that people tell,' I continued, 'what do you know of the history of the house? The things that used to go on there? I have heard of strange and dark rituals, people in robes chanting and ...'

My words trailed off as Mrs Pugh chuckled and rolled her eyes. 'Oh yes – that the Mordrakes kidnap wives and children, and worship the devil or something even worse, and make the crops grow or the rains come or whatever other nonsense? Don't believe a word of it, Mr Christie. Oh, I don't doubt that terrible things have happened in the past around here, the same as anywhere. There really were witches who met in the woods, you know, and the good Lord alone knows what sort of dreadful things they were doing. But that was a long, long time ago now, and the stories get all muddled up and exaggerated, if you ask me.'

'You don't think the Mordrakes could have been involved with witchcraft?' I asked, prickling with embarrassment to hear myself even ask such an absurd question with a serious face.

'It was the Mordrakes who got rid of the witches, when they civilised this place hundreds of years ago,' Mrs Pugh informed me authoritatively. 'Mr Bannatyne told me about it. Now you mustn't misunderstand me – I don't doubt that those woods around the house were a wicked place, once upon a time. And I think that old places, like Thistlecrook, they … they sort of remember the things that happened in them. Little traces of the past, they stick to a place, like dust, or soot that you can't get rid of. But, dear me, those little traces can't hurt us now, in the present, and they don't have the slightest thing to do with the people who live there now.'

I pressed my fingertips against my closed eyes. 'Yes, the people who live there now – there is nothing that you find odd about them, Mrs Pugh? In their arrangements … their routines? You've seen nothing that struck you as strange in the house? Nothing at all?'

She laughed, 'I'll tell you Mr Christie, I've worked for eight different households during my lifetime, all told, and every one of them was stranger than the last. There's nothing so queer as folk, you know.'

'Yes, but, at Thistlecrook House … I have seen … Has nothing struck you as wrong about the place?'

'What do you mean?'

'Well … the footsteps, for instance. At night, every night, someone paces the halls for hours on end, and –' I stopped, something making me hesitant and ashamed to tell of the shadows under my bedroom door.

'I don't stay at the house overnight, myself, but I know that poor Mr Mordrake suffers terrible insomnia sometimes. So does my George – after the war, you know …'

I felt a desperation take hold of me. My afternoon of circuitous enquiries had got me nowhere; I had learned nothing definite at all. I could not stand to leave Cobsfoot that evening empty-handed. 'In five years at the house, you have seen nothing, you have met no one?' I made one final push. 'You see, Mrs Pugh … situations in the household have come to my attention that I have struggled to make sense of … Things I have seen … I fear – that is, I have been sworn not to speak of certain arrangements, to anyone – but surely you must know what I am getting at –' I swallowed, and wiped my brow.

'Mr Christie, are you feeling all right?'

'I am – yes. Yes, thank you, just a little tired.'

'I am not sure I understand you,' Mrs Pugh said, staring at me now with parental concern.

'I shall try to speak plainly.' I swallowed. 'Only, what I ask you, will you give me your word it will remain between the two of us only? That you will not repeat it to Mr Mordrake, or Bannatyne, or any other?'

Mrs Pugh straightened her posture with an air of properness, though her eyes flashed with unrestrained curiosity. 'Well, as long as it is not illegal, or indecent, I shall respect your wish for secrecy.'

It would have to do. I inhaled deeply. 'I speak of Amy. What do you know of Amy?' The question croaked strangely in my ears, as if I was listening to another speak; my voice oozed thickly over my tongue. I seemed to be having more difficulty than was normal in remaining still and upright in my seat.

'Amy?' Mrs Pugh stared at me blankly. My heart fell.

'Amy … I don't know her other name. The lady who sits in the upstairs library – you must know of her.'

'Oh! The lady in the library!' She understood, at last. 'Amy, you say? You have seen her? And – goodness, she told you that was her name?'

'Yes! Yes, of course. But who is she?'

'My, no one knows for sure. There are so many stories. It's been such a long time since anyone has even seen her, so it has, I thought perhaps she was gone for good. And you even spoke to her! My word.'

'A long time since anyone has seen her? What do you mean?' I demanded, my body shuddering with electric anticipation. I felt so close to the answers I sought – and yet, suddenly I dreaded what I might hear – the truth that I knew Mrs Pugh was going to lay before me.

'Well, most never see her at all – I never have, not in five years in the house. There was a young lad, not long after I began working there, and he left soon after, he didn't last. He said that she … Well … I'd heard the stories, of course. Tsk, my girls won't even go into that room for fright – it's a struggle to keep it clean. I have to do it myself half the time. After all, I've no fear of what cannot harm me.'

'What – what are you speaking about?' I interrupted hoarsely. 'She is always there – Amy – someone must have seen her … a young lady, perhaps a few years younger than myself, with dark hair and dark eyes. I have spoken with her, t-touched her, it is inconceivable no one else knows of her. Where does she sleep, where does she eat –?'

Mrs Pugh had been smiling with excited enthusiasm, but as she listened to and watched my frantic account, her face clouded with comprehension, and then sorrow and pity.

'Oh, you didn't … You hadn't heard of the lady in the old library?' I could not speak to answer. I knew what I must hear next. 'The lady, she is not real. There is no one there. That is, not a person like you or me. She is an illusion, a … Well, I hardly know what to say.'

My voice failed me. I could only shake my head, mouth the word 'no'.

'Poor dear, she spoke to you, and you thought she was a real person? Goodness me!' Mrs Pugh smiled, laughed reassuringly, as though we were in on some jape together. But she must have seen I was incapable of making light at this moment. 'But – what did she say to you? Did she tell you who she was, or what she wants?' she asked eagerly.

I managed to mutter some vague words, I know not what, to dispel the housekeeper's interest. She twittered on for a while about local legends, and how every ancient house seemed to carry its own reports of mysterious sightings and so forth, but I would not engage with her – I could not. After a time, I simply leaned forwards to clasp my throbbing temples in my palms, and at last Mrs Pugh left me in solitude. God alone knows whether she thought me a simpleton or a lunatic, but it must have been one or the other, and either might have been correct.

The worst part of it was that I already knew, of course. Deep down, I think I must have known from the start. Mrs Pugh's words had come as no revelation to me. What other explanation could there have been? Always in the same room, never leaving to eat or sleep, the household staff never making even a passing reference to her, and the entreaties that I should keep my knowledge of her presence concealed. All Mrs Pugh had done was confirm my own darkest suppositions. And yet, the conversations we had held, the long discussions about our lives, and the outside world, her face – the blush of red in her cheek when she smiled and the glinting tears in her eye when she laughed – how could those not be real? Her hand in my own, the touch of her palm against my cheek, the scent of her long black hair – how could I disbelieve the evidence of my own senses? What Amy was, I could not yet be sure, but every instinct within me told me with certainty that she was no mere illusion, nor some cruel trick of my imagination.

The longer I sat, the darker my mood became, and my initial melancholy turned to bilious anger. Why should I take Mrs Pugh's word at face value, against the testimony of my own experience? The old housekeeper was in on the plot, too: she and Bannatyne and Victor, and probably all the others, conspiring to keep Amy, their innocent victim, confined, and to drive me to madness – to what end I could scarcely fathom. I seethed and clenched my fists, and cursed their wickedness, but in time this too passed, and my nerves cooled once more, and I reflected on the housekeeper's earnest face and guileless words, and I could not believe she had intended to deceive me. And then, there was the heaped evidence to back her claims, evidence to which I had hitherto turned a wilfully blind eye …

I sat there alone in the corner of the tavern, surrounded by the jovial merriment of Cobsfoot, for I do not know how long. Alternately I held my head in my hands and brooded, or stared about blankly at the chattering faces all around, flushed with drink, their words increasingly slurred, their laughter more jagged and unrestrained as the night wore on and their glasses emptied and were refilled, emptied and were refilled. In that moment, I envied and hated their easy contentment.

It was the sight of Mary, watching me from behind the busy bar, her expression serious and still, that brought me back to my senses and made me realize with a start how late the hour had grown. I rose and made my way unsteadily towards the door to begin the drive back to Thistlecrook

House before the last light of the long summer evening vanished and the forest turned treacherously dark. As I opened the door, I paused and looked over my shoulder, and saw that Mary was watching me still. She opened her mouth as if to say something, then closed it again. I left, letting the door swing shut behind me with a thud.

13.

I barely recall driving back from Cobsfoot to Thistlecrook House that night, only flashing images of the dark gnarling trees that blurred past the windows in the reddish moonlight as I followed the weaving and winding road, driving so fast and incautiously on the treacherous trail that it was surely providence alone that delivered me safely to my destination.

Bannatyne swooped upon me almost as soon as I entered the house, with the air of a man gravely wronged. 'You did not say when you would return.' He tutted. 'We had expected you to return for dinner – the master delayed his own meal for half an hour to wait upon you. You did not come, and so he ate alone.'

I was in no frame of mind to tolerate the elder's supercilious scorn, and hurried past him with only a cursory apology. The drive through the flickering, shadowy forest had done nothing at all for my headache, and I wanted desperately to lie down and close my eyes. Bannatyne would not let me ascend the staircase, however, without attempting to force some sort of meal upon me despite the lateness of the hour, not to mention the untold troubles he implied such an effort would necessarily cause him. My flat refusal of this strained offering seemed almost too much for the butler's injured pride to bear, and for a moment, I thought he was going to chase me from the house entirely, back into the night from where I had come.

I escaped, finally, and shut myself in my chambers with only my thoughts and my aching synapses for company. I collapsed into bed and writhed in a sleepless stew of fetid summer heat and my own fragmented consciousness. All I could think of was going to Amy – I needed to see her, to hear her voice and clasp her hand and know that she was real, that she was no phantom nor figment of my imagination. I felt certain, even then when my thoughts were at their most desperate, that she would be there in her library waiting for me, warm flesh and blood despite what Mrs Pugh had said. No mere illusion could enkindle such a need within my breast, I was positive; unless, of course, I had entirely lost my mind to madness – and I did not think that was the case.

At the same time, I dreaded to see her again too – after all, what could I say to her, now? I did not think I could look upon her and pretend blissful ignorance, not any more. And I could not forget our last meeting, the hostility of the barbed words she had directed towards me – would she even welcome my company, now?

That night I did not hear the omnipresent footsteps beating a patrol around the house; or else, perhaps I was so used to them, and so consumed by my own introspection, that I no longer noticed. I did not look to the crack of light beneath my door – I did not dare. When I rose the next morning, my unrested nerves still jangling like electrical wire, I saw that a sheet of paper had appeared on the floor by the bedroom door, which must have been slipped underneath during the night. I staggered over, stooped, and picked it up.

The side facing me was blank but I could see etched markings on the reverse; one edge was ragged as with a sheet torn carefully from a notebook. With a trembling hand I turned the leaf over – there was an image of a man seated in profile at a desk by a window, rendered in ash-grey pencil. The face – my face – was half turned from the viewer, but looked downwards with a frown of studious concentration. It was a rough sketch but competently accomplished, and, even delineated by just a few small pencil marks, the individual's features were recognizably my own: the artist had no small skill. Below the drawing, an elegant cursive hand had written the words:

You must forgive me. I spoke so unfairly.
Visit me this evening – please come.
Your friend.

I held that sheet of paper for a long time, staring at the image and the words, back and forth from one to the other. I held it until the surface of the paper wrinkled with small oval-shaped creases beneath the tight, pinching grip of my fingertips. I could not have imagined that one scrap torn from a notebook could weigh so heavy in my hand, could signify so much, nor hint at so many unanswered questions. I had tossed and turned all night wishing to go to Amy, and here she had come to me, in the form of a note delivered to my very door. Had I needed it, then surely here was the evidence – hard, physical proof in my fingers – that Amy was no mere delusion of my mind. And yet there was a part of me, a small part, that told me I should crush the scrap of paper in my fist and leave the entire damned household and all of its cursed occupants behind for good.

I placed the drawing neatly upon my dresser and began to prepare myself for breakfast.

* * *

That morning I found that Victor's mood had swung back to a jocular familiarity. 'Simon, my friend – good morning.' He greeted me enthusiastically, and proceeded to question me about my visit to Cobsfoot, and hold forth on the changes the town and surrounding region had seen over recent years. All without mention of my overextended stay in the house, the progress of my work, nor any other subjects that I might not have welcomed. I tried to resist his amiability, to set a wall of indifference against his easy charm. I mentally recited lists of his offences, both real and imaginary, to bolster my reserve. But inevitably, before long I was laughing at his jokes and chatting with him as though we were old companions. I could not help but be relieved to see him in a brighter mood, and to be the subject of his enthusiastic attentions once more. In some way, talking to Victor about matters of no relevance felt reassuring that morning, a welcome distraction following my day in town and all I had been told there. Any awkwardness seemed to be consigned to the past, for now. Perhaps, I thought, it would be best if what had happened between us was simply never mentioned again.

Even so, I did not allow myself to linger for long at the breakfast table and instead swiftly made my excuses and headed for my workroom. I was determined to pour my energies and my focus into my employment, to concentrate all of my attentions on the task at hand, in the hope of distracting my spiralling mind from its own ponderings and, I told myself, so that I might be completed soon and free to leave this dark and troubling place. But the contents of the attic, Mordrake's bloodthirsty collection, seemed endless. In the days and weeks that had passed, I had barely made a dent in the stacks of canvases. I would have been well within my rights to return to the auction house to explain the scale of the task, and agree an alternative to my staying under the roof of Thistlecrook House until the work was complete. Yet I found myself unwilling, unable even, to take this path, having trodden so far down my current route. I was submerged; I was in the deep. I had pulled at maddening threads, and now there was no choice but to unravel.

There was no use deceiving myself about it. It was more than mere morbid curiosity that kept me at Thistlecrook House, after all; it was Amy. I had to understand who she was, where she had come from, and how she had come to be here. And my vow still stood: I would help her, if I could, yes – but more than that, I just wanted to see her. I needed to see her, I needed to be in her company.

And so that evening I went to her, as her note had bid. I resisted Victor's attempts to detain me with wine and conversation after dinner had concluded, excused myself and recklessly proceeded directly to the upstairs library. My nerves were on edge as I paced the long familiar corridor: I confess that my walk to the library that evening was my moment of doubt, however fleeting. My heart pounded in my chest and I felt a tight grip upon my throat as I wondered – I dreaded – what I might find there when I opened the library door. And if, as I hoped and prayed, the room was indeed occupied as it always had been, what then would I say – what could I say – to Amy, without breaking my oath and inviting her scorn and disappointment once more – perhaps for the final time? I would find no answers if I did not retain Amy's confidence.

I found her in her armchair, wearing a green dress, her hair pinned back loosely so that it curled around her heart-shaped face in an elegant style I had not seen before. A book lay open in her lap, her small hands poised over its pages as though she would not only read but feel the texture of the words written there beneath the tips of her fingers. There she sat, as she was always to be found, and as real as any person I ever saw.

'Simon! There you are,' she said, a note of relief in her voice. She closed her book at once and dropped it carelessly to the floor, and rose from her chair with a bound. 'What's the matter? Why are you lingering by the door, there? Come in, and let me see you.' Her voice was warm but concerned, and without a hint of the poisonous reproach of our last encounter.

'Yes, here I am – and you are there,' I said. I felt suddenly lightheaded, and stepped quickly across the room towards the settee to sit down, but Amy caught my hand in her own as I passed. I paused, mid stride, and we stood there for a moment with our trembling fingers loosely intertwined. Her skin was warm against mine. I could not doubt these sensations. If this were madness, then surely it was of a blissful kind I had never heard of before.

Still holding her hand, I dropped to the settee, and she took the place beside me. 'Why, what is the matter with you?' she asked, the concern in her voice rising. 'You look dreadfully exhausted and pale. You have been working too hard, I am sure, on those vile paintings. It cannot be good for anyone to spend so much time with them. You must ask for a day off, promise me you will.'

'I am fine,' I answered, a little too roughly. 'Just a little tired. I have not slept well – I have had so much on my mind.'

'Oh,' Amy answered quietly. 'I see. I hope – I hope that I am not the cause. I said harsh things to you the last time you came to me, things that were unfair, and unworthy of me. Things that you did not deserve to hear. I know that you have been my friend since you came here – my only friend – it is just … Oh, Simon, I am sorry – say you'll forgive me, won't you?'

'There is nothing to forgive,' I told her, with a gallant effort. 'I was not without fault, and your words were not entirely undeserved. But what's done is done. The past is behind us, and will not change. What's the use in brooding on it? Let us move forwards.'

Amy looked down, and smiled, and laughed. 'Finely said, though it was not quite the acceptance I was hoping for. How strangely you speak, Simon! Tell me, what is on your mind?'

I looked into her deep, sincere eyes, and spoke slowly, carefully, 'I cannot answer that, Amy, without risking a betrayal of the promise I made to you. Therefore, I shall not answer. Let me instead say that I ... I visited Cobsfoot yesterday, and spoke to some of the people there. Naturally, we spoke of this house. I was curious, I admit, and I had questions that I needed to ask. I heard something of the history of this place, and of the Mordrakes, and the things that have happened here ... not always happy things. I heard of some of the legends and mysteries that cling to Thistlecrook House. The things that some people have seen, inside these walls ... and that many people have not seen ...' My voice trailed off, but it was clear that Amy had understood the insinuated meaning of my words all too well. The smile vanished from her face, and her fingers loosened limply in my hand, and then squeezed it all the more tightly.

'I see,' she said. 'I understand. Thank you, for not asking ... I ... I would ... I fear you may find it hard to believe, but there is actually so very little for me to say.' Her lip twitched nervously and she bit upon it, as though she feared what words might slip out.

It took much effort for me not to pounce upon this sudden openness to communication, this apparent softening of her defences. There was much that I could have said, or asked, in that moment. But to look into Amy's dark eyes, to see her happy in my company once more – for that evening, I thought that it was enough. 'I am ready to listen, should you wish it,' was all I said.

At this Amy smiled again, and nodded in silent appreciation. For a time we said nothing, and then we spoke tentatively, of other matters with no relation to the uncomfortable questions that yet lingered in the air, until at length the tension was dispersed from the room and we were in good spirits once more. We remained side by side on the settee – for that evening, Amy's armchair and her book, and my desk and sober household accounts were forgotten entirely.

I thanked Amy for her drawing and praised her talents gushingly – she blushed and shook her curls, and told me that I was a flatterer and she a mere rank amateur who had not picked up a pencil since she was a young girl. She had mentioned her childhood, in passing, on a few occasions, but I had never succeeded in gleaning from her more than the most indifferent details about it. Now, though, I felt emboldened to ask more. Perhaps it was her own, newly unguarded candour this evening that spurred my inquisitiveness; perhaps it was the maddening echo of what Mrs Pugh had told me, which would not quit from my ears. In either case, I dared to ask, offhand but cautiously watching for her reaction, 'I think that you told me you grew up far to the south, in Kent?'

'Yes, that's right … It was a quiet spot, a little town. I doubt you would have heard of it. It was a very dull place. Not half as interesting as growing up in a city like Edinburgh, I suppose. Some way outside Canterbury. I grew up there until I was sixteen – or, no, seventeen, I think. With my father and mother, of course, and my sister and two brothers … I was not very close to my brothers, who were somewhat older than me, but my sister and I were very close … her name was Abigail, Abby. Amy and Abby …' She smiled fondly, her eyes far away, her voice soft and dreamlike. 'My sister and I were altogether inseparable as children, and not very ladylike, or at least our mother told us we weren't. We kept ourselves busy running around the gardens, climbing trees and making up fantastic stories, a whole imaginary world that only the pair of us existed in. It all seemed so real – tall old trees that were our impregnable castles, beautiful and fearsome; squat, thorny old bushes that made for perfectly thrilling monsters and villains. I swear that we held entire conversations with the squirrels and birds, and I could almost hear them answering back …

'Well, I think we drove our poor parents half-mad with worry, that we were not growing up as young girls should, and that our fantasy worlds were somehow … unhealthy, I suppose. I imagine that is why we were sent to different schools. We stayed in touch by letter of course, but it was never as close, as intimate. I made other friends, and so did she, and the things we wrote to each other – our mad dreams and fantasies – started to seem silly and childish … And then, Abby married. The waiting between her letters grew longer and longer, and the contents of each one grew shorter. Until … one day my poor mother and father came to my school, when I was in my final year, and they told me that Abby had died. From consumption, a very short illness – it happened very quickly. She did not suffer, they said. Oh, it's all right, it was a long time ago, now, and I have made my peace with it …'

I have presented here, for the sake of brevity, a mono-logue that in fact took the form of a long-drawn-out dialogue. Amy did not tell me this sad story of her past read-ily, but I drew it from her through much coaxing and catechism: probing, picking up her stray comments and not allowing her to move the discussion to a different subject, though she tried repeatedly. I was no bully, I hasten to add – I only worked to overcome her instinctive hesitance. As I persuaded more details from her, expanding the mental picture she was drawing of her childhood, I felt my heart race in my chest, and I could feel some of the anxiety I had been carrying lift away; this, surely, was a true account of a personal history, of a lived experience described with a sincerity I could not dispute – it was not the stuff of Mrs Pugh's myths and phantoms.

Of course, when she reached the tragic conclusion to her tale and tears brimmed in her eyes, I could not help but feel wretchedly guilty for causing her to recall such memories. But my guilt, and her sorrow – momentary as they were – were prices I was ready and willing to pay in my search for the truth.

'And then, from Kent, you came to Cobsfoot?' I asked softly, when she said no more – but I knew the question was a step too far even as I asked it, and Amy looked at me gravely through the corner of her dampened eye and did not answer.

Finally, I permitted the subject to change, and our conversation moved to happier things. I told Amy about my trip to town – saving my discussion with the housekeeper, of course – and she soon forgot her sorrow in her eagerness to hear news from the neighbouring burg. She seemed well acquainted with Cobsfoot and its inhabitants, and it was now her turn to interrogate me. She demanded a full account of my every footstep about the place, and the people that I had seen and spoken to there. For each one she had some comment:

'Oh, does Mr Curtis still work at the post office? No? I shouldn't wonder that he has retired now – I expect his son has taken over.' And, 'That must have been Mrs Reveley you saw at the church – she played the organ until her arthritis seized up her fingers, the poor soul.' And even, 'Oh, Mary Johnston was such a sweet girl, I always knew she would grow up prettily – hasn't she? Well, I can tell by your face that she has. I expect she's broken half the hearts in Cobsfoot'. I smiled and laughed and nodded along with her excited questions. How she knew these names and faces, and why she talked as though recalling memories from long ago, and why she spoke nostalgically of Mary as a child, when surely Mary was the older of the two – these questions gnawed ravenously upon the edges of my concentration, yet I kept them to myself.

The shadows appeared outside my room again that night. My eyes opened, and I looked to where they were cast, black reflections shading the crack of moonlight that filled the blurry gap between the base of the door and the carpet's edge. I had almost become used to my unseen nocturnal visitor by now, found myself glancing to the edge of light almost compulsively, checking for those patient shades – but still the sight of their arrival thrilled my skin to gooseflesh in a shivered instant. And yet I felt an uncanny calm – as though I were observing a thing happening to someone else, as though it were not me who lay in bed under the lurking presence of an obscure and mysterious other.

As I lay and watched, the shadowed feet turned to one side in a slow shuffle, then set off down the corridor away from me. I listened as they padded softly down the hallway, until their sound faded to nothing and the house was dead silent once more. I rose from my bed, walked to the door, opened it and stepped out; I peered down the hallway after the direction I had heard the footsteps lead, but whatever or whoever had been there was no longer.

I returned to my room, went to my window and pulled aside the curtain. A man, silhouetted in the moonlight, was crossing the grass at a purposeful stride, headed towards the shining reflective surface of the lake beyond the trees. It was Mordrake, I was sure. In his hand was a lantern that cast a warm orange glow across the grass; at his side there loped a dark figure that for a startling moment I took to be Bannatyne, ever his master's shadow, hunched over onto all fours and cantering alongside in a grotesque parody of his usual subservience. At second glance, I saw it was a huge hound, deep-black and hairy, and not one of the pack I had seen about the house. Its tail curved downwards between its legs, and its highly arched back gave it an odd and sickeningly skittish, bouncing gait for a beast of such size.

Master and hound neared the edge of the forest, and the orange lantern glow vanished into the blackness. On sudden impulse, I turned from the window, threw on my dressing gown, quickly and quietly left my room, and hurried along the gloomy western hall, moving as fast as I dared without making sound to disturb the house. My slippered feet padded down the grand, ornate staircase, across the length of the main hall and to the front door, which was unlocked and yielded silently to my push. Around the side of the house and out across the grass I hastened, clutching my gown around me, though the night was warm and still. Puffing for breath, I reached the trees and pressed on where Mordrake had vanished, picking my way over roots and under boughs as carefully as I could, though it was treacherous in the dark, and the silent spell of night was broken by the racket of my blundering progress. Branches scratched and tugged at my flapping gown, and one of my slippers was lost to a snagging root – I continued undeterred. Ahead of me, beyond the tangle, I could make out flashes of the silvery surface of the lake, my only guide in the shadowed night.

I slowed as the light of the lake grew closer, creeping forwards carefully, hoping that my crashing advance had not been heard by the one I pursued. Emerging from the overgrowth at the lake's edge, I crouched and stared about, and wondered what on earth I was doing out here. Mordrake's lantern had been abandoned on the shore not far from where I squatted, but I could not see where the man, nor his enormous dog, had gone – in the darkness I could make out nothing at all but the flickering lantern, the gently rippling lake, and the faint outline of the swooning willow trees reaching out over its surface, illuminated in the white glow of the reflected moonlight. It was on that wide mercurial mirror that I eventually spied my quarry. Some distance from my position, a small vessel – a rowing boat – was moving out across the water, with Victor seated within; swift and smooth it glided, the oars lifting silently in and out of the water at its pilot's steady turn, the faintest trace of a wave arcing out from its bow in two sweeping lines. I watched as the vessel slowed, and then stopped. Then the boatman slowly rose until he was in a standing position, afloat at the centre of the lake. A voice carried through the still air, a voice that I could recognize as Mordrake's but whose words I could not quite make out. It sounded to my ear as a low, mournful chant, somewhere between a recited prayer and a slow, sad song, intended for the singer's ear and none other.

The dolorous incantation ceased suddenly, and all was silent save for the gentle lap of water. Then a new sound reached my ears, faint, light, like tinkling bells sounding very far away. Victor appeared to be leaning over the edge of his boat, peering downwards into the water at such an angle that the vessel below him looked ready to pitch over and cast him into the depths. With a chill, I thought it appeared as though he were listening: listening to the lake's reply. At length he straightened up again, and his strange recitation resumed, faster and – I fancied – more purposeful now. While he chanted, a faint ripple circled out from where his boat sat, followed by another, and another and another still: concentric circles expanding one after the other from the centre of the lake. Although it was distant, I believed I could make out the source of the ripples in a disturbance on the water, at a spot just beside Victor's small boat. Something was bubbling there, a foaming distortion, a shape breaking through the surface sheen and rising into view, slick and wet, long tangled tresses of hair streaming with water that ran in glistening rivulets down winding strands, hugging the curved shape of a form below: a head, and shoulders, and a body, rising from the surface of the lake …

A noise came from behind – a rustle of leaves, and a branch snapping underfoot. And then large hands fell upon me, gripping my shoulders in a firm hold and pulling me downwards, so that I fell, fell down to the dark ground below.

14.

The next I knew, I was awake in my own bed with the warm glow of the morning sun outside. My limbs and muscles felt tender and numb, my mind fogged by the sensation of having awakened abruptly from a deep and catatonic sleep – a sleep far deeper than any I had known since I arrived at Thistlecrook House. At first, I had only a vague memory of dreams, a troubling tableau that I had witnessed in my slumber – images that made no sense, ideas that had no order. Then, the vision of Victor afloat and incanting upon the mirrored lake returned to my mind, an image so insidious and frightening that I had to bolt from my covers and splash my face with cold water. I remembered hands seizing me, long nails pinching my flesh – but when I checked I could find no marks upon my person. With a racing pulse I reached a hand beneath my bed and breathed a sigh of relief to find that both of my slippers lay where I had left them, undisturbed and unsoiled. My dressing gown, too, hung on its hook, unblemished by scratching branches or telltale flecks of leaf or mud.

I told myself that morning that it had all been a dream. I had to; it was the only way I could make sense of the things that I had seen – or thought I had seen. That I had watched from my window as Victor and his hound hurried across the grass in the direction of the lake, of that I was reasonably certain. But whispered spells upon the lake, bodies rising from the water … At that time, I was sure my overstimulated imagination was playing tricks on me while I slept. And there were other things too, things I saw that night after all went black that I have not recorded here; snatches of images that remain too fragmented in my recollection to describe, and which – even now, knowing all that I know, with the scales of incredulity truly fallen from my eyes – I cannot to this day be certain that I truly witnessed.

Of course, I spent some time that morning questioning if I had not lost my wits completely. Amy, Victor, all of it. The footsteps at night, the haunting dreams and visions, the persistent headaches playing behind my eyes – these were not the signs of a well mind. But I did not believe that I was predisposed to such flights of fancy – there were no madmen or hysterics in my family history, to the best of my knowledge. And so much of what I had seen and heard could not be so easily dismissed. I only had to cling to what I was sure of, the things that I knew and held certain to be true, and I would get to the bottom of things yet. So I told myself.

At the breakfast table, Bannatyne imparted news that shook the household to its very foundations: a note, delivered by Laurie the cart driver in the early hours, announcing the parish vicar's intentions to 'drop by' and visit that same evening. The grim butler divulged the message to his master with all the severity of a man breaking the news of some major natural disaster, his face ashen and strained with consternation at the very notion of such an imposition – I even saw young Joseph visibly start upon overhearing. Mordrake received the information impassively, and gave no reply; Bannatyne hovered close for a few seconds, watching his master's face and seemingly awaiting further

instruction. When none came, the elder leaned forwards
and hissed, 'He cannae come at such short notice,' his
normally impeccably untraceable accent falling for a
moment in his distress.

Victor said nothing, did not even look at his man, but
shook his head slightly as if to signify it was not for discussion, then began to butter his toast quite calmly. Bannatyne
bowed rigidly and withdrew.

'Do you know the vicar well?' I asked, watching
Mordrake's expression every bit as closely as Bannatyne
had done.

'No, he's somewhat new, I believe. I am fairly sure I have
met this one … I forget. Perhaps he wishes to deliver a
verbal knuckle-rap for my tardy attendance at his services.
I am not much of a one for religious observation,' he replied
laconically.

'Some new company could be a welcome change of pace
this evening,' I commented. Victor glanced at me, raised an
eyebrow.

'Yes, I suppose so,' he muttered.

There was a pause. I felt restless and devilish that morning, and so I went on. 'Your ancestors must have been
somewhat religious, though, to have collected so many
images of saints and martyrs and so forth?'

'Hm? Oh, the paintings. I suppose. Although most old
paintings are on some religious theme or other, no? In
Europe, anyway. The Catholics seem to have an almost
insatiable appetite for the mortified flesh of their saviour.
It's quite an astonishing thing, really. Personally, I've never
understood the appeal of directing your prayers to a chap
trussed up like piece of meat.'

I laughed at this despite myself. Victor looked up at me in
surprise, a small pleased smile lightening his face. He turned
abruptly in his chair and began issuing a rapid stream of
orders to Bannatyne for the evening, which the butler

received with attentive relief. Evidently, a visitor to the house was a strange and exceptional thing, and special preparations had to be made.

Curious anticipation of the vicar's visit only added to the multitude of distractions already playing upon my mind, and my working day was once again significantly less than productive. The prospect of an unfamiliar face intruding upon this removed and insular environment seemed like an appealing novelty; that it should be a man of the cloth struck an even more encouraging chord with me, in spite of my own personal tendency towards agnosticism. Frankly, anyone new to talk to seemed like a welcome prospect.

While I worked through the day, I tried to imagine what the local vicar might be like; what sort of man would serve the historical, crumbling church I had seen in the town? Not a reverend who was equally decrepit, I hoped. And I wondered what insight or guidance he might be able to provide to my situation, if, of course, the opportunity to privately describe my concerns to him even arose, and if I was able to find the right words to do so. At the very least, a man in his position might know something more about the house, and the region, and the ominous part the Mordrakes had played in the history of both – details that I believed might in some way be pertinent to my own concerns. It occurred to me, too, that the timing of the vicar's unexpected visit might not be entirely coincidental. There was nothing so unusual about the parish clergyman visiting the local gentry, of course, except that by the reaction of the staff this was clearly a highly unanticipated event. And that he should call not so very long after my own arrival, and my recent trip to Cobsfoot – I wondered if these factors might all be related.

All afternoon, the household clamoured with greater servile hubbub than was usual. The house was, as a rule, a reasonably hushed and solemn establishment, but today footsteps came and went with alacrity, doors opened and shut, and voices – it was Bannatyne's harsh whine that echoed up the staircase most prominently – issued orders and arranged affairs for the evening's guest. Amidst it all, I plotted how I might manage to discreetly visit or slip a note to Amy, to inform her that I would be unavailable to join her that evening. I could only trust that the vicar's presence between myself and Mordrake would be enough to dissuade her of any perceived disloyalty on my part on this occasion.

The same painting I had set up for study at the beginning of the day still sat propped upon its easel, and my notebook lay defaced by only a handful of brief and cursory scribbles, when in the early evening one of the maids knocked on the door to tell me that the vicar had arrived. She looked vaguely terrified, though of what I had no idea – perhaps it was merely Bannatyne's contagious horror at the prospect of an interloper in the household that had spread through the entirety of the staff. I began to consider that the butler had been comparatively warm and welcoming of me.

'Shall I go down and join them now?' I asked, unsure, but the girl only shrugged her shoulders and curtsied helplessly. 'I shall join them in a moment – I just need to finish up,' I told her, then, no sooner than she had departed, I hurried out to make my way to the upstairs library. The hour was still far before my usual calling time and I found myself curiously reluctant to open the door, or even knock to see if Amy was within. Some sixth sense told me that she would not be, and I remembered how dull and lifeless the library had seemed to me the last time I found it empty – I now felt a quite severe aversion to witnessing it in such a state again. I did not pause to examine these thoughts too closely, however, and instead slipped a hastily composed note under the door explaining the vicar's unexpected arrival, and my unavoidable detainment for the evening,

and probably overdoing it a bit with the apologies and reas-
surances that I should infinitely rather have spent my time
in Amy's company and so forth. After my folded paper had
vanished beneath the crack of the door, I hesitated outside
the library for a moment, listening – but all within was
silent. I made my way downstairs.

I found Mordrake and his guest seated in the parlour. The
vicar was a small, fair, slightly anaemic-looking man, with
one of those disquietingly ageless faces, who was introduced
to me by the improbably pleasing name of the Reverend W.
Scattergood. We exchanged a rather unfortunate handshake, possibly too boisterous on my end and so entirely
lacking in boister on his that I felt compelled to abandon it
in embarrassment halfway, and released his limp fingers in
the midst of an incomplete upward swing.

'It is a pleasure to meet you, Mr Christie,' the Reverend
Scattergood told me in a thin and reedy voice evocative of
the dying breaths of a church organ. Then, cutting rather
straight to the point, he said, 'I must admit, and I hope that
Mr Mordrake will not take offence, but it was news of your
arrival that brought me out here. Or rather, reminded me
that my appointed visit to the good master of these lands
had become somewhat shamefully overdue. I like to make
a point of greeting any newcomers to the parish, even if
they are only … erm, passing through.'

'As any attentive clergyman would.' Victor smiled, directing me to a chair with a sweep of his arm. 'And although
Simon's business is sadly temporary, he already feels like a
fixture of the household. I have greatly enjoyed his company
here in Thistlecrook House. And, of course, your visits are
always a most welcome diversion, vicar,' he added
gracefully.

'I'm afraid I was quite unaware of your arrival in the
parish until yesterday, Mr Christie, when I heard of it
through Mary Johnston – who I am sure you recall. You

almost managed to slip through our quiet village unseen.' He smiled. I wondered why Mary should mention me to the vicar, and recalled the awed look in her eye when I left the Whistle and Duck so recently, her mouth half opened as though she was on the verge of some utterance. Victor was watching our exchange, looking from me to the vicar and back again, and all the while grinning quite strangely.

We chatted a while longer in the parlour, Victor and the reverend exchanging bland observations about the uncharacteristically persistent heat for this time of year, and minor titbits concerning the village and surrounding area that were wasted on me.

The vicar enquired about my work, and I explained what I was doing with the art collection. 'I have never seen the famed Mordrake collection – I should be fascinated to take a look,' Scattergood said.

'There are some wonderful religious pieces in there that I think you would appreciate, vicar,' said Mordrake, winking at me then laughing boldly at my startled expression. 'Simon and I were just this morning discussing the curious overlap between the artistic and religious spheres. Catholicism's taste for the pictorial. In fact, do you know that much of the family's collection was purchased in Rome, Venice, Milan – direct from the source, as you might say.'

'How marvellous. Of course, that would not be my precise denomination,' the Reverend Scattergood said mildly, 'but I am sure the paintings are marvellous. You say they have been kept in storage until most recently? I wonder … have you given any thought to putting on a display, a little exhibition, if you will? I am sure the town would be most interested – if it was not too much trouble for your staff, that is.'

Victor's wolf grin stretched from ear to ear. 'I think I might enjoy that,' he declared. 'A capital suggestion, reverend. Ah, if I am not mistaken, that will be Bannatyne summoning us to the dinner table. Why, the furrows in his brow look deeper than ever: two guests at once are pushing poor Bannatyne to his limits. Come, let's not keep the old scoundrel waiting!'

I didn't think I had seen Mordrake in such elevated spirits since the night of my own arrival at Thistlecrook House. He seemed to thrive on new company, I decided – an odd quality for a recluse, to be sure. But whereas his affection for me seemed, I believed, genuine, in the vicar's case he was plainly laughing at the man; he appeared to take delight in putting on the pretence of the good landlord and going through the motions of civilised company, all the while with a twinkle in his eye and his long white teeth showing in a malicious grin. And I was his compatriot in mockery, there to receive his sidelong glances and discreet winks – or, was he laughing at me as much as the vicar? In any case, the reverend seemed entirely too mannerly and well-meaning to even realize that he was being scorned.

The three of us repaired to the dining room and commenced our meal. Just as I had on my first night, the vicar hovered over the food indecisively for a while before declaring with a start, 'Why, Mr Mordrake, I quite forgot that you prescribe to a diet of vegetarianism. Well, this all looks delicious, in any case,' he added quickly. 'I admit, I am not sure I could manage without my Sunday roast. Mr Christie, has your time here converted you to a vegetable-based diet?'

'Oh no, Simon here is his own man, and not for converting,' Victor cut in sharply.

We both looked at him, and he gave a low chuckle and continued eating. 'Anyway, what does the church have to say about devouring all things bright and beautiful?' he asked.

'Oh, certainly the Bible tells us that no food is forbidden, and, well – to paraphrase it bluntly – that animals are there to be eaten,' the reverend said. 'And, I must admit, my own view is that it is in our nature to eat meat, just as it is in the nature of livestock to be consumed. It is perhaps a brutal way of thinking, but, well then, nature itself can be quite brutal at times, can it not?'

'It can indeed,' Victor's eyes positively shone. 'So, no food is off the table, what? The next time you visit I should have Bannatyne roasted up on a spit and served, in that case!' he declared with another barking laugh. 'He'd be a tough old bird to chew upon, I reckon, and dry – but with some sauce he'd do well enough, and there'd be plenty to go around.' The vicar and I both shifted uncomfortably. I thought the best thing might be to change the subject swiftly, and turned to the vicar to introduce some new topic of conversation – but before I could, he addressed our host in a tone of some distress.

'Mr Mordrake, I think I may have inadvertently caused you offence by referring to your dietary lifestyle. I certainly did not mean to imply anything –'

Victor cut him off. 'Nonsense, nonsense, reverend. It is you who should forgive my blunt manner; I am not used to decent company, as you can likely tell. As for me, you cannot possibly offend me … I don't care a whit for what others think, provided they only respect my wishes within my home.'

I pondered whether Amy might have read my note yet – wished I was sitting in the wordless comfort of her presence, rather than being caught in the midst of these two quaint opposing forces. It was going to be incumbent on me to moderate the evening's conversation, I could see. In any case, I was impatient to move things on to subjects of more interest and relevance to myself.

'In my time here,' I began abruptly, addressing the vicar, who turned his damp eyes to me with an expression of relief, 'I have learned a little about the fascinating history of the local area. It seems that this part of the world has an unusually bloody past.'

'Oh yes, the borders were quite a wild frontier for much of history. A very hostile place – things are much more serene, now, I am happy to say.' He smiled wanly. 'They used to call these the debatable lands – have you heard that term? I rather like it. On account of the conflicting claims and loyalties, you see … It seems hard to imagine, now, these quiet fields and hills overrun with royal armies, and bandits and feuding clans. Although, sometimes I look out over the landscape, and I think that I can still feel the traces of that sad past …' The good reverend blinked a few times, rapidly. 'I believe that the Mordrakes were one of the families brought to the area to enforce some sort of order, by – erm – James the First – is that not so?'

'Yes – so I have heard,' Victor said, shrugging.

'When I arrived at the parish, I inherited some fascinating books on the area written by local historians. I would be happy to lend them to you, if you're very interested in the subject?' the vicar said, addressing me. 'They are a little … Well, I think they blur the line between fact and fiction quite freely, but they're marvellously interesting all the same.'

'Fact and fiction? What do you mean?' I asked.

'What I mean is,' he seemed to weigh his words carefully, 'you see – I would say that some of the accounts described stretch the bounds of credibility. The old tales people tell about this place; you know how local legends and folklore can come to be accepted as fact, and distort the truth. It's all part of the character of the region, of course, and the stories are quite exciting in their own right – perhaps I am too much of a stickler for detail.' He smiled apologetically.

'I think that I know a little of what you mean,' I said, trying to restrain the enthusiasm in my voice. 'I have heard some stories about witchcraft, and … and rituals in the forests around here, hundreds of years ago – that sort of thing?' I found I did not dare look at Victor as I spoke.

The vicar frowned. 'Yes, there are tales like that. Some of it is really quite ghoulish. It was all a long time ago, of course, and,' he seemed to force a chuckle from the back of his throat, 'I suppose that these old myths are always more interesting and exciting than the reality.'

'Or perhaps the reality is stranger still, and the myth is just the easier tale to swallow,' I said, and thought I felt Victor look upon me with a sly smile. 'I should very much like to read those books sometime; thank you, vicar.'

'I should be most happy to lend them – you must come to the vicarage, at any time at all,' Scattergood said, placing his hands upon the tablecloth with his palms opened towards the ceiling in an odd, uncomfortable gesture.

There was a short pause, and then Victor broke his silence. 'It is all quite true, you know,' he announced. 'There really was a great witch-cult based here for the longest time, through the seventeenth and even into the eighteenth century, that practised all sorts of blasphemous arts and forbidden rituals. In the dark woods that surround us, indeed, there is a very old building, not far from here … And – why, even in this very house, they plied their dark magics.' His voice fairly boomed across the table, and his pale eyes flashed keenly and roved about the walls, as though he would spy the shades and phantoms of diabolical heresy crawling and slithering there even now. He wanted to embarrass and alarm the vicar, I thought, but there was a defiant certainty to his words that chilled me regardless.

'I used to be positively fascinated by the subject when I was younger,' Mordrake continued. 'A youthful curiosity for the macabre, I suppose. Of course, I still find it most interesting, from a historical perspective – it is as you say, vicar: the actions of the past are written into the very fabric of a place. They might still be felt by those who are willing to open their minds to it. These woods, and these stone walls, reverberate with the presence of the past, and the echoes of the deeds committed here ... or so I believe.'

'And the lake, as well? Can they be felt there?' I asked quietly.

'The lake was here first,' Victor replied.

'I heard ... that it was a Mordrake who led them in their rituals.'

At this Victor paused, only for a moment. 'Yes. For a time, my ancestors were the ringleaders. The very family that once brought the king's order to the brigands and raiders in this valley were to become the caretakers of its vilest secrets. A rather unfortunate legacy,' he added, with a deferential inclination of the head to the clergyman – and a sly wink to me.

At first, I had believed Victor spoke only to mock the timid reverend. But the realization came to me that his words were not for Scattergood, but for me. Just as he had done on the hillside, beside the burned church, and by the fireplace, on the evening of that same day, he was revealing his hand to me, slowly, deliberately. He was testing me, to see how far I was willing to peer upon that which was forbidden.

'What were they doing? What was the purpose of their rituals – their experiments?' I asked.

'Yes, experiments is the word for it. I am impressed by your insight once again, Simon. Experiments in communication, you could say. These were no mere hedge wizards, cutting herbs and mixing poultices – not by the eighteenth century, in any case. No ... they flocked to this place, itinerants and explorers. From far and wide, they were drawn here. So much of their work is lost to time, of course, but – they sought to communicate, and to experience, beyond the limits of the five conventional senses. To transgress time and place, to see and even move through spaces subliminal. And to listen, as well – to listen to those beings that dwell there.'

The vicar interrupted with a groan. 'Goodness, to think such blasphemies could be committed here in Cobsfoot – and in such a fine and civilised house as this!' He peered about the room suspiciously.

Victor gave a low, guttural growl. 'That is the conventional perspective, yes, although perhaps it only takes more imagination than your religion … Well, I must mind my manners, mustn't I? It is only that I have little patience for dogma when it interferes with progress … Tsk, but I should watch my tongue.'

'Why here?' I asked. 'Why were they drawn to this place in particular?'

'Why do you think, Simon? I have told you before, this is a very ancient place, and like all ancient places, there is a certain kind of power to be found here.'

'You speak as though there could be credibility to such lunacy.'

'I have read their accounts. The cult discovered much, uncovered many secrets that cannot be explained – if the things they say are true, of course. There is so much in this world that has yet to be understood or adequately described by accepted science. I am not so mad, nor arrogant, as to discount any possibilities out of hand.'

'Their accounts? You mean they wrote it down, the things they were doing here?'

'Naturally. When it was safe to do so. They were scientists too, after their own fashion. I still have the writings, somewhere hereabouts. More family heirlooms, you understand. I'm sure I could dig them out if you are interested, Simon, although much of it is … difficult to read. Their methods were unrefined. They believed that the walls of our world could only come down with a little … brute force.'

'It brings to mind these esoteric orders one reads of …
mindless, misguided debauchery.' Scattergood tutted. Victor
rolled his eyes.

'Let me see if I understand,' I said. 'It was the Mordrakes
who came to civilise these lands, once upon a time, but then
your ancestors fell to practising the same rituals and magic
they had once persecuted. What you call experiments. And
then what? I heard that … In town, there are some who say
that it was the Mordrakes, again, who put an end to the
witches for good. You yourself told me they used to drown
them at the lake.'

'And so they did,' Victor replied slowly. 'Drowned them
in their masses. A curious turn of events, no?'

'I wonder what could have caused such a change of heart
among your relations.'

'There is not much record of that. I imagine that there
was something of a cover-up, that the authorities didn't
want the attention – or the comparison with the hysteria in
the American colonies at the time.' Victor smiled and
shrugged, and sat back in his chair.

The vicar shuddered. 'How dreadful. Well, I for one am
grateful that we live in a more peaceful and Christian age,'
he declared. I said nothing, but watched Victor, who had
closed his eyes and allowed his face to relax into an inscrutable mask. It seemed he had said all he intended on the
matter, for now.

By this time, the table had been cleared of food, and it
was not long before the vicar had to make his departure. We
found ourselves standing alone, the vicar and I, for a brief
moment in the main hall while we waited for a servant to
bring his carriage to the door. Before I could say anything,
Scattergood leaned close to me and, in a voice barely above
a whisper, asked, 'Simon, is all well with you?'

'Why – yes, I think so,' I answered, surprised. 'That is – I
do not know. I think … there are things happening here,' I

added hesitantly. This was my chance to seek the vicar's counsel, but how could I even begin to explain?

He nodded, frowning with concern, a light of understanding and sympathy in his watery eyes. 'I shall tell you plainly. Mary Johnston came to me out of worry for you, and that is why I visited tonight. Mary expressed to me grave fears, only – well, she found it hard to explain what precisely concerned her. She said that when you visited the tavern last, you seemed exhausted and confused.' The observation stung a little but I could not counter it. 'And, she said that you left the Whistle and Duck in the company of a lady, whom she did not believe she recognized.'

'A lady? No, I left the Whistle and Duck alone that evening.'

The vicar shook his head. 'Mary was quite certain of it. She was most emphatic on that detail – uncannily so, I might say. She saw you leave the tavern, and greet a lady who was stood outside, waiting for you.'

I felt a tightness in my throat, and beads of sweat began to prick at my forehead. The faint stab of a headache formed behind my eyes. I had been alone in Cobsfoot, had I not? All of a sudden, I felt I could not be so sure. My own memories seemed vague, mixed up. 'Reverend … there is another, here –' I said, looking at the small, pale man in earnest.

'The boy is bringing the coach round,' Mordrake's voice interrupted us as he strode into the hall, beaming. The vicar's eyes remained upon me, pinched with worry, but he said nothing – he seemed to understand implicitly that what I had to tell was for him alone.

'Well, Mr Christie, it was a great pleasure to meet you,' Scattergood said warmly, taking my hand between both of his. 'I do hope that you are able to join the service this Sunday. And you must visit me at the vicarage to see those books I mentioned. As early as you like – I am at your disposal.'

He bowed, and shook Victor's hand and bowed again, and with that the vicar made his departure.

'What a pleasant and thoughtful man,' Victor said as we watched the coach trundle away into the evening's lengthening shadows. 'Tsk, it is growing darker already. The nights are drawing in, are they not? I do hope he makes it home through the woods without incident.'

'What makes you say that?' I asked, alarmed, but my companion just laughed.

'Yes, an enjoyable evening, and a most stimulating conversation,' Victor said, turning to me, and placing his hand lightly upon my shoulder. 'Simon …' his voice dropped to a soft hush, his eyes glimmering in the twilight.

I stepped back, out of his reach. Victor's hand fell back to his side, and he half smiled, and then sighed. 'Simon – you needn't tie yourself in such knots every time you find yourself in my companionship, you know. Do you regret what happened between us? It need never happen again, if that's what you want. But I implore you, you must never regret doing what felt right at the time. And wouldn't it be a shame to let such an inconsequential matter put paid to our budding friendship?'

I opened my mouth to speak, but words failed me. With a stiff bow, I bade him good night, and made my way up the stairs to my bedchamber.

15.

As I had hoped, the reverend's visit provided a welcome distraction – a single evening's disruption of my usual routine that allowed me to bring some order to my thoughts, and consider what options I might pursue next as my best course of action. I had no doubts at this point that Amy was being confined in some way within Thistlecrook House: kept there by Victor Mordrake for an as yet unknown purpose. But she was not a prisoner in any traditional sense – no bars or chains sealed her within her library, and nothing had prevented me from stumbling across her quite by accident so soon after arriving at the house, even when the household staff appeared oblivious to her presence. Here, my limits of rational and logical explanation were exceeded. Was it conceivable, then, that her restraint was metaphysical in nature? That she was not kept in somewhere, but rather, she was being kept out from everywhere – everywhere that might be perceived by sight, or sound, or touch. Except to me. The theory was wildly outlandish, something I should have dismissed with a derisive scoff only weeks earlier. But after all that I had seen and heard in this place, I could not dismiss it; in fact, I found myself surprisingly ready to believe it.

As to Victor, I was by this time convinced that he had inherited more from his ancestors than this crumbling house, a horde of sadistic paintings and a ghoulish flesh-bound bible. The fearful and ungodly research and rituals of the Mordrakes of old, their dark discoveries and methods – I was sure that such things were known to Victor also. And then, the painting that hung in the parlour, of his ancestor – so identical in features and expression … Reader, you may imagine the lengths to which my fantastical speculations led me.

As to next actions, my first resolution was to win over Amy's trust to a degree that she had not yet been willing to surrender. I believed that she saw me as a friend, and that she recognized I acted in good faith – and I thought she was close to confiding in me the truth of her predicament. But I could not and would not wait forever for Amy to take me into her confidence; assuredly, I needed to push the issue.

I became fixed upon the idea of seeing Amy in some other setting besides the upstairs library. Convincing her to leave her library, or even the house entirely, would test the limits of her confinement, if I was correct in my surmise that she was trapped here in some sort of way. Also, I hoped that opening our intimacy into a new setting – out into the vibrant outside world – might in some way cause her to open up her own self and prove more willing to divulge her closely clutched secrets. And I think, in part, I hoped that witnessing her outside her usual room might remove any final traces of lingering, nagging uncertainty that she could be merely some phenomenal delusion on my part.

Having decided upon this goal, the following evening could not come soon enough. Victor visited me while I was at work, again, and made irritating and inconsequential banter throughout the day, but I could hardly hold a conversation. I scarcely trusted myself to speak a word without letting slip one of the notions scuttling within my skull; besides, my mental processes were consumed with imagined dialogues planning how I might broach the subject of an excursion with Amy, and preparing contingencies for the varied reactions I could anticipate. I could not rule out the risk that she would see through my clumsy attempts to break down her barriers, and react accordingly, after all.

Finally, the evening came, and I joined Amy at our usual rendezvous. I had been so distracted throughout the day that it had slipped my mind entirely to wonder whether she had received my note of apology the previous evening, or to worry that she might be angry with me again for not calling on her. Fortunately, though, it transpired that the hastily written note had done its work. Too well, in fact, for she detained me with irrelevant questions about the reverend for some time.

'Who is the reverend for Cobsfoot, these days? Oh, he must be new to the area. But what a funny name: Scattergood! It's fitting for a clergyman, I suppose – he could hardly have been, I don't know, a high court judge, with a name like that. And what did the vicar have to say? Just a visit to the local master – yes, that makes sense, if he is new to the area. But what else – you discussed local history? I can't say I know much about that, if I'm honest – well, you know that I didn't grow up here … And what was the vicar's first name, do you know?' She chattered in this fashion for some fifteen or twenty minutes before I could move the subject on to my own agenda.

Having placed myself strategically beside the window while we talked, I gazed down upon the empty gardens outside, and made my gambit. 'It is another fine evening,' I observed casually. 'The weather has been so splendid recently.'

'Hm, yes, I suppose,' Amy answered distractedly.

'I had wondered – that is, I had been thinking –'

I was interrupted by a brief, guffawed outburst – I looked to Amy in alarm. She was watching me, with the fingers of one hand touched to her smiling lips.

'What is it?' I asked.

'I'm sorry. Only – you're speaking awfully strangely, and the way you're standing –' Her eyes were dancing with amusement, and she gave out another little laugh. But something in my expression must have given her pause, for her face grew suddenly serious – or mostly so – and she said, 'I am sorry – what did you want to ask me?'

I swallowed dryly. 'Well, only, with the weather so fine, I thought perhaps I – we – could take a walk. Together, both of us. I should be most pleased if you would accompany me,' I added quickly, wishing that I had been sitting down for this, after all.

'Oh, I see – why, yes, that would be very pleasant.' said Amy, looking away and blushing slightly.

'Ah – wonderful!' I exclaimed, doing little to hide my surprise. 'Yes, that would be most … most pleasant. Then, when … that is, no time like the present, I suppose?'

Amy stared through the window behind me. 'I do think those clouds look rather ominous, don't you? I'm not sure that this evening would be very wise.' I turned around – she was correct, dark clouds were beginning to loom heavily over the surrounding treetops. Even as I looked on, one or two drops of rain spotted against the windowpane.

'Oh, I see. Yes, all right,' I muttered. 'But when, then? Tell me.'

'Sit down, Simon – you look half-mad,' Amy commanded and I obeyed, dropping beside her on the settee. She took my hand in hers, and placed her other upon my shoulder, as light as a bird. Now seated, I realized that my pulse was racing, and my hands trembled so uncontrollably Amy could surely feel it in my touch.

'When, though? You will join me?' I asked again, like a child.

'Yes, Simon, I have already said I will,' Amy answered gently, and lifted her hand from my shoulder to brush her fingers through my hair. 'Sunday – let us go on Sunday.'

I realized I had no idea when that was – I seemed to have lost all track of the days of the week. Amy had my answer before I even asked. 'The day after tomorrow,' she told me. 'There now, it is decided. Poor thing, you look so tired. I hope that the fresh air will do you some good.'

'It shall, I am sure of it,' I replied. 'I feel more myself already, just thinking about it.'

Saturday came and went with little to recommend of it, its most notable quality being that it seemed to pass far too slowly for my liking. I was anxious for Sunday to come, and with it our appointed excursion; I spent most of the day that preceded it sighing, and fretting, and peering out of the window for any sign of an errant raincloud that could ruin my plans – as if the weather of this noble island could be predicted with confidence from one hour to the next. The only other point worth mentioning of Saturday was the arrival of a note from the Reverend Scattergood, thanking Victor for his hospitality and expressing gratification at having made my acquaintance. His communication came as something of a relief to me, after Victor's off-hand remark about him making the journey home safely – at least one anxiety lingering at the back of my mind could be scored off as unfounded and irrational. The reverend's note also reminded me, however, that my plans with Amy would preclude me from attending the Sunday service that I had been invited to: unfortunate, but I would just have to call on Scattergood at some other later date.

Sunday arrived at last, with the precise punctuality that might be expected of any day of the week. Under my attentive vigil, the sky held clear and blue, unmarred by any dark hint of rain, but my mind remained clouded by anxiety. I had been so keen to remove Amy from the household, to witness her in another environment – and perhaps, through a change of scenery, inspire a commensurate change of heart that might lead her to disclose some new, revelatory information – but now, as the hour drew closer, I found myself almost awed for fear of what form that revelation might take. I felt like a man of science on the brink of a new discovery, like one of the grey-browed, stern-faced philoso-phers in Victor's paintings, performing an experiment that promised to push not only against the bounds of human understanding but also decency.

For all that, it was only a walk in the countryside. I waited for Amy, at the time and place she had appointed. I had wondered whether we might have to sneak out unob-served, somehow, from under the noses of the staff and master – I decided to wait for Amy to broach that subject, if it needed broaching. As it was, she hadn't seemed concerned at all and had simply told me she would meet me in the main hall at twelve o'clock.

While I waited, and watched the hands of the grandfa-ther clock tick one minute past twelve, I marvelled at how quiet the household was: no discreet footsteps sounded on the groaning, echoing floorboards, no voices carried from the direction of the kitchens. Victor, Bannatyne, and possi-bly the younger boys too, must be out on some errand, I thought, or perhaps some of the staff had gone to church in town. I was alone with my fluttering heart and twisting stomach, just the tick of the grandfather clock to pierce the pin-drop hush. Even that seemed to sound the seconds more slowly than usual, every swing of the pendulum an aching effort. Two minutes past.

The silent spell was broken by the soft tread of a foot on the staircase above. I looked up, and saw Amy descending, wearing a tasteful blue dress with a dark jacket, and a small hat on her neatly pinned hair. I had never seen her attire quite so … well put-together, I suppose. She moved with a greater poise and purpose than I had witnessed in her before; seemed to carry herself with more ladylike reserve than I had observed in the cosy library. I suddenly found myself deeply self-conscious in the grace of her presence. She seemed to pause for a moment at the midpoint of the stair-case, as though to allow sufficient time for her entrance to have its desired impact, then stepped briskly down the remaining steps and joined me at my side. 'How do I look?' she asked, cheerfully. I think I may have been gawping a bit.

'Yes, very well,' I replied. Her eyes took in my own outfit – the usual summer suit – in a sweep and seemed to find it acceptable, just about. 'Though, it is still quite warm outside – you may not need your jacket,' I added.

'I always feel the cold,' she told me, and linked her arm with mine. She stood so close to me I wondered if she could feel the tremors of my thumping chest. Together, we made our way through the grand door, and into the outside world.

Our walk began with a leisurely visit to the estate's walled rose garden. Amy paused frequently to bend and admire the flowers, or remark on an unfamiliar arrangement; she seemed to know the garden well, but not in its current layout – I realized that the view afforded by her library window looked out upon another side of the building. She told me the names of the blooms, pointed out rare speci-mens and told me which exotic corners of the world many of them had been plucked from. I listened attentively to her every word, yet it was not the flowerbeds that held my attention rapt that afternoon, but the creature who walked at my side. So familiar, yet seeming different, somehow, beneath the midday sun; the drab, cloistered atmosphere of the library was undeserving of her, and though I could never have thought of Amy as drab herself, here in the open air, illuminated by the unobstructed sunlight that shone dazzlingly down from above, her long hair waving in the light breeze that encircled us, she seemed to move with a refreshing vivacity and lightness of spirit. Her voice was more musical than ever, her enthusiasm more girlish and charming. And though her eyes shimmered with merry laughter, it was not now cut with the sardonic edge to which I had become accustomed – she seemed filled with a happiness that was genuine and pure.

Amy noticed my diverted attentions. 'Simon, you're not even listening. You seem quite distracted.'

'I am listening – you were speaking of the herbaceous borders,' I replied, repeating the first expression I could pluck from my immediate memory. 'Although – you are right, I was distracted, though only by thinking how I am enjoying your company very much, on such a fine day as this,' I told her, and Amy smiled at me so radiantly that my head fairly spun with passion and I had to look away blinking for a moment.

We sat in the gardens for some time and spoke, quietly, intimately, though not on any particular subjects. I found myself now loath to ruin the mood of the day by pushing my own paranoiac agenda. For now, to be with Amy was enough. From the gardens, we made our way over the lawns, in full, bold view of the house's many windows, and from there into the encircling woods, picking up a rough and winding trail. In the bright sunlight, the crooked trees lost their usual menace: above our heads their branches shifted with soft creaks while emerald leaves rustled gently in the wind, and tiny birds tweeted and twittered their cares away and watched our passage with curiously tilted heads. About our feet, the forest floor rustled with scurrying beasts that darted hither and tither; Amy squeezed my arm and pointed to these minute denizens of the forest with delight.

We came upon a small cluster of rabbits, which we stopped and watched from a distance; they foraged the woodland floor contentedly, until some instinctual sense appeared to advise them of our presence and they hopped away unhurriedly. As their white tails disappeared into the foliage, Amy strained upon her tiptoes so eagerly I almost thought she would break away from me and pursue them into the undergrowth. Some short way on, I was startled by a movement at the periphery of my vision: a large, dark shape passing quickly through the trees some several dozen feet away, alongside us. For a moment, its shape and posture brought to mind the huge black crooked hound I had seen walking with Victor on that one night – but of course it could only have been a deer, surprised by our passing and slipping silently away through the trees. By the time I turned my head to get a proper look it had vanished; Amy turned to look, too, and we both stared into the empty forest for a time, and then continued on.

Deeper and deeper into the trees we ventured, the path we followed becoming less distinct until it seemed to me that we were picking our way between the boughs and branches unguided. Amy led the way, pulling me gently along a route that she seemed to follow from memory, or intuition.

'Have you walked through these woods often?' I asked, breaking the long, peaceful silence that had accompanied our travels.

'Oh yes, very often,' Amy began, then paused. 'Although, not for some time, now,' she added.

'You seem to know them well. I … wonder that you don't come out here more frequently, to enjoy the fresh air.'

'It is not so easy for me to come and go, now,' Amy said, quietly. Her voice sounded distant, and distracted – she was not fully listening, and did not seem to appreciate the purpose of my questions.

'Why is that?' I asked gently.

For a long time, Amy said nothing, and the only sound was the crunch of our footsteps upon the ground, and the ceaseless, looping melody of the birds singing in the tree-tops. I thought perhaps she would not answer, but then a faint reply came. 'I have to be careful. He is always watching me.'

'You mean Mordrake? He watches over you?' I tried to keep my voice low and level, to match hers, and did not look at her as I spoke. I had the disconcerting sensation that I was talking to someone in my dreams, that I was not really here, and might wake at any moment – or perhaps that she might.

Another long pause, and the gentle beat of our rustling footsteps. 'Yes.'

'He keeps you here – in the house, doesn't he?'

'He tries,' Amy said, and I wondered if whether the tone I detected in her voice was one of sorrow, or of pride.

We continued our advance through the forest. We passed the old Mordrake folly, as I had done in my first week at the house, when I had first walked the grounds and ventured into these twisting woods. Now, as then, its derelict form appeared before us through the trees unexpectedly; ornate and ravaged, it loomed upon its rise, a man-made anomaly of columns and carvings now reconquered by the forest. Amy paused, regarded its dark structure for just a moment, and then altered our path to walk a wide circumference around the base of its hill without turning her head in its direction a second time.

We left the ruin behind and Amy's pace seemed to quicken, the gentle pressure upon my arm by which she was guiding me becoming almost a tug, so that I had to focus my attention upon my footing to avoid a trip and fall. We were certainly far from any established trail, now. I did not see where Amy led us so urgently until we were almost upon it – though I might have guessed. Through the trees ahead of us shone the silver expanse of the lake.

I could not help but shiver when I saw it, and I almost made to pull Amy away, to recoil and turn our course from that portentous spot, but she was leading me so insistently there that I had not the will to prevent her. The lake: the site of so many of the tragic and indistinct rumours and legends that clung to Thistlecrook House, and where my dreams, my nightmares and my frantic speculations always seemed to lead me. I had come to instinctively shrink from the place, as some animals are said to shun those spots that carry the scent of death. Looking upon its rippling waters now, baking under a malevolent miasma, a chill crept up my spine in spite of the clinging heat, to think what secrets might lay concealed within its placid depths.

Had I planned our route myself, or paid more attention to where we were headed, I would not have taken Amy to this place. Yet she was the one who had brought us here, right to its lapping shore. We stood on the hard, caked mud and stared out over the water without speaking. When I could stand it no longer, I looked to Amy and saw in her eyes a hollow, abstracted stare that seemed to hardly be focused on any part of the scene before us. Her hands were clasped together before her at waist height as if she stood in half-hearted prayer, though her fingers moved restlessly, weaving and interlocking with each other then parting again, a nervous child's ceaseless fidgeting. The sunlight seemed to exaggerate her complexion so that her pale skin was almost porcelain white, her rose-pink lips moving slightly in an inaudible murmur.

'What is it?' I asked, my voice straining against the oppressive silence. 'What do you see?'

Amy said nothing. I thought that she did not hear me.

'This lake, what is it?' I tried. 'Amy, what is this place?'

This time, my words – my invocation of her name – seemed to penetrate, and she turned, slowly, to face me. When her eyes met mine, she blinked in surprise and gave a small sigh of recognition. I think she had led us here in some sort of trance that was only now lifted.

Amy blinked again, and her gaze returned to the waters. 'I have not been here for a very long time,' she said.

'What is this place?' I asked, again.

'I think … I cannot be sure. It's a place in between. Like the blank space at the bottom of the page in a book. It is hard to explain.'

This told me nothing. 'But you have been here before, haven't you?' I asked. 'Did something happen to you here?'

'The lake is a reservoir,' she said quietly, as if reciting words from memory, 'for – Oh!' Her eyes widened and then she turned in a sudden panic. 'We should go. I am tired,' she said, but I caught her arm. I was too close, now, to let go.

'Something did happen to you here, didn't it?' I demanded. 'The last time you were at this lake, perhaps? What was it?'

'I … I …' There were tears in Amy's eyes now, and she squirmed in my grasp, but did not pull away.

'Please … think, Amy,' I said, softening my tone but not releasing my grip around her wrist. 'When you were here last, was it – perhaps – it was not a day like today, hot and sunny and stifling, but it was in the winter, and the trees were hanging with snow and the sky was grey, and the lake was frozen over …' I was speaking as a madman, yet with complete certainty in the truth of my words.

'Simon, please –'

'Did Victor used to bring you here? This place means something to him, I am sure … You – and he – you were together, weren't you? You were his wife, Victor's wife. Amy, tell me the answer!'

'Yes ... yes,' she confirmed, defeated. I raised my free hand in triumph, holding my finger up in a gesture of victory, even as my stomach lurched with hateful resentment. To my horror, Amy actually winced as my hand went up, recoiling with fear at the ferocity of my monomania. She was frightened by me in that moment, I realized, and I hated myself – and yet ...

'I am sorry – you must forgive me, Amy – but I need to know – I have been driven half-mad through trying to understand. And I can help you, I am sure of it –' Her dark eyes, turned downwards, now looked up into mine with a glimmer of hope, though her other features remained stoically forlorn. 'Let me help you, won't you? Tell me what you remember.'

She only shook her head.

'It was you ... you who fell through the ice on the lake, here – this lake, a long time ago, wasn't it? Didn't you?'

'I ... I can't remember.'

'Try, Amy, please – you were his wife, Victor's wife, and you fell through the ice and you ... And now he keeps you here, somehow, doesn't he? It's Victor, he's done this to you!'

All at once, my fingers that held Amy were chilled to the bone. Where once they had fastened around the skin of her narrow wrist, they now clutched something wet, cold, and as stiff as a petrified lump of driftwood. I looked down in confusion, saw my own hand closed around a sodden limb, thin and brittle and ready to crack. Frost prickled against my skin; ice melted under my touch and ran dribbling through my trembling fingers. A spasm of dread clutched at my throat. When I looked at Amy again, she was not there: it was not her face that I saw, but a heart-shaped horror, its eyes bulging and blank, skin pallid and veined and lips blue as cobalt, framed by swirling tangles of long black hair that floated in a dark aura around that ghastly visage, suspended

on unseen currents. In terror I released my grasp and staggered backwards – but, just as quickly as it had come, the
illusion was passed, and before me stood only Amy, tears
brimming in the corners of her eyes. In her distress, she did
not seem to have witnessed my momentary shock.

She raised her hands – pink, alive – to her eyes, and cried
out, 'I cannot remember!', her emotion breaking free at last.
'I can't remember what happened to me. How can it be I
don't remember? We were married, yes, and I lived here,
once, but I know it was a long time ago. I have been so
terribly cold and alone for longer than I can say. What sort
of nightmare –' she stopped, gasped, with tears in her eyes.

'Everything I have told you is the truth: about me, my
family … but it was long ago, so long ago. And now … I
don't know why I am here, in this house, in the library
every day. I remember Victor, our wedding, and then – Oh,
God! It is as though I have been in a half-sleep, and
everything a dream, so that I don't know what is real or not
– and then things I remember that cannot possibly have
happened to me, things from another life – I … I remember
this lake, all frozen, like you said, in the white of winter; the
air was crystals and the trees all around so bent and black. I
came here to be alone, except …'

A shadow seemed to pass over her; she turned her wet
face to mine and stared into my eyes. 'And then – you. You,
Simon. You came into the library and I woke up. I don't
know why you did that to me.' Amy flung herself forwards
and I caught her in my arms, held her small frame tightly
against mine, felt her heaving sobs reverberate through my
chest until with time they slowed, and stopped, and her
body was calm once more, still pressed close to my own. I
was alive to every sensation of her form: my hands moved
over her, over the thin fabric of her clothes, the soft warm
skin and flesh underneath, and the bones and sinew and
pulsing heart within. And then, her hands were upon me,

too, moving, smoothing over my shoulders, her arms
around my neck and her fingers pushing through my hair.
Her head lifted and I gazed down into the deep wells of her
eyes, red-rimmed now with hot tears, but still black and
shining as the midnight sky.

'Let me help you,' I whispered, and she nodded, and she
closed her eyes and pulled my head closer until her lips
touched mine in a hot, sweet kiss. There, beside the lake,
held tight within my embrace, Amy was real.

16.

'Tell me what you remember about Victor,' I asked, stroking my fingers through the soft, flowing cascade of Amy's raven hair.

'Why, Simon? Where is Victor now? Not here with us.'

Her argument was persuasive – but I could not be so readily deterred. 'Just ... indulge me. How did you first meet him?'

You might suppose that the question was forced through gritted teeth, that I asked it out of bitter jealousy, or some masochistic wish to hear of my ostensible rival, but this was not the case. I was just curious; I wanted to know. I suppose that I should have blushed to have the gall to even mention the man's name while Amy and I lay contentedly together as we did – again, not so. I found that even now I could not think of Amy as Victor's wife – no more than she appeared to do, anyway, and it was evident that no erstwhile vows troubled her conscience. Mordrake might hold her key, for now, but he could not own Amy. No, Amy and I were no concern of Victor's. And besides, surely such moralising was for my father's generation.

Amy squeezed her arms tighter around me, pressed her face into my chest and sighed. 'I don't think I can remember much. I know that it was after Abby … after she passed, that he came into my life. He was kind when I first knew him … a different man, with a different name. He was so strange. He fascinated me, and I thought I must be fascinating too, that I should be able to hold his attention the way that I did. I couldn't imagine what he saw in me, but I liked how it felt. Well, you know how he is, how thrilling the feeling is when he focuses his attention on you – as though the sky full of stars is shining down upon you and you alone. And then, the heavens turn and you're still there, still underneath the same sky, but there's no light shining for you any more …' I shifted myself slightly beneath her embrace.

'I was still so young when I met him, just a child,' Amy continued. 'I don't think I knew that I had a choice in how my life could be. And then … he changed, so quickly. Perhaps that's not so unusual. His dark moods began, days and weeks where he would not talk to me, or even look at me, or else flew into such rages that I feared –' She broke off suddenly, shifted her hand to her mouth and tapped her fingers against her lips.

'Yes – I have seen something of his moods,' I offered.

'I thought that I had, too,' Amy told me sadly. 'I remember there were people, always people in the house …'

'People?' I asked, altering my position so that I could gaze down at her expression as she spoke.

'I – It's so confused. Just images, hazy, like dreams. But it is coming back to me, I think, slowly. I believe that I recall more than I did – only, how can I know what I cannot remember?' she asked, looking into my eyes as though she expected me to be able to provide an answer.

'What were the people doing?'

Amy did not reply, but made a gentle sound that might have been a hum or a sigh, and ran her fingers across my chest. 'More questions? Are you not indulged, yet?' she asked coyly. I laughed, straining my neck to kiss the top of her head and inhale the warm, narcotic scent of her hair.

'Experiments,' she said suddenly, her voice a tone deeper, more serious. The word sounded like a bell in my ears. 'They were ... there were people coming and going, always new faces and names to remember ... I never could. Soon Victor stopped introducing me. Their clothes, and accents, they were so strange, so exotic – people from everywhere. I didn't want to be part of it.'

'Part of what?' I prompted, when she paused again. Amy lifted her head to me, and beneath her dark crown of curling locks I saw her face had grown pale and was trembling. I drew my arms around her and we said no more.

The night after we had stood by the lake and kissed, sleep had come to me readily enough, for the first time since my arrival at Thistlecrook House. My dreams had been gentle and sweet, but I had been plucked from them at some point in the deepest darkness of the midnight hour, stirred awake by an abrupt and familiar sensation. Turning in my bed, I observed the dark shadows of feet stood outside my chamber door. My visitor was waiting outside – waiting patiently for me. Silently, I pulled my sheet aside and rose from where I lay, and padded barefoot across the shadowed room, reaching my hand out instinctively to feel for the door handle that I could not make out in the gloom. The door swung open without a noise. She looked up at me through large dark eyes, her nervous fingers playing with the ends of her hair that fell in tangled, untamed ripples. Without saying a word, I stood to one side, and Amy slipped past me through the doorway and into my darkened bedchamber.

At breakfast, not even Bannatyne's surly demeanour and bitter glances could ruin my effervescent mood. Mordrake was absent again, and his man seemed to feel emboldened to stare at me with outright hostility, and to rudely toss my breakfast dishes down on the table with a clatter. But I could not mind – if anything, the old fool's childish strop struck me as comical.

I spent the day inspecting a series of hellish scenescapes, all flickering red flames and bent devils leering with delight as they tortured the damned via a ludicrous range of inventive techniques. The composition, method, era all changed, but the anguished faces, distorted in agony and terror, remained a constant. Yet my mind was elsewhere: not even a palette indicative of the Northern Renaissance nor the light hand of a possible early modernist innovator could hold my attention. There were just two questions that turned over in my mind: when would I see Amy again? And – harder to think of but of more consequence – what should I do now? I was driven to distraction; I paced and muttered in my workroom, the artworks abandoned, a grotesque and demonic audience for my inward turmoil. What had I got myself into? What possible good did I think I could bring to this situation? What in blazes was this situation, even? Did I truly understand anything, yet? I walked chaotic figures of eight around the floor, eyes cast downwards, lost in dizzying thought. I began to believe, then, that perhaps this was madness after all. I was surely insane. The things I thought I had seen, and heard, and believed that I knew – what other explanation could there be?

But then I thought of her: her dark eyes brimming with a barely dreamed hope, and soft lips pursed into a smile – her scent, her touch, her taste. I stopped pacing. My brief, sweat-stained panic subsided, and I rediscovered my resolve, stronger than ever. Amy had placed her trust in me, finally: a poorly chosen vessel for her hopes, perhaps – an ill-equipped candidate to be her goodly knight. But I was determined that I should do all that was within my power not to let her down.

* * *

'Was it always you who walked outside my room at night? And who waited at my door?' I asked.

Amy made a sort of soft humming noise that I took for hesitant affirmation. 'At night … sometimes I could slip from my library, and try to come to you. But I had to be careful that the others wouldn't see me, or know that I was sneaking away.'

'The others? You mean Victor? And Bannatyne?'

'M-hm. Them, and … It's so dark in the house at night, and dangerous. You must be careful. Don't you go wandering,' she patted my cheek playfully. 'Ask me something else.'

I thought for a moment. We sat together in the rose garden, side by side on a low stone bench in the balmy afternoon sun, so close our shoulders were pressed together and her left hand lay clasped within my right. The air was still, calm, and quiet; we were alone. 'What do you know of Mordrake's paintings – the art collection?'

'What about it? I hate it.'

'Yes, but – it's so singular. To have amassed such a collection, of such brutal, terrible images – death, dying, torture and execution. They're so inhumane, so … wanton. Yet Mordrake's family must have been obsessive in collecting them for hundreds of years. The styles and compositions span eras and movements, from all through history across all parts of the world. To have even amassed such a hoard is an achievement in itself.'

'You sound almost impressed by it all. Was I to decipher a question for me in all of that?' Amy teased, stroking the back of my hand with her fingertips.

'Well – why? Why collect those paintings?'

Amy shrugged disinterestedly. 'The Mordrakes enjoy terrible art, I suppose.'

'Did Victor ever speak to you about the paintings?'

Amy fell silent, as she often did when trying to remember. At length her reply came, soft and dreamlike. 'He wanted me to take an interest in them, I think. I remember standing upstairs, up in the attic; he would show me horrible, violent things' – she shuddered – 'and talk to me about them, point out details, and ask me over and over again: do you see, do you see?'

'What did he want you to see?'

Amy shook her head. She could not or would not say. 'He thought … he spoke as though the paintings were a clue to something, or – as though there was a riddle, hidden there, in the canvases, or in the images that they showed. Or … I don't know … That is only my impression of it.'

I thought of what Victor had said to me weeks ago on the hill, in the countryside, while a cool breeze swept around us and panting dogs scampered at our feet: that mankind at its most brutal was mankind at its most honest. Were there answers to be found in the paintings? I knew, or believed, that art, all art, was more than the images it presented; that its value, its meaning was greater than the sum of brushstrokes on canvas. Paintings were a window into the very soul of the artist, and by extension all of humanity. There must be answers to be found, then, even in the most sensationally lurid of works. Perhaps Victor's questions were just different to my own.

Then, with a sickly lump in my throat, I asked, 'The things in the paintings … the rituals, the experiments – are those the sorts of things the people were doing here at Thistlecrook House?' A cavalcade of violent imagery passed before my eyes: executions, dissections, torture, summoning, sacrifice. The walls dripping thick with sticky red blood. The stories I had heard in Cobsfoot, of disappearances and abductions, arcane sabbaths, and strange beings in the woods. Surely it couldn't all be true.

Again, Amy's reply was not immediate. 'I don't know,' she said, finally, and then added quickly, as if not to disappoint me, 'I don't think I saw a lot of what went on. They wouldn't let me. I think Victor was angry with me, disappointed that I couldn't fathom what they were trying to achieve ... I still cannot. There is something about this spot ... there are ancient things here, ancient places with power, he said. Even then, the library was my refuge; I hid in there and tried to ignore what went on outside. I heard things – strange, frightening things, in the night. But I believe I saw nothing. I just don't know. I am sorry, Simon.'

I held her, soothed her quaking nerves, and assured her there was no cause for her regret. In truth, it came as a relief for me to hear Amy deny all knowledge. It eased my heart to believe that she could be innocent and ignorant of the dark and terrible crimes I suspected had been committed in this house's past. And if, at times, I wondered how it could be so – if I questioned how she could have lived in the midst of such multitudinous sin without seeing or hearing any clue as to its true nature – those doubts I left discarded upon my pillow each morning, uninterrogated.

I would have let the matter drop there, but Amy had one more thing to say. 'There were books,' she told me, reluctantly. 'If you truly must know ... Victor and his guests were forever reading, and writing. He tried to show those to me, too, I remember. Incomprehensible, mad writings that I could make no sense of, except that it frightened and disgusted me, the ideas they hinted at. You won't find them in my library, no. I don't know where they're kept. He's hidden them away somewhere, most likely. Oh, I wish you wouldn't – but ... if you're determined to understand what happened here, then surely there must be answers in his books.'

The following day, I snuck away from the work I should have been doing and returned to the musty rooms of the house's claustrophobic upper floor. I had a notion that if Mordrake truly kept occult and blasphemous accounts of the deeds committed in this house, then perhaps they would be secreted away in the cramped space above, as his demonic paintings had been.

I had made my best effort to shirk that top floor of the house ever since my distressing turn on the day following my arrival, trapped in the suffocating room with the vicious horrors of the Mordrake collection. Where possible, I had allowed Arthur and Joseph to carry paintings up and down the stairs to my workroom for me, rather than returning to the trove myself. Today, though, I found that the air was cooler and clearer, and I felt a sober calm within as I clambered the stairs, emboldened by the sense of purpose that brought me here. Yet I still slowed reluctantly as I reached the cramped corridor at the top of the staircase and approached the door to the room that housed the Mordrake paintings. Almost as soon as I laid eyes on it, pins of sweat began to prickle against my back and on my forehead. I resolved to walk straight past – unconsciously flinching from the doorway in such a wide berth that my arm rubbed against the wall opposite – but, as I drew level, an inevitable, fatalistic curiosity took hold. I paused, and glanced towards the door to the collection. It stood ajar by just a fraction – whoever had last been up here must not have shut it properly. I could reach out, now, take hold of the handle and pull it closed; or, the door would yield to my gentle push. My hand rose slowly, stretched across the narrow passageway and gave the door to the painting room a tentative shove.

It swung open slowly a short way and then stopped with a knock against something on the other side. Through the slender gap that had opened, I could see into a section of the room, jumbled with frames, rolled canvases, obscene statues and ornaments, all stacked one atop the other in the shadowy dim – exactly as I recalled it so vividly. I could hear faint voices downstairs, the clinks and thuds of daily domestic life; I even thought I detected the echo of voices raised in laughter, a rare sound in the house that for some reason set my teeth on edge.

I left the door to the collection standing partway opened and continued along the cramped corridor. Trying the doors of the other attic rooms I found that none were locked, but the rooms themselves lay empty, or stacked with old pieces of furniture concealed under layers of white sheets and translucent spiders' webs that hung in eerie, billowing shapes, like so many ghoulish wedding gowns. In one room I saw an antique child's cot, thick with blueish dust, and I vaguely wondered whom it had belonged to, and when.

I poked around each room in turn, picking my way through the disparate clutter and coming up empty-handed time and time again. There was no hidden warlock's library to be found here in the attic, no dusty trunk filled with rambling confessions. In one room busy with sheeted, spectre-like furniture, I observed that a number of metallic, hooped bolts or rivets had been fixed into the ceiling, as though something had been hung or chained there, once.

While I stared up wonderingly at these unusual fixtures, my conspiratorial imagination running riot, I detected the sudden, soft creak of a floorboard outside: the sound of a footstep treading the cramped attic hallway. I froze, and listened, my nerves instantaneously strained like piano wires. If I were to be discovered up here, what could I say? My presence was not strictly forbidden, but still, I could reasonably be expected to provide a plausible explanation as to why I had ascended to these lonely and unused uppermost rooms when I should have been working, and I had none.

The footsteps pattered and shuffled, up and down the hallway, back and forth, I fancied. I heard a door bang closed: that of the painting room, perhaps? And then the creak of the informing floorboard again, directly outside the room I was in. By good fortune, I had shut the door behind me as I entered, and had neglected to switch on the room's single electric light, instead relying on the small daylight allowed in through the ceiling windows for my investigation. The door thumped and then swung open abruptly; I swiftly ducked behind the nearest of the white shrouds that hung draped about the place. From where I crouched, I could peep over the sheet towards the door, and see where Bannatyne stood in the open doorway, for it was the butler who had appeared there, staring about the room, his nostrils flaring. I could only hope that in my darkened corner he would not see me. He turned his head slowly, staring about the shadowy and crowded room through squinted eyes; though his face was shaded, I could make out in his expression a stormy mask. His eye flashed with a bloodshot glint as it caught and reflected the little light. In his hand, too, something glinted: some longish object that he carried there at his side, while his other hand still rested upon the door handle.

For several moments Bannatyne loomed at the door, gazing into the darkness. And then, after an agonisingly long pause, his body seemed to bristle, and I thought he was about to step inside to commence a full search. But he only tensed upon the spot, his shoulders rising briefly, then gave a haughty sniff, and turned away, slamming the door shut once more. I let loose a sigh of relief. Once I was certain that Bannatyne had descended back to the lower parts of the house and the coast was clear, I wasted no more time tarrying up on the attic floor. The risk was too great, and in any case, I was convinced now that there was nothing useful to be found there.

That same evening, I rebuffed Victor's company at the dinner table, and deferred my nightly visit to Amy, to make a study of the ground floor bookshelves. Perhaps, I reasoned, Victor did not see fit to hide his secrets at all. Why should he, in his remote and seldom-visited home? And so I turned my attentions once again to the unconventional literary collection on display in Thistlecrook House. I had looked over the assorted spines upon Victor's shelves on previous occasions and found them obscure but unthreatening. Now, re-examining them with a more inquisitive, not to say suspicious, eye, their wide-ranging and esoteric subject matters struck me as some distance beyond eccentric. Aside from a number of histories both local and exotic, the shelves were almost exclusively taken up with scientific volumes covering subjects as varied as mathematics, physics, astronomy, and cosmology, some on such outcast theories as animal magnetism or dream interpretation, and also some works on the natural sciences, botany, and geology. These themes I knew little about, yet even with my glancing familiarity, the contents alluded to by the cryptic titles of the tomes struck me now as wildly unorthodox and experimental. I removed a selection that were written in English and flicked through them. The language was so technical and obtuse it was almost as good as gibberish, yet hinted at the most outlandish subject matter: theories and conjectures on the very fringes of recognizable science, which proposed the nonsensical as fact, and overstepped the acknowledged boundaries of human experience without a backwards glance. Some of the textbooks contained diagrams that I would have dismissed as childish doodling, were it not for their painstakingly academic presentation; the equations and formulas that surrounded these images meant nothing to me, but something about the diagrams of small humanoid figures caught in the midst of complex vortexes of lines, waves and angles – standing at the centre of overlapping spheres, or beneath vastly-proportioned triangulations that loomed above them like coned funnels – caused the hairs on the back of my neck to rise. I remembered Victor's words: 'experiments in communication'.

Most of the books appeared to be from the last century or so, but some were much, much older. One ancient codex in an archaic form of English compiled anecdotal accounts of conversations between medieval laymen and demons. Communication. Between its pages, as thin and dry as an insect's wing and almost crumbling to dust at my touch, one newer sheet of paper had been slipped with nothing written upon it but a list of place names. I studied that page carefully, wondering if the handwriting could be Victor's – it was certainly possible, although I had not seen enough evidence of his penmanship to be sure. Perhaps I should try to steal a sample from one of the mysterious dispatches he wrote from time to time.

A number of the books had short notes written inside their covers, or down the margins of the text, all in that same extravagant, looping hand: comments, synopses or recommendations on the writings within. A volume that appeared to marry astral currents and the position of the stars with the interpretation and influence of dreams was marked: 'The calculations are rudimentary, but there is much here'. Communication – I do not know whether the word rang in my ears as an echo of Victor's voice, or if I myself had uttered it aloud. For the most part, where I could decipher the careless handwriting, the content of these scribbled commentaries was as bizarre and incomprehensible as the books themselves; but one phrase stood out starkly to my eye, penned on the inside cover of a work that seemed to concern some sort of theoretical geometry, or architecture, or both: 'It is as we surmised – look for the spaces in between'.

I hunched over these varied texts, appalled by the wild fantasy of their contents that was matched only by the utterly serious conviction of the authors, until my skin crawled and I was compelled to return them to their shelves, none the wiser yet more convinced than ever of Mordrake's immersion in subversive wickedness. I could not believe that familial sentimentality alone had caused him to retain these lunatic volumes. As to the contents of the books, the mad theories proposed – I just didn't know what to make of it.

By the time I abandoned my reading, the evening light had faded to near darkness, and when I finally made my way to Amy's library, I was disappointed but unsurprised to discover that it stood empty, lifeless and still, save for the whorls of dust in the gloam of the encroaching night. I made for my own room, to wait for her there.

I became positive that Mordrake knew of Amy's and my intimacy. Day by day his mood sunk more into wordless animosity. He took to stalking about the house like an animal, his already somewhat lupine features hardening into a ferocious snarl whenever we crossed paths, which was frequently, for he seemed unable to leave me alone, as much as my presence seemed increasingly to infuriate him. He entered my studio and padded around behind my back while I worked, sniffing and tutting, inspecting the paintings I had out, those neatly stacked in the corner, and even scooping up my scribbled notes to stare at, only to throw them down again a moment later. It was all I could do to continue working in silence, trying not to allow his threatening demeanour disturb me into making some sort of incriminating slip. I felt he could read the guilt written across my face – or else smell its scent in the air between us.

He began to complain about the progress of my work, saying I was too slow and he would never be rid of me; he dropped hints and insinuations that I had exploited his hospitality, had taken his generosity and repaid it with self-satisfaction. Several times he asked when I would be done – I stalled, I made excuses, I referred to the expansiveness of the collection and the lack of any existing records or directories. I implied that I was almost ready to send a most promising report to my employers, but that with just a little more time the results could be so much more profitable for all. In truth I cared nothing for the collection, or my employment. Victor was right: I was working at a snail's pace. My only concern was Amy, my mind always on her.

'I long for my solitude,' became a recurrent phrase of his. 'I long to have my house back.' The truth was, of course, he could have turned me out whenever he liked – he was my host, after all. A word to Southgate's and I would be back to Edinburgh in disgrace, my prospects in the art world reduced to nil. He did no such thing, and I believed that his complaints rang hollow, though the threat was always there.

In the evenings I ran to Amy's embrace. Some days we met in the library, as usual; sometimes I found it cold and deserted, and went instead to my chambers where I would find her waiting, or where she would come to me later, announcing herself with a faint knock upon the door. I took this flexibility of location – this apparent increase in mobility – as a promising sign. Somehow, it seemed that Amy was no longer quite as confined as she had been when I first arrived in this place. I allowed myself to swell with pride at the thought that, in some fashion I could not fully understand, it was my presence, my support, that had liberated and energised Amy so.

'Victor watches me with suspicion. I think he knows about us – no, I am sure of it,' I told her.

'You must be careful. He is a dangerous man,' she replied matter-of-factly.

'What else do you remember of him?' I asked. 'You must recall something. Anything you can think of might be a clue.'

'A clue?' she asked, clasping my hand between both of hers and lifting it to press against her gentle lips. We stood at my window, staring towards the dark folded branches of the surrounding forest; somehow, at night, it always seemed to enclose the house more tightly than it did by daylight. As we watched I half expected to see the tall, loping figure of Mordrake emerge from the blackness there and come sweeping across the grass towards us, glaring accusingly up at the window where we both stood, as though my mental preoccupation alone could summon his presence.

'A clue as to what I must do to help you: why you are here, what Victor has done … is doing …' Even with Amy as my only audience, I found it challenging to put into words the absurdities of my suspicions. Half of what I meant went unsaid, and yet Amy seemed to comprehend. I had told her of the books, the bizarre and inexplicable theories they put forward, but they had stirred no further recollections in her and she could make no more sense of the madness than I could.

'I don't think the others trusted him, the other people who were here. They said that he took too much – or gave too much – perhaps both.'

'Too much of what? Took from where?' I asked, but Amy could not say.

'Perhaps that is why he is here, alone, now,' was all she offered.

'I told you that I would help you, and I shall,' I continued. 'We can leave here, together.'

She looked away, gazed out of the window in sorrow, or in hope. 'He would find us. Somehow, he would track us down, I know it. And I am not even sure that I could go. I don't know what would happen to me, if I tried to leave, if I went too far from my library –'

'There must be a way,' I told her. 'If I only understood what exactly Victor was doing, what he is up to. I have searched the house, as far as I am able, though it is not easy to look around under Bannatyne's nose. All I have found is eccentricities – behaviours strange and remarkable, but not criminal, not … Are you positive that you can recall nothing of his research here at the house?' I asked, for what might have been the hundredth time.

Amy's dark hair shook: she still did not. 'He wanted me to help him. He said … it was my duty, that it was the Mordrake legacy. But the things he was trying to achieve …' She shut her eyes tight, as though she would blind herself to what she saw in her mind.

'Yes?' I asked, eagerly.

'I'm sorry, Simon. All I have is a feeling, deep and dark and terrible – but I can't put it into words that would help you. I would have no part of it, and so he – Oh, it's useless. I'm sorry.'

'Why do you say he is dangerous?' I asked.

Her voice was suddenly solemn and grave, shed of the plaintive, almost sing-song tone of her remembrances. It sometimes seemed to me that Amy spoke with two voices: one that came from the distant past, that could only be vocalised by great strength of will, her words reaching me only as an echo, and a second voice that came from the here and now, clearer and more definite, its address formed with a precision of intent. 'I just know that he is a dangerous man, and powerful,' she told me. 'Please, say you won't do anything to anger him. He can't find us here – we are safe, as long as we are together.'

'What makes you say that?'

She sighed. Amy's patience for my ceaseless questions was long, but not without limit. 'Just believe me when I say it, Simon. He has not found me yet. He is not going to. And I am stronger when I am with you.'

'But you might be free,' I persisted, 'free to leave this house, forever. Victor can be stopped, somehow, I am sure of it. I only need to understand how – to be certain – before I do anything. Before I act. You can be free, and we … I just need to understand.'

She put her arms around me, squeezed me so that I could feel the pulse of her heartbeat. 'Let's not talk about it any more, not tonight. I have an awful feeling.' Her body shivered against mine, and I hugged her close. 'But all is well as long as we're together, Simon, my dear. You'll stay with me, won't you?'

I whispered that I would, and we kissed – but even in that honeyed moment I confess that my thoughts were elsewhere. Amy could tell me no more, and my searches were proving fruitless and increasingly hazardous. Bannatyne seemed to be in all places at once, always lurking whenever I tried to open a cabinet, or slip into a side room unobserved. I had no idea what I was looking for, or what I expected to find, in any case. And yet I could not shake loose the conviction that some secret remained waiting to be discovered, some hidden fragment that may in its unveiling cast a light of revelation upon this whole murky scenario.

It did not escape me that if Mordrake was indeed the one keeping Amy bound to this house, then perhaps he was the only thing keeping her so secured. An attempt to liberate her from his grasp might untether her completely, and put her somewhere beyond my reach entirely. It was a risk I could not discount – and yet, it was one I had no choice but to accept. Freedom could only be preferable to the lonely and meaningless confinement that was the alternative. That Amy should be liberated from the tyrant was my one resolve – whatever the cost.

17.

Victor was waiting for me at the breakfast table the next morning. His mood was agreeable for the first time in some days, and he attempted several times to engage me in conversation about incidental and indifferent matters, but I shunned his efforts with monosyllabic replies. He seemed unshaken by my terseness, however – amused by it, even – and persisted in addressing me with meaningless banter until I grew quite infuriated. I had to bite my tongue not to press a confrontation and demand to know what he was about: why he should huff and snarl one day and treat me as some unwelcome interloper, and then pester me with pointless remarks as if I were an old and comfortable companion the next. Good sense fortunately prevailed, and I instead surged off to my studio, and my work.

Even there I was not safe from the man's attentions. After I had been at it for an hour or so, the door opened with a creak and he entered. I knew it was him without turning to look; I did not acknowledge his arrival at all.

'Ah, the Rivera,' Victor commented from over my shoulder, addressing the painting I had set up for study: a plain-looking scene in jaundiced shades that showed a group of four young boys stringing up an unfortunate dog by a makeshift noose. From their dress, I had placed it somewhere in the Kingdom of Spain some two centuries ago, but I had been having difficulty identifying any distinguishing features about it that might point to a specific location, or the scenario, or the artist.

'You know who painted it?' I asked irritably, incredulously.

'Of course: Julius Rivera.' Mordrake shrugged, looking over the painting with an appraising eye. 'Mid-eighteenth century, I believe,' he added, then turned away and began pacing the room. I touched my pencil to my notepad, hesitating as to whether to write the information down, then placed both to one side.

'Can I help you? The faster I can work on, the sooner I will be out from under your feet,' I grumbled. I remained facing the painting, so that I could not see my employer's reaction to my blatant rudeness.

Mordrake said nothing. I sensed he was browsing the workspace, as was his wont when he made such visits: hands in pockets, rocking upon his heels – sure enough, it was not long before he began to whistle tunelessly. I tried to ignore his distractions, to continue my work despite him, but the man's very presence was anathema to me. After a time, he commenced to comment on the other works in the room, explaining their provenance to me one by one. 'Ah! This came from a particularly unfortunate young woman in Prague,' he said, of a stark yet abstract rendering of melancholia. 'And this is by one of the residents of Bedlam, I believe. Saint Cecilia, and look, this manic daub is supposed to represent her heavenly choir, too!' He laughed cruelly.

'I thought you had no great interest in art, or your family's collection?' I asked, finally relenting and turning in my seat.

'Oh, I don't, not particularly. But the stories of the artists – the stories of where they came from – those I recall vividly.' He grinned at me, his eyes flashing.

I scolded myself for giving in so easily and surrendering my attentions to the man, as he clearly desired. I presented the cold shoulder once more, but try as I might, my concentration remained fixated on his presence, the sound of his shoes shifting and squeaking on the floorboards behind me.

'Oho – and what is this,' Victor cooed some short while later. 'This I don't recall. Hm, not much to go on, a mere line drawing in pencil. Very basic, and quite uninspiring. What do you say, Simon, does the hand look familiar?' Grudgingly, I swivelled upon my chair yet again, a curse on my lips, but I could have fallen from my seat there and then when I saw that – somehow – Mordrake held in his hand Amy's simple, charming drawing of me seated at my desk, sketched onto a page torn from her notebook. He flourished the sheet at me with a triumphant grin.

Before I knew it, I had risen to my feet, astonished. Amy's sketch had been securely tucked into a drawer in my room, I was positive of it. I had never brought it to this studio – had I? 'Why, look,' Mordrake continued, 'someone has written something underneath. Ha ha, well, it seems someone was asking someone else for forgiveness. Perhaps some sort of missive between quarrelling lovers? How terribly amusing. But it is surely not part of the collection – I do wonder how it found its way here.'

'Let me see,' I gasped, and snatched the page from him. Rereading Amy's message, I was relieved to find she had not identified either of us by name, and there was nothing positively incriminating upon the page. Even so, Victor's wicked smile told me he knew exactly what it signified. Bannatyne, or some other, must have found the note among my possessions and turned it in to his master. But what to do? I could hardly accuse Mordrake or any other of subterfuge without admitting that I recognized the drawing and note both – and from there I could only confess all. Instinctively, I saw that this was the design of Mordrake's ambush, and committed to the other route accordingly.

'Hm, some hand-drawn sketch – it must have been slipped in among the other paintings, somehow.' I shrugged indifferently, handing the slip of paper back as though it meant nothing to me.

'So it must have,' Victor nodded, watching me closely. He turned the paper in his hand and peered again at what was scribbled there. 'A neat hand, but quite plain. Nothing remarkable about this one at all. I wonder how it managed to sneak in. Why, look at that – even in profile, the man in the drawing almost looks like you, Simon!'

'I suppose, a little.'

'How very amusing – very amusing!' Mordrake dropped the sketch carelessly on the mantelpiece and walked off. I could hear his laughter echoing down the halls even as the door swung closed behind him.

At dinner that evening, Mordrake's mood had evolved once more. He no longer fizzed with irrepressible, troublesome energy, nor did he seethe and brood animalistically – his expression was bland and mild, and he welcomed me with a civil 'Good evening, Simon,' as I entered, and poured me out a glass of wine.

I took the offered drink and thanked him cautiously. I had resolved during the afternoon hours following his ominous visit and the brandishing of Amy's drawing, that I must tread more cautiously than ever around the master of the house. His visit to my workroom was assuredly a threat and a warning, and I saw that I must not antagonize him unnecessarily as I had previously seemed hell-bent on doing. I could be no help to Amy at all if I made an open enemy of Victor, or was dismissed from his house entirely, unable to return to her.

'I believe that I owe you an apology,' Victor began, once I was seated. 'I am sure that my company over the past few days has been quite intolerable.'

'I am sure I did not notice anything of the sort,' I replied. Victor shook his head.

'You did notice,' he told me. 'Let us not mince words. I have had much on my mind. You have been on my mind, Simon. But in my self-absorption, I permitted my thoughts to get ahead of themselves. I … I held you accountable for things beyond your comprehension, and I blamed you for matters that cannot be helped, and that was foolish and imprudent of me.'

A pregnant pause followed, where he seemed to be waiting for me to ask what he meant by his words, or put forward some other question. I said nothing, and our knives and forks clacked arrhythmically against our plates in the awkward hush. It appeared that Mordrake had said his piece for the time being, and he moved on to other subjects for the remainder of the meal – affairs around the estate, ideas he had for the gardens, incidental topics on which I could engage with him politely and with minimal effort. As had happened previously, I found that when he turned his mind to acting the attentive host, Victor made for almost irresistible company. He had a hypnotic knack for making conversation easy: he was erudite and witty, and seemed to have an unending range of topics he could introduce whenever discourse began to falter, all of which were interesting to me and never failed to stimulate my renewed engagement. It was not long before, in spite of myself, I began to relax somewhat and forget my ill will. The two or three glasses of wine we shared over the course of the meal surely helped.

Victor poured me another as the staff cleared our plates. I rubbed my eyes, tried to tell him no, those I had drunk with our meal having already gone to my head, but the

words could not or would not come out. I looked to the
clock, thinking I had somewhere else to be, and then with
a start remembered Amy, who by this time would surely be
waiting for me.

'Do you have somewhere you need to be, Simon?' Victor
asked me. The sense of déjà vu was uncanny; I felt I had
lived this precise scene before.

'No, no.'

'Don't you?' he asked sharply, his eyes narrowing. And
then at once his tone was again as mild and soothing as
flowing water. 'How very tedious this has become. Aren't
you growing tired of it all? I know that I am. My patience is
not unlimited, you know.' Mordrake placed his hand on my
shoulder and gazed steadily into my eyes with condescend-
ing sympathy. I was surprised to find that we were stood at
the mantelpiece, with cigarettes perched between our
fingers that curled wreaths of smoke about the room. I had
not remembered rising from the dinner table. How much
wine had I drunk?

'It is all too bad, really. I regret', he was saying, 'that she
found you more quickly than I could have anticipated.
Perhaps I could have done something – I might have found
some words to warn you. I almost feel that I let you down.'

'What are you talking about?' I asked incredulously.

'But then, I wonder how much resistance you offered – if
any,' he went on, as if I had not spoken. 'And, for what? It
is difficult not to feel disappointed in you, truth be told.
What did she tell you, after all? What do you know of her,
truly?'

'She …' I repeated dumbly. 'Who … I don't know who –'

'Really, Simon?' Victor's eyebrow arched severely. As I
stared up into his eyes, so close to mine, it seemed to me
that they fairly blazed and stirred, like distant celestial giants
captured below his drooping lids. His red tongue darted out
and licked his lips, quickly.

'I don't –' I murmured, and with an effort pulled myself away from the fireplace where we stood, took two staggering steps backwards and almost toppled over a chair.

'You would do well to forget her. Come now, Simon – perhaps I can help ...'

My feet were suddenly rooted to the spot, frozen and unresponsive to my will. Victor stood in front of me again – he lifted both his hands and placed them gently down upon my shoulders. The room smelled of smoke, and eau de cologne, and full-bodied wine – a taste that seemed to fill my mouth, rising sickly from the back of my throat. Victor smiled at me, faintly, lopsided – a self-satisfied smirk of conquest. I felt passion rise within me at that grin – I was infuriated, and enflamed. But – I knew there was a reason to resist, a reason not to trust the piercing, crystalline blue eyes that held me pinned – I had to escape – there was a reason.

With an effort, I shifted my right foot, took another stumbling step back. Victor's hands fell from my shoulders as I turned away, mouthing my rejection.

'You should forget her – she is not what you think,' I heard him say, as I lurched from the room, slamming the door closed between us.

Unsteady on my trembling legs, and with both hands grasped to the banister, I found my way upstairs and practically tumbled down the hall towards Amy's library. I grasped the handle and twisted, wrenching the door open. But the hour was late, and the room stood deserted, and silent as a grave.

The next I knew I was in my own bed, cold and dark, and alone.

18.

I wasted the next day leaning from the opened first-floor window of my workroom, one hand dangling towards the ground below, the other lifting a cigarette compulsively to my lips so that I might inhale its noxious fumes as though no other air for me would do. The paintings, my work, stood abandoned behind me. In truth, I had hardly accomplished anything for weeks now. My assignment here was a failure, and my employment at the auction house was doomed. I would return to Edinburgh in disgrace: an incompetent who could not even hold down a job that had been gifted to him by virtue of his privileged acquaintances, and within his own limited field of specialism, no less. Back to the capital, my friends, and my family, with nothing to show for my expedition but the raving, fantastical stories of a madman. I hardly cared.

Victor knew about me and Amy – who could say how long he had known? He was toying with me, laughing at me, as a cat swipes a powerless, crumpled insect between its paws. So why didn't he strike decisively? He could throw me from his house at any moment – or worse. In my darkest moments I imagined that a dishonourable dismissal was surely the best outcome I could hope for. And yet, something stayed the master's hand.

My impulse was to go to Amy in her library, to find her and be with her, and know that she was safe and well. But even after all this time I had still never gone to her during the day, only by twilight. The handful of times I had seen her during the day it had always been at her instigation. If I went to the library now, I was sure that I would find it empty again, and I did not think I could stand that. Worse, I thought that blundering into her domain at a time when she did not expect me might risk leading Victor or Bannatyne straight to her, somehow. No, the stakes were too high. I had to wait, be patient, and avoid any impulsive moves.

I realized I was muttering aloud to myself. My nerves were shot to pieces, my capacity for rational thought frayed to nothing but threads. I ejected my half-smoked cigarette into the gardens below and began to pace the room, but found the walls too confining for my wandering mind – and so I made my way downstairs and outside.

I must already be insane, I told myself, as I stepped blinking into the afternoon sunlight. I had doubted it before, but now I was not so certain. A rational man would leave this place and seek help. In Cobsfoot: they could help there – the good Reverend Scattergood, or earnest Mary Johnston at the Whistle and Duck. It would be a long walk but I could reach the town on foot in a matter of hours, easily. But would the townsfolk even believe my story? If I marched into their midst unannounced, puffing and sweating and half-crazed, recounting tales of a mysterious woman whom no one else could see, and a man whose diabolical sins had only been glimpsed in my imagination … I had no substance, no proof with which to shore up my accusations; accordingly, I had no hope of securing aid.

Then again, I thought, why even seek help? Why not walk, and keep walking, until I was far away from this place and Victor Mordrake and Bannatyne and Mrs Pugh and

Joseph and Arthur and Thistlecrook House and the shining lake and Amy, all alone in her library? The madness of this blighted house had nothing to do with me: I had stumbled into it, and could stumble out again just as easily. I was no prisoner here. I even took a few crunching steps across the gravel driveway towards the ancient, rusted gates and the winding road that led through the forest beyond, my determination spurred by an impulsive desire to be rid of the whole wretched situation. But an imagined voice sounded in my mind, calling me by my name: Amy's voice, sorrowful, plaintive, desperate. How could I knowingly leave her behind, abandon her to Mordrake's designs? Somehow, my coming had awoken her – so she herself had told me – and, by my actions, I had surely endangered her, exposed her to the attention of her captor. With a burning face, I recalled how brazenly Victor had waved her drawing at me, how casually he had made reference to our relationship as we stood at the fireplace in the evening. And what had I done to deny it, what attempts had I made to deceive or misdirect? My dumbstruck silence had surely confirmed his suspicions as readily as an open confession. What kind of man would I be if I walked away from my own wreckage so callously now? Amy's features would surely haunt me for the rest of my days if I did not exhaust everything in my power to free her from whatever malign influence it was that kept her shackled.

My shoes kicked up a spray of dust as I swivelled an about-turn on the driveway and marched resolutely back towards the house. I returned to my work studio and there continued to pace, and brood, and tap my pursed lips in futile cogitation, watched all the while by the ghoulish audience of the Mordrake paintings: faces warped by misery and torture, grinning demons, leering persecutors, maudlin sufferers – meaningless strokes and swirls on canvas, set up for my study and now to my mind only a mocking jury for my own impotent anguish. In a rage, I fell upon them, pulled the paintings from their stands, heaped them facing away from me in the corner of the room and covered them with a sheet, so that they would witness my inadequacy no longer.

I missed dinner entirely that evening; I could not stand the prospect of running into Victor, of seeing his gloating face again. I had successfully avoided him at breakfast by rising early and sneaking to the kitchens to plead illness – no doubt all too believably, given my haunted visage – and young Joseph had obliged by bringing some breakfast to my room where I could eat in moody seclusion.

When I crept to the upstairs library that evening, I found it once again empty, dark, and desolate. I spent some time in there alone, inspecting the rolls of dust accumulated on the bookcases, and trying to resist the urge to call out Amy's name into the empty space. I sat in her armchair for a long while, deep in a maudlin despondency with my stomach rumbling noisily, until finally I returned to my chambers, light-headed with hunger and with no expectation of sleep. I passed the night listening for the sound of footsteps, for the gentle rap upon my door by which Amy would indicate her presence. Frequently, feverishly, I peered at the crack of light below the door, watching for the telltale shadows of a figure stood outside, feeling a deep, nervous unease as I watched, and waited. No shadows appeared, and the moonlight hours came and went in a terrifying silence.

I dreamed of Amy. I envisioned that I walked by the lake. I stepped along the bank, through ice-cold mud that oozed between the toes of my shoeless feet. She was standing in the lake, submerged up to her waist in the placid depths, turned away from me so that she faced out over the water. I wanted to call out to her, to make her turn, but I could not; I had no voice. The air was frigid and wintery; it burned my lungs to inhale and then rose before my eyes in showers of dazzling, microscopic crystals with every breath. Above our heads, the sky was dark, but no stars glittered – only an infinite black expanse, as though we stood at the very bottom of an abyssal well from which no glimpse of the world above could be possible.

I woke suddenly, jolted to consciousness by the sensation that someone had called my name, though it was still the small hours of morning and there was not a voice to be heard. Kicking my sheets away, I discovered that my feet were numbed, senseless blocks, as cold as ice, as though the chill of cloying, frozen mud clung to them still. I drew my legs up underneath me and lay in a groaning foetal position until the feeling in my toes returned, wondering what on earth such a poignant and troubling vision could signify. But I could find no sense in it, and soon I drifted back into a restless sort of sleep.

I was roused by a brisk knock that sounded upon my door. Despite the newly risen sun glimpsing through the window, and the forthright assertiveness of the knock, my gut lurched with the sudden, illogical hope that it might be Amy. Two full days had passed now since I had seen her – since I had held her last. I struggled out from the sheets that I had wound around myself during the night, and stumbled over at once to answer. It was only Joseph, who – good lad! – had brought some small breakfast to my room again, which I fell upon with a ravenous, primal hunger.

With some sustenance in me, I stalked directly to my workroom where I remained, restless and fidgeting, until I could stand it no longer. Sick with worry and foreboding, it was barely early afternoon before I quit my post and – in spite of all my previous arguments against rash action – made my way to the library.

In my passion, I threw the door open and it knocked against something inside with a bang; I was permitted the briefest moment of joy on seeing the room bright and fresh and a female figure stood within, spinning quickly upon her heel to face me. But my elation was burst as instantly as it had come by a shocked scream from the girl – who I recognized then was not Amy, but one of the housemaids – and my hopes dashed to utter, bewildered despair while the girl brought her hands up to her mouth in blind fright, releasing her grasp on the white sheet she had been holding so that it floated slowly, spectrally, to the floor. I stared about in enraged disbelief. The room, the upstairs library, our room, was in a state of transformation. The chairs and settee had been stripped of their covers. Amy's armchair lay hidden beneath the translucent veil of a dust sheet. The rug had been pulled up and stood rolled up in one corner, and the curtains and windows had been thrown wide open to let the sun and air, stingingly scented with summer grass and pollen, pour in most unwelcomely. Even the books had been pulled down from their shelves and stood piled in precarious stacks upon the very desk where I had made my study of the household accounts.

'What – what is the meaning of this?' I demanded of the maid, who stood in the centre of this ruin, her hands still clasped to her mouth and her eyes saucer-wide with shock and awe.

'I – I –' was all she could stammer uselessly, until finally her state of complete, paralysing terror penetrated the flinty shell of my consciousness and I realized, with no small shame, how my sudden entrance and enraged demeanour had frightened her out of her wits. With an effort, I mastered my initial fury and summoned some composure; I bowed to her, and repeated my question in a less vehement manner.

'I'm only doing what Mrs Fairfax told me!' cried the maid. 'I was sent to clean this room today. The master himself wanted it tidied, and the books moved out – with no delay, she said, and so I have been – it was Mrs Fairfax's orders!' She seemed on the brink of tears. I checked my impatience and did my best to soothe her.

'Who is Mrs Fairfax? Where is Mrs Pugh?' I asked.

'Mrs Pugh?' she replied, surprised. 'Why, Mrs Pugh left some time ago.'

'Mrs Pugh left?'

'Yes,' she told me, as though such knowledge was obvious. 'Her husband – that is, Mr Pugh – he fell ill, and they had to return down south to be with his family. Oh, but, my goodness, you gave me such a terrible fright,' the girl said, adding a jittery laugh that she seemed to force out as a balm for her nerves. 'And I hate this room so much, I hate it! But Mrs Fairfax told me, stories or no, I was cleaning in here today. That it was master's orders the room was cleaned out at once, and that was final, and I could answer to Mr Bannatyne if … And then when you burst in, I thought –' Her entire frame shuddered violently, from head to toe.

'You thought …?'

'Well … that it was her – the lady,' she told me meaningfully. I nodded, and thought to say something further, but I bit my tongue. With one final, resentful glance around the room – the defiled sanctuary that had once been mine and Amy's, and now belonged to no one at all – I bowed, and left.

From the ransacked library, I proceeded directly downstairs and into the dining room. The hour was still far too early for dinner, but Mordrake was already there, along with Bannatyne, who was solemnly laying out dishes of steaming vegetables, pastries and cheeses. The master sat slumped at the head of the table, elbow resting upon the arm of his chair and his head balanced at an almost horizontal angle upon a balled fist. Without shifting from this position, he nodded to me grimly, his lips curled to the thinnest shadow of a smile while his cruel, calculating, diamond-hard eyes directed me to take a seat where a place had already been laid for me.

'Where is she?' were my opening words, once I had sat down. My voice emerged dry and hoarse, but I was surprised at how controlled, and forceful, it sounded.

'Where is who, Simon?'

'Amy – Amy, damn it!'

'Amy …' His eyes widened a fraction, and he lifted his head from his fist, and nodded once. 'Amy, indeed …'

'You know who I mean,' I insisted. Bannatyne raised his stern gaze to me as he leaned over the table to place a dish. I sensed the tall, gaunt butler was poised to fall upon me like a bodyguard should my mood turn to violence. But in fact, in the cold heat of the moment – at the realization of this long-awaited confrontation – I felt myself possessed by an eerie composure.

'Yes, I am aware of whom you refer to,' Mordrake consented. 'Although I did not until this moment know that it was Amy. That is rather unexpected.' He closed his eyes and seemed to fall into thought.

'Well, and where is she? What have you done with her?'

'She is gone – that is all you need know. Back in her place, somewhere you need not worry about her. You must allow yourself to forget her, Simon. In truth, I have done you a great service, though I cannot expect you to appreciate it.'

I tapped my fingers impatiently on the silver cutlery set before me. My host's insolent crypticism was trying me to my limits. 'You should eat something, Simon,' he said, full of fraudulent concern. 'You look quite haggard, I hope you don't mind me saying.'

'What is all this? Just what are you?' I asked through gritted teeth. 'I know more than you think. I know –'

'What do you know?' Mordrake snarled contemptuously, his eyes blazing white. And then, in an instant, his manner was placid once more.

'I know – that Amy was your wife, once – that you married her and then tossed her aside. And then she ... died, she fell in the lake and drowned – and, that you, somehow, have kept her here, kept her as your prisoner ... I know what they whisper about this house back in town, and I believe that those rumours are true, every one of them. The witchcraft, the blasphemous rituals, your so-called experiments – who knows what form they took? I am not fooled; they are no mere stories that belong in the past. Those terrible crimes do not belong to your ancestors, but to you – it was always you ...'

Mordrake watched me as I spoke, nodding thoughtfully. Once my words had trailed off with uncertainty, he asked, 'Tell me, Simon, do you know these things, or do you only believe that they could be true? You really don't understand anything, not yet. But,' – his pale irises flashed – 'you could. I could show you, Simon. Don't you see? All of the answers that you seek with such commendable tenacity, they could be spread out before you, exposed and unadorned. And I could show you so much more besides.'

He chuckled dryly. 'Bannatyne here believes I must have grown soft in my advancing years, that I should indulge you so long. I wonder that he may be right. In times gone by, I would already ... Well, it is neither here nor there. But you do intrigue me, Simon my friend, and so here I find myself offering you one final chance. Witchcraft and blasphemy – tsk! Those are notions for ordinary folk, vulgar and jejune. You should forget these things that you think you have learned – that should be no great task. And little Amy – she really can't help you, I am afraid. Only I can show you what you want to see. You need only permit me.'

Bannatyne had stopped his service and watched while his master spoke, the old man's cavernous eyes opening wider with every word. He appeared to be on the verge of opening his tightly pursed lips and uttering something, some interjection to disrupt our dialogue, when Victor turned suddenly towards him and dismissed him with a sharp upwards nod. The butler paused for only the briefest of moments, then bowed and withdrew, and we two were left in solitude.

Victor sat now with both elbows upon the arm rests of his chair, his fingers steepled before his furrowed brow. He remained like that for a long time. Then he opened his hands, and sat forwards, slightly. 'I suppose that I should indulge your curiosity, a little, as a gesture of my sincerity. Yes, you are correct to surmise that I myself played no insignificant role in the discoveries that took place in this house. I did not work alone, though – I never have. They flocked here from all over the world, once. My fellows and I, we pushed the boundaries as far as they would go. I have already told you a little of this – of the things that we accomplished – and you scoffed, as any respectable man would. I do not fault you. But listen to me well, Simon – what took place here, in this house – what I have called experiments – these were no theoretical exercises. They were real, and they were successful. In this household's past, great deeds have been achieved that would thrill and appal you. With my own eyes I have witnessed sights you could not imagine in a thousand fevered nights. I have heard voices from outwith – voices as sweet as the most beautiful melody you ever heard, carried across the horizon upon the ocean's breeze, voices that will drip whispered secrets into your ear, and offer bargains, shrewd and cunning. I have slipped between the cracks and walked in fractured places that a weak man would lose his mind at the sight of. You stare at me now in disbelief. I understand, truly, Simon. But not a word of it is a lie.'

'You are mad,' I told him, shaking my head. 'You cannot believe – no more can you expect me to believe – that there is truth to these things.'

He laughed mirthlessly. 'You seem ready enough to believe the accusations you place upon me, as remarkable and unsubstantiated as they are. Why, then, are you so incredulous now? After all that you have seen and heard, can't you accept that I speak with sincerity and some authority on these matters?'

I could hardly argue with this. 'And so,' I asked slowly, 'what happened? Where are your accomplices now? What became of your followers?'

'The same thing that always happens. Nothing more unusual than human greed, and hubris. There were differences of opinion. They pushed one way, I pushed another. I pushed hardest. Things became ... a little ugly, for a time, I am afraid. That is a story for another day. Suffice it to say, once the damage was done, I found that my perspective had shifted somewhat. I had allowed things to spiral rather out of hand, and my appetite for it all had rather disappeared, you see. One can't keep these things up indefinitely, you know. I decided that a period of rest was called for. And so I settled, and vowed to live quietly, and shun the death and darker elements that had consumed me ... for a time. Of course, when the war in France rolled around, that quite put paid to that idea. When I saw for myself the things they were doing over there – good lord. I realized then that the world was changing; it had already changed, right under my dozing nose. There are things to be done. I would resume my work, Simon.'

'And what about Amy? How does she fit into all of this?'

'That's the real laugh of it – she barely does. To think that she would be the one who beguiled you so ... I admit, I did not see that coming. Perhaps that was why she was able to elude me for so long. Of all the possible – well, Amy was not the one that I expected. Amy was … a butterfly caught up in a cyclone. A spark falling from a Roman candle. Nothing at all.'

'Then why do you keep her here?' I demanded.

'Not my doing, old boy. Quite the opposite in fact. But that has all been dealt with. You really would do well to just forget all about her.'

He was leaning forwards over his place setting now, and held his hand towards me as though he would reach out and touch me across the far length of the table. 'Stay with me, here, Simon. It is the only way. Forget your false aspirations, and abandon the ridiculous road you are travelling down. Help me begin my work once more. Be patient, and obedient, and with time you will comprehend the truth of things. I see so much in you, Simon – we could accomplish great things together. Understand what I am offering you. I would lay out before you what most can only hope to glimpse in their sweetest of dreams. Men and women have journeyed across the earth, they have spent their lifetimes searching, they have degraded their minds with liquor and narcotics, for just the merest sliver of what I speak of. Our reality is so multifaceted it is a marvel. So much remains hidden, even to my eyes. Submit to my instruction, and I will show you. This is the best way, for everyone.'

I did not know what to think. My mind felt utterly blank, drained of all resistance or emotion. He was correct: I understood nothing, even after all this time, after all my futile investigations. And I believed that he was genuine in his offer to me, in the opportunities he presented. Even in spite of all of my fears and paranoia, I could not doubt the sincerity that had shone in Mordrake's eyes through all that he had said. More so even than that, I could not doubt that this offer was never again to be repeated if I did not accept here and now; what the alternative was, I could only guess.

'But – the cruelty, the brutality ... the things in the paintings,' I protested weakly.

'They are only paintings, Simon,' he told me, with a tone to his voice that was almost pitying. 'Though, indeed, the brutality was real. It is as I have told you before: this place, it is shaped by cruelty and by blood. It is drenched in it – that is what has awoken its promise, its potential. But those deeds are in the past. They cannot now be undone. I do not deny that ten thousand sins have been committed here; one hundred thousand virtuous deeds would not change that fact, nor wipe away their lasting stain. But,' his voice softened, 'you need not worry; my way is more delicate. I would ask nothing of you that should challenge your conscience.'

I cannot say that I did not waver, if only for a moment. I knew of doubt and temptation; my resolve was tested. And then, with a surging churn of bitter anger, I thought of Amy of her sorrow and patient suffering, hidden and forgotten in her lonely room, or whatever blank and surely even more desperately lonesome place she was in now. My core would not be shaken. 'I cannot. I will not,' I told him. 'If not madness, then the deeds you speak of must be the devil's own work. You cannot believe I would stoop to help you now, after all that you have done. Where is Amy? Where is she?' I banged my fist on the table, rattling the cutlery in an impotent fury.

Victor only sat back in his chair and shook his head regretfully. He dabbed a napkin to the corners of his mouth and rose from the table.

'It really is too bad. What is to be done with you? You cannot leave, not now,' he muttered to himself, not even deigning to look at me as he slowly wandered from the room and left me sitting there alone, a spread of food untouched and steaming on the table before me.

19.

Immediately following my confrontation with Mordrake, I was so filled with anger, and disgust, and – yes, I shall admit it – selfish dread for what may come next that I might have found the nerve to take flight from the house there and then. But the hour had grown unaccountably late, and the forest outside had turned to shadows. I stared out from the dining room windows at the shroud of night that had descended, through which I could just make out the shift and sway of the gnarled and clawed branches that surrounded the estate on all sides. With a shiver I remembered Mordrake's parting words, his barely veiled threat as he left the dinner table, and I wondered what resources the man – no, the demon – could have at his disposal.

Even so, my situation seemed so desperate that I might still have been tempted to risk the ominous wood under the darkness of night – except, even as I stood and frantically contemplated my options, the steady drumbeat of a rainstorm met my ears and before my eyes a torrential downpour moved in and enveloped the grounds. Very quickly even the trees became invisible behind a rising, murky vapour as the rain thundered heavy against the ground. Against the prospect of attempting to navigate the woods through such bleak and fever-inducing conditions, to stay one more night within Thistlecrook House was surely the preferable option – though I felt scarcely safer within than without.

Mordrake and Bannatyne both had vanished immediately after the meal, and I retreated to the familiarity of my rooms at a terrorized scurry, where there was little left for me to do but lie upon my bed, listen to the rain, and wait for sunrise. I did not reckon on sleep that night but it must have come, for once again I found that I stood on the frozen edges of the lake in the deepest reaches of a black and starless night, the air so bitterly chill that it clawed at my skin with rimed talons and choked painfully against my throat. Amy was there with me, in my dream, but, though I stood on dry land, she was half submerged and turned away from me so that all I could see was her falling black hair and her red dress, which billowed and rippled in the waters around her like a spreading bloodstain.

I watched her from the bank of the lake, pacing my legs up and down on the spot in a constrained march, trying to stir some warmth around my trembling form; how terribly cold the water must be, and yet still not frozen over, I thought. I tried to call out, but once again found that I had no voice to do so. I wanted to step into the lake, to go to her, but I could not do that, either – I feared that to dip a toe into those waters would plunge me deep into their oily depths, fathoms downwards, from which I could never hope to return. The surface seemed to brim and tremble with a barely contained energy, like a cup that has been overfilled and waits only for the barest nudge to overspill its sides.

Amy spoke to me. The sound did not come from where she stood, but seemed to emanate from all around, from the sky above and from the water and from the seething woods.

'Simon,' she said, 'Simon – is that you? I can't see you. I – I don't know where I am, Simon. He found me. It's so cold here, so empty … I'm all alone. There's no one here with me – I can't hear anyone at all. You have to come and get me.'

I tried to reply, to cry out to her, tried to make my useless legs take a step forwards, but nothing within me seemed to be working. 'I don't know how he's done this; I don't know where I am.' Her voice came to me flat, lifeless, and desperately sad. 'You have to look for me – please. Please come to me.'

I woke with my heart throbbing and Amy's plaintive words echoing sharply in my ears. These visions were no dreams, I understood now: Amy was calling out to me, calling out from wherever she was confined. Whatever Mordrake had done, it was still not enough to keep us apart. Across some unknown void her pleas had reached my ears, and I would be damned forever if I did not do as she had entreated of me. I would find her.

I spent most of the day in my room, lost in thought and making no pretence of going about my work. I formed vague and half-reckoned plans of action, then abandoned them with a sinking dread. I had a notion that I might make my way to the lake, stand on its banks in a recreation of my dreams – but to what end? No, I needed something more concrete to go on than hazy intuition before I ventured my next move.

As the afternoon wore on, I was drawn, by habit, by a grim curiosity, and by childlike attachment, back to the upstairs library. On this occasion I found it deserted: no housemaids, of course no Amy – and no Mordrake waiting for me as I had half anticipated. The room had been swept and dusted and the coverings changed, and was barely recognizable. I wrinkled my nose in distaste at its clean, clinical, and alien unfamiliarity. Amy's books were still stacked high upon my desk, waiting, I assumed, to be put away in storage somewhere.

I sighed, and wandered slowly around the space, running my hand over the furniture in small, futile gestures, as though their touch might evoke Amy's by association. I stepped to the window and looked down over the gardens. The previous night's rain had finally stopped, and the usual stagnant humidity had returned unabated, though the lawns still shone with a fresh, glossy veil of dew. As I scanned the view, the sight of a small cart creaking its way down the driveway came as a spur of vitality to my throttled mind: there was Laurie the delivery boy, rattling a course away from the house and off the property.

Seizing this unexpected opportunity, I flew downstairs as fast as my feet would carry me, out the front door, and bounded over the gravel in a series of long strides. 'Laurie! Laurie!' I called after the disappearing lad. He pulled his aged horse to a halt and half turned to me, his face red and eyes wide with surprise, though his mouth remained clenched in a noncommittal line. His horse turned its head towards me, too, and snorted with disapprobation.

'There was no one at the back door so I left th' messages just inside,' Laurie told me tersely as I drew close.

'What? It's only me, Laurie: Simon Christie. You gave me a lift here from the town, some few weeks ago.'

'Oh.' He looked me full in the face for the first time, and, recognizing I was not one of the staff, seemed to relax a little. 'Oh aye, 'tis you. Hullo. I was sayin', there was no one round the back so I just left the messages inside,' he told me again, as if such domestic arrangements were of concern to me.

'I'm sure that's fine,' I told him. 'Laurie, can you deliver a message for me, to the Reverend Scattergood? Tell him I would very much like to speak with him again, as soon as he is able. It is rather urgent. I should go to him, in town, rather than he come here – in fact, perhaps I could go with you now –'

'The reverend's no longer wi' us,' Laurie cut me off bluntly.

'What?' My blood turned cold. 'What do you mean? He has died?'

'Naw ... He had to leave. His relatives come an' took him home. He took a fall from his horse, and he landed badly, and he's been in a brain fever since.'

'Fell from his horse?' I asked in wonder. 'When did this happen?'

'Hm, just a week ago. He couldnae give the sermon on Sunday, we just prayed for him and sung hymns instead. Mr Buddon led the service.'

'A week ...' I repeated, trying to recall how long ago the vicar had visited – could more than a week have passed? The man must have been injured only days or even hours after I had seen him, and after his courteous note thanking Mordrake and me for his visit had arrived.

Laurie was watching me blankly, waiting for me to say something more. 'He fell from his horse,' I repeated, marshalling my thoughts aloud. 'Was it an accident, or did something happen to make him fall, do you know?'

'Erm, the horse threw him, I heard.'

'Tell me, was the reverend a good rider? Did he ride often?'

'Well, I couldnae ... I think he rode a fair bit, aye. He was fair proud of his horse. He said it was a fine gentle specimen – he'd even let the ladies and weans take it for rides about. Something must have given it a good fright to startle as bad as it did. But, they're daft beasts.' Here, Laurie threw a resentful glare at his own carthorse, which snorted in response.

'I see ... I – well, thank you Laurie,' I said, and let the boy go. I trudged my way back towards the house, my heart heaving painfully in my chest. So the Reverend Scattergood, my best lifeline, had been removed from play by a tragic accident, or so it would seem. I was seeing patterns and sinister implication in everything, I knew – but surely the coincidence was too suggestive to discount? The reverend himself had been but a faint hope; I did not know what he could or would have done that might have helped me resolve my dire situation. But the mere fact of his injury felt like a warning. A warning that, even if I were to leave Thistlecrook House and put a distance of miles between me and its shell of brick and mortar, I should still not consider myself safe from its long and dark shadow.

As I approached the front door in a state of wearied despondency, a thought struck me: Laurie had told me there was no one to receive his regular delivery of groceries and sundries. It was evident, from his perturbed manner, that this absence of staff was an unusual occurrence. I knew, from my walks around the grounds, that the deliveries came by the servant's entrance around the side of the house, beyond the kitchens. If Laurie had found that part of the house deserted then, perhaps, I would too.

I did not stop to question why the staff should be missing. Altering my course, I skirted around the side of the building to the small back door. I knocked sharply upon it: no answer. I tried the handle and found it unlocked; pushed it open slowly and called out: no reply. Laurie's parcels sat neatly stacked on the scullery counter. The kitchens were silent and cold; only the birds outside sounded freely their cheerful, uncaring verse.

I had rarely set foot in the back rooms of the house before, and found myself by instinct moving slowly, cautiously, like some common house burglar. Silently I stole my way through, with no real idea of what I was looking for, or what I hoped I might find – but these were rooms I had seldom visited nor found opportunity to explore, bustling with activity and industry as they generally were. This chance to search them unobserved seemed to be the precise sort of opportunity I had been waiting for.

This part of the house was more rustic than the rest – I had a sense that I stood now in the most ancient section of Thistlecrook House. I tried a heavy-set door that I assumed led down to the cellars, and found it locked tight. I opened one or two cupboards and uncovered only pots and pans, jars of preserves and dry goods. These were kitchens, nothing more, and I did not know what else I had expected. But just as hopeless despair once again began to rise within me, my eyes fell upon a board hanging on the wall, close to the back door through which I had just entered: rows of hooks, from which hung keys in all shapes and sizes. I hurried over to them and studied the neat labels written above each hook, indicating the lock to which the key dangling below was partnered. My eye was instinctively drawn to the largest, the most ornately misshapen and antiquated key: the label above it read 'Folly'.

With no further deliberation, I snatched the bulky, greenish artefact from its hook and hastened out the back door once more. With the key clenched in my fist, I set out across the rain-damp lawns in the general direction of the vine-tangled ruin of the old Mordrake folly, hidden deep within those witches' woods. It was the one locale I had not yet thought to explore, be that by oversight or unconscious aversion – for the thought of that ominous structure, strange and solitary and abandoned, even now filled me with a primitive dread, greater even than any suggested horror inside the house. Yet surely – surely! – there was some secret to be uncovered behind its chained and bolted entrance.

I had only a vague memory of where within the grounds the folly stood, but it did not take long before it revealed itself. I spied it through the trees, squatted upon its hillock like some slumbering troll from a child's fairy story. Rough stone steps, weathered smooth by exposure to the elements, led up towards its sealed gate. As I ventured closer, climbing the uneven staircase cautiously, I noticed with some alarm the smell of the thing – it had not impressed upon me on my previous visit, but the ancient structure positively reeked with a disquieting odour: something like mould, or dank, wet fur.

I swallowed, then crested the worn steps and squared up to the barred entryway that was wrapped in chains and fastened by a weighty padlock. Another thing I had failed to observe upon my initial visit: the old stone slabs all about the doorway had been defaced with markings. Small scribbly characters had been etched into the stone itself, some fashion of writing marked in chaotic scratches and nicks that led in an uninterrupted trail around the base of the door, up the sides of its frame, meeting at the apex of the arch above. Peering closer, I found the lettering inscrutable, matching no language or even alphabet I could recognize – and yet I felt positive that this was writing, all the same. A gentle current of wind rustled low through the trees, hissing against the stones and through the cracks in the ruin's structure, and shaking loose the lingering remnants of the rain that hung in the treetops and now fell pattering all around me. I hesitated, then put my ear close to the sealed doorway and listened to the breeze as it whispered wordlessly to the darkness that hunkered within.

With trembling fingers, I reached for the oversized padlock. The corroded key weighed like a burden in my fist – I felt an overwhelming urge to drop it, and leave that lonesome place. The green men, those blooming pagan faces carved into the folly's facade, seemed to all be turned upon me now, laughing and jeering from the stonework, their jolly, mocking smiles daring me to turn tail and run. I shut my eyes, thought of Amy, and steeled my nerve. I took hold of the old padlock. My fingertips had scarcely touched it when a voice called out to me from behind.

'What do you think you're doing up there?'

I turned quickly, furtively, caught in the act. Behind me was Bannatyne, standing at the bottom of the rough-hewn staircase and peering up to me with a hard stare. He was dressed in uncustomary rough tweeds, with sturdy gloves on his hands, and dangling from his right fist hung a long pair of gardening shears.

I found myself unable to provide an immediate answer to his challenge, and only gawped at him, frozen to the spot in a sort of half-crouched position, as if ready to flee or else throw myself at my accoster. Only my hand that clutched the folly key moved swiftly to my pocket. It was too shallow to conceal the bulky object's full length, and so I thrust my entire hand in and hoped that my sleeve would obscure the protruding end.

Bannatyne's wild eyebrows were raised and his irises glinted like daggers at me. 'You should not be here,' he drawled. 'What do you think you're doing?'

'Excuse me,' I said, realizing then with a sudden burst of arrogant defiance that there was no reason I should not be where I was. 'I merely wanted to take a closer look at this fascinating old building,' I told him, straightening my stance and holding out my empty hand in a casual motion. Let the servant challenge me if he liked.

'It is only an old ruin,' Bannatyne snarled, and looked away – I knew then that my reckless instinct to explore this spot had not steered me wrong.

'So I can see,' I said, then, daring to turn the tables upon my challenger, 'I could ask you what you are doing all the way out here. Why should a butler be outside doing a spot of gardening?' I found my eyes drawn to the long, flashing blades of the shears that swung by his leg. 'Doesn't Mordrake need you for something?'

'I have many duties around the house,' he replied, slowly. 'Sometimes I am called upon to cut away a weed or two.'

Neither of us said anything for a moment. 'What are you doing out here?' Bannatyne asked again, gravely.

'I – It was just curiosity, I suppose. I meant no offence.'

'What did you expect to find?' His voice was trembling with a sort of strangled energy, something close to rage. With a sudden lurching motion he climbed one step closer, then a second, and then paused, his gaze fixed upon me all the while.

'Well … I don't know. I was only curious, I … I'm sorry.' The sudden harshness, the implicit threat of his tone, wrung an involuntary apology from me. I glanced around as I felt a bead of sweat trickle down the small of my back.

'You are a guest. The master's home is not yours to explore at liberty,' Bannatyne rumbled. Then his tone changed suddenly – he lost all pretence of properness or decorum, and addressed me with unconcealed loathing. 'You think you're a clever one, don't you? You think you're so canny. But I know where you've been. I know. Nothing goes on here that I don't know about.' The butler climbed the steps slowly as he spoke, slithering towards me like some strange lizard, the shears hanging heavily at the end of his long arm. 'Aye, I've seen you, snooping around. I've been watching you. I ken what ye want to do,' he declared accusingly, drawing up directly in front of me, looming tall over my head, so close I could smell his stale breath and see the malignant fire flickering in his eyes. He swung the shears to his front and gripped their handles in each gloved fist, the wicked blades still pointed to the ground.

His purplish lips peeled back slowly to reveal gritted, yellow teeth. 'What the master found so interesting about you I'll never know. You're nothing but an insolent worm, aren't you? A worm who's crawled to where he doesn't belong. A wet little squib. You act like you know it all, like you were born to this place, but you've seen nothing. And you thought you could just wrap him around your little finger, didn't you? You thought you could squirm your way between us, take my place. Arrogant!'

I stood my ground, willing myself not to let the man intimidate me, though my voice came out small and trembling. 'Now look, I don't know what you're on about. I don't want anything from either of you. Just tell me, where is she, Bannatyne? What have you and Victor done?'

'Aye, you'll be forgotten soon enough, just like always. Then we'll have some peace around here.' Bannatyne swallowed thickly, and then he lifted his eyes with reverence to the structure behind my back. His brows raised as a thought seemed to strike him, and a cruel smile twisted across his features. 'Do you know what used to happen here? Do you even know what this place is? I think ye should see – I think I should show you. The master, he's sick of ye, he's no use for ye any more.'

'What happened here?'

'Yes – I'll show you what this place is,' Bannatyne hissed. He raised the shears between us, pulled the handles open then snicked them shut with a stabbing motion so that their dagger-like points snapped together only a few inches before my eyes. The long steel blades looked shining and new, and wickedly sharp. I flinched, and he laughed sadistically.

'Bannatyne,' I said faintly. The butler snapped the shears open and shut again, forcing me to take a step backwards towards the folly's shackled door. He took a step closer, trapping me in the archway. Like a cornered animal, I acted without thought, without hesitation. Before Bannatyne could pull his shears open another time, I reached out and seized the handles myself, so that we each had our fingers wrapped around them. We wrestled, pulling the fearful implement between us, the blades pointed towards the sky. I pulled as hard as I could, to wrench the weapon from his grasp, but Bannatyne's grip was clamped tight as a vice.

'You –' the butler snorted with indignation, and pulled back, straining against me to try and force the lethal blades open.

I did not mean for it to happen. He struggled against me so hard – I could not have known how little strength the old man in fact had. With all my might, and bolstered by genuine terror for my life, I shoved the shears up and away from me, hoping to push Bannatyne away also. But his legs were planted firm even if his arms failed, and the pointed tip of the closed blades pressed level with his chest and then thrust upwards. The thin, papery skin beneath Bannatyne's chin offered no resistance at all – nor did the tendons of his jaw, nor his dry tongue nor the soft cartilage of his palate. The gardening shears slid effortlessly upwards into his head, impaling it from below.

Bannatyne and I both released our grip at once – but the shears remained fixed where they were, the handles dangling from below his jaw. For a long moment Bannatyne only stood there – stood and stared at me with an expression of bewildered, accusing shock, the long blades sheathed firmly inside his skull. He gave a small, restrained cough, and a stream of black blood gushed thickly out from his mouth and down his chin. Something crimson and wet and solid slithered out from between his lips and slopped to the ground: the severed tip of his tongue, sliced clean through. I stared dumbly at where it had fallen onto the stone slabs, amid the leaves and the debris. Then, as if in slow motion, Bannatyne toppled backwards, his body falling rigidly away from me like a felled tree, falling down and cracking heavily against the stone steps below; he rebounded in an unnatural backwards flip, his long, thin frame twisting into a sick spiral and landing in a heap at the bottom of the hill beneath the shadow of the Mordrake folly.

20.

The woods had fallen to a deathly hush. The violent sounds of the fall, the thud, snap and crack, reverberated through the trees; and then nothing. The birds muted their song and held their wings from fluttering; the scurrying beasts nestled static, hearts pulsing in the undergrowth; even the leaves and the branches seemed to keep their peace, unmoved by the rustling touch of the wind.

I remained at the crest of the worn stone staircase, looking down, dumb and impotent, capable of doing nothing but stare at the crumpled pile that had seconds ago been a man. When my faculties at length returned to me, my very first overwhelming instinct, I am ashamed to say, was to turn and flee from the awful scene – but I swallowed this cowardice and crept down to where Bannatyne had fallen.

As I drew closer, I could not help but flinch at the broken, inhuman shape in which his body lay. His head, pale and deathly and all black and bloody about the jaw, had landed facing up towards the folly: towards me. His neck had jerked into an obtuse angle and the fatal garden shears remained fixed in their place, jutting out from beneath his chin like some grotesque, bizarrely oversized neckwear. His still-twitching eyes, I fancied, fixed upon me as I drew near.

His lips quivered – he lived yet! – opening and closing noise-lessly, reciting some wordless curse against me. Blood poured freely from his wound, and from between his lips, pooling around his head in a gory halo. His eyes glowered into mine with unrestrained loathing, and then they closed slowly, and the body gave a sigh and I knew that Bannatyne had died.

I stared at the corpse, my initial shock and revulsion giving way to curiosity. I had, of course, never watched a man die before. I am not sure what I had expected, but in the moment it had seemed strangely clinical to witness – the cessation of a biological function, nothing more. I was surprised at just how composed I felt, how rational my mind remained. I knew that I had committed a heinous crime, perhaps the worst crime of all – even if it had been an acci-dent. But there was no doubt in my mind that Bannatyne had threatened me most gravely, and that, had I not taken decisive action, it would have been my body lying shattered and pasted with warm blood deep within these woods, my own life severed by those same murderous blades. And in any case, the butler was undoubtedly complicit in his master's sins: in the foul deeds that had been committed in this wretched household, and in Amy's confinement and disappearance. As such, his demise was justified – I could not bring myself to feel guilt for the elderly servant's death. This was the logical and reasoned argument I presented to myself even then, with my heart still pounding like a steam engine from the heat of the deed. But I knew, too, that a line had been crossed. I had shed blood, now. I had become a part of the diabolical history of this place. And there was no turning back.

I shifted my focus back to the task at hand: the folly. My senses in that moment felt sharpened to a needle's point – like a hawk in flight, honed upon its prey, every instinct primed and focused on the hunt. And I was so close, now.

Intuition had led me to this spot, and Bannatyne's words had all but confirmed that there were answers here. I could not allow myself to be distracted from my original intent, not by the butler's crumpled and mutilated body, not by tedious moralising nor meaningless fretting.

I realized that I no longer held the folly key, that I had dropped it at some point in the struggle. Turning from where Bannatyne lay, I hastened back up the stone steps and located where it had fallen onto the etched stonework, among the dry leaves and twigs. Then to the padlock. I took hold of its metallic bulk, scraping the key against it as I tried to manoeuvre the two objects together with my trembling fingers. But it would not fit, both parts were so badly aged and corroded. Their rusted, jagged edges scraped and bit my skin. I could have cried out in frustration, or broken down in defeated sobs. The blood coursed in my veins at a roar; a dizzying hiss sounded within my ears, making my head spin. My own rushing bloodstream, or something else – something inside the folly, sounds from within that locked and chained structure – surrendered to the tangles of the overwhelming woodland. Did the crescendo of noise that flooded my ears come from within or without? As I wrestled with the stubborn key, twice I turned in fright, believing that someone or something was approaching from behind. I thought I heard soft, padding footsteps, and the hairs on the back of my neck rose as from static charge – but there was no one there, only the shape of Bannatyne's corpse, wreathed in a crimson pool that spread about him like unfolding wings.

Finally, the key slid into the padlock with a clunk. But the sight and the sound of the motion brought to mind all at once the image of the garden shears sliding neatly into Bannatyne's skull, and fixing in place. The full momentousness of the horrific deed I had committed only moments before struck me then, like a sledgehammer. All at once I

lost control of my senses, and released my hold on the lock
and key as my knees gave out from underneath me. I reeled
back, away from the opulently carved folly that now seemed
to shudder and echo in the fading twilight. I dropped to my
bended knees before that arcane spot, leaned forwards and
pressed my hands and forehead to the cool stone, and
exhaled slowly, trying to muster command of my faculties
once more.

When I lifted my head from where it rested, I was
shocked to see my hands coated in a red film of blood –
Bannatyne's, surely. I smeared my grimy fingers on the
ground so that the sticky fluid mingled with the wet dirt
and debris that lay there, seeping into the characters of the
indecipherable script etched around the base of the folly
door. I traced their lines with my fingertips. That unknown
writing now stood out bold and scarlet, obscene glyphs
marked out in blood – the butler's yes, but my own, too, for
I saw now that my fingers and hands were slashed and
bleeding freely, sliced to ribbons by the corroded roughness
of the key and padlock. I groaned to see what I had done,
and pressed my shredded palms together – and then for a
time knew nothing more.

I must have fallen into some nervous fugue, the kind I have
read of in persons undergoing extreme mental anguish, for
the next I knew I was back in my chambers in Thistlecrook
House. I had fled the terrible crime scene and somehow
scurried back to my room. Upon recovering my wits, I first
went to the door, checked that it was shut tight, and then
washed the dried brown blood and dirt from my hands. My
own cuts were not so numerous as I had first reckoned, just
a few long slashes, but savagely deep, and the porcelain of
my washbowl was dyed a deep pink that would not wipe
away when I was done. From there, I sat upon my bed for
several long minutes in useless, unproductive panic.

A man lay dead, by my hand. Even if it had been an accident, my decisive role was undeniable. But he had threatened me: it was self-defence. The way he had brandished those shears – freshly sharpened for the purpose, I reckoned – and the things he had said of the folly, what that place was and what had happened there … Even if I could not understand the full extent of his meaning, I did not doubt the fatal implication.

I attempted to weigh my options. To deny knowledge of the butler's death, or to attempt to cover it up or conceal the body somehow, seemed impossible. I did not reckon that my fractured nerves were up to the task of carrying off such deceit. And the thought, now, of returning to where Bannatyne lay, beside that ghastly ruin, filled me with a primitive terror that is difficult to describe. To think that I had come so close to unlocking it, to unbinding those chains and peering into the blackness within, made my flesh crawl.

All about me, the house was sounding with the noises of doors opening and closing, footsteps, clattering and muffled voices – I thought, or perhaps imagined, that I heard someone, a youthful voice, calling for Bannatyne by name. Wherever the members of the household had been earlier in the afternoon, they had returned, and it was now only a matter of time before the butler's absence was noticed and the body discovered. There was only one option left open to me that I could see – the last refuge of cowards and criminals: it was finally time that I must flee. What good could I possibly hope to do here, now? Events had spiralled so far above my head I could no longer hope to spy their true form from my lowly vantage point. I must leave Thistlecrook House, and its master, and Amy, too, behind, and save my own skin, if it were still possible, if Mordrake's reach might be so easily outrun. I thought of the Reverend Scattergood, felt a stabbing anxiety in my gut, and clutched my head in my hands with despair.

But such delay was foolishness. So resolved, I left my room for the final time, abandoning the possessions I had brought with me in favour of an unburdened flight. As I crept from my door, I believed I heard the sound of my own name, called from somewhere distant. With fatalistic inevitability, I trod the length of the corridor to the upstairs library, nursing a vain but unassailable hope in my breast. Of course it stood bare and empty. I stared about at its barren bookshelves, the cold, unoccupied armchair; I wished a hollow goodbye to the floating dust motes. Had it all been only for this? I left the library and wandered my way dream-like through the house, down the stairs and out of the front door.

I still did not leave the grounds, not yet. Pulled by some invisible thread, a fly stuck on a strand of spider's silk, I was led around the building to its southern side, where I stared into the knotted trees, beyond which lay the lake. I just stood there, staring, and waiting – I didn't know for what, until I heard it. A voice carried across the hot, stagnant air: a voice that spoke my name. Someone was calling to me. Amy was calling me. I followed, staggering across the grass towards the forest. The voice again. I broke into a half-run. The fading evening sun hung low over the trees, casting long, twisted shadows over the lawns, and over me, as I disappeared into the woven canopy of branches.

'Simon … Simon …'

I crashed through the undergrowth, impatient, ravenous; I pulled aside the foliage that delayed me until I could see the lake through the trees – and, yes – I could see her, too. Not so far away, a small figure dressed in red, facing away from me, her black hair flowing down her back. She was standing quite far out from the bank, so that her feet and legs were immersed in the lake past her knees, and the skirts of her dress billowed and floated around her. She was staring out over the water, which was rippling slightly –

broad, sweeping wavelets that seemed to originate somewhere near the centre of the lake, spreading in concentric circles.

'Simon …'

This voice came from behind – a different voice, not Amy's. I was so close to her now, though, and I kept on running, but stumbled and tripped as my feet sucked into the muddy bank. I put out my hands to break my fall and they splashed into the mud, splattering it all over my shirt front. Beneath my right hand, I felt the weight of a stone, sharp-edged and large enough to fill my palm. My fingers closed around it.

'Simon – where are you?' It was Victor. He stood behind me, puffing for breath. He must have chased me all the way from the house. Unsteady in the slippery mud, I rose to my feet and turned to face him – he did not look at me, but over my shoulder, towards where Amy stood.

'Simon,' Victor said, sadly, appealingly, but still looking at Amy. And then, 'What have you done?'

'Your manservant is dead,' I told him: a confession, and a boast, and a threat. Mordrake did not reply. He only looked to me for a moment, and then back to Amy again. 'I did not mean for it to happen,' I said. 'It was an accident. It was self-defence.'

'What – what do you hope to accomplish by this?'

I glanced over my shoulder, following his gaze towards where Amy stood in the water, still with her back turned, fixated on the lake, unheeding of our presence. 'Don't look at her,' I told him angrily. 'You – you will not keep her here any longer, you hear me? I'll not allow it.'

'You will not allow it,' Mordrake repeated tonelessly, looking at me once more, his face breaking into a mirthless grin.

'What is this place? This lake, here, what is it?' I demanded.

The grin fell, and was replaced by a mask of impatient indifference, cold and cruel. 'What does it matter? If I tried to explain it to you, do you really expect you could comprehend? I would be as well to attempt to explain a moonbeam to a field mouse.'

He sighed, frustrated. 'I offered to show you, Simon. You had your chance, and this was your decision. You chose her.'

Victor glowered venom at the small figure over my shoulder. 'Don't look at her,' I warned, again. My fingers tightened about the rock I held clutched in my fist, my arm snaked slightly behind my back so that Victor would not see it. 'Who … who is she?'

At this he laughed, with what might almost have been pity. 'You ask me now? If only you knew … If only you knew –'

'She is Amy … Why do you keep her here? What use is she to you?'

Victor addressed himself over my shoulder again. 'Do you hear this?' he called. 'Do you hear what you all have done to this pitiful creature? Bah! This is ridiculous. I have wasted enough time on your games. You cannot have imagined this would have gone any further – and what have you achieved, for your efforts? It must have been quite exhausting – you must have given so much – and merely to waste this one's life, and poor Bannatyne's.'

Mordrake stepped suddenly forwards over the muddy bank – in two pouncing strides he was upon me, and faster than I could react, his hand had locked about my throat, its long fingers choking me in a murderous grip. I gasped, transfixed by shock, and stared into his eyes in fear, but all I saw there was a chill, passionless steel. His other hand lifted and joined its murderous brother, pressing upon my windpipe, wringing the life from me until my vision turned to white, and then swam with red. I could not move; I could not even raise my arm to defend myself. And then, something drew his attention – Mordrake looked up sharply, glancing past me, towards the lake and where Amy stood, and his eyes widened in rage. I could not see what he stared at, but I could feel it. I could feel something, and hear it throbbing dully in my ears, as though we two stood upon the bow of a ship and were being buffeted by the powerful wind.

'It cannot –' Mordrake uttered, and then he fell silent, for my right hand, jolted into sudden service, flew up and dashed the rock I was clutching against the side of his skull. His cold, strong fingers released their grasp and he stumbled backwards and fell into the mud, his eyes blinking at me with dumb shock. A trickle of blood slithered down the side of his face from his left temple.

'Again,' Amy's voice came from behind, and I took a step forwards, raising the rock above my head.

'D-d-don't you understand – w-w-what it is?' Mordrake stammered thickly, his voice coming out in a weak, gasping splutter. I cracked the rock against his brow and he collapsed fully, his limp, prone body dropping backwards and sinking into the mud's thick embrace.

'Again.'

I dropped to my knees astride his prostrate form, lifted the rock high and brought it smashing down. Mordrake spluttered through the blood of his shattered face, his cracked teeth and jaw. 'You fool, you fool,' he moaned, his words barely intelligible through the wreckage, and then he said no more.

'Again. Again.' White eyes rolled in their sockets; feeble fingers clawed at my chest, and then curled into submission. Down and down I rained blows until I struck nothing but a pulpy mess. All I saw was crimson, and black, and pink and then white, until finally my arms gave up, spasming with exhaustion, and I could raise them no longer.

Wheezing, sobbing, retching, with spittle dribbling down my chin and tears pouring from my eyes, I stared down at the mess below me and could see nothing human in it at all. All strength was gone from my legs; I could not lift myself from where I sat, hunched over this shattered remnant of a man. Panting like a wounded dog, I turned my head slowly to where Amy stood, now by my side. She gazed down appraisingly at Victor and me.

'My Simon … my dear, dear Simon,' she said, and smiled at me. Her smile. Amy's smile. Once I thought I would have done anything to see that smile. Now, as I gasped and slobbered on my knees in the mud and blood, I wracked my brain to recall what that smile could ever have meant to me at all.

'What you have done for me … for all of us … it simply couldn't have come off better. I am so delighted with you, really I am. You played your part so perfectly, Simon.' She regarded the pile of gore beneath me, still beaming warmly. 'You have done us a great service, Simon Christie, and you will be repaid in full, I give my word. You have nothing to fear.' I could not take my eyes from her heart-shaped face, so pale and cool and emotionless, like a doll's, like a statue's. Behind Amy, in the periphery of my blurring vision, I was aware of movement: the surface of the lake was rippling, shifting, distorting. 'You can stay here, with us, if you would like, Simon. I would be so dearly happy if you did.' The water was alive now, simmering like the surface of a vast cauldron. 'But, I think – yes – you would prefer to leave now. I do not hold it against you. Though it pains me greatly, go with my blessing. All that is due shall be yours with time,' Amy told me placidly. I managed to tear my eyes from her and look out over the lake. The entire basin was writhing, squirming in a tumultuous rhythm, one enormous organism, a shimmering hive waking and lurching to life, all at once. Below the surface there were shapes, grasping, reaching, and straining against the oozing viscous liquid, clawing upwards towards the dusk sky; things with curled, clutching hands as thin and brittle as twigs; bulging, milky fish eyes; and wet, streaming coils of hair whipping about their heads as they rose, and rose, upwards and out from the water …

With whatever strength was left within me, I pulled myself to my feet and I ran.

21.

The year came to 1930. I was living back in the familiar
grey comforts of Edinburgh, making a home of a fashionable and spacious apartment in the New Town within
agreeable walking distance of my place of work at the
National Portrait Gallery. When my employment did not
require me to be present in person – which was most days
– I frittered away my time in the small arts and antiques
dealers dotted about the locale, or else at home, alone,
reading or attending to my correspondence, maintaining a
small garden that I took some pride and pleasure in, or
sometimes writing some few words of an article for this
journal or that. I had left my position at Southgate's several
years earlier, covered in glories and with a reputation that
would have opened any door in the art world. The discovery and sale of several significant, formerly undocumented
works by some of the greatest of the European masters,
long stashed away and entirely forgotten among the treasures of Thistlecrook House, had established my credentials.
A series of increasingly high-profile and remarkably
successful contracts and negotiations had followed, and
before long I was being feted by every dealer and buyer in
the country, if not Europe, if not the western world. But I

found that I had little desire to travel, no appetite for new and unfamiliar climates. The languid and well-trodden streets of the historic capital suited me fine. And with a position that afforded more than enough income to meet my humble needs in exchange for but a little of my time, and work that I found diverting and untaxing, I saw no attraction to lifting my roots.

For a time, I had attempted to enjoy the luxuries that my unanticipated successes – albeit within a narrow field – had brought to my door. Notable acquaintances, lavish parties, club memberships and other favours: I did my best to live as I imagined a man of leisure with youth, money, and friends to spare should. But, as many before myself have observed, the more I surrounded myself with people and things, the more alone and impoverished I felt within my heart. I soon accepted that the life of a New Town nouveau riche was simply not for me. I withdrew; I diminished. I found a comfortable way of life that suited me just fine, and I settled into it like a snug armchair.

My vocational success combined with a modest attitude to living came as great satisfaction to my concerned parents, with only one snag: I had turned my back on the wealth, celebration and acquaintances without securing myself a wife and family along the way. A bachelor I remained, much to my mother's consternation and frequent, vocal, despair. I suppose that a romantic reader might sigh at this; you may tilt your head in sympathy and understanding, and wonder that I could ever have hoped to love another after my time at Thistlecrook House. Or a cynic might say that the weird horrors I had endured in that place must have sickened and turned me against romantic attachment forever. But both would be a lie. The plain truth was that my ever-diminishing social circle simply never rotated me into contact with another whose company I thought I could enjoy, or even tolerate, for the rest of my life.

I make no attempt to deny that I thought of Amy often, of course. At first, daily, and sometimes these memories managed to be sweet and happy, in spite of everything. I remembered reading with her in the library, and walking the grounds in the sunshine, and our secretive nights together; and in those moments I somehow forgot, or neglected to remember, how things had all turned out. But just as often the memories froze my blood and drained the colour from my face, and I would be forced to excuse myself from whatever or whoever I was engaged with at the time and retreat into my own private nightmares. I tried to block the things I had seen – the confused, half-remembered horrors, blurred between dream and reality – from my thoughts. As the months and years wore on, it became easier. But even if I managed to successfully distract myself through the waking hours, by night I would always be visited by the sound of footsteps, and flashing pale blue eyes over a thin, indulgent smile and pencil moustache; a heart-shaped face framed by tresses of swirling, black hair; a bloodstained rock; and dark and dreadful things rising from a lake. I would awake coated in sweat and gripping my sheets in despair.

These terrors I could share with no one, naturally – they were my own burden to bear. I feared that if I tried to explain all that I had seen, all that I had lived through, then I should have been carted off to see out my days in the madhouse, for sure. Sometimes I wondered if that was not where I belonged. I consulted doctors, bid them examine me for signs of … anything at all. They all told me I was as fit as a fiddle, if a little highly strung. I sought out the services of a modern psychoanalyst, but he just kept asking me about my father, so I gave up on that approach. And besides, in my heart I remained as sure as I had ever been that I was not, in spite of it all, mad. All that I had seen, and done – Amy, Bannatyne, Victor, all of it – it had been real. It had really happened.

More even than these psychic anxieties, for several months after my flight, I lived in fearful expectation of an all-too-real knock upon my door, and the rough hands and accusations of police inspectors asking questions about the names Mordrake and Bannatyne, and what I knew of a place called Thistlecrook House, and two sets of human remains that had been found there. But no knock ever came. You perhaps expect that I dreaded less mundane repercussions from my time at the house, as well. That I feared the long tendrils of influence from that malign place – some carrion terror from the lake – would find me, one day, and seek revenge or hold me to account, like some shadowy, dogged pursuer from one of Poe's stories. But such ideas never troubled me. After all, she had told me that I was free to leave if I so willed it. Strange as it may sound, I never doubted her sincerity on that.

Of my escape from the house that mud- and blood-soaked night I could recall almost nothing. I remembered running through the trees in the pitch-black, the terrifying sense of pursuit. What I must have looked like when I crashed into Cobsfoot long after midnight I am loath to imagine; how I ever managed to secure onward transport to Edinburgh I have no idea. Having made my escape, there was a period of recuperation, back in the care of my parents, during which I could do almost nothing but toss and turn in my childhood bed and wait for the heavy hand of justice to catch up with me. In its place came the news – received just as my faculties had returned enough for me to begin to wonder what on earth I was to do next with my still-young life – that Southgate's had received note from a representative of the Thistlecrook estate stating that the owner would be making a number of sales following the most accommodating and productive visit by the representative sent by that organisation.

And so my name was made and my comfortable future laid out before me. Quiet, content, and lonely, I did my very best to move on. Time made it easier, and after enough had passed, I found that I began to struggle to recall the things that I had once wished to forget. Now and then, when I again doubted that it could all have been anything more than a dream, I would open the drawer beside my bed and take from it a small locked box, turn the key, and take out a scrap of paper that had been torn from a notebook, soft and worn at the creases where it had been opened and refolded countless times. I would let it fall open one more time, and stare at what was sketched there in faded pencil: a simple line drawing of a man sitting at a desk, and a conciliatory message written in a careful hand below. My only memento of my secret past, which I had discovered unexpectedly stuffed into my muddy jacket pocket many weeks after my arrival back in the capital, and which I had never permitted to stray far from my person since.

It was mere happenstance that led me back to Cobsfoot so many years later. I was on my way to Dumfries to visit a sick friend, and a series of landslips caused by a week's driving rain had diverted my rail journey significantly off course. It was not until the train pulled into Cobsfoot station, and I observed with an unexpected thrill the familiarity of my surroundings, that I realized where chance had delivered me. I supposed that some other punter must have asked the guard to make the stop, as I had years before. Perhaps it was the several maturing years that had passed, perhaps it was the rosy spectacles of nostalgia – whatever the reason, when I recognized the station, it brought to mind only the happy memories of my time on the border. An impulsive whim tugged at me like a hand upon my sleeve – like a tempting whisper in my ear – and I seized up what small belongings I had with me and disembarked.

Time had not altered the station at all – though I supposed it had not really been so long since my first visit, after all.

No fellow passengers joined me on the platform, and I wondered who, then, had requested the stop? But this time there was a guard on duty, wearing a long cape and hood that streamed with water from the downpour that still would not cease. Once the train had wheezed away, he approached me, rather formally, and we exchanged good afternoons beneath the shelter of the platform awning.

'Are you in need of directions?' the guard asked.

'No, I have been here before, thank you. Can you tell me: is the Whistle and Duck still open?'

The guard misunderstood me and looked at his watch. 'It's still a little early, sir. But the landlord Mr Bancroft rarely locks the doors, and I am sure he would be only too happy to oblige you if you were to drop in now.'

'Thank you. And … th-the old house, who lives there?'

'The old house, sir?' the guard looked confused. Perhaps he was not a local – I thanked him anyway and made to leave. 'If I may – you say you have visited Cobsfoot before?' he asked, before I could go.

'Yes, several years ago – on some business. I was only here for a short time.'

'I see. And is it business that brings you back?'

'Well, no – the train was passing through and I just wanted to visit the place again, I suppose.'

'I see. I'm sorry to pry, sir – it's only that there's been a little local difficulty, so I had to ask. Have a pleasant day.' He turned away abruptly before I could ask more.

If you had asked me to draw a map of the route from Cobsfoot station to the Whistle and Duck, I am certain that my fingers, seven years later, would have found the task impossible – but on that day, in person, my feet had no trouble in retracing the trail down the hill and to the small town square. Like the station, the town remained untouched by the passage of years: the same crisscross of streets laid out before me like a map when I looked down from the station hill; the same quaint little stone and thatch cottages; the rolling farmland all around and the distant church spire, half hidden by the weather. Indeed, the only perceivable difference from my first visit was the dense, persistent drizzle that rained down over everything, dripping off rooftops and pooling in every available nook and cranny.

With my head down and my vision impaired by the brim of my hat, I did not observe the three figures in the town square until they stood right in front of me. My first clue was a female voice that called out, 'There! Who's that one?', but I had not imagined she could be referring to me until I discovered that two burly men were blocking my path. Looking up, I saw a pair of roughish-looking young lads with flushed faces, but drawn and dark around the eyes. Behind them hovered a woman, closer to my own age, who was leering at me suspiciously from between her companions' shoulders.

'You, sir. You're a stranger 'round here, aren't you?' one of the men began.

'Well, yes. That is, I don't live here, but I have visited before, some time ago,' I replied.

'That so? You have relatives here or something?'

'No, I was here on business, of a sort,' I said vaguely, wondering what on earth this was all about.

The men exchanged a glance. Behind them, their female acquaintance called out, 'Ask him what he's doing here!'

'I heard the question and shall gladly answer you directly, ma'am,' I responded. 'I came here without planning it. The train I was on stopped at the station and I decided to come into town and see what has changed in the years I have been away. I doubt I shall stay very long. Now, what is this about?'

'You just thought you'd take a wee walk in the rain?' the second man asked, folding his arms and frowning. 'It's a queer day for sightseeing.'

I might have told him it was a queer day to be harassing strangers in the street, but before I could, his companion, who I quickly took to be the more sensible member of the group, asked me, 'You came direct from the station?' I affirmed this was true. 'Did you see anyone else at the station? Anyone or anything that struck you as ... odd?' Behind him, the woman had started to moan and sob to herself.

'No one but the guard, who I am sure will verify my story, if you like. What do you expect me to have seen?'

'It's nothing – I'm sorry to have bothered you.' The first man sighed, and turned to the woman. 'Jenny, he's not the one, look at him ...'

The same sense of inquisitiveness that had compelled me to disembark my train now implored me to question this strange trio further, but they were clearly in some agitation, and the drenching rain was already soaking me underneath my coat and hat, so I left them in the street and pressed on for the Whistle and Duck. I found the inn empty, save for an elderly bartender who greeted me with surprise.

Following my encounters in the village so far, I half expected the barman to interrogate me on my comings and goings and intent in the village, but he only offered me a drink and his commiserations on the miserable weather. 'The fire's just built, sir, the place'll warm up soon enough,' he told me. We exchanged some trivial small talk for a short while, before I asked if Mary was still employed at the place.

'Which Mary is that, sir? We've seen a fair few come and go over the years.' He smiled.

I could not recall her last name, if I had ever known it. 'She would have worked here six or seven years ago, now. So high, fair haired.'

The barkeep nodded and winked at me. 'Oh yes, Mary Johnston – or, she was at that time. She married and moved away, hm, some four years past. I might've known she'd be the lass you'd be asking about.'

'I didn't know her well, to tell the truth – we only met once or twice. I doubt she would have remembered me,' I told him – even as a fleeting recollection came to me of Mary's face, round-eyed and sheened with perspiration in the soaking heat of the night, as she and a crowd of others listened with tight-lipped frowns while I jabbered an incoherent account of the horrors I had witnessed, the blood still wet upon my shirt cuffs. I began then to wonder if returning to this place had not been a serious mistake after all.

'Are you all right, sir?' The barman brought me back to my senses. I must have drifted off into a reverie – one habit I had not been able to shake in the intervening years.

Before I could answer, the door opened and another person entered. The newcomer divested himself of his dripping, steaming outerwear, approached the bar and ordered a whisky. I saw it was one of the men I had spoken to outside, the younger and more aggressive of the two. He did not look at me, but took his drink and sat in the furthest corner of the room – the same spot where Mrs Pugh and I had once sat, years before. I could sense that he was staring at me intently from behind. The barkeeper watched him over my shoulder, sighed, and looked to me with an apologetic shrug.

'I spoke to him outside,' I said in a low tone, 'or rather, he and his fellows interrogated me. The guard at the station seemed on edge, too – what's going on here?'

'Ah, well, you see, it's a very sad affair all round … you mustn't take offence if people are a little jumpy to see a stranger …' The old man put up a decent show of being reluctant to partake in local gossip, but licked his lips and continued. 'You see, what it is, a young lass went missing about a week ago. Tragic affair. The Ritchie's eldest daughter, a sensible, quiet lass. The constabulary searched the place high and low but couldn't find a trace.' His voice dropped even lower. 'They said the odds of finding anything at all of her by this time were almost not worth considering. But the family' – he nodded to the man in the corner – 'well, they can't accept it, and that's understandable. That's the mother's brother, there. He'll be leery of you because you're a stranger. He's a decent man, normally, though, and he'll not do anything daft, don't you worry.'

'I see. How sad for the family – I pity him, more than anything,' I said. I considered whether I should offer the grieving uncle a drink, but thought better of it. He might only take the offer the wrong way.

In any case, as I listened to the barkeeper recount these provincial concerns, so unrelated to myself, I realized that I had no real interest in seeing Cobsfoot or its inhabitants at all. Any connection I had to the place, or those who lived here, was scant at best, and had only diminished in the interval of years. No, I had not got off the train to see Cobsfoot, I knew that. I had come back here for one reason, and one reason only.

My throat felt tight and dry before I had even voiced the question. 'And what of Thistlecrook House?'

A shadow seemed to pass over the barkeeper's face, just for a moment. 'What about it, sir?'

'Well … do the Mordrakes still live there?' I tapped my finger on the counter, and did nothing to hide the nervous agitation that was doubtless written plain across my face.

'Oh, naturally. That is, Mistress Mordrake still lives there, of course.'

'Did you say Mistress?'

'That's right.'

'But – and – it has always been Mistress Mordrake who lives there, yes?'

'That's right – for more years than I can remember now, anyway.'

'And she stays there alone?'

'Well, yes.' It would have been hard to say which of the two of us was more confused by the conversation. 'Do you know the family?'

I took a bolstering gulp of my drink. I could not keep my hands from fidgeting anxiously, or my knee from bouncing on its spot. 'I ... do, a little, yes. I heard ... I heard there was some trouble at the house, a few years ago – seven years ago. Do you know anything about that?'

'Trouble? Well, let me think, now ... nothing that comes to mind. We don't hear much of anything about the goings-on at the old house, truth be told. But if there had been any sort of trouble I expect we'd know about it quick enough. Oh, there are always rumours and so forth about what went on there in the past, but I don't put much stock in any of that talk. Some call Missus Mordrake a recluse, but she has always struck me as a very pleasant sort when I have dealt with her. And besides, how she runs her house is her own affair, and no one else's.'

'You have seen Mistress Mordrake?'

'Of course. She keeps to herself for the most part ... but she always comes to church on Sundays, and sometimes invites the ladies and girls back to her house to entertain them afterwards. I suppose perhaps she gets lonely, out there, all by herself, even if that's the way she likes it, and she must enjoy the company from time to time.' A look of sad fondness clouded the barman's eyes. 'She has even taken a meal in here ... from time to time,' he added with a touch of pride.

My mind was reeling at all he had told me, and yet ... somehow I was not surprised at all. In a way, I had expected to hear all of this – I had already known.

'I heard that someone ... her brother, I think ... drowned in the lake, years ago,' I asked. The words sounded wrong to me even as they passed my lips – or were they? My recollections were hazy, muddled. I pushed my glass away from me, still half-full.

The barman's frown deepened even further. 'That old lake behind the house? There's all sorts of legends about someone drowning there, to be sure, but not in my lifetime. I think that was some noble's wife, hundreds of years ago. How was it that you said you knew the family, again?' The barman's narrowed eyes flickered over my shoulder to the bereaved uncle in the corner, and I felt instinctively that the balance of sympathies in the room had begun to shift – and not in my favour. It had been foolish to come here, I realized, arriving unexpectedly and asking quaint, suspicious questions of the locals.

'How can I get out there – to Thistlecrook House?' I asked quickly, changing the subject. There seemed to be no sense in delaying the inevitable, now that I was here.

Somewhat reluctantly, and perhaps mainly to be rid of me and my erratic questions, the barman helped me to arrange onward transport. He was able to telephone the house and a driver was sent for me with no further questions. Perhaps I should not have been surprised that the conveniences of modern life had reached as far as Cobsfoot, and yet I was. A sallow-faced young man puttered a familiar, antique motor car into the town square some time later, and mutely conveyed me along the winding road through the woods that divided the old house from the town. I gazed out of the window as the coiling branches of the twilight-shaded trees blurred past me on the swerving route. My mind wandered, and scenes and images of my time here seven years ago drifted unbidden through my thoughts. They seemed like dreams now, half-remembered scenes with only a finger's touch of reality … or had they been real, and the intervening years were the illusion? I sank back in the comfortable leather seat and experienced the snug, blissful sensation of waking the morning after a long journey to find yourself at home and in your own bed, having dreamed of nothing else for so long that you can scarcely believe you are finally, truly, returned.

'How long have you worked for Mistress Mordrake?' I asked the youth at the wheel.

'Three years, very nearly, sir,' he replied.

'And she is good to you? You like your job?'

'Oh yes – very much so.' His eyes met my own in the rear-view mirror.

'Did you ever know her husband – or her brother?' I asked sleepily.

He glanced again. 'No … I think – I have heard that she had a brother, but he died during the war, I believe. Of course, that was long before I came here.'

'Yes, that's right,' I agreed, laying my head back and closing my eyes for the remainder of the short journey. In no time at all, we arrived, rolling through the familiar high-arched gate and crunching up the gravel driveway. I got out of the car and stared up fondly at the house's domineering architecture and the jagged peak of the gable roof that seemed to stab towards grey sky above. A swirling mist of rain still fell, not so heavy as it had been but clinging, and cold. I stood there getting wet, and gazed at the old house, and I smiled to think that I should momentarily be back beneath its roof. Not long now, a voice within seemed to say, until I would be back in my old room once more, or at work sorting through the multitude of art and scribbling notes on what I found. Or seated comfortably in the upstairs library, examining the household accounts while Amy read her novels, the two of us together again in perfect, wordless contentment.

22.

The grand and imposing door was opened by a youngish servant whose face I recognized, but could not at first place. He nodded, and bowed: my arrival was expected, but he did not know me. I knew him, though – when I was able, after a moment's hesitation, to attach a name to the familiar face I was taken aback by cheerful puzzlement. 'Why, it's Arthur, isn't it?' I said. He was a little older, naturally, his face a touch careworn, but this was unmistakably the same lad who had worked here before, under the previous butler, whose name seemed also to escape me for the time being.

Arthur frowned at me slightly, and I laughed. If the years had rendered his face less familiar to my eyes, I expected the effect was at the very least doubled on mine. 'Oh, I shouldn't wonder you don't recognize me – I only stayed here for a short time, and it was quite long ago. But I am pleased to see a familiar face at Thistlecrook House. And you have risen in the ranks since my last visit, it seems.'

Arthur's expression remained impassive, and he bowed slightly formally. 'Excuse me sir, I didn't recognize you at first,' he said, though I was sure he still didn't. Hard to believe, I thought, after all the commotion when I was last here. 'The lady is in the parlour, if you would,' Arthur said and gestured me through. I followed obediently, but with some hesitation, my movements stalled by the prickling memory of something that had happened when I last came to this place, some unpleasantness that I could not at that moment quite remember.

Upon stepping into the main hallway, I could hear the tinkling notes of a piano drifting lightly through the house, a pretty and pleasing melody, though something about that, too, struck my ear as odd. I could not recall there having been a piano in Thistlecrook House previously. I entered the parlour slowly, frowning, trying to collect my thoughts – but in vain, for as soon as my eyes fell upon the personage that inhabited the room, all other paltry concerns fell away, dismissed from my mind as the irrelevances they were.

She sat at the piano, her back to the door – she knew that I had entered, but did not look at me immediately. No, she teased out that perfect moment, continuing to play until she finished her piece. It was not a song I knew. The pretty melody was something new and unfamiliar – something of her own composition, I fancied. I remained by the door and watched her hands glide over the keys, back and forth, until they touched the final notes to her tune; and then, once it was over, save the sound left reverberating in the air between us, she ran her fingers lightly over the top of each key in its turn. Only then did she finally turn to face me.

A skewed rectangle of light falling through the windows even on such a dreary day flashed through her raven hair as she turned upon the piano stool. Her hair had been cut shorter, just past her ears in the Hollywood fashion of the time, and bounced in waves around her heart-shaped face, rich black against the pale skin. That face, exactly as I remembered it; the face I had seen behind my eyelids every night for the past seven years; a face seemingly untouched by the hand of time that had altered my own, and Arthur's, and surely all else in the world's – but not hers, never hers.

The fashionable clothes she wore; the jewellery fastened around her neck and her wrists; that quiet, contained assurance with which she now held herself; the dignified poise of one who is in perfect control: those things struck a new and unfamiliar chord in me. But her otherworldly aspect – the glow of her midnight radiance – that part of her remained unmistakably the same. She smiled slightly, knowing that I gazed upon her in awe, but kept her own eyes downcast for just a moment longer, and then they lifted and lit upon me.

I hastened obediently across the room and placed myself before her – she turned completely upon the stool and took my two hands in her own without a word, her mouth breaking into a joyous grin. My heart raced in my chest; my knees shook with such emotion that I thought I could not stand it for long.

'Simon Christie,' Amy said warmly, gazing up into my eyes. 'Thank you, Chapman,' she added quickly to the butler, dismissing him. 'Sit down,' she told me, rising from the piano stool, and we moved to the settee, still clasping each other's hands, each gazing lovingly back at the other. 'You have finally come home to me.'

'I am sorry I could not have come sooner; I had things to take care of –'.

Amy shushed me.

'You needed time – you had things that you had to do. I understand. It means nothing now. You are home. You know,' she chuckled a little, 'I still have your possessions that you left behind. I had Chapman tidy them away, but the cases are still in your room, waiting for you. Just as though you never left at all.'

I listened to her words, sweet and soothing, a balm to my tired soul. I stared adoringly into her dark eyes, black and bright like cut onyx. But even as I watched, and listened, and gloried in Amy's presence, I nonetheless found that my attention was being drawn to a bowl of red roses that had been placed upon the window ledge behind where she sat. It was nothing – an insignificant detail – and yet somehow it managed to niggle upon my consciousness most infuriatingly even in the full passion of that moment. What was a bowl of flowers when I sat finally reunited with the woman I loved, the only woman I had ever loved, the woman I was devoted to and whom I would serve for ever more? Amy was all I would will my eyes to see. And yet, I could not help but think that there was something quite remarkable about the red blooms of those flowers.

I made myself look away. Above the fireplace there hung a large painting, a landscape depicting the severe majesty of Thistlecrook House itself, viewed from an oblique angle on a striking winter's day.

'You have redecorated the place,' I said to Amy, gazing at the painting.

'Why – yes, that's right, a little. The piano is new.'

'And this painting,' I said, rising from the settee, 'this is also new. Another hung here before, a … a portrait.' I looked to her where she remained seated. Her mouth still wore a wide, fixed smile, though her eyes did not.

'A portrait? No, I don't think so,' she said lightly.

'Yes … there was, it was a portrait, of … a man. I can see his face, though I forget the name …'

'Perhaps there was – I can't remember now. What does it matter, Simon?' She laughed. 'How can you think of that, when we are finally together again?'

Amy stood quickly and seized my hands once more.

'So tell me, what news from Edinburgh? I want to know every detail – but there will be plenty of time for that, of course. For now, just tell me – have you been satisfied with your life there? Did it make you happy?'

'Why, I'm fine. I have no complaints. I have my work and my health,' I answered vaguely. 'Only … I suppose that it all sometimes feels somehow empty. I find myself spending my days just trying to come up with ways to keep myself occupied.'

'But you have been successful in your career. You are respected, and you have wealth, and friends.'

'Yes … yes, I have a good life, I know,' I replied. But my mind was back on the flowers. I turned to face them, turned away from Amy and gazed towards their stark blossoms, layers of vibrant, velvety cherry-red: so familiar an image, yet one I could not quite place …

'There were no flowers here, before,' I remembered quietly.

'Simon …'

'He would not have them … the man in the painting.' I looked at Amy, who was smiling no longer – she stared at me curiously, with one eyebrow raised minutely. I pointed to the space above the mantelpiece. 'His image hung there. He lived here once – he would not have allowed these roses! Where is he now?'

'Simon, sit down. You are exercising yourself so needlessly,' Amy purred softly, her hands folded before her and head tilted slightly to one side, the very image of a mother patiently monitoring the rising tantrum of a petulant child.

'And why did you call the butler Chapman,' I continued, agitated now, as confused memories came back to me piecemeal, 'when surely his name is Bannatyne? The butler's name was Bannatyne!' I spun back to the flowers, lurched over to where they sat on the window ledge. I placed my hands down on either side of the bowl and stared into it like it was some cauldron in whose rich crimson contents I would divine whatever truth was being hidden from me. The heady aroma of the blooms filled my nostrils, swirled my senses, and suddenly I found that I gazed down not at the folding petals of a bowl of roses, but upon the gruesome, bloody pool of a shattered skull and brains, the meagre remains of a face battered to unrecognizable pieces by the muddy rock that I gripped even now in my own red-stained hand; a cubist nightmare in shades of ruby and pinkish-white. In terror, I released my grasp on the murderous stone and fell reeling backwards – the sharp shattering of the rose bowl as it struck the floor, sending its fragrant contents scattering and spinning all about my feet, recalled me to my senses.

I turned upon Amy once more – she took a step towards me and I a step back, back towards the window, stepping through the fallen flowers that were now dispersed across the floor. I found I could not make a sound, but my terrified face must have spoken my thoughts loudly enough. Amy remained quite still, watching me with an expression of cool indifference.

'Really, you needn't be so dramatic about it all.' She tutted impatiently. 'So you have managed to see through a little; truly, you have more wits about you than most. I do wish you would wipe that triumphant expression off your face.'

She lowered herself back onto the settee. The door opened silently and the butler interposed with a small cough. 'Is everything all right, madam?' he enquired, adding, with a sweeping glance that took in the room, its flower-strewn floor and me, stood paralysed at the centre of the wreckage, 'I believe I heard something break.'

'Yes, it's quite all right,' the mistress told him, with the polite yet wearied tone of a host determined not to let their guest's lack of civility put a strain on their own. 'You can tidy up later. Thank you, Chapman.'

I watched the butler – it was not the aged Bannatyne, but young Arthur after all – withdraw.

'Please, Simon, close your mouth and sit down with me. You look most indecorous stood there, gawping like a fish,' Amy told me.

I obliged, kicking my way through the fallen red roses as I returned to my seat – not for her sake, but only because I believed that I needed to sit down for a moment. Rain pattered softly against the grey windowpane. Memories and images were crawling back to me now, slowly – but they were just fragments of a greater whole that I could not yet see in its entirety. I remembered the night beside the lake, brimming with blood and mud, and kneeling over a fractured, broken skull while Amy herself loomed over me, watching, willing. I remembered her blank, loveless smile, like that of a china doll. I dared a sidelong glance to where she sat now: I feared that to look at her direct would be too much for my faculties to bear, would pull me back under whatever spell this wretched place had cast. Was it the same Amy, after all? The face was familiar, but her pose, her movements, her manner, even her voice all seemed different, somehow. I reached for my cigarette case but it was not there – I remembered that I had given up years ago.

'Who are you?' I asked finally, staring blankly ahead.

She laughed lightly, teasingly. 'Why, I am Amy – surely you have not forgotten me, Simon.'

'But – what are you, truly? Were you ever the Amy I knew – who I thought I knew? Was there ever a wife who drowned in the lake?'

'Oh yes. A wife, a sister, a daughter – and a thousand others whose stories have been forgotten, if anyone remembered them in the first place. I am your Amy. I am the woman you knew, and everything I told you of her was true. She lived, she breathed, she – loved. But,' her voice grew softer, she looked away demurely, 'I am more than that. I am … We have … There are depths that you do not know.'

Scenes and events, people and places that had once been so familiar to me, that had dominated my thoughts obsessively and dragged me halfway to madness, swam up before my eyes like drowning men bobbing before a shipwreck, like claw-fingered bodies, rising with inhuman animation and milk-white eyes from beneath the water. 'The lake … you mean those depths?'

'Those – yes, in a manner of speaking. It is difficult to describe.'

'Then try.'

She sighed. 'Well, I hardly know where to begin. Ask me something else, won't you?'

I looked around numbly. 'You live here alone? Only … Arthur, and your servants? But, there were so many of them – I remember … I thought that I saw so many figures – so many women, coming up from the lake that night. Were they real? Where are they now?'

'Yes, they were real, and you did see them,' she told me. She almost sounded proud of me, I thought – proud that I should be able to remember what it seemed the rest of Cobsfoot could not. 'They are still here. Around, and about. Only, not in any way you would recognize. They were set free that night – we liberated them, together, Simon. They lent me the power to make it happen. And now, they are a part of this place – a part of this house, a part of me. But mine is the only body you shall see, the only voice you shall hear. I do my best to represent them all.' She tried to sound humble as she said this – tried and failed.

I remembered a voice telling me, once, that many had died at the lake, too many to count. Executions, murders, and offerings; innocent and guilty alike, they had all been sacrificed to its cold embrace.

'The dead … in the lake, the drowned witches, and victims … you freed them?'

A small sigh. 'Oh, something like that. And you helped me, remember, Simon.'

Memories and insane notions I had kept locked up for over half a decade were all coming back. Worse, they were starting to make some manner of sense to me, now. I closed my eyes and spoke, letting my thoughts run loose from my tongue without second-guessing whether they could be true. 'You were one of them ... one of the dead. And you were the one who broke through. Broke through and reached – me. He was looking for you, but couldn't find you ... because of who you were. He expected to find someone else. And now he is dead, and the others, they are all freed. But they stay here – they are a part of this place ... by choice? Do they want to stay, or do you keep them here?'

Amy clenched her fists. 'Oh, why must you be so inquisitive! You shouldn't trouble yourself over such things. Really, what can it matter? You are with me again, here and now – what more can you want?'

I rubbed my eyes, felt trickles of sweat roll beneath my shirt. 'I want to understand what I have been part of! What you ... What happened to me. You must be able to appreciate that – and, I think, surely, you owe me that much?'

'But I like you Simon, and I want you to be happy, and I rather think that if I told you everything then you would be very unhappy indeed,' Amy told me plainly. 'Can't we just be content, here, together? Is my company not enough? Is your love for me not enough?'

'Your love for me?' I repeated wonderingly, and, back on my feet, began to pace the room in fitful strides, knocking the fallen roses to and fro and crushing their blooms uncaringly beneath my heel. I still did not dare to look at the figure on the settee in anything more than sidelong glimpses, and so I stared about the room instead, and came to realize that nothing within it was familiar – the rugs, the furnishings, the paintings on the walls and the decorations upon the mantel, all had been replaced since my first stay.

'The people of Cobsfoot, the staff, here, in this house – they don't know anything about it? They ... they don't remember the things that happen here?'

'They don't recall things that would make their lives more complicated, or difficult. And aren't they happy? They live simply, contentedly, and I am good to them – what else can they ask for? Haven't you been happy, as well? Though we were separated, haven't the years treated you well?'

I shook my head. 'But to live under this … beguilement. They are manipulated: they have no free will!' I looked at Amy for the first time since I had commenced my frantic pacing, and was surprised at how small and dainty she looked, perched upon the edge of the settee, watching me with a sort of fascinated, indulgent patience.

'They are perfectly fine,' she replied, with a somewhat defensive pout. 'They are quite free do as they like. You have spoken with some of them, you tell me – are they sheep, or human beings, living their lives as they please?'

'What sort of power is this? How can it be possible?' I asked.

'You are interested in power? There is a great deal of it in this place – I can show you; I can share it with you.'

I sighed, pressing my fingers against my eyelids.

'That is no answer. Is this black magic, or something worse? The tales they tell in the village – the witchcraft and the rituals, the experiments. Everything I have tried to forget for the past seven years, every terrible detail that has haunted me in the night, the questions that have kept me from my sleep – must I accept that it was all real? All of it … true? And you – you can be no mere woman, surely, to have done such things. You were never just an innocent wife who fell through the ice, were you?'

'Oh, but I was! Amy was truly quite the lost lamb when she first arrived here. She never did fit in, poor thing. She has … I have learned so, so much, since I died,' she told me, grinning like an imp from ear to ear.

I stared at her in horror. 'Are you a witch, or a demon?' I asked harshly. Amy only laughed at me.

'Oh, Simon, how prosaic! Really, you must be a little more imaginative. You must have spent too much time staring at Victor's old paintings, I think.'

I had not been able to recall the name until she spoke it. 'Victor – yes … Victor Mordrake. My God.' I remembered, too, the fear, and reverence, and suspicious hatred that I had once held for the man – all of these emotions poured back to me in the same moment, with the hearing of his name. 'And who was he? Was he really keeping you here, or was I deceived on that as well?'

Amy yawned quietly. 'He is a rival, I suppose you might say. Another one attracted by the possibilities of this spot; not the first, not the last, but – persistent. The balance of power has shifted, back and forth, for a long time. For a while, he … yes, he held some advantage over me – over all of us. I was constrained,' she admitted with a slight frown. 'But now the pieces are reset, and all the advantage is mine – thanks to you, Simon! It is all thanks to you,' she smiled at me warmly.

'You speak as though he were not dead.'

She laughed. 'I wish I knew. It would not surprise me at all if he were to make his reappearance, someday – but not for a long while, I think. Why? Does your conscience prick at you?' Her tone suddenly became one of genuine concern. 'You really mustn't let it – what you did for me was truly chivalrous. That man deserved his fate, believe me.'

I thought of bloody red pulp oozing and curdling in the mud, and wished I could believe her. One hundred further questions burned in my skull, but I felt suddenly wearied. We could have gone on all night with our meaningless back and forth, and I would have arrived scarcely any closer to the truth. Amy had no inclination to provide me with any straight answers or clear explanations, that much was obvious – and why should I expect her to? Besides, even if she did expound upon some small detail here or there, could I hope to comprehend its meaning or significance? The barest slivers of knowledge that had been revealed to me previously had almost driven me from my senses completely. Perhaps she was right – perhaps Victor had been right all along. My happiness did not depend on my comprehension, but my acquiescence. I fell onto the settee beside her and buried my face in my hands.

'I am glad you are amused by it all,' I groaned. 'My life has been ruined. I could have been a fine, upstanding member of society – normal, and completely unremarkable. I could have done well for myself, lived a peaceful life, content and ignorant of any of … this. Coming here, meeting you, it destroyed me. Why me? Why did Victor invite me here at all?'

'That, I do not know. I have often wondered myself, in fact. Perhaps he had his own designs for you that we will never know of. He told you he wanted you to help him resume his work, yes? That may have been true. Your curiosity, and your wilful determination against the deceit inherent to this place would certainly have appealed to him.' I felt Amy's hand on the back of my head, stroking my hair, soothing me – mentally, I recoiled at her touch, but my body accepted it with a shiver of pleasure.

'Or,' she continued, 'perhaps he was just a lonely man, and he only wanted some company. I cannot say.'

I did not want to ask the question, but I had to. My voice croaked from the back of my throat, 'And, what about you? Why did it have to be me? There were … others, weren't there? I wasn't the first to see you; Mrs Pugh told me that.'

Her head shook. 'Only in glimpses. No one else knew me the way that you did, Simon. Truly. Perhaps … the others, perhaps they tried in the past, I don't know. But not me – not Amy. As for why it had to be you,' she smiled then, sweetly, 'I don't know that, either. But I am glad it was. I'm glad it was you who found me. Maybe that was just how it had to be. Maybe we were always bound to be together, to find each other – across time, and across space.'

'Being sent here was my death sentence,' I told her miserably.

Amy did not say anything for some time, just continued to smooth my hair gently. I wondered if she felt guilt or pity for me. I hoped that she did.

'Do you know,' she said eventually, her voice as soft and smooth as velvet, 'it is true that this place sits somewhat … askance from the world outside, and that permits me to exert certain influences over others. I do not deny it. But Simon – I never called you back here. When I told you, years ago, that you could leave this house with my blessing, I meant it. I should have missed you terribly, but I would not have denied you your liberty, after all that you did. And yet here you are again. You came back to me, by your own choice.'

I moved my fingers to my temples and pressed upon them, an instinctive gesture, though having done so I realized that for once my head did not throb with pain. Amy took my hands into her own, and held them. We sat then, side by side, for some time, our hands folded one atop the other, Amy gazing at the side of my face while I stared hollowly ahead.

'I am sorry I could not tell you everything from the start, truly I am,' she said, 'but I think you understand my reasons, now. I did not set out to hurt you. My feelings for you were real – my happiness in the time we spent together was real. It was … the first and the truest happiness I have known for the longest time, Simon. You cannot know how lonely I had been.' I felt her fingers tighten possessively around my own. 'Even so – even for all that – I would have let you go, if that had been what you wished. But you want to be here with me, don't you? You came back to me freely, after all. We can … It can be just as it was before. Most of the paintings are still upstairs – they haven't been touched since you left – and I still deplore them, truly I do. You could finish your work, catalogue them and sell them for me. And then you could help me buy new ones! We can decorate this place for ourselves, make it our own home, no longer Victor's. And we can read together, in the upstairs library, just as we did before. Wouldn't you like that, Simon?' She squeezed my fingers pleadingly, but I disentangled them from hers, stooped, picked up a rose from near my foot, and twirled it before my eyes, examining the glossy crimson petals.

'I would like it … That should please me very much, I think … and yet – how can I forget the things …'

She reached for the rose in my hand, and I let her take it from me. She held it before her eyes for a moment, staring at its bloom impassively, then snapped the stem between her thumb and finger and let the broken pieces fall. 'The past is behind us, and will not change,' she said. 'What lies ahead is all that matters, so why go into it facing backwards? We both did what had to be done, and the consequences have been written. You may either accept them for what they are, or wring your hands with guilt and self-denial. But, dear Simon, why torture yourself any longer? We could be happy together, at long last, just like you always wanted. We will not be troubled here, there is no one who will bring up the past – no one, save yourself. As for me, I will waste no time mourning those who would have kept us apart, if they could. My one and only regret should be if you cannot see things the same way.'

Though her words were hard and cold as ice, her tone was warm, and appealing, and – I thought – hopeful. She meant it, I believed that. Amy's want for me was as great as mine for her; somehow, the fact that she was willing to let me leave, and slip from her grasp entirely, seemed all the more proof of it.

'Two men died by my hand,' I murmured. But the truth was that what she said made a morbid sense to me. I had carried an inward burden for seven years, a guilt for which none but myself would hold me to account. Perhaps it was time to let it go. And I had not been happy, I saw that now. I had not known real joy since I left this place – since I left her behind. The accomplishments of my career, and the ascent of my social standing, they had meant nothing to me – I had drifted through life unable to connect with my fellow human beings, having witnessed the briefest hint of something more, as tantalisingly incomprehensible as that glimpse had been. Now, sitting with Amy, I felt an inner peace, as much as I tried to fight it. It was a peace that I had known only once before, and fleetingly, during my short life. The existence she spoke of, quiet study in the house, reading in the library, a life at her side and in her devotion – well, it was truly all I could wish for.

Amy reached out and placed her hands on either side of my face, turned my head so that my bewildered, tired eyes stared into hers – those deep, mysterious pools, now brimming with compassion and understanding, a slight, patient smile on her red lips … what did any of it matter, but her? I had done it all for her sake. My crimes had been committed in her name. Amy. I had killed for Amy, and I knew I would again, if she willed it.

Her fingers slipped to the back of my neck, pushed through my hair. She closed her eyes slowly, and pulled my head closer to hers. Our lips met, and the world below me fell away as my senses plummeted into an ocean of bliss. It had all been for her. All for her.

'Come now, it is late,' Amy said finally. 'Chapman shall ring the bell for dinner, momentarily. We should prepare ourselves – you will stay with me for tonight at least, won't you? It is too late for you to get the train now, anyway. You may leave me tomorrow if you wish to – you have always been free to come and go as you please. But say you will stay with me tonight, Simon,' she asked, as though there could be any answer but yes.

That evening we ate a fine rack of lamb that Chapman and a young serving girl I did not know set out before us. I thought it would seem strange to take a meal with Amy, in the dining room – and yet it was not at all. It felt as familiar as a childhood memory, as though we had dined together one thousand times before. Amy asked me endless questions about my life in Edinburgh, my work, my social engagements – such as they were – and my family; it was as though she wished me to account for the past seven years within the space of that single meal. But her manner was neither prying nor suspicious – she listened to my answers, no matter how ordinary their substance, with eager fascination. It seemed to me that I had not spoken on any subject, and certainly not about myself, at such length or in such detail for many years. I asked Amy one or two questions of my own about the intervening years, about changes in the house and changes in Cobsfoot, without pressing too hard on any precise matters; Amy answered me with a refreshing openness and candour.

After our plates were cleared, we took a glass of wine, and Amy suggested we might walk the grounds a little. 'The rain has stopped, and we have another hour or so of sunlight – the nights have not drawn in quite yet,' she said. Despite the exertions of my lengthy day, I found that my energies were not drained, in fact quite the opposite, and so I readily agreed.

The afternoon's soaking drizzle had turned to a light mist that hung over the treetops as we walked a circuit around the house, and then into the surrounding forest, arm in arm beneath the dripping canopy. We said very little at all; nothing was needed. I felt a contentment to the very bottom of my heart that words could only fail to describe. We rambled through the trees, forging our own path amid the undergrowth and the swirling mist that enshrouded us on all sides, concealing the outside world behind its white vapours so that there were only we two.

We walked until we came to the lake, and then stood on its banks staring out over the water, our breath coming out in little clouds. The night air had begun to turn chill, and I felt Amy shiver at my side; I put my arm around her, and she rested her head upon my shoulder.

Without taking my eyes from the lake, I said, 'I will stay with you – tonight, forever, always'. Amy raised her head; she took my hands in hers and we turned to face each other. She looked into my eyes, and smiled.

'You will love me forever?' Amy asked, and I nodded my surrender. We turned back to the deep, still waters and stood there side by side. The mists had parted, and above our heads the stars twinkled and glowed in a sweeping, prismatic wash of light set into a sky so perfectly clear I felt we were looking to the edge of heaven itself. A rising silver half-moon shone as the centrepiece, its face bisected with precision, one side afire with pale luminescence as the other vanished into shadow, darker even, somehow, than the frozen and empty infinity that encased it. At our feet, the wide expanse of the lake reflected this celestial tapestry within its perfect, shimmering mirror. There, upon its bank, we stood, and we watched, and waited.

An exclusive early look at
Mathew West's new novel,
The Water Child, coming
in spring 2023

The Water Child

Mathew West

Part One

1.

Portugal, 175~

The largest window in the house is in the parlour and it looks out over the ocean. In fact all of the windows in the house look toward the ocean: in the parlour, in her drawing room, her bedchamber and in John's study – all of the windows in the rooms that she makes regular use of, anyway. Wherever she is when she is at home, all she need do is turn her head and there it is. The vast Atlantic shifting and flashing beneath the sun, a brilliant, glittering tapestry that stretches towards the blurred haze of the horizon.

A hot slice of sun falls at a slant through the glass, shining a bright diamond shape across the parlour floor. Cecilia stands carefully positioned at its edge, her toes just clear of the burning patch. Without knowing she is doing it she shifts her feet every fifteen minutes or so, adjusting her position to account for the sun's perpetual motion through the sky. Within the shade of the house it is cool – outside, in the full glare of the afternoon heat, it is close to unbearable.

She is staring at the water. She stands with her hands clasped before her – not in prayer, though a passing observer who happened to glance in from the outside might easily mistake her stillness for that of a churchyard statue. She watches the waves. This is where she can most usually be found; at her window, watching the bay. Waiting. Her gaze passes over every ship that approaches from the horizon with a vague flutter of hope that its small, abstract shape might somehow kindle a spark of recognition inside her.

Her house is located at the very pinnacle of the town, proud at the summit of the cliff, below which a tumbled confusion of dry red rooftops that zig and zag in crazed, angular patterns lie in a chaotic heap, stretching down towards the glimmering sea. Viewed from above it appears as though the entire town must have been caught up in a landslip and the local people now live in the jumbled detritus of their former homes. But the buildings are simply very, very old, and they lie where they always have, built centuries past when the town was nothing more than a fishing village, well-sited beside a natural harbour.

But now, springing up all around and above this ancient town there are new buildings, tall and grand – buildings like her house. The air smells of freshly-sawed wood and new paint. At all hours of the day you can hear the knock of hammers and the toothy rasp of jagged saws slicing into timber: the sounds of construction, the sounds of expansion. The majority of these new buildings stand at the cliff-top: ornate jewels upon a crown of blooming prosperity.

From her window Cecilia can see the docks: the broad, bustling port that has brought such wealth and commerce to this once-sleepy town on the Westernmost coast of Europe. A conveniently-located, freshly-minted pin at the centre of the wheel of eighteenth-century trade. The town is built by the gaping mouth of a river where it empties gurgling into the Atlantic. A natural curve of the rocks provides it with a degree of protection from the tide, which once made it ideal for catching fish, and now makes it an ideal destination for merchant ships to drop anchor. They arrive from every place carrying anything you can think of, and more besides.

Bobbing within the bay Cecilia can make out the towering mastheads of the innumerable vessels which sail in and out from port every day, evidence of the town's place at the vanguard of civilisation. Their riggings – miles of ropes tied taut and cast black against the dazzling water – fill the bottom of Cecilia's view as she gazes from her window. They look rather like spiders' webs, she thinks. Her father once told her that a ship's ropes are made from nothing more than a hardy type of grass. Sometimes she tries to imagine how many swaying fields it would take to weave just the lengths of rope she can see from her window. Enough to cover over the whole of England, she supposes.

Other vessels lurk further out in the bay, jostling for a place in port, waiting for their turn to pull in and weigh anchor and unspill the treasured contents heaving within their holds. They arrive bearing jewels and ornate stones carved or raw, metals both precious and practical, beautiful fabrics and fragrant spices, herbs and incense that perfume the stale air inside the ships' bellies.

But today Cecilia is not looking at the berthed ships, nor the harbour, nor the new buildings built along the seafront nor the old buildings that cling resiliently to their cliffside. She is staring past them all – past them, and towards the open ocean. Beneath the blazing sun its surface ripples with endlessly mixing swirls of blues, greens and greys, never seeming to settle on one tone no matter how intently you screw your eyes. Relax your vision, and all you see is blue. The sea and the sky become one; a single mass, like a great sheet of lapis lazuli. All across its surface ships crawl like insects – like ants scuttling on a leaf. Any of them could be the ship that she is waiting for. But even watching from her parlour window she knows, in her veins, that none of them is.

With a sigh Cecilia turns her back upon the window and her view. The comparative darkness of the room briefly obliterates her vision, until her eyes gradually adjust. When she has blinked away the blindness she is startled to discover that she is not alone. Her maid, Rosalie, a local girl – or, local woman, for Rosalie is at least the same age as her mistress, if not older – is standing patiently in the doorway. Cecilia wonders how long she has been there. She wonders how long she herself has been standing, watching the ocean, silent and unmoving.

'Y-yes? Do you need something?' Cecilia asks.

Rosalie fires off a rapid patter of syllables, rising and falling inflections which Cecilia cannot make sense of. It is English, but spoken too quickly and accented for her to follow. She asks Rosalie to repeat, which she does, patiently. Her question is only about that night's meal. Cecilia indicates her preference – or at least, she thinks she does, and then she makes to leave the room, faintly embarrassed that her maid has been watching her stare out the window so idly. But there is more. Rosalie indicates with the crook of her finger that she wishes her mistress to follow.

Cecilia allows herself to be lead upstairs with the uncomfortable sense that she should not allow her staff order her about the way that Rosalie does. She had some servants in her home when she grew up, naturally, but only to cook and clean and never to wait upon her hand and foot the way that Rosalie is employed to do. The entire arrangement fills Cecilia with a quiet discomfort. Sometimes she thinks that Rosalie is too brash, too confrontational to be proper. *Everyone told me not to hire a local girl*, she remembers as she climbs the stairs.

In her bedroom Rosalie presents the problem. A pair of Cecilia's shoes, pumps in burgundy cotton with neat ribbons to tie around the ankles. Or, they had been. The cotton is faded and marked by blotchy patches all around the sides. The delicate silk ribbons are curled and wrinkled, and fraying at the edges. They had been nice shoes, once – fine footwear, not suited for walking down at the shore amidst the sand and the stones. But Cecilia had been wearing them by the black rocks some days ago when a large wave had caught her off her guard, surging past her feet and ankles and even touching the hem of her skirt, so that they were all soaked through entirely. She should have told Rosalie at the time, instead of kicking the shoes under her bed while they were still warm and damp. Probably there was something that could have been done to save them, before the salty teeth of the sea dried into the fabric and began to destroy it.

'They are ruined,' she interrupts whatever Rosalie is saying. 'Throw them away. There is nothing else to be done.'

Her maid objects, but Cecilia quickly turns away and departs the room, evading further questions that he does not want to answer. Questions like: how did your shoes come to be soaked in seawater? What were you doing by the shore, so close to the waves? *Just throw them away*, she thinks, *and do not ask me to explain*.

When she first took Rosalie on they had conducted the preliminary interview in English, naturally, and Cecilia is positive that Rosalie had spoken it quite well at the time. But somehow between the interview and the hiring all of that shared communication seems to have slipped away, and now the two women spend the majority of their interactions struggling to make each other understood. Perhaps Rosalie simply expects her to be able to comprehend more Portuguese than she can, having lived here for many months now. But then Cecilia reminds herself that she is the employer, and it is not proper for her to be overly concerned about such matters.

In any case Rosalie does basically everything that is required around the house without Cecilia ever requiring to understand what she is up to. There are others who help sometimes: an old man with snow-white hair and a crooked back who tends to the garden, and an old woman who helps in the kitchens. Sometimes a new girl will appear and spends the day stripping bedsheets or peeling potatoes, and then vanish. She thinks they might all be related to Rosalie in some way: uncles and aunts and cousins. Certainly she did not hire them. She allows Rosalie to keep track of it all and tell her what is required each week for wages, which is never very much. That is enough to keep the household – such as it is – running.

She is still thinking about the burgundy shoes when she wanders aimlessly into the dining room. Perhaps the fabric could be saved, or the ribbons replaced; these things are not cheap. Perhaps Rosalie is already rubbing away the encrusted salt and snipping off the tattered ribbons so that she might save the pumps for herself, or as a pretty gift for some relative. Cecilia hopes that she is.

John had been with her when she bought the shoes. Not long after their arrival in this place. Now she feels a pang of regret to think of them being tossed away. John had said something complimentary – perhaps something about the colour? – and so she had bought them. It had been foolish to wear indoor shoes down on the rocks. But then, she had not really been intending to visit the shore when she left the house on that morning. She seldom does.

2.

The house that afternoon feels too quiet, too confining. The air inside is hot and stale, despite every window being thrown wide open. Through their apertures Cecilia can hear the constant symphony of hammers and saws as the town around her audibly expands.

She spends some time wandering around, standing in doorways and staring about absently – staring at the furniture, the decorations and fixtures with which she and John had filled their new home many months earlier. Perhaps half of what she sees they shipped over with them from England. As she moves from room to room she touches those things that they bought from home; a single touch of her hand, to make them real. Two high-backed chairs made from cherry wood. A small table beside the fireplace, still scattered with toast crumbs from her breakfast; the silver sugar tongs that were a wedding gift from her Aunt Lara. Fat flies buzz around the sugar bowl which Rosalie has neglected to tidy away.

Their other furnishings were purchased here in town: rugs and furniture and ornaments which they traded in the exotic and startling marketplaces during those exciting few weeks after they first arrived in port. Italian, Chinese, Indian styles sit side-by-side; her house is like a mongrel, a halfway proper English home cluttered with curios and artifacts from a mish-mash of other cultures.

She finds that today she does not care for any of her furnishings at all. *When John comes back we will buy all new ones*, she tells herself.

She picks an old book that travelled with her from England off the shelf, and settles down to try to read. Less than twenty minutes later she returns it to its place with a maudlin sigh.

Without thinking she finds herself back at the large parlour window, gazing out towards the ocean once again. The day has worn on, somehow, in spite of her own inertia. Time does not wait for you to fill it with meaningful activity. The sun has already started its afternoon descent across the wide open sky. She can tell just by looking at the streets below that, by now, the edge has been taken off the shimmering heat. Sharp, jagged shadows like sharks' teeth spike and stab across the descending angles of the rooftops of the town. In the distance – from the harbour – she can hear the faint clang of a tolling bell, carried up the cliffside upon the ocean breeze. Farther out the sun is throwing long shadows off the tall ships as they glide in and out from port, so that each one looks like a sickle-curved slice of dark against the radiant blue water; as though some divine being has reached down with a celestial knife and cut a series of notches out from the surface of the ocean.

She walks out of the house just as she is, without changing a thing – without pinning a cap to her head, or slipping on a light shawl. Even after all this time the dense heat hits her with a surprising force. Outside her house the streets are wide and regular, as might be found in any modern European city; but two left turns and a short, brisk walk brings her to the long road that leads down the cliff, through the old town that has stood here since time immemorial.

As she follows the descending road the modern buildings abruptly give way to an aged and archaic labyrinth of squat homes, piled haphazardly one atop the other in a warren of skewed side-streets and shadowy alleys; but her route is a straight line through them, following the steep cliffside path directly to the waterfront. The road has been worn so smooth with the passage of innumerable feet over centuries that Cecilia must slow her pace to a crawl as she descends its treacherous incline, to avoid a slip and a nasty fall. Even so, every time she makes this descent she is tempted by a perverse desire to break into a run and let the momentum carry her all the way down, faster and faster, to the bottom of the steep cliff and all the way to the water.

Today, however, she takes the descent slowly and carefully. At this time of day the only faces she sees are elderly locals, who watch her curiously as they lean from windows or shuffle past at a bent stoop. It is only when she begins to draw closer to the water, and the briny scent grows sharper in the air, and gulls wheel and flap overhead scanning the streets for any flecks of food, and the crashing surge of the nearing tide fills her ears even over the vibrant din of the working harbour and streets filled with commerce – it is only here that the town comes to life. As the cliff's steep gradient levels out the streets begin to buzz with vitality and threat. Here, close to the docks, where the river water pours forth into the great Atlantic, is where the two conflicting currents of the town – the old and the new – collide with the greatest force.

Her ears are assailed by a babble of every language known to man – or so it seems to her. People try to proposition her: street vendors hold out their wares and call for her attention. One man slips suddenly very close to her side and hisses something she cannot understand through his teeth; Cecilia walks on, pretending obliviousness. A short way on she is forced to step to the very edge of the street to let a trio of sailors pass by, arm in arm and drunk and singing, a veritable wall of tattooed muscle. As she watches them pass there is a tap on her arm and she turns in fright, thinking it is the unpleasant man again. But it is a tiny old woman, wrinkled like a walnut, who mutters something in words Cecilia does not know.

'I am sorry ... I am English,' she apologises, holding her hands out and smiling weakly, and she moves on.

She comes to the docks. Cecilia moves silently, almost invisibly, slipping and weaving her way deftly between the teeming, labouring sailors. Some wear splendid uniforms but most are clad in vagabond scraps of clothing. Some wear almost nothing at all, displaying their tattoos – vibrant and frightening images that coil up their thick arms, their chests and even their necks and faces – tattoos that tell tall tales of who they are and where they have come from, and make wild promise of where they will go next.

Cecilia spent her entire childhood, from birth to marriage, in an English port town, and she had thought herself well-accustomed to the nautical world. But the sights she recognised at home did not prepare her at all for these foreign seafolk. They had terrified her, at first. But John had reassured her. He told her, whatever they might look like, these are working men. Their livelihoods – and their very lives – depend upon their labour in port, and not even a pretty girl passing by will give them much cause to break focus. It is advice that she has found by and large to be true, provided she steers clear of any sailors who are too deep into their drink.

Close to the docked ships the steaming scent of hot tar scalds her nose, stronger than the smell of the sea; stronger even than the stink of dead and gutted fish, or the musky reek of working men's sweat. The market streets smell of spices and incense and perfume, but at the docks every intake of breath is a hazard. The smells there will amaze you with their vileness. They soak into your clothes and your skin. At first she found the assault on her senses revolting; but now she finds a strange sort of comfort in its controlled, orchestrated chaos. It is amazing, the things you can get used to.

She walks the length of the wharf at an unhurried pace, trying her best not to get in anyone's way, and watching her step carefully for missing planks in the boardwalk. Where there are gaps you can see the foaming sea, right below your feet. Beside the water the air is mercifully cooler, and the towering ships standing lined in their berths cast a cooling shade. The mighty vessels rise from the waters like titans stepped out of some myth, but it is a myth of the future, not of the past. Their complicated masts and riggings pierce the sky above her head, stabbing upward into the clouds. She knows that the very highest sails bear thrilling and outlandish names like moon-rakers and sky-scrapers – names to make you wonder at the audacity of the men who built these machines in reckless defiance of nature's dominion. If you crane your head back and try to see to their very tops it will make you trip over your own feet, like peering upward at a church spire when you are standing too close. Cecilia keeps her eyes downcast and watches her footing, instead.

She reads the names painted onto the prows of the ships as she passes. *La Jean Baptiste. The Piccadilly. Dona Maria.* She admires their curious figureheads, some crude, some ornate, some painted and some bare, depicting ladies in finery and wild mermaids and horses and other, fantastical creatures. *Le Cheval Marin. Corazon de Oro.* Names that have travelled to this place from all across Europe, or further still. Some she could not even guess at a pronunciation. The names are strange, and the ships are strangers. None of them is John's ship. But, still she keeps looking, keeps reading. She reaches the end of the wharf, the last of the ships lined up – she has walked almost to the very edge of the town, now, when–

'Mrs Lamb? But it can't be her. Why, it is! Cecilia Lamb!' a voice cuts through the harbour din as swift as an arrow, penetrating by dint of familiarity of accent and language.

Cecilia spins sharply and immediately sees a carriage standing a short distance away, where the coastal road that leads out of the town runs almost parallel with the wharf. She recognises the carriage at once – and, in the same instant, regrets responding so quickly to the sound of the voice. Perhaps if she had hurried away without turning to look she could have vanished before they could be positive that they had recognised her.

The carriage belongs to the Delahuntys. At the window, alternately pointing and waving to her, is her friend Mabel, who smiles at Cecilia with a pleasure and excitement marred by only a faint shade of confusion. It is too late to do anything but smile and wave back.

Cecilia takes a few steps towards the carriage and almost crashes into a passing sailor, who snaps at her like a dog. With her heart racing and her head down, she scurries the rest of the way more carefully.

'Why, I knew it was you, Cecilia my darling!' Mabel trills. 'Mr Delahunty and I are on our way back to the house – we have spent the day at the Moroccan quarter. Isn't it just too much of a marvel? Have you seen, they have the most fascinating market: we must take you there one day, mustn't we, dear?' This she addresses to her husband, a rather plain, paunchy, somewhat older man in his mid- to late-thirties, and not particularly handsome, Cecilia thinks.

'Get in, get in,' Samuel has clambered down from the carriage while his wife talks, and now offers Cecilia his hand to assist her up. 'We'll give you a ride back up the hill.'

'Mrs Lamb, my dear, what on earth are you doing down here beside the harbour?' Mabel asks, alarmed, as Cecilia sits down in the seat opposite.

'I expect she got turned around in these infernal alley-ways, didn't you?' her husband interjects. 'Though, you should take care at the docks. It is … Ah, a bit rough around here, you know.'

'Indeed, did you find yourself here by accident? Well, I can understand that, it took me simply *months* before I had a sense of the place. Even now I hate to go too far by myself.' Mabel's eyes flash as she takes in Cecilia's slipshod appear-ance. 'It *is* rather too warm for a bonnet, today, isn't it? I almost left the house without one, myself.'

'Yes – that's right, I must have got turned around, trying to find my way in the market,' Cecilia answers quietly, as she tries to settle herself. The atmosphere is uncomfortably cloying with all three of them inside the carriage. As they begin to trundle up the curving road that will lead them back up the cliffside – back to their homes in the new town above the bay – she cannot help but cast a glance from the window. A final, longing look at the tall ships lined up, and the labouring tattooed seamen and the screeching, scaveng-ing gulls and the spilled fish innards coating watery planks.

'I must have got lost,' she tells them, watching from the carriage window as the road curves away from the harbour scene that she knows so well. She cannot seem to take her eyes from the shore, not until it has slid from her view with the turn of the road; even then she can still smell it and taste it, and feel it stirring within her blood. She thinks that she hears a voice behind them, calling her name. A voice like John's, calling out for her amidst the chaotic burble of the harbour. But she doesn't turn her head. She used to look – perhaps the first hundred times she heard him calling to her she would turn around, look for his face in the crowd – but she would never find him. He is never there.

Harper
North

Book Credits

HarperNorth would like to thank the following staff
and contributors for their involvement in making
this book a reality:

Hannah Avery

Fionnuala Barrett

Claire Boal

Charlotte Brown

Sarah Burke

Alan Cracknell

Jonathan de Peyer

Anna Derkacz

Tom Dunstan

Kate Elton

Mick Fawcett

Simon Gerratt

Monica Green

CJ Harter

Graham Holmes

Megan Jones

Jean-Marie Kelly

Oliver Malcolm

Alice Murphy-Pyle

Adam Murray

Genevieve Pegg

Agnes Rigou

Florence Shepherd

Angela Snowden

Emma Sullivan

Katrina Troy

Sarah Whittaker

For more unmissable reads,
sign up to the HarperNorth newsletter at
www.harpernorth.co.uk

or find us on Twitter at
@HarperNorthUK

Harper
North